D1229699

WINTERKEEP

Exclusive FairyLoot Signed Limited Edition

Published by Gollancz and FairyLoot, 2021

Kristin Cashore

WINTERKEEP

KRISTIN CASHORE

First published in Great Britain in 2021 by Gollancz
an imprint of The Orion Publishing Group Ltd
Carmelite House, 50 Victoria Embankment
London EC4Y 0DZ

An Hachette UK Company

1 3 5 7 9 10 8 6 4 2

Copyright © Kristin Cashore 2021

The moral right of Kristin Cashore to be identified as
the author of this work has been asserted in accordance
with the Copyright, Designs and Patents Act of 1988.

All rights reserved. No part of this publication may be
reproduced, stored in a retrieval system, or transmitted
in any form or by any means, electronic, mechanical,
photocopying, recording, or otherwise, without the
prior permission of both the copyright owner and the
above publisher of this book.

All the characters in this book are fictitious, and any resemblance
to actual persons, living or dead, is purely coincidental.

A CIP catalogue record for this book is
available from the British Library.

ISBN (Hardback) 978 1 473 23277 8
ISBN (Export Trade Paperback) 978 1 473 23278 5
ISBN (eBook) 978 1 473 23280 8

Printed in Great Britain by Clays Ltd, Elcograph S.p.A

www.gollancz.co.uk

For Kevin

The KNOWN WORLD

PIKKIA

NANDER

ESTILL

THE DELLS

MIDDLUNS

WESTER

Bitterblue City

MONSEA

SUNDER

OCEAN

LIENID

MANTIPER

KAMASSAR

BORZA

Torla's Neck

TEVARE

WINTER-
KEEP

Ledra

BRUMAL
SEA

WINTER
SEA

TORLA
&
The ROYAL
CONTINENT

A NOTE TO THE READER

IT'S DOUBTFUL THAT the worlds of my fantasy novels have a method of date-keeping equivalent to our Gregorian calendar or our seven days of the week. It's almost certain that the nations of Monsea and Winterkeep, which reside on continents that developed independently, would not have the same calendar as each other. When I use the Gregorian calendar and days of the week while relating the stories of these characters, consider it a friendly translation I'm providing for you, from their world to ours. I want your mind to be free to enter these characters' lives — not tangled up in confusion about what day or month it is.

Please also note that there is a cast of characters at the end of the book.

PART ONE

PART ONE

THE KEEPER

THE MAN WITH the white streak in his black hair was diving too close to her again. He was a powerful swimmer, for a human. He kept pulling down through the water with strong arms and hands, propelling himself with big kicks.

The sea creature tried to quiet her trembling limbs, so that if the human got deep enough to see her, he would think she was just a mountain of moss on the ocean floor and would turn away and stop scaring her.

Then the human shot back up to the surface. The creature relaxed, relieved that humans needed air. Especially this human, who was different from the others. Most humans jumped out of a boat, thrashed around in the water looking like birds trying not to fall out of the sky, then dragged themselves back into their boats, satisfied. The sea creature never saw them again.

But this human returned frequently, and dove with a purpose that frightened the creature, for she kept treasures here on the ocean floor, gathered them, guarded them, and this human knew about one of them. He didn't know about her. No one knew about her. But he wanted the object that was her favorite treasure. She could feel him thinking about it. She wound her long tentacles around it, trying to hide it from sight. It was a ship.

This ship, two-masted with swirling sails, had dropped nose-first from the waters above not too long ago, and landed beside her. All the creature's treasures—nets, harpoons, anchors—sank like this, from the bright water above. But ships were rare treasures, and this ship was extra-special, for when she pressed one of her eyes to a porthole, she could see a secret world inside. A pink room with tiny sofas and armchairs attached to the floor, paintings on the walls, lamps; a skylight crossed with bars and a door with a sparkling knob and hinges; and two pink-skinned human bodies, which were beginning to look soft and puffy. She called it her Storyworld.

The most special and unusual thing about her Storyworld was that there was a padlock on the outside of the door, trapping these bodies inside. Usually, when a ship sank, the people jumped into the water or the lifeboats, trying to live. They didn't close themselves into a room with a padlock.

The human with the white streak in his black hair, who had brown skin, dove deep again, looking for the ship. He thought about a woman sometimes as he dove, a human woman with dark braids and gray eyes who wore glimmering rings on pale brown fingers. The sea creature understood that he wanted the ship so he could give it to the woman. The sea creature didn't like this woman, not at all.

The diver's own boat was a small oval above. She thought about grabbing its anchor and pulling. It was not the sort of thing she ever did. If she pulled his boat under, he would probably see her, and she never attracted anyone's attention. But then, eventually, he would drown, and that would make him stop looking for her favorite treasure. In fact, he himself would make a fine treasure. In addition to the nice way his hair floated around his face, and in addition to his tiny, perfect muscles, his tiny, perfect hands and feet, a red jewel sparkled on a ring on his thumb. The creature would like to slide that ring from his thumb and wear it at the tip of one of her thirteen tentacles. She loved the sparkly things humans wore. And then the man would bloat, and rupture, and rot, and eventually become a smooth, shiny skeleton in tattered clothing, and she loved that about humans too. She could add him to her collection of bones. Encircle him with her tentacles, keep him safe.

Then a pod of silbercows approached, so she decided to leave the human's small oval boat alone. Silbercows never let humans drown, if they could help it. Silbercows were about the size of one of the sea creature's eyes. They made platforms with their backs and lifted drowning humans to the surface, thinking encouraging thoughts at the humans. Also, now the chance of being seen was too great. Silbercows had better underwater vision than humans.

Again, the human broke his dive and ascended to the surface. Next, the human seemed to be playing with the silbercows, swimming and rolling with them, laughing, shouting in happiness. This happened pretty often with this human. The silbercows liked to visit him, and he always laughed a lot.

Then, without warning, something extraordinary happened. Two new humans crashed into the water from above, attached to long ropes. They grabbed the laughing human, struggled with him. He fought, punched, kicked, twisted. He was marvelous; she waited for him to break away. But then he seemed to run out of air, for his body went still. The other two humans shot out of the water on their ropes, lifting his body with them.

The creature was so flabbergasted that she rose some distance from the ocean floor, balancing on her thirteen tentacles and reaching around with her twenty-three eye-stems. Through the wavy glass of the water above her, she could make out the form of an airship heading north across the sky.

Then, remembering the silbercows and not wanting to be discovered, she sank back into the darkness at the ocean floor. They didn't notice her; their purple-blue faces were stretched above the surface, their big, dark eyes watching the limp man being carried by the airship. Their mental voices were raised in a song of distress. They communicated in pictures and feelings, not words, but the creature understood their meaning. *We see you, friend,* they were crying. *We know. We will tell.*

THE CREATURE, WHEN she scavenged for treasure, went to dark places, because she didn't want the silbercows to see her. The silbercows were surface animals, creatures of the light; she was a creature of the depths, a sneaker, a crawler, a dragger. There were animals who saw her in the places where the creature liked to go, pulling herself forward with her long tentacles, but they weren't the kinds of animals whose attention mattered.

Today she crossed the field of pink and white flowers and slunk into the forest of filaments and reeds, where the seahorses peered out of their swaying caves. Seahorses forgot about things once they could no longer see them. Sometimes, when they saw her, they unwound their tails, shot back into darkness, then forgot and came forward again.

The creature was thinking about the human with the white-streaked hair, the humans who'd grabbed him, and the silbercows who'd called out to him. *We see. We know. We will tell.*

See what? Know what? Tell whom? The creature didn't want the answers to these questions. She was relieved to live in the deep, away from the light where animals interacted and interfered with each other.

She reached the place where clumps of moss gathered against the base of coral mountains. The sponges who lived here had tiny, bright, sharp minds full of silly words. *Keeper! Friend! Hero! Keeper! Music! Laughter! Dance! Keeper! Keeper!*

They sang in a chorus around her every day as she brought moss to her mouth with her tentacles. She was so used to their song that she paid it no attention. Sponges weren't very smart. Once, when she'd tried to eat one on a sudden, curious whim, it had screamed with laughter as she'd tried to pull it from its pillar, as if she was tickling it. *Keeper!* it had cried. *Games! Jokes! Fun!* She'd given up, let it go, and returned to ignoring them.

Usually, after she ate, she scavenged for treasure in the murky pits beyond the coral mountains. Today, though, the creature didn't need to scavenge, for the same currents that brought her food had brought a treasure. It was a little thing, a ball of metal, bobbing and tapping against the coral. Human-made, but not an object the creature recognized. Egg-shaped, with a tiny circle of metal at one end that was attached to some sort of pin. The circle and the pin were shiny, which was pleasing, though nowhere near as pleasing as the sparkly red jewel on the thumb of that diving human.

The creature picked the thing up and held it to her eyes. She caressed the metal circle, wondering if something happened when you pulled it, for sometimes human-made objects did things, if you touched them in the right place. One of her treasures was a box that opened and closed. Another had a chain wound around a cylinder, and a handle that made the whole thing turn; at the end of the chain was an anchor that thumped and dragged along the ocean floor when she played with it.

She would save pulling the metal circle as a treat for later. She carried the thing home and added it to her treasures.

IT WAS NIGHTTIME when the creature woke to an unfamiliar perception. On the moonlit surface far above, the silbercows were crying out in their sleep.

Confused, she stretched her neck and swiveled her eyes. Overhead, lights flashed, thuds sounded, and suddenly, screams of silbercows stabbed at her mind. The screams galvanized her body, sharp and electrifying, the silbercows crying out in heartbreak, desperation, as had never happened before. The creature was so overwhelmed by the pain of the silbercows that she did something she'd never done. Rising to the surface, she lifted her eyes above the water.

Below a blanket of stars, humans in small boats were thrusting spears into silbercows.

The creature ducked below the surface again. What was this? No one ever killed silbercows! *Hide,* she thought to herself. *Hide! Make it go away.*

But as she tried to sink back down to her treasures, four silbercows, escaping, zoomed past her. They saw her, suspended in moonlit waters. They stared at her in amazement.

Pretend I'm not here, she begged them, trembling in every limb. *Pretend you can't see me.*

Are you the Keeper? they cried, throwing their pain at her, washing against her with their fear. *You must be the Keeper! You're our hero! Save our friends!*

The creature didn't know what they meant. Three of them were bleeding. One had blood pouring from a wound in his shoulder. *I'm not called Keeper,* she said. *I don't have a name. You're confusing me with someone else.*

Help us! they cried. *What's wrong with you? You're the hero of Winterkeep! You're supposed to protect us!*

Deciding to pretend she couldn't hear them, she sank down into the blackness of the ocean floor.

CHAPTER ONE

GIDDON WAS CARRYING a sleeping child through a rocky tunnel when he got his first clue that something was wrong in Winterkeep.

The child's name was Selie, she was eight, and she was not small. In fact, Giddon was starting to wonder if she was growing while he carried her. Surely she was objectively heavier now than she'd been when she'd held her arms up to him two hours ago, a gesture that hadn't surprised him, for the children always wanted Giddon to carry them through the tunnels. He was bigger, more interesting, and less anxious than their parents, or so the children thought. Giddon was actually quite anxious during these missions for the Council, these smuggling journeys through the tunnels from Estill to Monsea, but he buried his worries deep, where they couldn't reach his eyes or his voice. It was more helpful to seem calm and reassuring.

So he carried Selie calmly, with exhausted shoulders and dead arms, wading through streams, trying to measure the fatigue in the drawn, white faces of her family, stepping carefully from rock to crevice to stone on an uneven path lit by the lantern of Selie's older sister, Ranie, who, at nineteen, kept giving Giddon sly, flirtatious glances. He was used to this too on these missions. He'd gotten in the habit of mentioning his beloved girlfriend frequently in conversation. Giddon didn't have a girlfriend. It was another thing he pretended, to keep things simpler.

He put up a hand to stop Selie's head from lolling. *Children are bizarrely flexible,* thought Giddon. Sometimes it seemed like her head would roll right off her body and plop onto the rocks. And Selie was the reason for this journey through the tunnels to Monsea, for she was a Graceling, Graced with mind reading. In Estill, Gracelings were the property of the new government, which exploited their special abilities however it saw fit. There were all kinds of Graces, ranging from skills as banal as imitating bird calls to more useful capacities such as speed on foot, predicting the weather, fighting, mental manipulation, or mind reading. In Monsea, where Queen Bitterblue made the rules, Gracelings were free.

The Council—which had no other official name, just the Council—was a secret international group of spies, rescuers, fighters, plotters, consultants, headed by Giddon and a few of his friends—Raffin, Bann, Katsa, Po—that came to the aid of anyone anywhere in the Seven Nations suffering unjustly under the rule of law. The Council had started small some fourteen or fifteen years ago—Katsa had started it—but now its reach was vast.

Giddon and his friends had, in fact, assisted the Estillans with the coup of their corrupt king. But then the makeshift republic that had taken the place of Estill's monarchy had turned out to be more militarized than the Council had anticipated. And the Council never held with governments owning Gracelings.

So here Giddon was, secretly sneaking Gracelings away from the Estillan government he'd helped to establish. Trying to avoid the Estillan soldiers armed with swords and bows who had begun patrolling the Estillan forests recently, asking for the identification of anyone they met.

Giddon's sword was heavy at his side. He found some strength to hold Selie tighter, in case she was cold. It was early May, and frigid underground. A steady trickle from a hidden ledge above had been plaguing them for the last twenty minutes and Giddon had found it hard to keep the child's hat and scarf dry. Some two hours from now, the path would change, turn into the steady, downhill slope that would deliver them gently to the forests outside Bitterblue City. And Giddon would bring this family to the Council allies in Monsea who were awaiting them, then return himself to Bitterblue's court. Fall into bed, sleep for a year. Then go find Bitterblue.

"Did my father remember to give you that message?" Ranie said to Giddon, speaking so quietly that he had to move closer to her, lean in.

"What message?" he said, liking, despite himself, the way voices rumbled through these tunnels, turning into whispers, like the trickling water.

"Papa?" said Ranie, turning back to speak to the balding man who plodded along resolutely behind them, a sleeping baby strapped to his front. Beside him, his wife marched with an expression on her face like she would walk forever, if that's what it took. It was an exhausted but determined sort of expression that Giddon recognized. He suspected she was walking on blistered feet. Parents did heroic things for their children.

"Papa, didn't you have a message for Giddon?" said Ranie.

"Oh, yes," said the man, blinking as if waking, then seeming startled by the volume of his own voice. The tunnels could do that, lull you into a sense of being inside yourself. Conversation could seem like violence.

"It's a message about those two Monseans whose ship went down in Winterkeep," said the man. "You know about that ship, the *Seashell*?"

Giddon suddenly saw Queen Bitterblue at the door to his rooms, clutching a letter, her tear-strewn face upturned to him. Bitterblue's envoy to Winterkeep, Mikka, and one of her advisers, Brek, had died in that shipwreck on the other side of the world. And it had been an accident—Giddon had assured her over and over, hugging her in his doorway—but still, she'd blamed herself, for she'd been the one who'd sent those men away, to a death so far from home.

"Yes," Giddon said grimly. "I know about the drowned Monseans."

"I'm supposed to tell you that they had some news about something called zilfium."

"News about zilfium?" said Giddon, who found this message rather opaque. Zilfium, to the best of his memory, was a kind of fuel that was important in Winterkeep, but he couldn't remember why. "What news?"

"I don't know," said the man. "I only know that they wanted to tell Queen Bitterblue some news about zilfium, but then they went sailing that day and drowned. So the queen should learn what she can about zilfium."

"Who told you to tell me this?" said Giddon.

"The man who brought us to the start of the tunnels, where you met us," he said. "Bann, the one who's the consort of Prince Raffin of the Middluns. He said he had it from Prince Raffin, who had it from a letter one of the Monseans wrote to him before he drowned."

Council messages were often passed like this—from mouth to mouth. "Did Bann give you anything for me in writing?"

"No, nothing," said the man. "Only what I've said: that before that ship went down, the Monseans had wanted to tell Queen Bitterblue some news about zilfium, so maybe Queen Bitterblue should look into zilfium."

This message was intensely annoying, and Giddon didn't think it was merely because he was wet and exhausted and carrying a child made of lead. One, he didn't understand it. Two, he suspected some part of it was missing. And three, the reminder of her dead men was probably going to make Bitterblue cry.

Ranie was walking close to him again, and speaking so quietly that he had to bend down to her. He began to wonder if she might be doing this on purpose.

"What's zilfium, Giddon?" she asked.

A stream of icy water hit the back of his neck. "I'm not sure," he said crossly.

"She *is* doing it on purpose," said Selie sleepily in his ear, making him jump. He'd been sure the child was asleep.

"Doing what?" he said, somehow finding this to be the most aggravating thing yet. Mind readers!

"Ranie's talking in a low voice so you'll get close to her," Selie whispered, too quietly for anyone else to hear. "Also, I know your girlfriend is imaginary."

"Oh? And do you know you're as heavy as a horse?"

Selie was giggling. "Don't worry," she whispered. "I won't tell."

WHEN, HOURS LATER, the party emerged from the tunnels into the pink morning light of the Monsean forest, tears began to stream down the face of Selie's mother. She crouched onto a carpet of rotting leaves, sat, and said, "I just need to rest my feet for a moment, children."

"Let me take a look," said Giddon, lowering Selie stiffly to the ground. Selie made a protesting noise, clinging to him. "I need you to walk now, Selie," he said. "You see the forest? This is Monsea. What do you think?"

The forest here was practically identical to the forest in Estill where they'd entered the tunnels: tall, thick trees with the pale green buds of early summer, dark, scraggy pines. Wind, birdsong, trickling water, squirrels.

But Selie began to cry. "It's ugly," she said, and Giddon understood. It was the nature of escape. A person consumed with the need to flee didn't have the luxury of realizing how far away her home would seem, once she stopped running.

"Come, Selie," said her mother, holding an arm out to the child. "Come keep me company while Giddon prods at my feet."

"Your faith in my abilities is touching," said Giddon. "Let me just go collect some sharp sticks to stab them with."

Selie, still crying but now also giggling, tucked herself against her mother's side, where she sniffled, receiving kisses, while Giddon took off her mother's shoes. When he found her feet so bloody that it would be difficult to remove her socks without pulling her skin away, he chided himself for not checking sooner. Then he considered the distance still to go. The contact Giddon was bringing them to would have clean, fresh water, medicines, a bed for this woman to lie down upon. It wasn't far, and the others seemed able to walk.

The baby was fussing. The woman reached her free arm out for the infant, then gave him her breast. The father and Ranie hovered nearby, as if wanting to be useful.

It would be best to wait to remove these socks. *Thank goodness I'm big,* Giddon thought.

When the baby was done feeding, the woman handed him back to her husband. Then Giddon gave her a pill for pain, lifted her into his arms, and carried her the rest of the way.

CHAPTER TWO

IT WAS LATE morning when Giddon, finally alone, caught sight of the bridges that crossed the river to Bitterblue City. It meant he was almost to his bed. He was riding a horse the Council contact had lent him and his thoughts were sluggish; he was trying to push thinking aside for now, with plans to welcome it back after he'd slept. But he couldn't stop all thoughts, like, for example, the realization of how nice it was to be carried by this wonderful horse after hours of carrying others. Nor could he avoid thoughts of Bitterblue as he directed the horse onto the white-and-blue marble road of Winged Bridge.

Bitterblue had lost one of her advisers on this bridge. She'd tried to stop him, all by herself in a snowstorm, but her adviser had thrown himself over the edge. She'd been only eighteen. That suicide had been one of the legacies of the reign of Bitterblue's father, King Leck, who'd been a terror, a psychopath. Five years later, things were better for Bitterblue, but she still carried the weight of all the damage her father had done to Monsea. There'd been no one to carry Bitterblue through it all. She'd carried herself, and now she carried her kingdom.

Giddon was also thinking about Winterkeep, a Torlan nation halfway across the world. It had only been a few spare years since the currents of the Winter Sea had thrown a Torlan fishing vessel onto Pikkian shores, and everyone's understanding of the world had grown.

Giddon's continent was composed of nine countries—the Seven Nations, the Dells, and Pikkia. Torla was apparently composed of five: Winterkeep, Kamassar, Borza, Tevare, and Mantiper. Winterkeep was the closest Torlan nation to Monsea. This made Winterkeep the natural first destination for Bitterblue's envoys, traders, and spies. The Seven Nations had Gracelings. The Dells and Pikkia had monsters, vibrantly colored and mesmerizing, who could numb your mind to their attack. But according to the reports, Winterkeep was a land of miracles. Keepish people spoke to telepathic sea creatures and kept telepathic foxes as pets. They flew across the sky in ships attached to balloons. Their government was a democratic republic composed of people who liked one another. They had an academy for young people, run by the same scholars who ran the government, and renowned all across Torla. They had advanced medicines and powerful fuels. They wanted to meet Monsea's queen. Would she come?

For three or so years, Bitterblue had been receiving such letters. She and her friends had begun to learn the Keepish language—for a while, it had been a bit of a fad—and import Keepish goods. The silks of Winterkeep were bright and beautifully woven and their oils produced a clear, warm light. Winterkeep also had a vast range of teas that were medicinal or recreational, some merely delicious. The Torlan nations were close enough for trade, but seemed to have no thoughts of war. The Keepish were dark-haired like the Lienid, dark-eyed as well, with browner skin than anyone from Giddon's continent. The Torlan continent had at least five languages and the Keepish were eager to communicate with their new neighbors across the sea. In Monsea, as in all Seven Nations, the native language was called Lingian, shortened from "Gracelingian." At the request of the Keepish prime minister, Bitterblue had sent teachers to the Winterkeep Academy, to teach Lingian to the Keepish.

Everything had been exciting and hopeful. Until her envoy and one of her advisers had taken a pleasure cruise in the Brumal Sea and gone down with their ship. Before getting a chance to tell Bitterblue news about zilfium, apparently.

When Giddon reached Bitterblue's court, he slid off his horse. A groom materialized, taking the responsibility of the animal away from him with such efficiency that he could have wept with relief. He dragged himself through the castle, down corridors, up staircases, talking to no one, looking at no one. He found his rooms, blundered inside, ignored the mountain of letters on the table, the cat on the armchair who shot him an aggrieved look. He was asleep before he'd even landed on the bed.

IN EARLY EVENING he woke, feeling like a new man. He glanced around for the cat. Lovejoy, the world's oldest, scruffiest, and grouchiest animal, belonged to the royal librarian and always entered and exited Giddon's rooms by his bathing room window. The window was five floors above the ground and the cat did a terrifying shimmying maneuver down the slope of a nearby roof in order to avail himself of it. The first time Giddon had seen the stupid cat half sliding, half barreling down the roof with legs akimbo like he was having a skiing accident, Giddon had yelled at him, then gone downstairs and yelled at the librarian, then determined to keep his window closed. But then Lovejoy had just come clunking against the closed window, the fur of his face and body pressed flat as he glared in at Giddon, outraged. Giddon, who'd been in the bath, had surrendered. He kept the window open now, and tried not to jump out of his shoes whenever the cat came flying in like a piece of mail through a mail chute.

Lovejoy was lying in the middle of the pile of letters on the table, blinking at Giddon.

"Did you miss me?" said Giddon.

Lovejoy stuck one foot in the air and bit his own bottom.

"I missed you too," Giddon said. Then he pushed himself up and went to the bath.

SOMETIME LATER, HIS skin scrubbed white again, his dark hair combed, and his beard trimmed close, Giddon went searching for the queen.

He found her in her lower offices, standing beside her adviser Froggatt's desk, looking over his shoulder, studying some papers with him. Small, gray-eyed, serious, her hair in its usual dark braids. Something inside Giddon relaxed and something else tightened.

She glanced up and her whole being brightened. "You're back," she said. "How was your trip?"

"It went well," he said, then noticed a man at the far end of the room who was talking to two royal advisers. He was whip-thin, his light hair graying at the temples, his smile a humorless flash of teeth. His name was Lord Joff; he was from Estill's south, near the tunnels; and he was one of the minor Estillan nobles who'd secretly sought the Council's help deposing their king. And now he was one of many investing his personal fortune in the growth of Estill's army, which kept expanding and strengthening. Recently Giddon had begun to wonder if liberating Estill from its king had been the Council's first truly grave mistake. What if Estill retaliated against Bitterblue and Monsea for aiding the escape of its Gracelings?

Why was he here?

"That's good," said Bitterblue, who'd noticed Giddon's fixation on Joff but wasn't drawing attention to it. Then Joff glanced up. At the sight of Giddon, Joff's eyes narrowed, pale blue chips of ice. Giddon stared back at him implacably.

"Giddon?" said Bitterblue.

"Do you have a minute?" he asked her.

The queen nodded at Froggatt, who was eyeing Giddon with displeasure. The advisers might not know all Giddon got up to, and they certainly didn't know he was sneaking Estillan Gracelings across their borders, but they knew enough of the rumors about the Council to consider him an inappropriate friend for the queen. "Excuse us, Froggatt," she said. "Giddon, come upstairs."

She led the way up the spiral staircase to the castle's highest tower, where she kept her private office. The light was always brilliant in this room, with windows facing every direction. Tonight, the western sky was painted with streaks of violet and orange.

"How are you really, Giddon?" said Bitterblue. "How were the tunnels? You look tired."

"I'm fine, really, but why is that Estillan in your office?"

"I saw you trying to kill him with the power of your eyes," said Bitterblue. "My advisers are harboring a delusion he'll turn my head."

"What?" said Giddon, honestly a little shocked. "They want you to marry a known Estillan revolutionary?"

"They want me to marry an Estillan noble with influence in the new Estillan government, which would make Estill our military ally."

"Does he want to marry you?"

"He claims it's why he's visiting."

"But *why* would he want to marry you?"

Bitterblue giggled. "Don't worry, I'm not insulted."

Giddon was grinning. "You know what I mean."

"Yes. I'm sure he intends some advantage to himself or Estill, but I don't know which advantage, and unfortunately, I'll never know, because I'm not going to encourage him. Is Joff what you wanted to talk about? I got the impression it was something about your trip."

"Oh, yes," he said. "What's zilfium, exactly?"

"Zilfium?" she repeated, rubbing her braids the way she did when her neck was hurting. "It's a rock that's a powerful Torlan fuel. It's used all over the Torlan continent, except in Winterkeep, where it's illegal."

"Why is it illegal in Winterkeep?"

"I believe it's because zilfium use pollutes the air," said Bitterblue, going to the large desk that sat in the middle of the room. She began to shuffle through papers, the gold rings on her fingers catching the light. "Maybe the water too. Winterkeep mines zilfium and exports it, but they don't use it there. I have more information here some-where. We can call for Froggatt—"

"Before you do," said Giddon, "we have a message from Raffin. He says one of your men who died in Winterkeep wrote him a letter. Whichever man it was—"

"That would be Mikka, my envoy," said Bitterblue, her voice suddenly quieter. "He had a correspondence going on with Raffin and Bann about medicines. He was an outdoorsman. He used to go hiking for days, then send them packages full of seeds and leaves."

"Ah," said Giddon. "Well, Mikka wrote to Raffin that he had news to tell you about zilfium. Did you get any news about zilfium?"

"None. What kind of news?"

"I have no idea. But Raffin says you should look into zilfium."

"Look into it?" said Bitterblue, who was still shuffling through papers. "Look into it how?"

"Again, I have no idea."

"What a silly message. Why can't I find anything on this desk? Oh, weaselbugger!" said Bitterblue, then strode to the stairway and bawled "Froggatt!" down the steps.

A moment later, Froggatt appeared in the doorway. "Yes, Lady Queen?" he said, peering at her over his droopy whiskers.

"Where's my information about zilfium?"

Froggatt turned and ran downstairs again.

"Katu is always talking about zilfium," Bitterblue muttered, starting on a different pile. "Not that he's bothered to write to me in forever."

Giddon made his face even and friendly. Katu Cavenda was a

Keepish man, wealthy, an adventurer, who'd come to Monsea sometime back and become Bitterblue's instant boyfriend. He was irritatingly young and likable, irritatingly handsome with his Keepish
looks, his soft Keepish accent, and the streak of white in his black
hair that pulled everyone's eyes to him. He was also a perfectly nice
person. Giddon's friend, really; he'd taught Giddon to sail a boat,
right here in the river.

"What does he say about it?" said Giddon pleasantly.

"That everybody fights about zilfium in the Keepish Parliament,"
said Bitterblue, then tilted her head as if remembering. "A lot of
people in Winterkeep want to legalize zilfium use."

Froggatt bolted into the room again, huffing and pink, bearing a
sheaf of papers, which he placed into Bitterblue's hands.

"Thank you, Froggatt," said Bitterblue. "Will you please tell everyone to stop for the night and go have their dinners?"

"Of course, Lady Queen."

"That means you too."

"And you, Lady Queen?"

Froggatt wasn't a particularly tall man, but everyone was taller than
Bitterblue. Nor was he old, but there was something fatherly in the
tone he always took with the queen, folding his hands and tucking his
chin against his chest, peering down at her and patiently waiting.

"I'm quite hungry," said Giddon, who wasn't really.

"Yes, all right, you've both made your points," said Bitterblue,
pretending to be annoyed. "Go away, Froggatt."

"Have a lovely night, Lady Queen," said Froggatt, giving Giddon
one last, pointed glance of disapproval.

"Did you see that look?" Giddon said after Froggatt had gone.
"When I took his side about dinner!"

"They're being so grouchy," said Bitterblue, "ever since I refused to
spend more time with a horrible Sunderan earl."

"They want you to marry an Estillan revolutionary *and* a Sunderan earl?"

"He kept talking over me," said Bitterblue. "Then, when I finally told him to stop interrupting, he said, 'I like a woman with a temper,' in this creepy way that made it clear he was talking about sex." She was flipping through the papers Froggatt had given her while she talked, her eyes scanning them quickly. "Here it is," she said, stopping at a certain page and reading. "'Zilfium deposits occur naturally all across the Torlan continent. Winterkeep's environmental laws prohibit the use of zilfium in Winterkeep, but it's mined there and sold to Kamassar and the other Torlan nations, where it's used to power trains, ships, plows, machinery in factories.'"

"Winterkeep has airships," said Giddon. "Don't the airships use zilfium?"

"No," said Bitterblue. "Airships are powered by the wind, and held aloft by some gas that doesn't pollute the air. Airships are uniquely Keepish, and a zilfium-free technology."

She dropped the papers onto the desk, then raised her eyes to his, steady, calm. "There," she said. "I've looked into zilfium. Do you suppose that's what Mikka wanted?" Then she smiled, her tired face opening with humor, and Giddon was no longer worried, and suddenly happy, hungry for dinner.

"Most certainly," he said.

"I guess we should write to Raffin and ask him if he can be any less obscure," she said, taking his arm. "Let's go eat."

BITTERBLUE'S GRACED SPY and half sister, Hava, was at dinner. So was Bitterblue's cousin Prince Skye, who hugged Giddon just as if they hadn't had dinner together in this same room a week ago. Like many from Lienid, Skye was demonstrative. Giddon had always welcomed it; it made him feel like he had a brother.

Bitterblue was cutting herself a second piece of sweet vinegar pie when a letter fell out of her pocket.

Skye reached down and grabbed it. "This is Saf's handwriting!"

"Oh, yes," said Bitterblue. "I forgot I had that."

"Did you read it yet?"

"No."

"Why is he writing to you?"

"How can I know that if I haven't read it yet?"

"Well, when are you going to read it?"

"I'll read it now," said Bitterblue, giving Skye a look, "if it'll make you stop behaving like a fretful puppy." She used her knife to break the seal, then pulled out a single sheet of paper written in the most illegible scrawl Giddon had ever seen. No one wrote as badly as Saf, who was Bitterblue's . . . friend? Giddon wasn't sure of Saf's status at the moment, beyond that he and Bitterblue had been lovers once and that he was a reckless, purple-eyed ass who'd decided a few months back, for no good reason, to take work on a ship sailing to Winterkeep. Presumably, that was where he was writing from now. Saf and Skye were great friends, and had spent the last few years sailing together on Pikkian mapmaking missions in the northern Winter Sea. Giddon supposed Skye must miss him.

"Well?" said Skye.

"Give me a minute. It's ciphered," said Bitterblue, whose eyes were racing back and forth across the page. Bitterblue had a mind for ciphers; she was the only person Giddon knew who could decipher a letter quickly in her head. And the key she was using to decipher Saf's letter was certainly "Sparks," Saf's nickname for Bitterblue back when they'd loved each other. So maybe they still loved each other. Which was fine.

"He's in Ledra," said Bitterblue, naming the capital of Winterkeep. "He's basing himself there for a bit, while he decides what to do.

The first paragraph is about zilfium. Isn't that a funny coincidence, Giddon?"

"What's zilfium?" said Skye.

"Fuel," said Hava in a bored voice from the sofa, where she was lying on her back, staring at the ceiling, pretending not to listen.

"He says the Keepish Parliament is going to vote about whether to legalize zilfium use in Winterkeep, and they want to know where the Royal Continent stands."

"The Royal Continent" was the Torlans' name for Giddon's continent; they'd thought it was quaint that most of the nations upon it were monarchies. It was a name that had always had an air of condescension to it, in Giddon's opinion, much like the official name for Giddon's language, Gracelingian, which had also been assigned by outsiders. But that hardly mattered now. What mattered was that as Bitterblue began deciphering the letter's second paragraph, her eyes widened.

"Giddon!" she said. "He says he's made friends with Katu, and Katu thinks there's something suspicious about the ship that went down with my men!"

"Suspicious!" said Giddon, sitting straighter. "On what evidence?"

"Saf doesn't know," said Bitterblue. "And—wait—he says Katu has disappeared!"

"Disappeared!" said Giddon. "What does that mean?"

"Everyone in Ledra says Katu's gone traveling," Bitterblue said, her eyes still flying back and forth across the page. "That he's taken his boat north. But Saf had a date with Katu to go sailing, and Katu never canceled the date or said goodbye. Katu had been searching for Mikka and Brek's sunken ship, the *Seashell*. They were going to go out together. Katu was going to show Saf where he was searching for it, since Saf's such a strong diver too. But now Katu's gone, and Saf has a funny feeling. He says he's going to look into it."

"What!" cried Skye, reaching for the letter. "Look into it how?"

"He doesn't say," said Bitterblue, handing him the letter, which was pointless, since it was ciphered. "But he says he wrote to you separately, Skye."

Skye studied the letter with an expression of rising aggravation. "Then where's *my* letter?"

"Giddon?" said Bitterblue. "What do you think? Does any of this make sense? Saf might be the type to look for trouble where it doesn't exist—but is Katu?"

Something about Bitterblue when she focused on him always made him want to rise above his lower instincts, for fear of hurting her, or disappointing her. He could never tell if it was the pucker of worry she let him see between her brows, or the appeal in her eyes, or the way her voice changed, as if she was ready to believe whatever he said. He wanted to be worthy of the trust she'd bestowed—arbitrarily, it seemed—upon him.

So he thought carefully about the disappearance of one of Bitterblue's lovers, reported by another of Bitterblue's lovers.

"I don't think Katu makes things up or drops appointments," he said. "And I don't think Saf would repeat Katu's suspicions if he didn't trust Katu."

"That's what I think too," said Bitterblue.

"If there's something suspicious about that ship going down," said Giddon, "then I'm more curious than ever about what Mikka wanted to tell you about zilfium."

"Yes," said Bitterblue. "And I'm worried about Katu. He hasn't written in forever."

"Balls to Katu," said Skye contemptuously. "What about Saf? What does he mean, he's *looking into it*?"

"Skye," said Bitterblue gently. Reaching out, she touched her cousin's dark hair, touched his worried face. The Lienid wore gold in their ears and on their fingers. Skye was a handsome man, glowing with gold, his eyes gray and his skin sun-brown. Bitterblue, who was half-Lienid, shared his coloring and wore Lienid rings. The two of them gleamed together.

"There's no cause for you to fret," Bitterblue told him. "You know how Saf is."

"That's exactly why I'm fretting!" said Skye. "What's he doing? Diving into the Brumal Sea in random locations, drowning himself?"

"I think Saf is undrownable," said Bitterblue, returning to her pie.

"And where's my letter?" said Skye. "And why is he endangering himself searching for one of your boyfriends?"

"Skye," said Bitterblue, whose fork was now frozen in the air between her plate and her mouth. "What's this about?"

"He promised me," said Skye, suddenly standing, so fast that his chair tipped over. "He swore to me that if he went to Winterkeep without me, he wouldn't do anything dangerous!"

"Skye!" said Bitterblue, who was now staring at her cousin in amazement. "Are you in love with Saf?"

Abruptly, Giddon stood. "Hava," he said, his mouth full of pie. "Let's go for a walk."

"I don't want to go for a walk," Hava said. Then, at Giddon's severe look, she added, "Fine. But bring pie."

After slapping more pie onto his plate, Giddon strode to the big doors and waited. With a great, impatient sigh, Hava grabbed a fork from the table and followed him. Giddon wanted to stay, so he could know how Bitterblue felt about her cousin being in love with Saf. But he would give them their privacy. It was what someone with more noble instincts than his would do.

CHAPTER THREE

"Saw that coming," Hava said as they walked away from the queen's rooms.

"You did?" said Giddon, truly surprised. "How? Have you been spying on Skye?"

"Of course not," she said scornfully. "How would that look?"

"You could make it look however you wanted it to look," said Giddon, for Hava was a Graceling who was Graced with a kind of hiding that allowed her to change what people thought they saw when they looked at her. If she wanted to, Hava could stand in a room with Saf and Skye pretending to be a curtain in the window while they said and did all sorts of things, never knowing she was there. Every Grace was different, and each was variably useful. Saf had the Grace of giving people wonderful dreams, which Giddon found irritatingly romantic. Hava's Grace, on the other hand, made her an excellent spy.

But of course she would never spy on Skye and Saf.

"I don't use my Grace without my sister's permission," Hava said in a scathing voice. "Can you see her asking me to spy on her own cousin? Especially on his love life?"

"No, of course not."

When Giddon sank into silence, Hava took a few sidelong looks at him and seemed to thaw into a more sympathetic person. Taking charge, she led him around corners and up and down several flights of stairs. Eventually, she brought him to the art gallery that Giddon knew was her favorite place in the castle. Hava's mother had been a sculptor. Her father had been Bitterblue's father, King Leck, though this was a secret. Giddon was one of few people who knew. Hava's mother was dead, for King Leck had killed her, many years ago. He'd killed Bitterblue's mother too. Then he himself had been killed, turning Princess Bitterblue into a ten-year-old queen.

In a room crowded with her mother's sculptures, Hava sat on a raised section of floor and patted the place beside her.

Sitting numbly, Giddon held the plate out between them. For a while, they did nothing but eat pie.

"Anyway, Bitterblue doesn't care about Skye and Saf," said Hava, finally picking up the dropped conversation.

"How can you say that? Didn't you see the expression on her face just then?"

"Because she was surprised, you blockhead. Not because she's still hung up on Saf. That was over four years ago!"

"Was it really?" Giddon said, scratching his head in confusion.

"You're hopeless," Hava said, holding a forkful of pie out to him, even though he had his own fork. He opened his mouth, deciding to accept the pie as a shameful token of his hopelessness, which Hava had laid bare in that way Hava always had. Bitterblue's half sister didn't look like Bitterblue. She was tall, pale, and straw-haired. Hava also had one eye copper and the other bloodred, for Gracelings had two-colored eyes. Hava was only twenty years old, but often seemed older and cleverer than Giddon, who was thirty-one. Except when she was being a brat, which was often enough. Though even her brattiness left him feeling six years old sometimes.

"All right," he said. "Tell me what you know."

"Saf and Skye have been together for two years or so," Hava said.

"A little longer. Saf keeps breaking up with him and coming back. Saf's a lot younger than Skye, you know. And he more or less hates that Skye is a prince."

"He could always stop falling in love with royalty."

"Oh, grow up, Giddon," said Hava, which made Giddon snort. "Anyway, that's pretty much all I know, beyond what Skye just said. They made an arrangement that Saf would go to Winterkeep without Skye, for six months at the most, because Saf needed some time."

"Time to do what?" said Giddon. "Sleep with everyone he met?"

"Why would you care if he did? Time to think, you idiot."

"How do you know all this?"

"Oh, I don't know, maybe because I'm not stuck behind a fog of my own projections?"

Giddon snorted again.

"Haven't you wondered why Skye is hanging around?" Hava said. "He never stays here this long. But a letter from Winterkeep gets to Bitterblue City five or six weeks faster than to Lienid, don't you see?"

Giddon supposed he was beginning to see.

"Why are *you* hanging around this court?" Hava added significantly.

"You know I can't go home," said Giddon. He'd been a lord once, with an estate in the kingdom of the Middluns. A beautiful estate, with forests and farms and horses, and hundreds of people in his care. King Randa had banished him, stripped him of his title, then razed his castle to the ground, to punish him for his Council work. The people who'd depended upon Giddon had had to accept Randa as a landlord, or else find new homes and work. "And I need to be near Estill," he said. "You know we're worried about their new government. I'm keeping an eye out."

"Wouldn't you have a better view of Estill if you were actually in Estill?" Hava said. "Rather than sitting across from my sister every night at dinner?"

"Brat," said Giddon.

"Bully," said Hava. "I'm done with our walk now. I'm going back to see what happened."

After she left, Giddon sat alone for a while, finding his better self before he allowed himself to return to the queen.

USUALLY, GIDDON HAD easier access to his better self.

Didn't he?

After all, he spent most of his time trying to figure out how to solve people's problems without creating worse problems. Sometimes they were small problems, like what three kinds of batter should make the layers for the queen's twenty-third birthday cake. This was not a Council matter, of course, but that didn't mean he wasn't the man for the job.

One morning, in the week after Bitterblue received Saf's letter, Giddon overheard Helda, the elderly woman who took care of Bitterblue's domestic needs, muttering indignantly to a member of her staff in the corridors.

"She's refusing a party," Helda said. "She doesn't want a big dinner, either. She wants her usual, quiet dinner here with her friends, and for us to act as if she isn't the most important woman in the world. Well, I know she loves sweets. But she never admits a preference. She wants all her cooks to feel equally wonderful. She takes care of everyone, all the time! How am I to make her feel taken care of on her birthday?"

"Um, excuse me, Helda," Giddon said, glancing around conspiratorially to make sure he wasn't overheard. "All three layers should be chocolate, with buttercream frosting. And encircle it with bite-sized vanilla cream puffs."

Helda narrowed eyes on Giddon that contained a certain spark of interest. She leaned back. "And how do you know that, Giddon?"

"She gets very quiet and focused when we have those things at dinner," Giddon said. "And she scrapes her plate clean. Haven't you noticed?"

The next look Helda gave him made him flush with heat and decide he was needed elsewhere urgently. But on the night of Bitterblue's birthday, the chocolate cake and cream puffs made Bitterblue take Helda into her arms and kiss her cheek. Giddon couldn't stay that night, because he had more people to shepherd out of Estill. But he was able to leave knowing that her long day had been punctuated by a small delight, because of him.

Always, Giddon was careful not to look too closely at how those moments felt. He understood the pointlessness of it. Bitterblue was a queen, which meant she was expected to marry a man. Her advisers thrust men at her constantly, and he'd noticed that none of them were disinherited, banished lords. He knew she tried her best to like some of them. He even knew, because she made no secret of it with him, when she involved herself with any of them, or with anyone else.

Sometimes, she came to him for advice. He was almost nine years older and she wanted the benefit of his experience. This made him feel ancient.

"Have you ever been quite in love with someone," she asked him once, a couple years back when she'd been seeing some lord from the southern coast, "then realized they're not actually as kind or grown-up as you thought? And in fact, you were in love with an idea of who you thought they were, instead of who they actually are? And now you have to tell them so, but there's no point in being hurtful?"

And yes, he had been in that situation. In fact, he was pretty sure he'd been on both sides of that situation. But it was hard to trust his own best instincts in giving her advice, since in those moments, it became achingly clear to him how badly he wanted her to jettison whatever man she was talking about.

But he considered the question seriously, because she looked unhappy, and because she trusted him.

"I know it's hard to feel like you're being kind," he said, "when the truth you need to tell is going to be hurtful. There's just no way around that. But when I look back, I most appreciate the people who were straightforward about it, you know?" Even a little merciless, if he was being honest, but he didn't say that out loud. He didn't trust his own intentions in advising Bitterblue to be merciless with some man she was kicking out of her bed. "It's good to avoid ambiguity," he said. "It helps everyone move on."

And then he waited, with various levels of agitation and self-enforced patience, until the man in question stopped being talked of, disappeared from court, and seemed unmissed. And then the next one came along, and he felt his age, the small income the Council granted him, his unworthiness, again. She was probably going to marry Katu Cavenda, once they figured out where he'd gone. Or she'd marry some earl, or at any rate, some man with a fortune and an unblemished past who deserved her, as much as anyone could deserve her. A good man.

Giddon had discovered, in his Council travels, that he could be many different men, depending on whom he was with and what they needed from him. He didn't like all the Giddons he could be. Some were manipulative or forceful. Some were even violent, which always reminded him uncomfortably of his past, for in his life before the Council, Giddon had been a bully on behalf of King Randa. Long, long before the Council had made him understand some things about himself, and kings, and power, and bullies, he'd been a small-minded man who did small things. Bitterblue knew. He didn't have many secrets Bitterblue didn't know. He was lucky she considered him a friend.

This is enough, he thought. *A life where I'm helping people, tricking corrupt kings, even dismantling monarchies is enough. What sense would it make anyway, for a queen to marry a lawbreaker?* And then he would tell himself that it was time to write to Raffin and Bann, Katsa and Po, and propose a new assignment for himself, somewhere else.

Somehow, though, he never found the time to write those letters.

LATE ONE MORNING in August, three months after Saf's letter had arrived, Bitterblue came to Giddon's door.

Minutes before, he'd returned from the tunnels again; he'd just stripped off his shirt and dropped into bed when she knocked. He smelled like horses and mud. In fact, as he blundered across the room to answer the door, he found a streak of mud on his chest, which didn't even make sense. It wasn't like he led Estillans through the tunnels shirtless.

Then he opened the door, saw Bitterblue, and woke up.

She blinked at him. "Oh good," she said. "I heard a rumor you were back."

"Come in while I find a shirt," he said.

"Don't do it for my sake," she said, which was one of the only flirtatious things she'd ever said to him in their entire acquaintance and subsequently threw him into such confusion that he decided to disappear into his bathing room on the pretense of cleaning up. Luckily he was filthy, so it was a believable retreat. Of course, while he was splashing water on himself, Lovejoy burst through the open window, nearly giving him a heart attack.

When he came out a moment later, dressed and with what he hoped was an imperturbable expression, Bitterblue was curled up in his big chair with Lovejoy purring in her lap. It made his heart hurt.

She waved a letter at him. "You know Skye's in Winterkeep now?" she said. "He's written a letter and I haven't opened it yet. I wanted to read it with you. In case it's bad news."

He paused, studying her. "You're worried about Katu," he said. "You're serious about Katu, aren't you?"

"I'm serious about making sure he's okay," she said, that pucker appearing between her eyebrows. "And I'm terrified of learning that my men were drowned on purpose. If they were, I won't be able to forgive myself."

"Bitterblue," he said, sitting on the big chair beside her. "If something like that happened, then it's entirely the responsibility of the person who drowned them."

"I know," she said, then raised her eyes to his face. "But you know how it is."

Of course he did. The queen felt responsible for everyone. "I know."

She opened the letter and held the page out for him to see, her fingers flashing with gold. "The key is 'bratty little brother,'" she said, which was adorable, as it had to be a reference to Skye's brother Po, who was a grown man and the furthest thing from a brat. But it was also superfluous information, as Bitterblue would decipher the entire letter in the time it took Giddon to make out the first line.

"Saf's decided Katu really has left Winterkeep without saying goodbye," she said grimly, reading. "Katu left no forwarding address and his boat is gone. His family and friends say he's off adventuring, as usual. Saf checked with Katu's banker and apparently Katu's drawn money from banks in Kamassar and Borza, with his own checks."

"Well, that's reassuring," Giddon said.

"But how could he leave without canceling his appointment with Saf?" said Bitterblue. "And without writing to me?"

"Maybe he wrote to you and his letter got lost."

"Yes, maybe," she said, still deciphering the letter. "I hope so. Skye says here that Saf has been swimming with the silbercows."

"The telepathic seals, or whatever they are?"

"They're bigger than seals, and purple, but yes. He says the silber-cows keep showing Saf an image of a many-windowed house on a cliff, and a shadow in the sky that looks like an airship. Then, a disturbance in the water nearby. A serious disturbance. Like, everything changes."

"What do you mean? Changes how?"

"He says that in the image, the ocean is normal, then suddenly there's a blinding light and no water and the silbercows are in pain."

"Okay," said Giddon, to whom that meant nothing. "All we need now is a vague remark about zilfium and the letter will be completely incomprehensible."

"He says that now the Katu mystery is solved, he and Saf are going to Mantiper together. The Mantiperans are looking for a sea passage east to Lienid. Saf and Skye are going to join the efforts."

Mantiper was the Torlan nation farthest from Winterkeep, so far east that Saf and Skye would likely be gone for a long time, sailing in uncharted waters. "That sounds dangerous."

"Yes. But it sounds like they're happy," Bitterblue said with a small, winsome smile. "Ah," she added. "Here's a bit about zilfium. He says that no one in the Keepish government likes to talk about this, but the Torlan continent is running low on zilfium. Some mines in Winterkeep and Kamassar are closing." Then she stopped, stared. Something changed in her face. "Giddon," she said.

"Yes?"

"Saf says zilfium is most often found near native silver."

"What does that mean?"

"Zilfium rock and native silver are formed by the same geologic activity. Where there's native silver, there's likely to be zilfium."

"Okay," said Giddon, not understanding why her face grew oddly furious. Then remembering that the largest and richest deposits of native silver on the Royal Continent were in Monsea.

"Do you think that the mountains in Monsea have zilfium?" he asked her cautiously.

"Would you excuse me for a minute?" she said, standing stiffly, so that the cat went sprawling.

"Of course," he said, but she was already at the door, the cat yowling around her feet. A moment later, the door slammed behind them both.

Abruptly alone, Giddon didn't know what to do with himself. He was so exhausted that while he was trying to decide, he began to fall asleep in the big chair. He'd just made it across the room and fallen onto the bed when she knocked again, then came storming in without waiting for his answer. She stopped in the middle of the room and stood there with her eyes on fire and her fists clenched, and Giddon was amazed, as he always was when she was angry, at how much power, fury, and force her person could convey.

"Do you know," she said, "that a number of different Keepish importers have been buying the rock detritus from my silver mines for the past three years, for almost no money?"

"What?" said Giddon blearily, stupidly, but then he understood.

She pulled a piece of paper out of a pocket and waved it at him. "I thought it was odd," she said, her voice rising, "but I've been too busy to focus on it. I figured they used it for some building process. Winterkeep doesn't have our mountains, they don't have our rock."

"Of course," said Giddon. "It was natural for you not to focus on it."

"They have been stealing our zilfium!" she practically yelled, her body electric with rage. "They've been taking advantage of our ignorance of a resource far more valuable than silver! Tricking me, our miners, our scientists. You should see the names on this list! It's practically every important family in Ledra! Balava Importing. Tima Importing. There's even a Cavenda company on this list, probably some horrible relation of Katu's! What kind of people do this? What kind of *nation*? My kingdom can't help its backwardness," she cried.

"We were trapped under the reign of a psychopath who made monuments to himself and buried science and burned books and murdered anyone who tried to break free of it, for thirty-five years! Winterkeep has airships and brilliant schools and brilliant industries and I can't even teach my people to *read*! And they saw that, and they saw my silver mines, and they decided to trick me out of wealth I had that I could've used. To fund a school, one as brilliant as the Winterkeep Academy!"

Giddon knew the tears running down her face were tears of fury. At the Keepish; at her father, King Leck; at her life; on behalf of the lives of everyone in Monsea who'd suffered. He went to her and put his arms around her.

"Tell me whom to kill," he said.

That made her laugh, and the laughter transitioned her to the other kind of crying. The harder kind for Giddon, because it was about her grief, and he couldn't lessen that.

"You're doing everything any human being could do for Monsea," he said. "More. You are being amazing."

"Giddon," she said, soaking his shirt with her tears. "What if Mikka and Brek died because they were going to tell me that my own nation is rich with zilfium?"

"Then someone in Winterkeep is a murderer and is going to pay," he said.

"But I sent them there."

"It's not your fault."

"But—"

"It's not your fault," he repeated firmly. "It's your burden. But it's not your fault. There's a difference."

She sniffled for a while, thinking about that. "Yes," she said. "I see what you mean." Then, a moment later, she said, "Giddon, did I wake you up? Twice?"

"It's okay."

"I haven't even asked you how it went this time in the tunnels. I'm sorry."

"It was fine," he said, though it hadn't been, not really, for the soldiers in the Estillan forests had been harder to skirt than ever, and the increase was rumored to be at the orders of Lord Joff, home from his trip to the Monsean queen. Why? Also, along with their blades and bows, the soldiers were carrying a flag Giddon hadn't recognized. One of the refugees had told him it was the flag of the new Estillan regime. It was just a flag—Giddon kept telling himself it was just a flag—but it was eerily like the Monsean flag. Bitterblue's flag showed a mountain peak rising behind water with a single gold star above, shining in a dark sky. The new Estillan flag showed a similar mountain peak rising behind hills, and a similar star above, except that their star was shaped like a sword with a cross guard. And the sky was red like blood.

"I'll tell you the details later," he said.

"I'm glad you're home," she said, throwing Giddon into another confusion, because he had no home anymore; he spent his life on the road, in the company of strangers. This court was merely where he was staying, until the Council needed him to be someone else, somewhere else.

"I'm going to Winterkeep," she added, pulling away from him and mopping her face with her sleeve.

"What?" he said, startled.

"I've been receiving invitations from the Keepish Parliament for some time now. I think it's time I went there myself, and made some things clear. Meet the importers on this list who've been cheating me, and learn more about the ship that went down. Make sure Katu is really okay."

"Bitterblue," he said in alarm. "Aren't those jobs you can delegate?"

"My last two delegates drowned."

"Well then, could it be dangerous? Send someone."

"They're not going to kill the Queen of Monsea," she said scornfully.

"All right," he said, changing tactics, "but aren't you needed here? Since when do you have the time for a trip like that?"

"How could it not be worth a queen's time to see the workings of more advanced nations?"

"But don't you get seasick?"

Bitterblue began to laugh. "Listen to you," she said. "I'm going, Giddon."

But I like myself best when I'm around you, he didn't say. *I try the hardest when I'm with you. Don't leave.*

"Giddon?" she said, turning those steady, trusting gray eyes upon him. "Does the Council have any interest in seeing Winterkeep?"

CHAPTER FOUR

LOVISA CAVENDA SLIPPED down the corridor and stopped outside her Politics of Trade classroom, tucking herself against the wall.

A professor walked by, not even glancing at her. Lovisa could make herself as still and uninteresting as a wall fixture. It was one of the benefits of being small.

She was early, as usual. The previous class was still in the room. Behind the closed door, she heard the even cadence of her mother's voice, her faint northern accent, strong and assured; the occasional laughter of the class, engaged in the lesson. Every class taught by Lovisa's mother, Ferla Cavenda, had a waiting list as long as this corridor. Students threw themselves against her high standards and competed for her approval. They wanted to be challenged by her.

Bullied by her? thought Lovisa, who'd grown up in Ferla's house and knew the line was indistinct.

A pair of younger students, heads bent together and giggling, came down the corridor, not noticing Lovisa until they were practically upon her. She memorized their faces, their clothing, their silly conversation about someone they both had a crush on; then leveled an expressionless gaze upon them when they finally saw her.

Dropping into a startled silence, the two students hurried on. Lovisa watched them go, suppressing a shiver. A fire was crackling in the foyer fireplace around the corner, but September was chilly in Ledra.

Then someone else came down the corridor and Lovisa stood up straight. It was her own father.

"Papa!" she said. "What are you doing here?"

"Lovisa," he said, coming to her with open arms, pulling her into a hug. He was a big man, stylishly dressed in a long, dark fur coat as usual, gold scarves at his throat and his black hair cut close. He smelled as he always did, like the warm, spicy teas he drank, and his brown face was different from hers in its striking handsomeness, strong boned and finely chiseled like a sculpture.

"How have you been?" he said.

"I'm fine," said Lovisa, then repeated, "What are you doing here?" Her father was a politician and a businessman. She rarely saw him during the week. "Is anything wrong?"

"Of course not," he said. "I merely thought I'd take my wife out to lunch. Would you like to join us?"

"I have class."

"You should come home for dinner tonight, sweetheart."

Behind the closed door, her mother's voice grew louder, then the door opened and Ferla's bonded blue fox bolted out of the classroom and down the passageway. *Good riddance,* Lovisa thought, watching the animal go, for she had no fondness for her mother's fox. Blue foxes in Winterkeep, which were actually more gray than blue, had the ability to bond telepathically to humans. The bonding was an opening of an exclusive mental pathway between one human and one fox, initiated by the fox. It allowed the fox and the human to share their thoughts and feelings with each other, for the rest of their lives. And Ferla's fox served as Ferla's smelly, devoted spy, nosing around, snooping, and telling on Lovisa and her little brothers whenever they misbehaved.

Ferla glanced out into the corridor. When she saw her daughter, her expression remained impassive. Then she saw her husband and surprise touched her small face. Some silent communication passed between them.

"I'll be with you in a moment," she said quietly, then turned back to the room to dismiss her class. "Next time we meet," she called out, "I expect an opinionated debate on the topic of chapter two." Students picked up their belongings and began moving, chatting, forming groups, spilling out into the corridor. By the time Lovisa and Benni entered the room, Ferla had gathered her things and was heading toward the door.

"Good morning, Lovisa," she said, turning the force of her attention upon her daughter. She raised a hand to touch her husband's chest as he kissed her on one brown cheek. The students still remaining in the room slowed their movements, watching discreetly. Everyone always like to watch Ferla and Benni Cavenda when they were together, for both were members of the Keepish government, but they represented parties that were bitterly opposed. Ferla was a Scholar. Benni was an Industrialist. Ferla was also the nation's current president; though, with a few important exceptions, that position was mostly ceremonial. Benni was an elected representative of Parliament. Ferla and Benni agreed on hardly anything politically, and made a spectacle of it sometimes while Parliament was in session. It turned out you could make yourself famous, even successful, powerful, by marrying the enemy and having your wars in public. Yet there were no political fights at home. It had always been that way: At home, her parents had no differences.

"Good morning, Mother," said Lovisa.

"How is your paper coming along for Politics of Trade?" asked Ferla. She was a small woman who never seemed small, not even beside her big husband, for her chin was high and her face proud and certain. Her dark hair was pulled severely back from her forehead, streaked with white at the temple like Lovisa's. All of Ferla's four children shared her smallness of stature, but only Lovisa had the white streak.

"It's going well," Lovisa said.

"Good," said Ferla. "I've asked Gorga to share it with me."

A screw tightened in Lovisa's throat. Her professor, Gorga Balava, was a forgiving grader, whereas Ferla had an eye for reading Lovisa's work and detecting exactly where she'd been lazy. She'd written a section of the paper just this morning, and maybe it had been too easy. She'd have to take a closer look.

"Say hello to the boys for me," said Lovisa as her parents moved toward the door.

"Come home for dinner and say hello to them yourself," said Ferla, speaking with the kind of friendly challenge she accorded to her students and her colleagues, and her daughter when they were in public. This was why Lovisa always came to class early. She wanted the sense of belonging bestowed by her public mother.

Ferla and Benni left the room together. Then Gorga Balava pushed through the door, a small man with a ring of graying hair, a bonded fox of his own at his heels. Lovisa didn't like anyone's fox, because all foxes snuck and hid and she hated not knowing if a conversation was happening right in front of her that she couldn't hear. But Gorga's fox was less annoying than the others, because their relationship seemed based less on secret communication and more on the professor's indulgence. For example, this morning his fox was prancing around in little fur booties, sparkling with gems. Ridiculous.

"Nice to see you, Lovisa," said Gorga.

"You too, Professor Balava."

"Was that a union of rivals I saw leaving just now?"

"I'm afraid so."

"I don't suppose you overheard any of their conversation?"

"No, sir."

"I don't suppose you'd tell me if you had?" said Gorga, with a flash of a smile that contained warmth, a kind of teasing. Almost every teacher in the academy's school of politics and government also worked in the Keepish government in some capacity, large or small, and Gorga was no exception. He was an elected representative of Parliament, like Benni. An Industrialist, also like Benni. And everyone in government, regardless of their party, was nosy.

"I saw them exchange meaningful glances," Lovisa said, making a joke of it, but remembering the look that had passed between her parents. Her mother's face had contained a question, and her father's, an answer, one that had caused Ferla to light up with curiosity. Lovisa was adept at reading silent conversations. Maybe that was why foxes made her so irritable. Their conversations with their humans were uninterpretable.

"Are you ready to talk about the upcoming zilfium vote?" asked Gorga.

Lovisa sighed. "I knew there was some reason I didn't bother to do the reading."

"I don't believe you didn't do the reading, Lovisa."

And he was right. Lovisa always did the reading, because that was the path to perfect grades. But Lovisa couldn't care less about the upcoming vote scheduled for December on whether to legalize zilfium use in Winterkeep, because there was no point. The results were already certain. The Industrialists, who were the pro-zilfium party, did not have enough votes to win. It was too bad, because Lovisa had a feeling she'd like the zilfium trains that the other Torlan nations enjoyed. Her uncle Katu, who was her mother's baby brother and a world traveler, had told her all about them. He'd once ridden a train across Kamassar and Borza, then on into Mantiper. For all Lovisa knew, Katu was on a train somewhere right now, for Katu had set off again a few months ago on a new adventure. Maybe he would write soon, and tell her where he was. Lovisa hoped he would. Katu was so much younger than his sister—in his mid-twenties, really closer to Lovisa's sixteen than to Ferla's ancient grown-up-ness—and so different from Ferla that he'd always felt like more of a cousin than an uncle.

"Zilfium trains smell like burning and excitement," Katu had told her once as they climbed aboard his boat. When Katu was home, he often took Lovisa and her three little brothers sailing.

Lovisa had snorted, whacked his shoulder idly, and demanded to know what excitement smelled like.

"Like the sun on metal," he said, "and a saltwater wind."

"You're just saying that because you're wild about boats."

A smile had transformed Katu's face into light. Lovisa's brother Viri, who was five, had repeated, "Wild about boats!" Then Viri had stood up straight as a soldier, tiny, brown, and freckled, waving his arms around as the boat moved under him, repeating it again, chanting it to the sky. "Wild about boats! Wild about boats!" The other boys, Erita and Vikti, seven and nine, had joined in the chant. Being with Katu made the boys hyper, silly. They always seemed a little drunk around him. Katu, who thought life in their household was grimmer than it needed to be, did nothing to discourage it.

"I'm wild about my niece and nephews," Katu had responded as he began to check the winches; then, rolling his eyes good-humoredly at the boys, "Or maybe they just make my head spin." And Lovisa had wished, if he was so wild about them, that he would take them the next time he ran off. Or at least take her. She wanted to climb the mountains of Kamassar and hug the coasts of Borza in a big, long metal contraption that sounded like grinding steel and smelled like excitement.

"Make my head spin!" the boys began chanting, while Katu,

laughing, worked around them. He hoisted Erita onto his shoulder so he could reach the dock line and Erita broke into delighted squeals. Katu was compact and strong and looked like Lovisa's mother, especially the white streak in his hair, but he was so easy and friendly, so much less serious. The ruby on his thumb sparkled as he unhitched the dock line. He'd once, in Ferla's hearing, called the ring "the only nice thing our father ever gave me," which was ridiculous, for their father had given him a zilfium and silver mine he shared with his sister, not to mention the house that sat above it. But Katu spoke that way sometimes about the father Ferla idolized—called him a tyrant, a bully, and a bore—impressing Lovisa with this person who said what he wanted, did what he wanted, and wasn't afraid of Ferla's temper.

The other students in Politics of Trade were filtering into the classroom, glancing at Lovisa, greeting their professor, finding their seats. Lovisa took a breath. Then, deciding that she wanted to know the real reason her father had come looking for her mother, she asked to be excused to the restroom.

INSIDE A PARTICULAR restroom on the second floor, Lovisa reached her hand up and felt along the marble ledge of one of the privy stalls. Finding the small wedge of wood she kept there, she jammed it hard under the door so that no one, person or fox, could come in. Then she bent down under the long sink basin and put her ear to the heating grate in the floor. Lovisa had a way of noticing what was on the other side of ceilings, floors, and walls. Two years ago, on one of her first days at the academy, she'd figured out that this restroom was directly above her mother's office.

Immediately, she heard the rumble of her parents' voices below, the sound rising through the heating pipes with a tinny distortion. Hot air gusted into Lovisa's face, making her eyes water. But her mother's voice was clear.

"I admit it's not a terrible plan, Benni," she said. "But it has a lot of variables. You tend to assume things you can't be sure of yet. You're rushing."

Her father's voice rumbled, his words imperceptible.

"That will be up to you," said Ferla. "I can't solve your storage problems. Come over here, would you? Stop fidgeting."

Benni's voice rose more audibly through the grate. "Could I store it in the attic room? It would be in a banker's box. No one would look twice at it."

A banker's box was a small safe with a combination lock; Benni had two, which he used for categorically dull things. Usually cash.

"I don't love that idea," said Ferla. "When the time comes, you can stash it in your library. Even better, my study."

"It would only be for a short time. We don't have a good place in the house for these kinds of valuables. I think the attic room is best."

"We'll discuss it later," said Ferla. "The issue is unlikely to arise for quite a while. Why are you here, Benni? I don't believe your future storage problems brought you here from Flag Hill."

"You're right," he said. "I think we should accept an invitation for dinner tonight at the house of Quona Varana."

"Quona Varana!" said Ferla, her voice resonant with both disbelief and scorn. The Varanas were an important Ledra family—Sara Varana, a Scholar, was currently prime minister, which meant she led Parliament and directed most of the actions of the government's executive branch. Minta Varana, sister to Quona and Sara, was Winterkeep's foremost airship engineer. Varane, the gas that kept airships buoyant, was named after their family.

But Quona was something else entirely. In a family of Scholars and inventors, she'd first become a doctor of animal medicine, then decided to live by herself in a house on a cliff above the sea with about a dozen cats. She had no interest in politics. She was a professor in the school of animal medicine at the academy and floated around campus wearing skirts covered with fur.

"Why does that woman keep inviting us to dinner?" said Ferla.

"Who doesn't invite us to dinner, my dear?"

"Why would you *want* to go to her house for dinner?"

"Because she also invited the envoy from Estill," said Benni.

Briefly, Ferla was silent. "Why should I care that Quona invited the Estillan envoy?"

"It might matter," said Benni.

"To whom?" said Ferla. "Maybe they're just friends. Maybe he's a cat fanatic. It's Quona. Anyway, I just invited our daughter home to dinner tonight, Benni."

"Lovisa will survive," said Benni.

"Are you ever going to tell me the real reason you've crossed town?" said Ferla, her voice beginning to sharpen. "You'll never convince me it's because you want to have dinner with Quona Varana."

"You're right, as usual," said Benni, his voice growing both warmer and quieter. Lovisa shifted uncomfortably, trying to press her ear more firmly against the grate, because something told her that whatever her father said next was going to be the puzzle piece that connected everything.

"I've had a letter," Benni said. "The Queen of Monsea is coming to Winterkeep for a visit."

This time, Ferla's silence lasted longer. Lovisa wished she could see her mother's face. She wondered if it was lit up like her own.

"You don't say," said Ferla, surprise in her voice. "When?"

"Now. She'll be on the sea already. She expects to arrive in three or four weeks."

"Well," said Ferla, who was beginning to sound as happy as Lovisa felt. "Do you think Parliament will agree to let us host her?"

"They must," said Benni. "You must use your influence on Sara

Varana, for we simply must have her at home. It's such an opportunity for diplomacy."

"Yes," said Ferla, her voice deepening. And then Lovisa heard muffled noises, a series of murmurs, then a gasp, and sprang away from the vent so fast that she cracked her head on the marble of the sink's underside and had to suppress a cry of pain. Ugh. Her parents. It was disgusting how often their conversations randomly turned into things she did *not* want to hear.

She pushed herself up from the floor, pressing her fingers under the tight twists she wore in her hair, trying to rub the sore spot. In the mirror, she saw a young version of Ferla, which depressed her. She also saw a pattern of crisscrosses and circles embedded in her cheek from the grate, and sighed. She was stuck in here until that mark faded.

But the news was worth it. The Queen of Monsea was coming to Winterkeep, and might even stay in her house! Important delegates invariably ended up at the Cavenda house. That was because Lovisa's parents represented opposing parties. Placing someone like the Queen of Monsea in the Cavenda home would leave neither the Scholars nor the Industrialists feeling at a disadvantage.

The Cavendas had also hosted Prince Skye for part of his visit, the one who was the Queen of Monsea's cousin. Lovisa had found herself going home for dinner often, wanting to sit across from the man with the Lingian accent, the gold in his ears and on his fingers. He'd said that his father, a king, lived in a palace that sat atop a spire of rock. He'd said that he had a brother who was a Graceling, Graced with fighting. He'd had a Graced boyfriend too, a man named Saf, the first Graceling Lovisa had ever met. Saf had had blond hair like no one Lovisa had ever seen before, skin paler than his hair, eyes of two different purples, and the Grace of giving people dreams. He'd asked her once, over dinner, if she wanted a dream, and she hadn't known what kind of dream to ask for. While she'd stalled, thinking, her little brothers had asked him for dreams of the Keeper, who was the undersea hero in the fairy tales the silbercows told. Then the conversation had turned to explaining the Keeper legends to the guests, and Lovisa had never gotten her dream. The boys had, though. They dreamed of the Keeper every night now, if they wanted.

A visit from a queen of the Royal Continent would be a real adventure. Wouldn't it? This was the sort of thing that happened in a life like Katu's. In fact, Katu knew the Queen of Monsea personally. He'd visited the Royal Continent not long ago; he'd told Lovisa about Gracelings. About the little queen who lived in a castle, spending her days in a soaring tower that rose above the city bridges. About Royal Continent magic.

From her parents' overheard conversation, Lovisa hadn't gotten the puzzle piece that made everything clear. She still didn't understand about Benni's plan, the banker's box, or Quona Varana's friendship with the Estillan envoy. But she would file those tidbits away, in case they became useful later. You never knew what detail might fit perfectly into a future puzzle.

It did occur to her to notice that her father, like her mother, had invited Lovisa home for dinner as well, even though he'd never intended to be there. That stung a little.

But Lovisa would forgive him anything to have the Queen of Monsea living in her house.

CHAPTER FIVE

BITTERBLUE HAD FORGOTTEN how seasick she got. Had it always been this bad? She was certain that as a child, her head had stopped spinning after just a few days. Now her sickness kept going away, then coming back; going away again, then always coming back.

When the first ten days of the journey to Winterkeep had passed like this, she'd suddenly become terrified that she might be pregnant, a fear that had not reduced her nausea. It would've been the baby of a young lord named Pella from central Monsea who was intelligent and funny and attractive and whose child she absolutely, positively did not want.

Once the scare had passed, she understood that she needn't have worried. Bitterblue was always careful to take the medicines. Still, it had frightened her, and made her remember how angry Pella had been when she'd broken things off with him.

"You're cold," he'd said to her in a sudden, harsh voice, surprising her, because Bitterblue was quite sure nothing but warmth had passed between them. Pella had a warm, grinning mouth and the most beautiful shoulders and arms, the warmest hands. She knew that he'd known, for she'd made *sure* that he'd known, that their affair was temporary. He'd told her it was what he wanted too.

"What do you mean?" she asked. "You know I'm not cold."

He pushed to his feet, curled his lips with contempt. She'd never seen him do that before and it was stunning. They were alone in Bitterblue's sitting room. It was late; the lamps threw their reflections against her windows. Bitterblue, confused, stood up too, and saw her mirror-self rising across the room.

"You pretend you're giving your heart," he said.

"I never pretend," she said, really hurt now, because she was always honest with lovers; it was a lesson she'd taken to heart long ago. "I think you're the one who's been pretending something!"

"Well, you see the truth of me now," he said, and she did. "You use people," he said. "You never give."

"That's unfair!" cried Bitterblue, who'd loved exploring his body, learning what made it sing. "I am a generous lover!"

"You never give your *heart*," he said, then swept away through the big doors, visibly upset, probably giving the guards outside her rooms plenty to gossip about.

Alone, Bitterblue sat with a blanket pulled around her shoulders, working through his words. She was certain that he'd been unfair. He'd wanted more than she'd offered. When she hadn't given it to him, he'd lashed out, as if it was something he was entitled to. This was part of the reason Bitterblue liked Katu Cavenda so much. He took responsibility for his own feelings. When it had been time for Katu to go home and they'd parted with no promises, he'd pulled her close. "I can't wait to see you again someday," he'd whispered, breath soft against her ear, "and see what happens." Pella could have parted that way. Instead, he'd been unfair.

A few minutes later, Helda padded up the hall from her own rooms in a robe and slippers. Of course she did; Helda always knew what was going on. She touched Bitterblue's hair and sighed gently, her own white hair pulled back messily and her pale face lined with sleep.

"Can I get you anything, dear?" she said, and Bitterblue started to cry.

"I never intended to hurt him," she said, then glanced up at Helda. "Or wake you, dear Helda."

"I'll make you something warm to drink," Helda said, giving her shoulder a squeeze and shuffling away. The warm drink, placed gently into her hands, comforted her. Nonetheless, Bitterblue sat for a long time, thinking. She'd begun to wonder if Pella's accusation—not the earlier ones, but the final one—might be true.

On the ship, after the pregnancy scare, when it all came back to her, she did what she always did: She asked Giddon his opinion.

"Do you think," she said, "that I'm incapable of giving anyone my heart?"

First, a series of indescribable expressions crossed Giddon's face. Then he said something so on the nose that she went silent, keeping his words close, pulling them out frequently afterward, thinking about them as she lay, nauseated, in her cabin bed.

"Maybe you have too much experience of the bad things that happen when you love someone, and too little experience of the good things," he said. "Maybe you're protecting yourself."

Bitterblue thought it was a polite way of saying "Your father murdered your mother." She suddenly wondered if her mother, Ashen, had been horrified to find herself pregnant with Bitterblue. Or had her father, with his Grace of telling lies that were believed, told Ashen she was happy? Maybe Ashen hadn't had the option of being horrified. Or maybe Ashen *had* been happy, truly happy, because of how much she'd loved the child inside her, regardless of the father?

In which case, maybe Bitterblue was a monster for not wanting Pella's, or anyone's, child. And maybe she was a coward for not opening her heart.

"When you love someone, you lose them," she said quietly to Giddon. And then she was almost relieved at the waves of nausea that hit her, because she was able to focus on the physicality of retching into the basin Giddon handed her, instead of the terrifying memories of the day she'd lost her mother.

It was all too much to process at once. It had always been too much to process.

ON THE FINAL day of the voyage to Winterkeep, Bitterblue woke early, feeling no better than she ever did.

In the other bed, so close that Bitterblue could touch her, Hava was asleep. Bitterblue hadn't heard her come in last night. Hava loved to be on deck, watching everything that was happening. At home, Hava left the castle for days, sometimes even left the city, without telling anyone. It was her job as a spy. She always came back with helpful information but it was still nerve-racking, to have no earthly idea where she was, or if she was safe. Hava was too good at leaving. On the ship, she seemed to have plenty to interest her, and Bitterblue always knew she was near.

Bitterblue wanted some fresh air. Just a little fresh air, so that when they pulled into the port of Ledra later today, she'd be less likely to vomit on someone's shoes.

She touched Hava's sleeping shoulder, once. Hava made a small, contented noise in response, but didn't wake. Bitterblue found her boots, then the knife holsters she always wore under her sleeves.

Leaning on walls and doors, she made her way down the long corridor, then upstairs to the deck. Immediately, cold sliced through her clothing and the wind whipped her hair out of one of its braids. Wind this cold was shocking, especially given that it was only the first of October.

Giddon's laugh rang out somewhere nearby. She looked for his tall, solid form, wanting to tuck herself into his body for warmth, for protection from the wind. Giddon would be with her for the entire trip, making her laugh, helping her care for Hava, giving her his honest opinions when she asked. She hadn't believed that the Council would let Giddon go. She'd written beautiful thank-yous to Raffin, Bann, Po, and Katsa. Bitterblue felt greedy, like she'd stolen him.

He was in the bow, talking to the captain and one of Bitterblue's guards, the ship's cat winding around his feet. A rose glow from the eastern horizon touched his face. She heard snatches of his voice, thrown back to her by the wind.

She wouldn't interrupt. Clinging to whatever she could grab as the floor bucked, she edged onto the afterdeck and looked out over the water behind them. This very same water was touching the water that touched the water that lapped up against the docks and cliffs and hills of her very own nation, her home. Somewhere in the world, back the way they'd come, was a place where the ground was solid beneath her feet, where she knew what she was doing. More than that: Monsea needed her. She was the keeper of its people, no matter where they roamed. She would find out what had happened to Mikka and Brek, her two men.

She saw a wave rolling toward the ship, bigger than the others. *Much bigger,* she realized with a blip of surprise, just before the ship ducked to meet it. The deck surged up, then fell, the sailors in the bow shouting their amusement, everyone unhurt, everything in its proper place, as always; except that Bitterblue was gone.

IN THE WATER behind the ship, Bitterblue shouted and screamed. But the wind bore the ship and her words away, and nobody heard her.

It seemed impossible. "Giddon," she shouted, thrashing and flailing, absolutely incredulous that they didn't realize they were leaving her behind. "Giddon!"

She swam after them. *They'll see I'm missing,* she thought. *They'll turn around.* But the waves lifted her regularly as she swam, giving her a view of the vanishing ship, and nothing changed, except that she got colder, and more flabbergasted.

"What do I do?" she cried. "Giddon!"

Still in a state of disbelief, she kept swimming.

BITTERBLUE SHOOK WITH cold. She was still swimming, more or less. Trying to stay above water, trying to continue on a straight path, feeling like she'd swallowed half the ocean, icy pain throbbing in her ears. Had they noticed yet that she was missing? Didn't anyone *ever* check on the queen? How could they be so careless?

I'll swim all the way to Ledra, she thought, allowing no other thought into her head, no other possible ending to this story. *I'll fire every one of them when I get there, for leaving me behind.* It was harder and harder to move her shoulders, slap the water with arms and legs she could no longer feel.

They're all fired, she thought. *As soon as I get there.*

SHE WAS HAVING a sort of dream, about the time her friend Katsa had saved her from her father, after her father had killed her mother. Katsa was a Graceling and had carried her to sanctuary across an impassable, frozen mountain, running on snowshoes, yelling, keeping her warm and alive.

Don't you give up, she heard Katsa yelling. *Keep swimming. Keep swimming!* Which was a strange thing for Katsa to yell, if they were crossing a mountain, but Bitterblue was used to Katsa's teacher voice during training sessions, so she did what she was told. She kept swimming. And swimming, and crying. Her arms wouldn't move. She couldn't do it anymore. She breathed water. She sank.

Something bumped against her, hard. Bitterblue came awake, choking, thrashing. *Katsa?*

Something bumped against her again, from below. *Keep swim-*

ming, it said. Then a purplish mountain formed beneath her, lifting her up to the surface, soft, slippery, and warm. It had a head and flippers and was swimming strongly forward. Bitterblue didn't understand what was happening.

Too cold, someone said. *We must hurry.*

In the water around Bitterblue, she saw the faces of what looked like seals, but bigger, and deep purple, pearlescent, almost blue. They were staring at her with dark, placid eyes as they swam beside her. *Don't give up,* one of them said.

Something about the way they talked made Bitterblue feel like the top of her head was coming off. "I never give up," she said. "Everyone's fired."

Keep moving, another of them said. *You must keep warm.* But Bitterblue couldn't move, she could only lie prostrate on the purple creature below her, letting her arms and legs trail into the water and closing her eyes.

Open your eyes! someone yelled, and her eyes popped open.

Swimming beside Bitterblue, one of the creatures stared at her hard, its whiskers long and droopy. Its whiskers reminded her of her adviser Froggatt, who was probably still asleep in his bed on the ship, and who was fired.

Don't fall asleep, the long-whiskered creature said to her. *You mustn't fall asleep.*

"I'm so tired," she said.

If you fall asleep now, the creature said, *you won't wake up.*

"But I'm so cold," Bitterblue said, then noticed snowflakes falling on the creature's head, melting into its fur. She reached a hand toward its head, then cried out in a ragged, broken voice as one of her rings, her most important ring and dearest treasure, slid from her finger, bounced on the purple mountain she was riding, and slipped into the water.

"Mama!" Bitterblue cried, because it was her dead mother's ring, gold, with inset gray stones to match the color of Bitterblue's eyes. It was the only piece of her mother she'd brought on this journey. "Mama!" she moaned as she tried to slide from her mountain and dive after the ring, stopped by the long-whiskered creature who surged up beside her.

Numbly, Bitterblue rested her cheek, watching the snow form a small mound on the head of her long-whiskered friend. She supposed snow was forming soft mounds on her own body as well. She couldn't feel her body. She heard lapping water as the creatures around her moved, felt the gentle care of the creature who balanced her on its back. *Stay awake,* Long Whiskers said, over and over, regularly, like the low beat at the base of a song. Idly, it occurred to her that she was hearing all of their voices inside her own head, not really in words, but in pictures, pictures of herself swimming, strong, warm, awake. She remembered then that she knew about these creatures: Keepish silbercows, who were telepaths. Their oil, after they died, made an exquisite golden light. Bitterblue had imported some for her court. Saf had swum with them too.

Maybe none of this is happening, she thought, just as an enormous whale appeared in the sky, with two people suspended below it in a sort of boat. *I'm entering the hallucination stage,* Bitterblue thought, remembering the things Katsa had taught her about hypothermia.

The two flying people were yelling at each other and doing something with ropes. One of them, tall, athletic, brown-skinned like Katu, was lowering herself on a ladder down to Bitterblue, then trying to wrap Bitterblue in some sort of rope halter.

"I've reached the hallucination stage," Bitterblue tried to say to the hallucination of the woman, in case it was helpful for her to know. "This isn't happening." She supposed she was too cold to live now. She wouldn't get to fire all her people, because she was going to die.

She wouldn't get to see Winterkeep, or kiss Katu again, or confront those importers, or find out what had happened to Mikka and Brek aboard the *Seashell*. She thought of each drowned man now, remembering that their deaths were her burdens. She wouldn't get to carry the burdens of her kingdom, ever again.

Bitterblue began to cry, because she understood, now that it was happening, how her friends would grieve. Was anything more horrible than losing someone, and not even understanding why? Hava would be inconsolable. Hava would run away; would she ever come back? "Giddon," she cried. She'd been worried, for a long time, that the Council would take him away from her soon, assign him to some other court. She didn't want him to leave. Now she was the one leaving him. "But I don't want to go!" she cried.

Suddenly she was in the air, hanging above the water, leaving the watching silbercows behind. She looked into the eyes of the long-whiskered one who'd tried to keep her awake. The creature gazed back at her with perfect calm. Then everything went black.

CHAPTER SIX

SOMETHING STRANGE WAS afoot today. Lovisa Cavenda had a
sense for these things, like a snake perched upright with its tongue
touching the air.

At dinner, in the dining room of her dormitory, one of her friends
overturned a cup of tea. When no one came from the kitchens to
clean it up, Lovisa stood. "I'll get someone," she said, crossing to the
kitchen doors and entering quietly.

Two women stood at a counter. "They didn't even miss her until
they sighted land," one of the women said. "Someone went below
to wake everyone, and she was gone. Then they were a long time
searching the ship, because, of course, they assumed she was on
board somewhere."

The other woman, more of a girl, really, made a small, distressed
noise. "But she wasn't?"

"No, the poor dear! A few of them actually jumped into the sea,
looking for her. My sister was in the harbor when the ship docked.
She said they were all in hysterics."

"That's the saddest thing," said the girl. "How old was she?"

"Young! Twenty-three, twenty-four?"

Throwing her braid over her shoulder, the girl noticed Lovisa
standing by the door. "Oh," she said, flustered. "I'm sorry, miss. Can
we help you?"

She was plain-faced like Lovisa, but her discomposure made her sweet, pleasing, and, Lovisa suspected, eager to please. She looked genuinely distressed about the story she'd heard.

Lovisa was worried too, though she hadn't decided yet what it meant. The Queen of Monsea was twenty-three. But so were a lot of people.

"We have a spill," she said. "Could someone clean it up?"

With distracted murmurs, the girl bustled off in search of a cloth. Lovisa returned to her table, where none of her peers seemed aware of any sailing accidents that had befallen any queens.

LATER, LOVISA SITUATED herself in an armchair in the dormitory's second-floor foyer, right beside the window and the fireplace, her lap full of homework. She wore a robe with a fur collar that she tucked close against her throat, protection against the cold that radiated from the glass. She liked to work here for an hour or so most evenings. It gave her a view on everyone's comings and goings. Tonight, she was waiting for the return of Ta Varana, who'd gone home for dinner. Ta's mother was Minta Varana, the esteemed airship engineer. More importantly, her aunt was Sara Varana, the prime minister. If there was news to be had about the Monsean queen, Ta would probably have it.

Around eight o'clock, the doors below opened, then crashed closed. Ta always slammed doors as if she believed they'd been constructed for the sole purpose of getting in her way. Lovisa readied her face as, with big, protesting breaths, Ta stomped up the stairs.

"Oh, hi," she said to Lovisa when she reached the foyer, her eyes lighting up at the prospect of someone to talk to. Ta had a flush of pink in her brown cheeks and her lips were shiny, painted the color of a raspberry. Her hair, which she wore in long, swirly waves, spilled out of the hood of a fluffy white fur coat that probably cost more than all Lovisa's coats combined, and Lovisa had very nice coats. Ta Varana, like all the Varanas, was a big presence in a room, and extremely, noticeably pretty.

"How was dinner?" said Lovisa, being careful not to sound too curious.

"Less tedious than usual," Ta said. "Did I miss anything?"

"Good cake."

"My aunt was at dinner," said Ta, certainly referring to the prime minister. Which meant that this conversation was going to be even more informative than Lovisa had hoped. "So *our* cake was excellent," she went on, "and our house was lit up like the sun. All of Flag Hill is lit up; everyone's showing off their airships. Did you know the Monsean delegation arrived today?"

"No," said Lovisa, sounding bored.

"You didn't? Aren't they staying at your house?"

"Are they? I can't remember," said Lovisa, a screaming lie. "Some delegation was supposed to stay at our house. Maybe it's the Monseans?" Then she waited, suspecting that Ta would supply everything else she knew willingly, without being asked.

"The Queen of Monsea is dead," Ta said.

Plunged into disappointment, Lovisa fought to rouse herself, knowing Ta would want a surprised reaction. "What? What do you mean?"

"She died," said Ta, with the satisfied smile of a gossip who knows she's scored a point. "They think she went overboard, but they don't actually know what happened. When the ship got close, they realized she was gone. They think she went out on deck and fell in. But I think the Magistry should consider other possibilities."

The Magistry was the Keepish police. "Like what?" said Lovisa.

"Maybe murder. People murder queens. Maybe suicide. Her

father was that psychopath King Leck, remember? A few people from the delegation came to dinner and I thought they were acting suspicious."

"Suspicious how?" Lovisa asked, because she couldn't resist hearing Ta's opinions on how people were supposed to behave.

"One of them, the queen's doctor, I think, was way too polite and pleasant for someone who's just lost his queen. You know? Wouldn't you expect someone to show some feelings?"

"Definitely."

"Another one, a big, tall guy named Gidlon or Gildon or something, was all glassy-eyed and pale, and he hardly said a word. I mean, even paler than most Monseans, like he was almost transparent. And he kept shivering too."

"Like someone in shock?" Lovisa offered.

"Or someone who can't believe he just threw his own queen overboard," Ta said. "Don't you think?"

"Definitely."

"A bunch of the Royal Continent envoys were there too. The Estillan, the Dellian. The Lienid envoy kept crying. The Monsean queen is half-Lienid, you know."

"Mm-hm." Lovisa remembered her parents talking about the Estillan envoy. "Was your aunt Quona there?"

"Yes."

"Did she have anything to say about it?"

"Um, she's an animal doctor," said Ta. "What would she have to say? There's a Graceling in the delegation too, but she wasn't at dinner."

Lovisa was beginning to be rather envious of this dinner. "What kind of Graceling?"

"I don't know. But the big guy asked about your uncle."

"Katu?"

"Yes," said Ta. "Apparently they know him. They wanted to know if he was back from his travels."

"He's not," said Lovisa, badly wishing she knew where to write to Katu. He would want to know about Queen Bitterblue. And he would understand how Lovisa felt right now, like a door that had seemed about to open had slammed shut.

"Is your mother all right?" Ta went on, eyes gleaming. "She got a message during class this morning and ended it early. Then she was late for dinner. Like, very late. We were already done with the soup."

Lovisa had gone to Politics and Trade class this morning early as usual, then wondered why the classroom was empty. It had been one of the first clues that something was different today. And it was, in fact, unusual for Ferla to be late for anything, especially a dinner at which powerful people were present. "As far as I know, she's fine," said Lovisa, then waited.

"Supposedly she was dealing with some problem at home," said Ta. "Your father wasn't at dinner at all."

"Oh, wow," said Lovisa. "One of my little brothers is sick. I wonder if he's okay."

Ta wandered away, satisfied with herself, leaving Lovisa to ponder her mother's tardiness to dinner and her father's absence. One of her brothers *was* sick. But Lovisa doubted Vikti's cold would keep her parents away from a dinner with the prime minister and delegates from the Royal Continent.

She was half looking out the window thinking this over, half reading her Sentient Animal Law textbook, when another student who'd been missing from dinner appeared on the path below. Nev. Finally. Lovisa had noticed Nev's absence, a little clock in the corner of her mind paying attention to the passage of time. It was well past curfew. This mattered for a student like Nev, who wasn't the niece of the prime minister. Nev could get into trouble for being out so late.

Lovisa watched Nev approach. Even through the thickening snow, her tall, straight-shouldered form was unmistakable; that one-named girl always looked as if the freezing cold, her hatlessness, the lateness of the hour, and any other unpleasant circumstance was inconsequential to her. She was a scholarship student from the north, Torla's Neck, a province in Winterkeep near to the Kamassarian border. Lovisa had been to Torla's Neck several times, because it was the location of the house and mine shared by her mother and uncle. Ferla and Katu had grown up in Torla's Neck. The province was rough, wild. A place with few wealthy families, few restaurants; a place with glaciers, and rocks, and forests, and mines. Not a place that justified Nev's proud shoulders.

Nev stopped in a circle of light cast by one of the streetlamps and raised her face to a window somewhere above Lovisa's. Mari Devret's, probably. Lovisa had watched Nev climb to Mari's window more than once when Nev and Mari had been dating and Nev had been doing whatever it was Nev did that made her miss curfew so often. Breaking curfew without a pass from a professor meant a demerit, which carried a fine that Lovisa was sure Nev couldn't afford. Too many demerits led to expulsion.

But Lovisa doubted that Nev would call on Mari Devret for help with that now. It hadn't been a friendly breakup. Lovisa knew, because Mari was one of her oldest friends, that Mari had been too surprised and hurt for that. It had been months ago and he was still moping around, like a sulking child. There were other rumors too, mean stuff that Lovisa collected and filed away, but didn't necessarily believe.

She's . . . pretty? Lovisa thought, studying Nev's brown face. No. Nev wasn't pretty, but she was something, her black hair cut close to her head, her strong mouth and her high chin arresting. Handsome. The shadows of a snowy street suited her too. Her rough coat, made of patchy furs she'd probably trapped herself, always had a way of making her look strong, rather than poor.

Then, suddenly, Nev was staring straight at Lovisa. She gave no sign of greeting, just stared.

I could open this window for her, Lovisa thought. *I could go get Mari's ladder, or someone else's.*

Instead, she stared back, curious to see what Nev would do.

To her surprise, Nev turned straight for the dormitory doors. Lovisa heard them open and close below, heard Nev's muttered conversation with the monitor, but couldn't make out the words. She adopted the guise of being deeply focused on her Sentient Animal Law textbook. When Nev climbed the steps and reached the landing, Lovisa ignored her.

Then, as Nev brushed past, Lovisa smelled a strange mixture of scents on her clothing. Blood, the cold, and the sea. Nev was in the school of animal medicine, and sometimes Lovisa couldn't help her own horrified fascination.

"What happened this time?" she asked. "You smell even worse than usual."

Nev stopped. She slid eyes to Lovisa that conveyed nothing, not one jot, of what she was thinking. Then she glanced at the textbook in Lovisa's lap. "I doubt you'd find it interesting," she said, her northern lilt stronger than Ferla's or Katu's. Most northerners worked to sound more like Ledrans when they were in Ledra. Not Nev.

Lovisa noticed a bandage wrapped around her left palm. "I'm interested in how it's humanly possible to smell so bad."

"It's not," Nev said. "I'm not human. Now you know my secret."

Nev wasn't usually quippy like that. She looked tired, her bland expression more deliberately constructed than usual. It was interesting. "Did it turn out well," asked Lovisa, "whatever it was?"

Nev hesitated. "Yes and no."

"Oh," said Lovisa, noticing a smear of sand stuck to some unknown sticky substance on Nev's trousers. "Too bad. Were you on the beaches?"

"For a bit."

"Did you hear any of the hubbub about the Monsean queen?"

"No."

"Apparently she fell out of a ship today and drowned."

"How sad," said Nev.

Lovisa felt a small, unwilling smile forming on her face, from the pleasure of a conversationalist who was as good as she was at seeming indifferent. "Where'd you get a pass?"

"A professor."

"*Which* professor?"

"Quona Varana."

Of course. "Is Quona Varana the person who always keeps you out so late?" said Lovisa, unable to hide her curiosity.

Then, at the sound of footsteps on the stairs above, she deadened her expression. A couple of boys carrying papers and books clattered down into the foyer and gave Nev small, particular smiles. These were Mari Devret's friends, rich, popular boys, probably coming from studying in Mari's room. Their smiles weren't friendly.

"Hello, Lovisa," said one of them, a smirky boy named Pari Parnin. None of them greeted Nev.

"Move along, Pari," said Lovisa, unimpressed.

The boys disappeared down a corridor. Nev chose that moment to move along too, turning for the stairs, not saying good night to Lovisa, who watched her go, wondering if Nev relaxed her shoulders once she'd entered her own room and closed the door on the world. Also wondering if she'd eaten anything in lieu of dinner. Did Nev keep a stash of food? Lovisa always kept food in her pockets. It made her feel prepared.

Two more boys came down the steps, greeted Lovisa, and left, this time without any unfriendly smiles. Ever since Nev had broken things off with Mari, a rumor had been circulating about Nev's skills in bed. Her lack of skills, actually. Lovisa strongly doubted that Mari had started it, for he wasn't the type to circulate cruel rumors that probably weren't even true. Lovisa suspected Pari Parnin.

Regardless, it was what those boys' smiles had been about earlier, when they'd seen Nev. The kind of smiles that say *I hear you're no fun.*

Lovisa stared into space, her mind returning to matters of greater interest. Was her house in Flag Hill now full of grieving Monsean delegates? How was her mother, the Scholar, turning that to her advantage? How was her father, the Industrialist, counteracting her mother? When there were foreign delegates in the house, it was always interesting to watch for the secret, self-interested undercurrents in her parents' outwardly gracious behavior.

Also, why had her father skipped dinner and her mother left class? Why had her mother been late? Was the stress of Ferla's responsibilities as professor and president finally getting to her? A crack in the armor, deep enough for people outside the house to notice? If so, it would be the first such crack Lovisa had ever seen.

Was there a Graceling living in her house right now? If so, what colors were her eyes? What was her Grace? So few Gracelings passed through Winterkeep. People were talking recently about a Graceling woman living in Ledra who had the Grace of finding lost things, but Lovisa hadn't met her.

Lovisa didn't want a freezing, windy walk, nor did she want her mother's company if her mother was under a lot of stress. She especially didn't want the spying gold eyes of her mother's fox. Blue foxes could live how they liked, bonded or unbonded; Sentient Animal Law protected their freedom to choose. Most foxes bonded to no one, choosing to remain independent, living in the wild or in fox sanctuaries where humans catered to them. But other foxes liked the companionship of bonding, or the feeling of usefulness, or the treats. In return for a cushy life in a private house, the fox was loyal, and, if its human had particular requests, obedient.

Of course Ferla Cavenda had wanted an obedient fox who could sneak around and speak to her and her alone. She'd visited fox sanctuaries for months before one had expressed an interest in her companionship. Then that fox had lived in the Cavenda house for almost a year, while Ferla doted on him with a sweetness that had obscurely alarmed nine-year-old Lovisa, for Ferla never showed that saccharine sweetness to her children. It had crawled with falseness. But it had worked. The fox had finally chosen to bond to Ferla. From that day forward, Lovisa had felt eyes on her back.

Despite the promise of those eyes, tonight Lovisa was curious. She could never help herself when she was curious.

Pushing up from her chair, she went to her bedroom for warm clothes, a coat, and her bag, schooling her face to look homesick. Lovisa would sleep at home tonight.

CHAPTER SEVEN

LOVISA'S NIGHT DID not go as planned.

Most of the estates in the neighborhood of Flag Hill stood behind stone walls, with gates that were left open during the day and locked at night. The expectation was that an unannounced visitor like Lovisa would ring the bell at the Cavenda gate, then wait for a guard to come let her in. And of course, that was what she intended to do. But first, she found the unlit section of wall with the pokey rocks and used them to climb over.

Pokey rocks, she thought as she found purchase on one rock, then the next, hoisting herself up to the top of the wall. That was the name she and Mari Devret had given these rocks when they'd climbed them as children. Their feet had been smaller then, of course, more nimble, but Lovisa's feet were still pretty small. And her skirts were in fact wide pants legs, her leather gloves good for gripping and wiping away snow, her shoes snug and flexible.

Once on her own grounds, she was careful to avoid the light from the wall lanterns and the house windows. If one of the guards caught her, it wouldn't be a calamity, but it might make her mother start paying closer attention to what Lovisa did. The thick falling snow helped to obscure her. She hoped it would cover her footprints.

She circled the house. Her father's library on the first floor was gently lit, as if he were sitting in thought with a cup of tea. Her mother's study on the second floor was glowing with the kind of light that only came from silbercow lamps, a rich, golden warmth. Lovisa was hardly ever invited into her mother's study, but what always hit her first was the smell of the silbercow lamps, deep and earthy, like summer soil. Silbercow oil was highly regulated by Sentient Animal Law and exorbitantly expensive, but Ferla wasn't one to deprive herself.

Up at the top of the house, a dim light shone in an attic window at the back. Lovisa felt an anxious tug, wondering which of her brothers was up there tonight in Ferla's attic room, and why. It was a customary feature in a Flag Hill house, a small room in the attic, far away from the front door, unreachable by intruders. Most people used it as a storage space for valuables, but Lovisa's mother used it for discipline. It wasn't a terrible room, in and of itself. It had a bed and desk, a rug, a book or two, a lamp. When Lovisa was little, Ferla might close her in there briefly with her homework, some crayons for drawing, a hot drink and extra blankets if the day was cold. "You need some time to yourself," Ferla would say, clear and strict, "to think about what you've done." It was lonely, but it was fine.

But Ferla had a temper. It could burn low for hours. For days, even, heat snaking along her voice, glimmering in her eyes, slowly growing. Eventually, it would explode into a conflagration that could be felt all over the house. It was invariably one of her children who set it off, by being loud or asking one too many questions, by whining or crying, by interrupting her when she was with Benni. On those days, the punishments were different. She would close Lovisa in the room with a flint, a candle, and no food, taking the books and the lamp away, locking the door. "This is harder for me than it is for you," she would say. "This is soft compared to what some parents do. When your uncle and I were children, our father would put us in a cave. It was cold and hard. Our only visitors were birds and our only view was the sun over the ocean as night fell. Do you understand, Lovisa? Do you understand that your life is soft?" She would shut the door, turn the lock, then not come back. When her anger burned itself out, she would send one of the guards to release the child. Lovisa would have to guess at how to ration the candle, not liking the darkness, but never knowing for sure how long her punishment would last. Sometimes it stretched well into the night. She'd learned to control a nervous bladder, and to hide food in her pockets all the time. She'd learned a lot of things.

Lovisa continued around the house. She noticed, with surprise, that no lights shone in the guest apartments on the third floor. Were the Monseans already asleep? It occurred to her that their presence in the house boded well for whichever boy had misbehaved. Ferla did not lose her temper in front of foreign delegations.

Atop the house, the Cavenda airship was tethered, a bulbous beast, dark against the falling snow. Lovisa doubted she'd be able to see it if she didn't already know it was there. In daytime, the decorations of its balloon were visible: a purple, blue, and gold scene of silbercows swimming with the Keeper, as on the Keepish flag. Airships like this were Winterkeep's pride. The technology was proprietary, no other Torlan nation had them, and Ta had been right when she'd said that Flag Hill was showing them off tonight. Her parents' airship might be in darkness, but a number of the houses Lovisa had passed had lanterns glowing on their roofs, illuminating the most expensive possession a Keepish citizen could own.

Lovisa scaled the wall again, in the back of the yard where the rocks made it easiest on this side. Then she circled around to the front, where she went to the gate, rang the bell, and waited.

THE BLUE FOX who was bonded to Ferla Cavenda loved it second-best of all when Lovisa came home. Lovisa was one of the more interesting Cavendas, a born liar like Ferla, but better at it, because she didn't need people to admire her.

First-best, of course, he loved the airship, into which he was never invited. He snuck up to the roof sometimes and sat inside, imagining the wind whipping against his fur as he flew toward adventure.

The fox was dozing on the hearthstone of Ferla's study fireplace when he sensed Lovisa on the grounds outside, snooping. Sometimes Lovisa did that, climbed over the wall and circled the house before announcing herself at the gate. She snooped in the politics and government building too; the fox always knew when she was listening through the vents. Humans didn't appreciate how much foxes could perceive. This suited foxes, for humans would sneak a lot less and be a lot less interesting if they knew. It was one of the secrets of foxkind.

He wasn't surprised Lovisa had come home tonight. Lovisa had an instinct for when drama was brewing, and it was certainly brewing tonight. Ferla was a tornado of rage that coiled tighter and tighter as the evening progressed. Benni Cavenda, her husband, swept in from time to time to announce something boring about stupid zilfium. When he did this, Ferla would stare at him, throwing daggers with her eyes, until he went away. Ferla was furious at everyone and everything. The fox didn't always like being bonded to Ferla Cavenda, but he did like these moments, for Ferla was a human composed of sharp motivations, passions, and ambitions, like a tangled pile of pins, always interesting. He might not always understand what her thoughts meant or what they referred to, but he always understood how she felt about them. And she had a warm, cozy house; an airship; a beautiful fur coat with a hood he could nestle into; and a family with a penchant for drama.

Casually raising his head from his paws, he touched Ferla's mind with a question. *Shall I make a round of the house, to see that all's well?*

All is not well, she stormed. *I don't care what you do, Fox. But you'd better be available if I want you.*

I'll check back often, of course, the fox reassured her quickly, wishing, as he always did, that she would ask him his chosen name. All the other bonded foxes he knew, including his seven siblings, had humans who called them by their chosen names, but Ferla always just called him "Fox." *A round of the house, no more,* he said, *to check that everyone's behaving as you would wish.*

Scowling, Ferla grunted, then ignored him. With a small sigh of regret for the hearthstone, he rose to his feet and tiptoed to the door. Pushing through the fox flap, he stood in the corridor, bracing himself against the cold air that plagued a fox in almost every part of this house in winter, for heat rose and cold sank, and a fox was low to the ground. It would be warmer once he'd snuck into the heat ducts, though sneezier. It was an unfortunate irony in the life of foxkind that achievable comfort was often inversely proportional to achievable interestingness. He thought that even his seven siblings would agree with this, and they were the most spoiled foxes in Winterkeep.

The blue fox entered the heat ducts through the secret hinged vent grate in the low wall of the second-story privy. It was his most recently converted vent grate and he was proud of it. Hinging a grate took a blue fox days and was neither comfortable nor interesting. First he had to hurt his mouth and risk breaking his teeth pulling out nails, then he had to thread yarn through the grate, again with his mouth, and wind it tightly in place. No one in the Cavenda household knew that he was capable of any of this. Not even Ferla; especially not Ferla. It was very satisfying.

Once in the heat ducts, he could reach every room in the house. He could check on any of his secret tools, which he kept in various nooks and crannies. He could also follow any individual human around the house without that person knowing. No one made the heat ducts more worthwhile than Lovisa Cavenda. She had a fire inside her that burned as hot as the fire inside Ferla, but she kept it to a low, steady blaze, always controlled, always hungry. Always just nearly about to make something happen. He loved her visits home.

The fox worked his way to Benni's library on the first floor, guessing that that was where Lovisa would go first.

WHEN LOVISA ENTERED her father's library, her father wasn't there.

In the middle of his desk sat a stack of papers covered with his big, bold handwriting. No doubt, her father was drafting another argument in favor of the legalization of zilfium use: She could see the word *zilfium* repeated several times. She felt a little sorry for him, and for the irony of his position. By chance or fate, in the elected, fifty-member Parliament, there were currently twenty-five Scholars and twenty-five Industrialists, dead even. In the case of a tie, the president was permitted to cast a tie-breaking vote. And of course, the president was Benni's own wife, a Scholar who would vote against him.

The door opened and her father pushed in. "Lovisa! We weren't expecting you. Is everything all right?"

"I just wanted to sleep in my own bed tonight," she said.

"It's late," he said, bending down to hug her. "Did you walk all the way from campus, alone?"

"Yes," she said, rising on her tiptoes to hug him back, pressing her face into his scarves. "And as you can see, I was perfectly safe. No marauders in the streets."

"I wish you wouldn't," he said, still holding her. He smelled like his teas, as usual, but his voice was a little too hearty and his breath too quick.

"What's wrong, Papa?" she said.

He gave a short laugh, kissed her forehead, and let her go. "My perceptive girl. Have you heard about the Monsean queen?"

"Ta Varana told me."

"Yes," he said. "Well. Everyone's pretty upset, including your mother. It's a tragedy, of course, but also, we had real hopes of getting to know her, establish a strong working relationship with her. The Royal Continent has a lot of war and instability, but Queen Bitterblue has long been one of its steadier leaders. It's just so unfortunate."

"Is that why Mother had to leave her class this morning?" said Lovisa. "Ta told me about that too."

"That was Vikti," said Benni. "His health had taken a turn for the worse. But he's better now. Nothing to worry about, sweetheart. Would you like to go see him?"

"I don't want to wake him," she said. "Have they all been behaving themselves?"

"Viri was making your mother's life difficult earlier, I believe, but everything's fine now."

Then it must be Viri up in the attic room. Viri was the youngest, only five. If he was up there, he'd be shivering right now, his arms wrapped around his knees, tears running down his face. Lovisa would have to find a way to check on him.

But she pretended not to care about that, because Viri could get into more trouble if she was caught helping him. "What about the rest of the Monseans?" she said. "Are they here?"

"I'm afraid not," said Benni. "The plans have changed."

"Why? Because they're not useful to you and Mother without the queen?" Lovisa, who wasn't afraid of her father, grinned up at him.

"My mischievous girl," he said, touching the white streak in her hair.

"Where's the delegation staying instead?"

"With Quona Varana."

"Quona Varana!"

"Yes," said Benni, a mournful tone to his voice. "We're all a little concerned."

"But how did that happen? They'll sneeze themselves to death!"

"Well," said Benni, "now that the queen is gone, everything's changed. There's apparently a member of their party—a young Graceling woman—who's distraught and would benefit from time alone."

"In a den of cat fur?"

"Quona's house is not that bad, Lovisa," said Benni. "Quona has so many rooms that each cat could have its own. Think about it: An isolated house on a cliff above the sea is probably perfect for them right now. I understand that the Estillan envoy suggested it at dinner tonight, then Sara and Minta seized on the idea, and you know the Varana sisters can be a force of nature."

The shutters around Lovisa's life closed tighter. She'd counted on meeting the Graceling, at least. And sitting across from the Monseans at dinner, hearing stories about a continent that still had kings and queens, wars, but also magic. And having something exciting to tell Katu, when he came back. She wondered suddenly if Nev, who was one of Quona's students, would be more likely to meet the Graceling than she was.

Typical, she thought bitterly. "Why was Mother late for that dinner?" she said. "Ta was asking me about it."

He touched her hair again, gently. "I'm sure she just lost track of time," he said. "It's been a distressing day. I myself stayed home. Your mother is in her study, Lovisa, if you'd like to say good night."

A stairway behind one of Benni's bookcases that swung like a door led directly up to Ferla's study, connecting their private spaces. It always made Lovisa feel like Ferla might be spying on her conversations with her father. And sometimes, her father's words felt like a warning. Your mother is angry; your mother could be listening; don't press your luck. Benni had long been Lovisa's safe harbor during Ferla's storms. As a child, she'd used to escape to this library. He would tuck her into his favorite red-and-gold armchair, share the tea he was drinking, give her a book to read. If her mother came looking for her, he would stop Ferla at the door and tell her he was handling it. Shut the door, kiss Lovisa's forehead and say to her, "Your mother loves you."

"I think I'll just get ready for bed," she said.

"Did you tell someone to light your fire?"

"I will."

"Your mother and the boys will be very happy to see you at breakfast."

"Me too, Papa," said Lovisa, wondering how much sneaking she could do tonight without encountering any guards, or Ferla's mangy fox. She needed to get to Viri. She could talk to him through the door, tell him his favorite fairy tales. Viri always laughed at Lovisa's versions of the Keeper stories, for hers were particularly irreverent. The underwater creature, who was supposedly the protector of the planet according to the silbercows, was as big as a mountain. She protected the silbercows, and in return, the silbercows took care of the sea and recruited their friends the humans to take care of the earth. So everyone was taking care of everyone, which was good, because if they didn't, the Keeper would rise up, kill all the animals and humans, and flatten everything.

That was the part of the fairy tales that made Lovisa want to be irreverent, that lingering hint that if this hero wasn't placated, she would destroy the world. Everyone idly mentioned that part, then moved on to the fun parts, like the Keeper tickling the undersides of human ships, or singing mesmerizing songs that soothed the enemies of the earth and sea. But the Keeper wasn't powerful because she was just. Her power came from being *big*. Anyone that big could gather worshipers and call herself a hero. It made Lovisa wonder if a hero was ever anything more than a bully.

So, in Lovisa's stories, she made the Keeper a clumsy bully who was prevented from destroying the world by tripping over her own feet, and so on. And her brothers protested, laughed, and squealed.

Lovisa's bedroom was on the second floor, not far from her parents'. She took the back, less-guarded stairs up to the nursery wing on the third floor to do some reconnaissance. Past the schoolroom, she cracked Vikti's bedroom door open. Vikti, who was nine, was snoring loudly in his bed, like a boy with a very congested nose. A small worry Lovisa had been carrying melted away at the sight of what looked to be a garden-variety cold.

She opened Viri's bedroom door next. Viri was the one who got sick all the time, probably because he was always putting his books and his game pieces—and his clothes, and his fingers—in his mouth, as if he was hungry, or needed the comfort of chewing on something. He was ashamed of it, because he got yelled at for it, but he did it anyway.

He wasn't in his bed, which confirmed what Lovisa already knew.

Slipping out, she paused in the corridor when she thought she heard a scampering noise. She turned in circles, looked under a nearby table, but no fox was in sight.

Deciding not to risk waking Erita, who was seven, Lovisa retraced her path. She needed a reason to be in the attic so that Viri wouldn't get in trouble if she was discovered. She was sneaking down the back staircase again when an excuse appeared on the steps below: the youngest house guard, the one with the broad chest, the close-cropped hair, the northern lilt to his speech, and the beardless face. She couldn't remember his name, only that his sister was also one of the Cavenda guards, and that he smiled at her sometimes, with a gleam she thought she recognized. A gleam she didn't think her parents would like, if they saw it.

An idea appeared in her head, fully formed.

"Hello," she said lightly.

"Hello, miss," he responded, a tiny smile softening his lips.

She stopped on the step above his, so that their heights were more even. His brown eyes contained flecks of amber and he smelled like a wood fire. "Don't tell on me," she said, nodding toward the upstairs. "Please?"

"Tell on you for what, miss?"

"I was looking for you."

"Were you?" he said, after the slightest, surprised hesitation. "Is there something I can do for you, miss?"

Now she hesitated. "I don't know. You might not like it."

His eyes touched her face. "I doubt that," he said quietly.

He understood what she'd intended him to understand, and Lovisa was a little alarmed with herself. She'd done this before, with boys and girls at the academy, generally out of curiosity, to know what her friends were talking about when they talked about sex. This was more calculated, which made it different.

"Would you meet me in the attic at one o'clock?" she said. "I'll show you then."

"Of course, miss."

And she continued down the stairs, planning to get to the attic early to visit Viri. Then the guard would arrive, so that if her mother or the fox arrived too, she could pretend she was there to meet him. Ferla wouldn't like it, but Viri wouldn't be punished for it.

FIFTEEN MINUTES BEFORE one o'clock, Lovisa crept out of her bedroom with a lamp.

She took the back stairs and passed through the nursery wing again, then the house staff's wing, shining her light under every table and chair, into every corner, looking for the fox. Not finding him. She left the door to the attic stairs open, then ascended to the door above, steeling herself against the eeriness of the attic, always strange at night with its high ceilings and exposed beams. She left that door open for the guard as well. As she stepped into the attic, she swept her light around, still looking for the fox.

"Viri?" she said, crossing the floor, then crouching down at the door to the punishment room. She tried the latch once, just to be thorough, but of course it was locked. She knocked lightly, then waited, surprised when there was no responding scuttle. No high-pitched voice saying her name, no tears. She pressed her ear to the wood. "Viri?"

She heard a strange sound then: a muffled, metallic screech, followed by a thud. "Viri?" she repeated, confused.

Then, at the sound of scampering paws, she sprang to her feet, and two things happened at once. First, she heard boots on the stairs. Second, her mother's fox appeared out of nowhere, standing braced before her, his glimmering eyes catching the light of her lamp. She had the strange sense that he'd fallen from the sky.

That was it, then. Now Lovisa was going to have to make a show of her liaison with the guard, and just hope the fox hadn't seen her trying to get into that room. Crossing to the stairs, she turned out her light. "Pervert," she whispered savagely at the little creature, a pointless jab, because foxes didn't understand language and could only read the mind of the person to whom they were bonded. But she knew he'd be able to see this next part well enough, even in the dark.

"What did you say, miss?" whispered the guard as he stepped into the attic.

She pressed herself against him. They both had unlit lamps that clattered together; they put them down clumsily, kissing and touching each other. Lovisa's main objective was to give the fox the right kind of show, exactly the misbehavior that would convince her mother that she'd come to the attic for this very purpose. She thought they should probably stay there, kissing, for a little while, but that they needn't do much more. The guard didn't try to press her; he was much less grabby than she was used to. But she felt him grow hard, and she heard the soft, desiring noises he made. His hands were gentle. Wishful, but cautious. It was different from anyone else she'd kissed. His restraint gave her room to feel something. When she'd estimated that they'd kissed for the right amount of time, it was actually hard to stop.

"That's enough for now," she said.

"Yes, miss," he said breathlessly. "Of course, miss."

She picked up her lamp and handed him his, motioning for him to descend the steps. Then, after he'd gone, she lit her lamp again briefly, to verify that the fox was still in the room. Once she'd spotted him under a table, his eyes flashing up at her, she stepped onto the stairs and shut the door on him tightly. At the bottom of the stairs, she shut that door too.

Then she scurried after the disappearing guard, caught his hand, and, hardly recognizing herself, pulled him along the corridor, past the house staff's wing to the schoolroom, which had a door that could lock and a thick, soft rug.

She knelt, pulling him down beside her. He was surprised. "Are you sure?"

She reached for his hand and put it inside her robe, moving it against her breast, a technique that had worked on everyone before him. It worked this time too, but this time was different, because his hand was shaking and his breath was catching. Something about the way he sounded, or smelled, or just *was* as he touched her, excited her. She understood now what some of her friends meant when they talked about sex as if it was something they badly wanted. She had wondered if they were lying, to make everyone else envious. She still suspected some of them were lying. But she understood the wanting now.

Afterward, they whispered to each other about doing it again sometime soon, and Lovisa meant it. She returned to her bedroom, tired, then unable to sleep, nagged by an unsettled feeling she tried to ignore. She tossed and turned. Then she sat up, remembering the tea she needed to drink to guard against pregnancy.

Slipping out of her room again, she carried a tea sachet from her schoolbag downstairs to the kitchen. The kitchen in the middle of the night always seemed three times bigger than it did during the day, and it was all her domain. She could raid the pantry, light a fire in the massive oven and sit as close to it as she wanted, think and plan in solitude. She was queen.

Queen, she thought, remembering the death of the Queen of Monsea, and all the questions she'd had before she'd come home, gotten distracted, and had sex with one of her parents' guards. She still didn't know the guard's name. Was that normal? Was it fair to him? What was wrong with her? *Focus.*

Quietly, Lovisa boiled water, set her sachet to steep, then sipped the odd, bitter tea, wondering why doing so didn't remove her worries about the guard. She couldn't stop replaying what they'd done. His small kindnesses, his excitements. The questions he'd kept asking. Was she comfortable? Was she cold? Did this feel good? Were his hands too rough? No. They hadn't been too rough, but his mouth had grown rough, a mix of tender and rough all at once that had made her dizzy with want.

Something moved in a distant corner. Lovisa nearly jumped out of her skin before realizing that it must be the fox again. Except that she'd closed the fox in the attic.

I'm so tired, I'm hallucinating and scaring myself. I need to go to bed.

On her way back to her room, she had another fright when she encountered one of the guards on the dark stairway. First she gasped, but then she laughed, because it was him, it was *her* guard. In relief and surprise, she kissed him again. Again, his mouth was soft and urgent and his hands had the same effect. To her astonishment, they ended up back on the schoolroom floor. Lovisa couldn't believe her own body.

After he'd gone away the second time, she stood outside her brothers' bedroom doors, trying to understand herself. Needing an anchor, she peeked in again on Vikti, who was still snoring evenly. It helped to see him there, stuffy-nosed and familiar. Then she peeked in on Erita.

In Erita's bed, Erita and Viri were sleeping together, Viri curled in a tiny ball, Erita curled around him, as if Viri were his treasure. Lovisa was so surprised that she turned her lamp on briefly, to make sure.

Yes. That was Erita and Viri. They would get in trouble for sleeping together like that, if anyone found them. And something about their smallness in the bed, the tightness with which they were wrapped together, made her feel small too. Involuntarily, she touched her hair, which was bound into the usual twists around her head that framed her face and made her look young and unthreatening. Her hair had weathered tonight's activities well.

What was she doing? Standing here, staring at her brothers, thinking about her hair, when she'd done what she'd done tonight? She hadn't expected to like that guard so much. A sick feeling inside her, a kind of discomfort about having used him was starting to turn into a misery on which she didn't want to dwell. She would learn from whatever happened, but she wouldn't dwell. And next time she needed an alibi she would choose someone she didn't like the way she was starting to like that guard.

If Viri wasn't in the attic room . . . then, what was that light? That clunking sound? She realized now that she'd been trying to solve the wrong puzzle. This was about that snatch of conversation between her parents, that day weeks ago, when her father had come to campus looking for her mother. Some storage problem Benni had. "Could I store it in the attic room?" he'd asked Ferla. "It would be in a banker's box. No one would look twice at it. We don't have a good place in the house for these kinds of valuables."

"I don't love that idea," Ferla had replied. "We'll discuss it later."

Now the snake inside Lovisa touched its tongue to the air, mildly curious. Benni shipped fuels, metals—but gold and silver, too, and sometimes even jewels. Did he have something others wanted to steal? Something interesting? The secrecy of the thing tugged at her.

Could it hurt to know what her father was keeping in the attic room?

Lovisa, who was thinking more clearly now about what the fox had seen her do, had a feeling that her mother's vengeance in the morning was going to be unsparing. Well. If she was already in trouble, why not risk more?

Almost disbelieving what she was about to do, Lovisa closed Erita's door, checking the latch to ensure the fox couldn't get in. Then she went back to her own bedroom and collected a few supplies.

CHAPTER EIGHT

LOVISA HAD TWO goals.

First, she snuck down the corridor with the guest apartments, where the Monseans would have been staying had the queen not died. In one of the bedrooms there was a window with a latch that she and Mari had deliberately broken as children, for there was a trellis and a tree outside. They'd never actually climbed up to the window and snuck in, but Lovisa wanted to know if anyone had fixed the lock since. She went to the window, checked that the latch was in the locked position, then tried the frame. The window opened easily. Good.

Next, she went straight to her parents' bedroom on the second floor. She took a moment in the corridor to light a single candle. Both of her parents drank teas to help them sleep. Hoping the teas were working tonight, Lovisa opened their door and passed inside.

In the flickering light of her candle, Lovisa saw the sleeping faces of her parents in their mountain of a bed. Her mother's face, small and tight and so much like her own, was angry. Her father's was slack and foolish, which made Lovisa inexplicably sad.

She went to the chest at the foot of the bed, where her mother always laid her clothing. It was an odd quirk, in a woman of such wealth and with so many responsibilities, to insist on managing her own wardrobe. But one thing Ferla never seemed to mind was more work.

Lovisa sat on the floor, then quietly, methodically, made her way through her mother's pockets. She found some money, which would serve as her excuse if she got caught: She was here to steal money, she'd say. Ferla would never question monetary greed as a motive, seeing as it was one of her own motivating principles.

The remaining items in Ferla's pockets included her identification papers, a leather wallet wrapped with a cord, and a pen nib that scratched Lovisa. She'd never seen the wallet before. Quickly, she unwound the cord. The wallet popped open, for it was crammed tight with candies, of all things—hard, black, northern candies, called samklavi, that tasted like ammonia and burning and that no one in the world liked, except, inexplicably, her mother and Katu. Lovisa hated samklavi so much that she wound the wallet closed and shoved it back into her mother's pocket in disgust.

She reached into the next pocket. Finally, her fingers closed over the large, sharp key that she knew, from a childhood of punishments, opened the door to the attic room.

Pulling a small box from her own pocket, Lovisa opened it, noting with relief that it was just big enough for her purposes. Each half of the box contained wax, for making impressions of keys. Mari had given it to her as a present when they were children, heroically offering to rescue her from the attic room when necessary, if she would only make a key. They'd worked out a way to communicate with flashes of light from a candle held to the attic room window. Two flashes meant "Stand by," three flashes meant "Rescue me at midnight," four meant "I'm on the verge of starvation." It was why they'd broken that lock, so that Mari could climb the tree and the trellis, sneak in and rescue her. But it had been a game, a fantasy. Lovisa had never actually attempted to replicate her mother's key until now.

After making wax impressions of both sides, she checked the key for signs of wax and, finding none, slipped it back into her mother's pocket. She also returned the money that would have been her excuse had she been caught. Then she snuck out. On the way back to her own room, she encountered no fox and no guards.

Once she had a key made, Lovisa could wait until everyone was out, especially the fox, and satisfy her curiosity about what her father was keeping in a banker's box in the attic room. Lovisa knew the combinations to her father's banker's boxes; she'd spied them out long ago. Maybe, next time one of her brothers was in serious trouble, she could even join him, bring him snacks, act out the Keeper stories with him. She could bring him paper and crayons too, for they all loved to draw. The Keeper was never specifically described in the stories the silbercows told, beyond being big, but Viri usually drew her with twenty-four spiderlike legs around a bulbous, one-eyed body. "Icositetrapus cyclops," Lovisa always said, a name for a twenty-four-legged, one-eyed creature that she'd made up after doing some research in the academy library, and he would dissolve into laughter, as if it were the funniest thing in the world.

With her own way in and out, Lovisa could be the spy, instead of the spied upon. The rescuer, instead of the prisoner. She could do what she liked.

In her own bed, the face and the voice, the body of her sweet guard wouldn't leave her alone. What would happen to him when the fox told Ferla about the kissing?

Lovisa was so exhausted that even her guilty feelings couldn't keep her awake.

THE BLUE FOX was in the airship on the roof, standing at the bow in the dark, like a courageous captain exploring the night. He was reflecting on the last few hours.

He'd had to make a lot of tricky, sudden decisions tonight. Lovisa

Cavenda had kept him on his toes, literally. At one point, he'd had to streak through a heat duct and leap down from the attic ceiling, so that she would see him, and believe that he was spying for her mother.

He didn't want to tell on her for the kissing with the guard, and bring her mother's wrath down upon her. But he needed to do something that would keep Lovisa from being so curious in the future, and nothing could restrict Lovisa's movements more effectively than telling on her to her mother.

So he would play Lovisa's game, because yes, of course he knew it was a game. He knew that Lovisa had gone to the attic thinking one of the little boys was there, needing comfort. He knew that the guard had been her cover, for foxes, all foxes, could read the thoughts of all humans, not just humans they were bonded to. This ability was one of the secrets of foxkind, and guarding this secret was one of a fox's gravest responsibilities. Of course, his ability to read human minds depended on how open the human kept her mind, and it also depended on how complicated the thoughts became. Even his own human, Ferla, could become hard to read when she wasn't explaining things to him specifically. But the fox could follow basic plans taking place inside the house.

So he would play, because maybe this would keep Lovisa out of worse trouble. Anyway, now that she'd seen him, he *had* to play. Lovisa would expect him to tell. If he didn't tell, then everything about his loyalty to his bonded human would be brought into question, an unthinkable consequence with the potential to damage the welfare of all foxkind.

Almost letting her see him in the kitchen after the kissing, when he was supposed to have been trapped in the attic, had been an accident. He was so distracted tonight. He supposed this was the inevitable complicated life of a fox who had chosen to bond to someone like

Ferla Cavenda. Most of his fox friends and relations had simpler existences. They didn't need to spy on everyone and interfere. They liked their humans, only ever disobeying occasionally, maybe for the sake of extra treats or a warmer hearthstone. Not because they were trying to keep terrible things from happening!

But there wasn't much point in questioning something it was too late to change. At the time, the fox had bonded to Ferla because he'd felt it was his only choice. The day it happened, he'd been scampering down a corridor, trying to decide whether to sneak into the airship now or later, when he'd stumbled upon something interesting: little Lovisa, with her ear pressed against her parents' bedroom door. How oddly proud he'd been of her in that moment. Such a young human, yet she already knew her parents had interesting secrets. And she knew to pretend not to know. Foxes were born with that kind of knowledge, but how had she figured it out? Were little humans born that way too?

He'd reached out a mental thread to see what she was thinking. Before he could gather any details, however, three things had happened, very fast. First, a biscuit had slipped from Lovisa's fingers and slapped down onto the marble floor. Second, Lovisa had broken away from the door and fled, faster than the fox had ever seen a human move. Her feet, socked but shoeless, had made the smallest thudding noises as she ran.

Third, the bedroom door had been flung wide and Ferla had thrust herself into the aperture, peering quickly up and down the corridor with a focus and ferocity that had made the blue fox think of an avenging bird of prey. Ferla's eyes had narrowed on the fox, then on the dry, crumbly biscuit.

Instantly, the fox had understood that things could be bad for Lovisa if her mother suspected her of eavesdropping. Without consideration, he'd begun jumping and prancing, slapping his little feet against the floor as hard as he could, trying to mimic the sound the biscuit had made before. Then, remembering that a fox was probably expected to eat a biscuit, he'd bitten down on it, which had turned out to be a true sacrifice, for it had been stale and disgusting.

Ferla's lips had stretched into a bright, false smile. "Is there something you want, my beautiful darling?" she'd said, in that cloying voice she'd always used back when she'd wanted him to bond.

No, he'd said, responding inside her mind for the first time ever. *I've just been out here, dancing with a celebratory biscuit. Did I bother you? I'm sorry. I'm dancing for happiness, because I've decided to bond to you.*

The thrust of Ferla's joy—or greed? (it was always complicated inside Ferla)—had almost thrown him against the opposite wall. She'd motioned him into the bedroom, then pointed triumphantly at his little body, for the benefit of her husband.

"It worked," she'd said to Benni. "I told you I would make it work."

Benni had started to laugh. "I give up," he'd said. "You win."

Then she'd gone to Benni and kissed him and the fox had watched the two of them come together in a heady kind of pleasure that had felt more interesting than it usually did between them, like a meeting of both trust and mistrust, mutual competition, and surrender.

And now, here he was. Tomorrow would be a long and challenging day. It was time for him to check on all the house's secrets, and go to sleep. He jumped out of the airship, found the loose shingle, squeezed through, and began his rounds.

Some minutes later, the fox scampered back to Ferla and Benni's bedroom. He took the normal route, through the corridors. Pushing through the flap in their door, he crawled into his own little bed beside the fire, luxuriating in the warmth.

He raised his nose once, sniffing. The room smelled like a visit from Lovisa.

What had she done now?

Sighing, the fox stretched his tired mind around the house. But when he found Lovisa, she was in her own bed, asleep.

He wished sometimes that he didn't care. His fox friends, especially his siblings, warned him that he *shouldn't* care, especially not for a human to whom he wasn't bonded; that caring led to dilemmas. But Lovisa and the fox had been children together. The fox had seen what it was like to be a child in this house. He'd watch her learn to lie, hide, sneak, just like a fox did. Then he'd watched her fall in love with each of her brothers, and begin lying, hiding, and sneaking on their behalf.

Could he help it if it had created a connection, a different kind of bond?

Suddenly the fox remembered something. Lovisa believed herself to have closed him in the attic. In the morning, he would have to be discovered closed in the attic.

How tiresome. The fox dragged himself to his feet, knowing he should probably go there now, in case anyone woke up and found him where he shouldn't be.

Adventure Fox, he thought to himself wearily as he made his way through the heat ducts again. This was his chosen name. Not Fox, but *Adventure* Fox. Adventure for short.

Though he wouldn't mind if the coming days involved a tad less adventure.

IN THE MORNING, Lovisa went down to breakfast not knowing what to expect. To her relief, she found the dining room empty of everyone but Viri and Erita.

Their eyes widened at the sight of her. "It's you!" they said, both small, dramatic in their happiness, their freckled faces glowing with the hope that she was staying for a while. Most Keepish people had brown freckles in brown faces, but Viri's and Erita's were darker than usual, more noticeable. It was cute.

"It is I," she said, sitting down with a smile, waiting for someone to pour her some tea. "Did either of you spend any time in the attic room yesterday?"

"No!" said Erita. "We're not stupid. Mother is angry, so we've been good. Mostly! Vikti has a cold."

"Poor Vikti. Where's Mother?"

"Yelling," said Viri.

"Oh? Who's she yelling at?"

"A guard," said Viri. "She fired him."

It shouldn't surprise her; she'd made a conscious decision to sacrifice him. Still, a ball of sick dropped to the pit of Lovisa's stomach. "Why?" she asked, trying to sound nonchalant.

"I don't know," said Viri. "She was whisper-yelling. Are you staying all day? It's Wednesday. We have outside exercise on Wednesday and we could make a snow keep."

"*I* know," said Erita importantly. "He's a slut with no self-control."

"*What?*" said Lovisa, choking on her tea.

"He put his dirty fingers on something he didn't deserve," said Erita.

"You heard her say that?" said Viri, awed.

"Yes. You were in the bath."

"What did he put his fingers on?"

"Something he didn't deserve," Erita repeated, stressing each syllable significantly. "I already said."

"But what does that mean?" said Viri. "What didn't he deserve? Did he steal?"

"I thought maybe he touched her fox. Mother is weird about her fox."

"But maybe he had to touch it," said Viri as a shape appeared in the doorway over his shoulder. It was their mother. Lovisa went cold. Not seeing her, Viri said, "Sometimes you have to touch the fox, like, if he's in the way, or if he's bringing you a letter from Mother. Are you staying all day, Lovisa?" he repeated. "And what's a slut?"

"Yes, please," said the calm and precise voice of Ferla. "Tell us what a slut is, Lovisa."

The boys turned, startled, to look at her. Her expression was closed, almost haughty, and her hair was pulled back from her forehead as tightly as usual. She wore a sweeping coat of brown and silver fur, as if she were already on her way out, and her blue fox sat in her hood, peeking over her shoulder. The fox's gold eyes watched Lovisa steadily.

Lovisa swallowed. "I'm sure I don't know."

"And I'm sure you do," said Ferla. "Answer your brother. He wants to know what a slut is."

"I don't," said Viri in a tiny voice. "It's okay, Mother. I don't want to know."

"I distinctly heard you asking, Viri," said Ferla. "Are you too cowardly to hear the answer? Ask your sister again."

Now Viri was crying. "What's a slut," he said to his plate, wiping tears from his face.

"Ask the question as if you're curious, Viri. The first time you asked, you sounded curious. And ask it of your sister, not of your plate, because I'm certain she knows."

Viri was crying harder now, his breath squeaky and desperate. His fingers had crawled to his mouth. Lovisa sat perfectly still, knowing that if she did or said anything that deviated from her mother's script, it would probably make things worse for Viri.

Ferla crossed the room and slapped Viri's face. His crying turned to a scream. "Take him away," she said in a disgusted voice to a frightened-looking attendant, who helped Viri up and rushed him out of the room. Lovisa guessed he would spend the day alternating between vomiting and hysterics.

"Sit down, Erita," Ferla said when the older boy tried to slip out of his seat too. Erita was doing a better job of not crying, but his face was tight, his eyes big. "I want you to hear Lovisa's definition of a slut, so that later, you can tell your brothers. Lovisa? We're waiting."

Lovisa forced her voice calm. "A slut isn't anything. There's no such thing. It's just a nasty word people use to try to make other people ashamed for wanting to be happy."

Ferla swept around the table and was reaching for Lovisa before Lovisa even understood what was happening. Ferla's fingers clutched the twists in Lovisa's hair and pulled her up from her seat so fast and hard that Lovisa couldn't help crying out in pain. Ferla began dragging Lovisa across the room by her hair, her fox bobbing around on her back, comically, like he was enjoying some kind of carnival ride.

"You little slut," Ferla was whispering between her teeth, spitting from the force of her words. "You can kiss as many academy students as you want, you can have sex with them, you can even get pregnant and have their babies, I don't care, but the next time you put your dirty mouth on an employee, I will wash your mouth clean myself, do you understand?"

"Yes, Mother," Lovisa gasped.

"Go to your father," Ferla said, shoving her through the doorway and into the corridor. "He wants to speak to you."

"Yes, Mother."

Ferla spun back, returning to the dining room. Lovisa heard her clipped voice say, "Eat your breakfast, Erita, and stop sniveling."

For a moment, Lovisa stood, shivering in the corridor. She touched her hair, checking to see that it was still in place. She wanted to take it down and massage her scalp. She wanted to be in her bed in her dormitory bedroom, where things like this didn't happen.

Then, feeling calmer, she crossed to her father's library. It was over now; Lovisa wasn't afraid of her father.

"Papa?" she said, pushing the door open.

"Lovisa," he said, looking up from his desk. "Come in."

He folded his hands over his papers, watching her with a grave expression. Attentive, fatherly, concerned. Lovisa was ashamed suddenly of the part she was about to play, lying to her father, but at least the shame was helpful. She allowed it to show on her face.

"Lovisa," said her father. "Your mother and I are considerably disappointed in you."

"Papa, I only kissed him," said Lovisa.

"There is no 'only,'" said Benni, "when a young man we've entrusted with this family's safety has his hands on our child."

"Are you sure you're angry with me? It sounds like you're angry with him."

"He's an employee," said Benni. "We've dealt with him. He'll never see the inside of this house again, or the house of any reputable family. His sister is one of our guards too, did you know that? We've had to give her a warning." He paused, studying her reaction. "What do you think of that?"

"It's unfair, Papa, to both of them. It wasn't his fault, and it certainly wasn't hers. And we can't help how we feel."

"So. You imagine yourself to have fallen in love," he said, sounding satisfied.

"Papa," said Lovisa reproachfully. "How would you like it if I told you that you imagine yourself to have fallen in love with Mother? You can't tell me whom I should love."

"Indeed," he said, making a triangle with his hands and resting his chin upon it. "You'll think I'm heartless, Lovisa, but a daughter of the Cavenda family cannot fall in love with a house guard. Do you imagine your mother and I would set you up to live together?"

"Why should you? Do you think I won't be able to find a profitable industry?"

"In fact, I think a lot of doors in Ledra would close to you if you lived like that with your own house guard. You excel in your politics and government classes, Lovisa. You know we expect you to follow in our footsteps, whether it's as a Scholar or an Industrialist. Either way, it'll require wiser decisions on your part."

"Doors will always open to me, Papa!" Lovisa said. "I'm a Cavenda. If I married a house guard, I would still be a Cavenda." In Winterkeep, when two people married, the surname of the wealthier person became their family name. The name Cavenda came from Lovisa's mother.

"Parents can take a name away from a child," her father reminded her quietly.

Lovisa looked into her own hands, trying not to show how astonished she was. Parents took names away from a child only if they were officially disowning that child. It was hardly ever done, except, perhaps, in cases of the social shame that came from raising a criminal. And not a minor criminal; one who murdered or raped, did truly inexcusable things.

Before Lovisa could think of the right response, the door swung open and Ferla swept in. Ignoring Lovisa, she advanced on Benni's desk, glaring at him. Her hood lay against her back heavily, which meant that her fox was still riding inside it.

Benni stood to meet his wife, and when she held out her hand, silently took the object she offered, a bit flustered. Ferla was visibly seething at Benni, which was unusual. Even at the heights of her temper, she was rarely angry directly *at* Benni. Had he done something to upset her?

Then Ferla spun around and marched toward the door without speaking. A moment later, they heard the front door slam. That was unusual too. Her parents always kissed goodbye in the morning.

In his hands, Benni held the leather wallet Lovisa knew to be stuffed with samklavi candies. He slipped it into a pocket, then smiled at Lovisa.

A smile, when he'd just threatened to take her name away?

It was exhausting, sometimes, to hold up the pretense of being unintelligent about certain things. "I don't believe you'd ever take my name away, just because I loved someone," she said. "I'm not a criminal."

Benni peered at her so keenly that Lovisa feared she'd accidentally said something intelligent. She gave him her blankest expression.

"Did you know that I lived at home during my tenure at the academy, Lovisa?" he said. "I did so at my parents' request, so that they could teach me the shipping business."

It was difficult for Lovisa to keep her expression smooth in response to any suggestion she live at home. Benni came from a family of shipbuilders, shipowners, and importers. He owned dozens of ships and he was never satisfied, always wanting to move into newer, bigger, more profitable kinds of shipping. Ferla's mine—the one she shared with Katu—was a steady supplier of silver. It had been rich in zilfium too, in Ferla's father's time, though the zilfium had recently reached the point of depletion. The diminished value of the mine was one of the many reasons Ferla worked so tirelessly and pushed those around her so hard, trying to live up to the standards of her father.

Lovisa had no interest in either of her parents' family industries. Not that she had any interest in her own course of study either; she'd chosen the school of politics and government out of a bored sense of obligation. Maybe also because it was easy. "I think it's better for my schoolwork if I live on campus, Papa," she said. "I'd better get going, or I'll miss my first class."

ON THE WALK back to the dormitory, Lovisa felt like a different person from the girl who'd left campus the night before.

She'd had sex twice with a guard whose career was now ruined; she'd stolen from her parents while they slept; and she'd prepared a secret path into the house with a plan to sneak into her mother's prison soon.

What were her parents fighting about? What was her father storing in the attic room? And why had her mother passed her father candy, wrapped up in a wallet as if it were a state secret?

In one pocket, the box with the key imprint bumped against Lovisa's leg. She reached in to touch it. Then, from another pocket, she unearthed some biscuits, which she ate in lieu of breakfast.

CHAPTER NINE

BITTERBLUE WOKE TO dim gray light, the scent of lavender, and the feeling that her hands and feet were on fire.

"I don't want to die," she cried out, confused, then hearing her own voice and understanding she mustn't be dead. Feeling soft, silky blankets and pillows around her; realizing she wasn't drowning.

She was in a small room, its walls touched by weak light filtering through a high window. The lavender smell came from the bedding, but there was another smell underneath. A more pervasive smell, as if the lavender was meant to mask something less pleasant. More animal.

"Winterkeep," Bitterblue said, remembering. "Is this Winterkeep?"

Other memories began to form. The ship. The wave. The incredible moment of being tossed through the air, like a doll stuffed with beans, then splashing into the sea. Being surrounded by those purple creatures, just at the moment of giving up. *Silbercows,* Bitterblue thought, remembering more about Winterkeep. *They rescued me and brought me to people in an airship. They showed me pictures in my mind. They saved my life!*

Bitterblue shoved her blankets back and swung her feet down, thinking she would go find everyone, tell them she was awake. But when she tried to stand, her feet screamed with pain and she fell back onto the bed.

"Ow!" she cried. "Hello? Giddon?"

When no one came, she took stock. She was wearing someone else's pajamas and her toes were bandaged. Frostbite? Chillblains? Her fingers hurt too, as did her nose and ears, but they weren't bandaged. Touching her arms, she noticed that her knives were missing. Then she realized that her gold rings were gone too; then remembered her mother's ring.

Oh, no, she thought, imagining the ring falling into darkness, thudding against the floor of the Brumal Sea. *I'm sorry, Mama,* she thought, with the desolate sense that she'd abandoned her actual mother in a cold and lonely place. *I hope there are interesting things to see down there.*

"Giddon?" she said out loud. "Where is everyone?"

Grumbling about how she always had to do everything for herself, Bitterblue put her feet to the floor again and, carefully, tried to stand. It hurt, but she could do it. She shuffled forward a step or two, until it became too painful. Then she knelt, tried crawling, which was equally painful because her hands ached. Slowly, she made her way to the door. She reached for the knob.

The door was locked.

That was strange.

Giddon? Why would the door be locked?

She knocked on the door with her elbow and called out once more, but nothing happened.

Shifting toward a different understanding of her situation, Bitterblue studied the room. The only furniture was the bed. There were no lamps. She thought the thick rug might be the source of the unpleasant smell. She saw a chamber pot peeking out from under the bed. The window was high in the wall, too high for Bitterblue to reach.

And the door is locked, she told Giddon. *And you're not here. And I've been left with no food or water or lamps, and someone has taken my rings.*

Something inside Bitterblue was becoming interested and still. She shuffled back to the bed, noticing the distinctly Keepish softness of the silk of her sheets, the bright Keepish shade of crimson. Pulling the covers around her shivering body, she lay down, then proceeded to think. About her drowned men; about zilfium, and people importing it from her mountains. About why someone in Winterkeep might want the Queen of Monsea locked in a room.

SHE WOKE TO the tiniest sound, a scratch or a scrape, and sat up fast. The room looked the same, but the light had become more diffuse. She could see a pale blue sky through her window.

Then she saw something gleaming white on the rug. Someone had slipped a piece of paper under the door.

Well. At least that's something.

Steeling herself against the pain, Bitterblue climbed down to the rug again and crawled to the door. *Po told me once that there's no shame in crawling, when you can't walk,* she said to Giddon, picking the paper up.

It was a picture of Bitterblue City, a print, one she'd seen before. In fact, she'd sent Mikka and Brek to Winterkeep each with a copy. This version of the picture, however, had been altered. Her castle and the bridges all flew flags, drawn in graphite, that hadn't been in the original. Some of the flags showed a scene of silbercows in the ocean, a gigantic, underwater creature below them: the flag of Winterkeep. Some of the flags showed hills rising to a mountain peak, and above the peak, a single star shaped like a sword with a cross guard. Giddon had drawn this flag for her. It was the new flag of Estill.

Bitterblue's hands held the paper tightly, for she could not help but understand this. It was a declaration of war.

PART TWO

THE KEEPER

THE CREATURE WHO lived at the bottom of the sea gazed at the little metal egg with the sparkly ring and pin, fondling it with the tip of one of her tentacles.

She hadn't pulled the pin yet to see if anything happened. She was waiting for the moment when she really needed cheering up. She thought it would come soon, for she did not like her new, disrupted world.

For one thing, there were the four silbercows who'd escaped from the massacre, who'd seen her, and chastised her for not helping. They'd told all the other silbercows about her, calling her that name they insisted on using, Keeper. Then silbercows had come in droves to stare at her and say "Keeper" at her. Some had touched her. Some had even tried to talk to her, which had been the scariest thing of all and had made her vibrate and cry and feel so dizzy that she saw stars. And they kept pressing in, asking her to do things, "Keeper" things she didn't understand, like play with whales or sing. It was terrible. Nothing felt more lonely than being surrounded by silbercows who thought she was somebody else, instead of who she really was, some-one they could see if they just looked, a large but ordinary creature with a round body, thirteen tentacles, and twenty-three eyes, who loved her treasures and wanted to be left alone.

One day, while they were all pressing in, a song of sadness burst out of the creature. It was the first song she could ever remember singing, beautiful and wordless, all about who she was. It started as a screech and a buzz, then a rumble, then a jagged explosion of sensation that felt really good to her, really true and brave. The silbercows leaped back in alarm. Then all of them except for the original four sped away. She kept singing. It felt so right.

When she stopped, the four silbercows stared at her with enormous eyes, alert and tense, as if bracing for her next song. *I'm done,* she said, which seemed to help them relax. Then, in a conversation amongst themselves, they decided that she couldn't be the Keeper after all. Silbercows didn't speak in words, more in images and feelings, but the creature understood from their conversation that the Keeper was famous for having a mesmerizing singing voice. Her singing voice, in contrast, made them feel like they were going to turn inside out and explode.

The creature was extremely relieved. She would've sung a song sooner, if she'd only known. Fewer silbercows came to stare at her after that. Mostly it was just the four. And that was better. But it was still too many. One of them had the pucker of a long scar on his shoulder, and a very stiff and achy flipper, from the massacre. The second had deep scratches on her side and the third was missing part of her tail fin. The fourth silbercow seemed strong in body, but there was something wrong in his eyes, and he never talked. She liked that one best, because he never talked. He even brought her a ring that had slipped from the finger of a drowning human they'd saved. It was gold with inset gray stones. The creature wore it on the tip of one of her tentacles. Often, when she was alone, she stretched her tentacle up and watched the ring glimmer with shifting light as the water around it moved. It made her very happy.

But she was rarely alone now, not with these four visiting her constantly.

There were strange sounds in the ocean now too sometimes. They were faint and very far away, like a distant whisper, making her think she was imagining things; but then the floor under her body would shake with the smallest rumble, and she would know. Something loud was happening, somewhere in the ocean. Something new.

She asked the silbercows about the noises once. But they got so quiet and serious, they said *Yes* and *We know* and *We'll tell you.* Then they started to show her pictures that she badly did not want to see, pictures of coral and seahorses and silbercows suddenly torn apart, so that she cried out, *Never mind.*

But you should know, they said.

No. I don't want to. I'm not interested. I don't care, she said, and when they kept trying to tell her, she began to sing. Her singing made them dart back. When she got to the end of the song and they gathered around her again slowly, they no longer tried to show her those terrible pictures.

You are definitely not the Keeper, they said, which pleased her.

I told you I wasn't, she said.

But just because they agreed now that she wasn't the Keeper, it didn't mean they understood who she was. In fact, they seemed to spend a lot of time trying to decide amongst themselves who she was. It made her anxious about what they would decide. She wished she knew how to make them go away, and stay away.

ONE DAY, THE silbercows asked permission to look closer at her treasures.

You can look at them, she said, obscurely nervous. *But you can't have them.*

For a while, they poked around among her anchors, nets, and tattered sails. They were very interested in her Storyworld, especially the two rotting corpses inside the cabin. They pointed out that some-one, certainly humans, had chopped gashes into the ship's pale gray hull. They touched some markings on the ship's side, saying that the markings were a name, but that they didn't know how to read it. They seemed curious to know who those corpses were, and why they were padlocked inside. They also wanted to know why *she* was interested in them. Was it because *she* knew who they were?

The creature responded that she didn't. She just liked their ship, which was a window into another world. It had fallen down slowly from that world, as if it were looking for her. It was as if the world above had blessed her.

The silbercows asked her if it was possible that she was a kind of keeper, just not the Keeper they'd thought she was. Could she be the keeper of the secrets of humans? The keeper of human sadnesses and failures?

The creature didn't understand this, at all. She'd never considered humans, beyond that she liked their shiny, perfect, tiny things, she liked being connected to the world above, and she liked watching their flesh melt into bones. Also, her treasures were happy, not sad. *I'm the keeper of their things,* she said. *I love their things.*

The silbercows asked her if she understood that her treasures fell from another world because of calamities in that world; that if human things sank to the bottom of the sea, it was because something in the world of humans had gone wrong. *We talk to humans sometimes who tell us about it,* they said.

You seem to talk to everyone, she said, rather reproachfully.

We don't talk to all humans, they said. *Only the humans who are good listeners. The point is, humans might be able to tell us why there are bodies inside your Storyworld.*

The creature was beginning to dislike the conversation again, and wondered why the silbercows were always so gloomy. *I would rather talk about how sparkly my ring is,* she said, stretching her tentacle out, wondering if she was going to have to start singing again.

But then something happened that changed everything. One of the silbercows, the one who didn't talk, found the little metal egg with the sparkly circle and pin. He sprang away, shaking. When the others saw it too, they cried out, and sprang back with him.

What? said the sea creature. *What is it?*

It makes fire, they cried out. *It makes the ocean disappear.*

That little thing? she said, not believing them.

Something big is trapped inside it, they told her. *Poison and horror and pain. It comes out when you pull the ring. It burns!* And then they showed her the pictures again that she didn't want to see, and she started to sing, but the silbercows didn't go away, they just kept pressing the pictures into her mind. The ocean torn apart with a terrible light. The noise and the shaking, and silbercows crying, and everything gone. *Stop,* she cried, *please.*

It's not safe to keep that thing near you as a treasure, they told her.

Not safe? Should I take it somewhere else? she asked, noticing that, ever so slowly, the silbercows were backing away.

If you do, they told her, *wherever you take it won't be safe.*

Should I throw it on land?

No! That could kill humans!

Should I bury it under the ground?

Maybe, they said doubtfully. *But what if the water uncovers it again, and someone pulls the ring?*

But then what can I do? cried the creature. *I have to keep it near me, and guard it! I have to keep it safe!*

The silbercows, who were still backing away, told her that it could never be safe. Then they told her that they had to go away now, because they couldn't be near it.

Then, to her amazement, they turned and fled.

FINALLY, THE CREATURE had what she wanted. Solitude.

The ocean floor spread out around her, quiet and dark, and life was how it had used to be.

Except now, when the creature held her Storyworld to one of her eyes and looked inside it, she remembered that the silbercows had wanted to talk about who the two bodies were. Why they were there. The creature still didn't want to know those things. But it had changed her Storyworld, that there were stories connected to it that she didn't know.

And when she lifted her ringed tentacle to the brighter water above, admiring its sparkle, she missed the silbercows trying to press upon her the story of the sad human who'd lost it. When someone tried to press a story on you, you needed to be able to refuse. But it was also nice to know that the story would be there again for you another day, if you changed your mind. If you were ready.

The creature was lonely, for the first time.

She began to play games in her mind, invent fantasies, of ways to make the scary egg treasure go away, so that the silbercows could come back. Not come back often, but visit sometimes.

Eventually her fantasies turned into ideas, which she studied and revised, until one day, her ideas became a plan.

On that day, the creature began to push one of her tentacles—not the ringed tentacle—into the sand beneath her body. With all her strength, she pushed down, drilling a deep, thin tunnel in the ocean floor. She drove her tentacle into the ground as deep as it could go, surprised by how hard it was inside the earth, how cold. At the bottom of her tunnel, with her tentacle fully extended, she scraped out a little well.

Then, ever so carefully, she pulled her tentacle back out again. She picked up the scary egg treasure. She lowered it through the tunnel and placed it into the well.

Then, her tentacle plugging the tunnel, she pulled the ring.

THE PAIN WAS terrible.

The pain was so terrible that when the silbercows arrived, flying toward her with big, alarmed eyes, she told them that she thought she might be dying.

What did you do? they asked her. *We heard the big noise. We felt the ocean shake. You don't look like you're dying. What did you do?*

I buried the treasure in the ground beneath me, she told them, *and pulled the ring.*

The silbercows were boggled by this. They stared at her, blinking, then they stared at one another and talked amongst themselves. They told her that she was a hero.

I'm not, she said, crying from the pain in the place where a horrible poisonous fire had burned away her tentacle. She was really quite sure she was dying. She didn't want to live.

Maybe you're the Keeper after all, they said.

No! she said, unable to bear this. *Not that again! I was just lonely!* And then she began to cry. Her crying turned into a song of loneliness, sadness, and loss, because she'd lost her tentacle. She'd hurt herself, to make her home safe for the silbercows, and now they were misunderstanding her again. She sang louder and louder. Her singing turned into a wail.

The silbercows didn't leave. They stayed with her while she sang and wailed, watching her quietly, waiting. They flinched sometimes at the noises she made, but they didn't leave.

When she was done, they carefully examined her tentacle with their noses, which were soft. It wasn't a tentacle anymore, really, they told her. It was a black, burnt nub.

Will it ever stop burning? she asked.

We don't know, they said.

I'm uneven now, she said. *My body is uneven.*

Yes, they said, touching her gently, touching their noses to her nub. *We're uneven too.*

Do your wounds still hurt?

Much less, they said.

Am I dying?

We think you're going to live.

The creature found that she was relieved to hear this. She thought that she would like to live at least long enough to see if her wound could ever hurt less.

Listen, she said, because something else was hurting her. *Will you tell me . . .* She paused. Briefly sang a few notes for courage. *Will you tell me why the humans would make a thing like that?*

CHAPTER TEN

A BLADE OF LIGHT woke Giddon, blinding him, then dragging him into a consciousness he did not want.

Everything hurt, especially his neck, especially his hands and feet. They'd had to drag him out of the frozen sea yesterday like a drowning dog; they'd had to go through an entire rigmarole to warm him, for he'd made himself sick, trying to find her even if it killed him. Hava's face had been tight and scared with worry for him when they'd pulled him back aboard. He was supposed to be taking care of Hava, and instead he'd given her something else to fear.

"Bitterblue," he said. "Bitterblue." Then he wept, as he hadn't been able to yesterday, desperately, like a man who was choking, pressing his face into pillows so that his neighbors wouldn't hear.

WHEN GIDDON BEGAN to understand, with some alarm, that his cistern of tears was bottomless, he forced himself to sit up and calm down. This had never happened before, that he hadn't been able to cry himself out. A new discovery about himself that he'd have to learn to manage.

Bitterblue, he said. *I've mucked it up already, without you. You would not be proud.*

Except that he knew she would be proud, always, whether he deserved it or not.

Tears began to trickle again. He cleared his throat, wiped his face, and took a breath.

All right, he said. *Tell me what to do.*

The answer came in her clear voice. *Make sure Katu is safe. Take care of my sister. Write to my uncle and our friends and tell them what happened to me. Keep an eye on my advisers. And find out about Mikka and Brek: Investigate those importers.*

The family names on the importer list had included Cavenda, Tima, Balava. There had been people with those names at dinner last night.

Giddon was going to kill the importers.

He reached for his clothes.

BY THE TIME Giddon stepped out of his bedroom, he had his face in order.

He was on the second floor of Quona Varana's tall, many-windowed house above the sea. Light streamed into the corridor from the gigantic stairway at the far end, where the walls were made of windows. The light was an assault.

A straight-backed, bearded man in white stood in the corridor and nodded a greeting as Giddon approached. His skin was brown but his hair and eyes, his beard, were the same dark shade as Giddon's.

"Breakfast is served in the dining room downstairs, sir," he said in Keepish.

"Thank you," Giddon replied in Keepish, pausing to knock on Hava's door. She'd skipped that interminable dinner last night. Refused to leave the ship, then kept turning into a sculpture anytime anyone tried to talk to her. So they'd left her behind with the sailors, then Giddon had returned after dinner to collect her. Once he'd explained that they'd be staying in a quiet, isolated home, then begged, pleaded with her to come, she'd done so, silent and cold, going straight to bed when they'd arrived.

"Hava has already gone to breakfast," the man said.

"Has she?" said Giddon, worry twisting inside him. "Was she wearing a coat?"

"No, sir," said the man.

Then maybe she really had gone to breakfast. Though Hava could make a man see a young woman without a coat, if she wanted to.

Giddon walked on quickly toward the staircase. At its top, a cat sat at attention, its rump on the floor, its nose in the air, its white fur, even its posture and gravity, mirroring that of the man in white, almost comically, as if it believed itself to be directing guests to breakfast as well. Then it saw Giddon and darted down the steps in front of him and the illusion was broken. Giddon was comforted, obscurely, by its familiar, catlike behavior.

There had been a few blue foxes at dinner last night—though their fur had been a dark gray, not actually blue—and he hadn't liked the feeling of their intelligent gold eyes on him, the sense that they might be "bonded" to some person at the party with whom they were having a secret conversation. Of course, everything about dinner last night had been difficult. Giddon had felt as if he were clinging to propriety by a thread; he'd wanted to crawl under the table and roll into a ball.

Through the south-facing windows, he could see the Cliff Farm that, Quona had explained, was owned by the Winterkeep Academy and was used by the school of animal medicine. Its barns, painted pale blue, were perched on a cliff of gold grass above the sea, fat cows grazing idly. Giddon had never seen barns with huge glass windows before. Suddenly he hated the farm, because it was part of an educational institution more successful and blessed with resources than Bitterblue had ever been able to dream of.

His breath whooshed out in relief when he found Hava in the dining room, tearing bacon with her teeth like she was trying to punish it. Her shoulders were hunched, her pale face in a snarl. He sat across from her, not pressing her to speak when she ignored him.

Guide me, he said.

You're doing fine, Bitterblue said. *Just let her be.*

BREAKFAST WAS OVERRUN by cats.

The meal took place in a beautiful room with tall windows that striped the table with sunlight. The food was good. The tea was delicious. And Giddon had grown up in a castle with dogs; he was friendly with many cats; it didn't alarm him for something furry to brush past his legs under the table, or for small eyes to watch him from a windowsill. But there were just so many. Two in the room when he arrived, a ginger and a mottled black batting at each other with concerted antagonism that turned suddenly into complete indifference, and their numbers kept growing. By the time Quona Varana came in, at least seven cats were present, and he could hear others scurrying in rooms nearby. One had fallen asleep on Giddon's foot. This was fine with him.

Quona took each of the visitors' hands in a quick, firm grasp—first Bitterblue's advisers Froggatt and Barra; then Coran, who was both an adviser and the queen's doctor; then Giddon; then Hava. Giddon, who knew handshaking wasn't a Torlan custom, was so touched by the gesture that he almost started crying again.

"How are you all?" said Quona in stiff but unhesitant Lingian, sitting down, then attacking a hard-boiled egg with a spoon. "Did you sleep? Are you comfortable? I hope you don't mind the cats." She was a woman of perhaps forty, with dark hair pulled neatly back and black eyes in a brown face. Her voice was deep and forceful, her focus on them rather startlingly intense. She asked her questions like she had an agenda and was ticking things off a list.

"I'm quite comfortable, thank you," said Giddon, "and I like cats."

"Good," she said, eating quietly for a minute or two. Occasionally a cat jumped into her lap and she swept it onto the floor again with a quick remonstrance in Keepish. "Bad cat!" or "Behave yourself!"

"Do you have any foxes?" asked Giddon, wanting to know if he needed to guard himself, though unsure against what. Could foxes read everyone's minds?

"I do not," said Quona. "Though if I did, I would have only one. There are many laws governing the relationships between humans and foxes, and one is that no human may be bonded to more than one fox. Do you understand about the foxes?"

"About . . . the laws?" said Giddon, confused.

"About how their telepathy works," she said. "You'll be encountering foxes during your stay, so it's important to understand. You don't need to fear their intrusion, for a fox can't understand your thoughts or words at all, unless it's bonded to you. A fox might choose to bond to you in the course of your visit—it's unlikely, but possible—but if so, the fox will tell you. And then, it's like human conversation. They'll know what you tell them, and you'll know what they tell you. You won't be able to see into each other's souls, or any such nonsense, but if you need a letter delivered or want to know if your staff is dawdling, they can be useful. It's quite straightforward. At least, this is the common knowledge about foxes. None has ever bonded to me, so I can't speak to how it feels. Do you want one to bond to you?" she asked abruptly.

"Not particularly," said Giddon.

"Congratulations," said Quona. "You're the only person in Winterkeep who doesn't, perhaps besides me. I prefer my cats. But maybe, as you come to understand the importance of blue foxes here, you'll change your mind. I'm told they are loyal, obedient, and unbribable by your enemies. If you do change your mind, give them treats. They're pleasure-seekers."

Hava seemed to rouse herself. "Aren't you an animal doctor?" she asked Quona, leaning forward with her chin in her hand. She did that sometimes—rarely—when she wanted to challenge someone with the strangeness of her mismatched eyes. She blinked at Quona, copper and red.

Quona met her gaze. "Yes. I have an advanced degree in animal medicine," she said. "It's also my academic subject. I teach Winterkeep's brightest future animal doctors."

"And isn't your sister the prime minister of Winterkeep? Doesn't your family usually go into politics?"

Quona flashed a toothy smile. "Absolutely," she said. "Politics, or airships."

"Why didn't you go into politics or airships? Don't you like your family?"

"Hava!" said Froggatt in a scandalized tone, his first contribution to the conversation. Poor Froggatt. Giddon guessed he'd been crying this morning too; his eyes were puffy.

"Don't you 'Hava' me," Hava snarled at him.

"Hava," said Giddon tiredly, before he could stop himself.

"Oh, Hava asks a valid question," said Quona. "I am, without a doubt, not what my family hoped I would be. I'm about as qualified to be a politician or an airship magnate as I would guess you are, Hava, to be Queen of Monsea."

Quona had no idea that Hava, like Bitterblue, was the daughter of King Leck, but it was the sort of offhand remark that could send Hava running. Giddon glanced at Hava nervously.

"But don't misunderstand: I'm very proud of my family," Quona continued. "Like a true Scholar, Sara is devoted to the protection of the environment. She's not the first Varana to be prime minister, nor will she be the last. And our family invented the airship, which is a zilfium-free technology and the fastest means of transportation in the world. The mixture of gases that keeps airships buoyant, varane, is named after us. Unlike zilfium, it's environmentally safe. So," she said, switching topics. "What do you all intend to do today? How can I help? No one will bother you. Keepish society knows not to come to my house without invitation."

"We have letters to write to our colleagues at home," said Froggatt, "and meetings to set up here. We believe the queen would have wanted us to move forward with her diplomatic intentions."

"Good men," said Quona, nodding grimly at Froggatt, Barra, and Coran. "And you?" she said, considering Giddon and Hava. It was interesting that she'd intuited, correctly, that the advisers were one team, Giddon and Hava another. Froggatt, Barra, and Coran knew little about the zilfium trick that had been played upon Bitterblue and nothing about her suspicions regarding the sinking of the *Seashell*. Nothing about Katu, either. The advisers were here to behave like diplomats. Giddon and Hava, in contrast, were going to sniff out those zilfium importers, and choke them.

And yet, Giddon also had letters to write, to his friends, the people who'd loved Bitterblue the most, besides him.

He couldn't write those letters yet.

"We intend to visit Periwinkle, the Lienid envoy, today," he said. "At dinner last night, he suggested we stop by." Periwinkle, who had dripped with tears all throughout dinner, would recognize the surnames on Bitterblue's list of importers, and maybe he would know the given names that went with them.

"Excellent," said Quona. "The office of the Lienid envoy is in the Keep. Would you like to fly there in my airship? Avoid the ambles?"

Giddon didn't know what the ambles were, nor did he particularly care. Last night, they'd traveled to this house in Quona's airship. How surreal it had been to float across the sky in a wooden ship attached to a balloon, with sails tacking and jibing like they did on water. So windy and cold, with sudden drops and climbs, as if the air was composed of invisible hills. When it had been time to land, one of Quona's fliers had shot some sort of tiny anchor, attached to a line, into a net on Quona's roof. A guard on the roof had disattached the anchor from the net, then attached a dock line to the anchor. The fliers had hauled the dock line up into the airship, then kept hauling on it to bring the airship down to the dock. It had been unlike anything Giddon had ever experienced. *You would've hated it,* Giddon thought to Bitterblue, suddenly furious that she'd missed the wonder of flying. She would've been amazed by it too. She would've asked a million questions, while clinging to Giddon and Hava and shrieking. She should have been allowed to have all those feelings.

Giddon could sense that his face had turned to marble. "Is it a long walk to the Keep?" he asked, trying to banish the anger from his tone.

"Perhaps an hour," she said.

"We'll walk," said Hava, in a short, unfriendly voice.

"Shall I draw you a map?" she said.

"We have a map," said Hava.

"If a fox were bonded to me," said Quona, "I could ask that fox to direct you there."

"We have a map," Hava repeated sharply.

"I understand," said Quona, an innocuous comment that nonetheless caused Hava to stand up and stalk from the room. The cat that had been lying on Giddon's foot stirred, then moved away, leaving him feeling untethered.

"I'm sorry," Giddon said weakly. "She's very upset."

"Of course she is," said Quona. "Aggression is a natural tactic in her situation, if ineffective. And how are you feeling this morning? I understand that you were in the water yesterday for a very long time."

"I'm fine," said Giddon, who didn't want to remember.

"Are you one of those people who pretends to be stronger than he is?" said Quona. "That's a reasonable tactic too, of course. One must choose a path, then stick to it."

Punctured, Giddon spent a moment carefully folding his napkin. He blinked, baffled by his new inability to control his tears.

You are not pretending, Bitterblue told him. *You* are *strong.*

You don't see inside me. You don't see my small, mean thoughts.

I am *inside you, silly,* she told him.

"I hate this place," said Hava as they walked to the Keep. "And I hate her."

The footpath to the city led first past the Cliff Farm, which, despite its beautiful, glass-windowed barns, smelled earthy and sour, just like farms at home. With a slow, deep breath, Giddon made a promise to himself to get through this day without saying "Hava!" reproachfully more than three times, including the time he'd already done so at breakfast.

He said, "She is a bit—"

"Braggy?" interrupted Hava. "Cat-obsessed? Nosy? I'm not going to be queen."

Giddon had been waiting for this. "Hava," he said, "I promise that won't happen."

"I won't do it," she said insistently. A tear ran down her cheek, then vanished. Giddon recognized the signs, the strange wavering in the air if you knew to watch for it, his own sudden disinterest in looking at her too closely. She was using her Grace, probably hiding more tears.

He swallowed the gorge that rose sometimes, if you were too aware of what she was doing. Then he turned back to admire Quona's house, as if it interested him, as if he weren't trying to give her a moment to gather her composure. The house clung to the cliff, looking like part of the landscape. Its windows gleamed. On the roof, above a single, small window, sat Quona's airship. Its balloon was long and gray, decorated with many tentacles, a representation of that creature that had some significance in Winterkeep. Some legendary sea monster? Giddon couldn't remember.

When he glanced back at Hava, she was still changing her face. "I know you won't be queen," he said. "No one knows who your father was, Hava. Even if they did know, they wouldn't expect you to be queen. Bitterblue had protocols in place in case of her death, and they don't involve you. You know that."

"I would leave," she said, her voice cracking.

"I know you would," said Giddon. Then he used all the strength he had to keep from saying more. Not to beg her to stay, not to forbid her to run away; not to impose any will that wasn't her own, because that was the surest way to lose Hava. But he needed her to stay. He needed it so badly that he clenched his fists around the map he was carrying, to keep from reaching out to hold her there.

"It was an unfortunate thing for Quona to say," he said. "But she said it in ignorance. It was also unfeeling," he added, "to all of us, given the circumstances."

"I hate her," she said again.

"I'm not wild about her myself. But I think she means well."

"I don't. I didn't believe a word she said. Every word was insincere."

"Well," said Giddon. "I do believe she likes cats."

Hava snorted. She was showing him her real face now, complete with tears. She raised a sleeve and smeared them away. "This is awful," she said. "I hate this."

Giddon took another breath. "Yes. Me too." *What do I do?*

You could try giving her a job, said Bitterblue.

He handed Hava the map, now slightly crumpled. "What do you think is the best route to the Keep?"

THE FIRST PART of the journey, down the footpath that ran along the cliff above the sea, was straightforward enough. Before and below them, the city of Ledra spread itself out, towers and domes, parks and gardens, taking shape as the day brightened. The footpath turned occasionally to short, wooden bridges that crossed over crashing water below. Some of the bridges moved when you stepped on them. *You would hate the footbridges,* Giddon thought. *But you would love the views.*

"Do you notice there's a fox following us?" said Hava.

"There is?" said Giddon. "Whose fox?"

"How would I know that?"

Giddon shrugged. "With whatever magical power made you notice the fox?"

"You mean eyesight?"

"Is it actually following us," said Giddon, "or just going the same way we're going?"

"It's not like it's carrying a sign announcing its intentions," said Hava in a quelling tone.

Giddon glanced around, but all he saw was the dramatic landscape. "All right," he said. "Keep me posted."

Once they reached the city, it became more necessary to consult the map. At one point, winding their way through Ledra's labyrinthine streets, they took a wrong turn. Then, when they tried to retrace their steps, two people in uniform at the base of a staircase asked them for their pass.

"Pass? What do you mean?" said Giddon, in his most polite Keepish. "We just came down that staircase."

"You're in the amble now," one of the guards said. "You have to walk through in the same direction as everyone else, unless you have a pass."

"I'm afraid I don't understand," said Giddon. "What's an amble?"

"Royal Continent," said one of the guards, nodding knowingly. "You don't know our shopping areas. You enter at one end and exit at the other."

"An amble is a shopping area?" said Giddon. "Where's the other end? Is it at the end of this street?"

"No, it's beyond that. Just follow the traffic."

From where Giddon was standing, the traffic didn't seem to have a particular direction. There were more people on this street than on the other streets they'd walked along, all kinds of people, some speaking languages he didn't know, but most were milling around what he now recognized as shops for clothing, fabric, flowers, food. Almost all the shops had counters open to the street, then a door that customers could enter if they wished to see what else the store had to offer. Now and then, an airship passed overhead. He wanted to board them, and go somewhere else.

"Is the Keep accessible from inside this amble?" asked Hava.

"No," said the guard, "of course not. This is the Flag Hill amble. The Keep is over near the academy, to the east."

"But—" said Giddon.

"Thank you," said Hava, then grabbed Giddon's wrist and started pulling him down the street.

"Hey!" he said. "No grabbing!"

Hava rolled her eyes and kept pulling him. "The Keepish sailors on the ship talked about the ambles. It's like a maze. We'll never get anywhere until we get out of it."

"All right," he said, feeling hopeless and tired suddenly, because apparently he was in a city of invisible traps. He wanted to go home. But where was home? Once, this had been a difficult question; now it was unbearable.

Hava let go of his wrist, then looked at him hard.

"I'm fine," he said.

"Sure you are. Come on, I think the traffic's moving this way."

Giddon followed her, resenting the beauty of the Flag Hill amble. The winding alleys and narrow staircases gave the city a character that, combined with glass windows, shiny brass lamps, neat painted signs for upscale shops, made it seem prosperous, expensive, in a way that Bitterblue City was not. At a tea shop, the drinks smelled bright, sharp, unusual. Bitterblue loved trying new foods and drinks. If she were here, they would stop. At a game shop, unfamiliar board games lay in a window open to the street, jeweled pieces lined up like cheery little soldiers. In different circumstances, Giddon might have bought one of the games for them to try later.

Though he might not too, because at every cross street, guards stopped them from exiting the amble, asking for their pass, and this nettled him. He noticed that people were allowed to *enter* at those points, of course. You could get in, but you couldn't get out.

He wanted to know if people lived on these streets, people who had to weave through a maze every time they left home, maybe in the opposite direction from where they needed to go. The amble took turn after arbitrary turn down alleys lined with shops, sometimes up long staircases with shopfronts to either side.

"How does anyone live here who can't climb?" said Giddon, who was getting tired of going up and down stairs. "What happens when you get old, or break your leg?"

"I don't know," said Hava, climbing beside him with an intent expression.

"Do the people who live above these shops have to walk the long way through the amble?"

"I think residents and businesspeople carry a pass," Hava said. "Noa said something about it on the ship. She grew up inside one of the ambles."

"What if you have a medical emergency? What if you're giving birth?"

Hava clapped him on the shoulder. "I promise I won't let you give birth alone."

"Brat."

"Bully."

The familiar teasing hurt. It was part of a happiness that was gone now. Giddon pushed on.

At the top of another staircase, down an alley and around a corner, they reached an arch guarded by two uniformed people. A square was visible beyond.

"Do you think we've made it through?" said Giddon.

"I surely hope so."

"Proof of purchase," said one of the guards as they approached.

"Proof of purchase?" Giddon replied.

"You must purchase something in the amble before exiting," said the guard.

"Are you serious?" Giddon said, startled by this. "If you enter a shopping area, you have to purchase something? Is this a law?"

"It certainly is," said the guard. "What part of the Royal Continent are you from, sir?"

"But what if I have no money? What if I'm poor?"

"Begging your pardon, sir, but you don't look poor."

"I purchased something," interrupted Hava, then handed an object to the guard that seemed to be a tiny, silver figurine of a fox, its eyes made of yellow diamonds. Giddon noticed that she was changing how her face looked. Her eyes were gray, and Ungraced.

"This looks like a game piece from a City game," said the guard, fingering the fox. "A valuable City game. Is this from Bazil's Game Shop?"

"Yes," said Hava.

"And you only purchased one piece?"

"Yes."

"That's odd, isn't it?"

Hava shrugged. "I only needed one piece."

"Hm," the guard said doubtfully. "For all I know, you brought that game piece into the amble with you. I don't need to see the purchase. I need to see the *proof* of purchase."

"Is this it?" said Hava, holding up her hand.

At the sight of the bright, white paper with a colorful shop insignia held in Hava's hand, Giddon glanced away, for it made his gorge rise.

The man handed the fox back to her, a new disinterest on his face. "Very good," he said. "Move along."

Giddon waited until they'd crossed the square. Then he allowed himself his second frustrated "Hava!" of the day.

"Yes?" she said, tucking the shiny little fox back into a pocket.

"What if he'd tried to take that proof of purchase from you?"

"You saw that he didn't."

"How did you even know what it should look like?"

"Weren't you watching the people in the amble? I saw a dozen shopkeepers hand a dozen proofs of purchase to people."

The main thing Giddon had noticed in the amble was that every small, dark-haired woman was Bitterblue to him, until she turned and showed the wrong face, or spoke in the wrong voice, or moved the wrong way. "You have money," he said. "Why are you stealing from Keepish artisans?"

"Because I wanted it," she said, "and because I hate this place. It killed my sister."

The answer undid Giddon, who didn't have a Grace to hide the tears that filled his eyes. He blotted them quickly with his sleeve. *Bitterblue?* he said. *I'm afraid she'll take anything I say right now as a reason to run away.*

I think you have to accept that she may run away, Giddon. It's not in your power to stop her.

Giddon blotted another tear.

"Hava?" he said.

"Yes?" she said, warily, not looking up from the map.

"You can talk to me."

Her mouth went hard. "Bully," she said. Then she pulled inside herself, that way she did when she wanted to pretend he wasn't there. It wasn't something she did with her Grace; it was just something she did. She turned and began walking.

"Wait," Giddon said, taking her sleeve.

"Hey! No grabbing!" she said, yanking her arm away.

"Wait!" he said again between clenched teeth, for he wasn't stopping her because of their conversation. He was stopping her because he'd just caught sight of someone in the square, someone he almost didn't recognize, so strange was it to encounter her in Ledra.

"What is it?" said Hava quietly, understanding.

"There's a pale, blond woman walking toward a staircase," he said, turning to admire a fountain nowhere near the woman, "with a tall brown man in a long fur coat, you see? The woman is wearing a light yellow coat."

"I saw her," said Hava, who turned to admire the fountain with him. "So?"

The more Giddon thought about this, the stranger it was. "She's an Estillan Graceling," he said. "Her name is Trina. She's one of the first people I ever led through the tunnels to Monsea. Last I knew, she'd found employment in a hotel in eastern Monsea, near the silver mines. So what's she doing here?"

"What's her Grace?"

"She can find hidden objects."

Hava paused, giving a little annoyed shake of her head. "Be more specific."

Giddon remembered the passage through the tunnels with Trina, who'd been quiet, almost aloof. She'd had no family. Nor had she shown much interest in the others who'd made up the escape party, until one of them had referred to her Grace as a party trick. Then her uneven eyes had flared.

"Say you've lost something," he said, "like a piece of jewelry or a memento. Or say there's something you want, but you don't know where to find it, or even if it exists, like a starfish on a beach, or"—he used the example from the tunnels—"a seam of gold in the walls of a tunnel. As long as she understands the essence of that object, she can find it."

"Could she find Bitterblue's body?" asked Hava abruptly, and Giddon was undone again.

"I don't know," he said. "Maybe? The ocean might be too deep."

"Should we ask her?"

"Will you slow down?" said Giddon, who badly didn't want to think about that yet. "First, could we figure out why she's here?"

Together, with casual disinterest, they watched the woman and the man approach a deep blue building with gold trim, halfway up the staircase. Giddon realized, with another spark of recognition, that he also recognized the man. "That fellow was at dinner last night," he said. "His name is Arni Devret. His wife, Mara Devret, is a politician. She was one of the more thoughtful people at the table." In fact, Mara had deflected the conversation away from Giddon in the moments when Giddon had most needed to be left alone.

Outside the blue building, Arni Devret and Trina said their goodbyes. Then he entered the building and she walked up the staircase to the street above, on her own.

"I suppose Trina could stand before Bitterblue's silver mines and know if they contained zilfium?" said Hava.

CHAPTER ELEVEN

CURIOSITY PROPELLED THEM up the staircase to the building, which was tall and narrow, wedged between other businesses. A small sign on the wall read "Bank of Flag Hill" in elegant, gold-gilded letters.

"Shall we see what we can learn about Trina?" asked Giddon.

"On what pretext?"

"We want to walk to the Keep without getting caught in any more ambles," said Giddon. "He can give us directions."

"Weak, but acceptable, if it's the best you can do." Hava tried the door. "Locked."

"Is there a knocker?"

"Here's a bellpull," she said, yanking on a thick gold chain that hung beside the door. "Oh, balls," she said as the chain came away in her hand. Above them, sparks sounded, then a row of lamps whooshed into flame.

"Hava!" said Giddon, for what he knew was his third and last time.

"Listen, how was I supposed to know?"

"You can't just yank at things in a strange city!"

As Hava shot him a look suggesting that this was the stupidest aphorism she'd ever heard, the door opened. Arni Devret stepped out, big and broad, with eyes that were mild like Bitterblue's. Did everything in this city have to remind him of Bitterblue?

Arni knew Giddon immediately. "Giddon!" he said.

"Hello," said Giddon in Keepish. "How are you, sir? I'm afraid we've lit your lamps."

"Oh?" Arni said, glancing upward. "So I see."

"I'm afraid we've also broken your lamps," said Giddon, nudging Hava, who held the gold chain out to Arni.

"I'm sorry," she said in Keepish. "I thought it was a bellpull."

"Bellpull?" repeated Arni in slight confusion, his dark eyes touching the chain, then resting on Hava's face.

"A chain you pull that makes a bell ring inside," she said.

"Oh! A doorbell," he said. "Think nothing of it. It's the most natural mistake. You weren't at dinner last night, but I believe you must be Hava?"

"Yes."

"I'm Arni Devret. How are you feeling today, Giddon? Recovered from the water?"

"I'm well, thank you," Giddon said evenly, wondering if everyone in Ledra knew about his near-drowning escapade. *I'm going to ask the Council to send me someplace new,* he told Bitterblue. *Some corner of the earth where no one's heard of us. Or maybe I'll go home. To my real home, I mean. King Randa has accused me of treason. If he catches me on my lands, he'll execute me. Should I go home?*

Then he was ashamed of himself for asking her that.

"You both look cold," said Arni.

Giddon supposed he was cold. He wasn't paying much attention to his body. When Arni ushered them inside, he numbly followed.

Arni Devret was, apparently, the owner of this bank. After asking a small man wearing glasses to bring them tea, he led them up a flight of stairs to what seemed to be his private office.

"I believe your wife was kind to me last night," Giddon said.

"It was cruel for Minta Varana, or any of the Varanas, to expect you to sit through a formal dinner on such a day," said Arni gravely, herding them past a desk the size of a bed, to a group of armchairs arranged before a fireplace. "Some of us were there for the sole purpose of policing their conversation."

"Oh," said Giddon. "I had no idea."

"Scholars are opportunists," said Arni. "Sit down, please. The Devrets have always been on the side of the Industrialists. My own wife is an elected Industry rep in Parliament; it's the party of practicality and progress. Now, what can I do for you?"

"We wanted to meet with the Lienid envoy at the Keep," said Giddon, "but we've already gotten trapped in one of your ambles. We were hoping you could direct us around the others."

"Oh, dear," said Arni, rising and striding away. After ruffling through the drawers of his desk, he came back with a small stack of cards.

"Keep one of these with you," he said, passing half of the stack to Giddon and half to Hava. "Give one to everyone in your delegation. Show them to the guards anytime you find yourself at a crossroads where you're not allowed to proceed."

Studying one of the cards in his hands, Giddon read the heading "Amble Pass." Under the heading, printed letters proclaimed: "The individual bearing this pass has an official function in this amble on behalf of the Bank of Flag Hill, a registered business."

Giddon touched his fingers to the elaborate printed border on the card, the date of its expiration, and the raised seal that said "Ledra Magistry. Penalty for misuse."

"Wouldn't we be misusing this?" he asked. "We don't have business with your bank."

"Oh, the penalty is generally for counterfeiting a pass, not carrying one. The guards never question your business. Most Ledrans carry a pass they picked up somewhere."

"Do you mean most wealthy Ledrans?" asked Hava.

Arni's mouth twitched into a smile. "People who live here know the locations of the ambles," he said. "Those who lack passes know how to navigate around them. Now, have your tea, and once you're sufficiently warm, I'll accompany you to the Keep. My son, Mari, is an academy student. It'll give me an excuse to visit him."

As they drank, Hava asked Arni so many questions that Giddon was able to retreat into a kind of stupor. Raise cup to face, tip liquid in. Think nothing, feel nothing. Parts of their conversation jabbed him into sudden awareness that Bitterblue would never learn what Hava was learning. The difference between Scholars and Industrialists. Which of the two parties tended to hold more power, win more elections, and influence more policy: the Scholars, though Parliament was evenly split at the moment, which made Arni hopeful. Whether it was unfair to the Industrialists that the Keep sat adjacent to the academy, which was the Scholars' domain: Yes.

"But Winterkeep had a monarch once too, just like you," Arni explained, "hundreds of years ago. Our kings and queens established the academy, and lived there, in the Keep. All the nation's nobility were educated at the academy. Our scholars, with a small *s*, were the advisers to the monarchs. Winterkeep has a long history of a government run by scholars, which eventually led to the Party of Scholars. The Party of Industry has had to struggle to establish itself from the beginning of the two-party system. Personally, I think our progress has been admirable."

"Quona Varana told us that the Scholars are the party of the environment," said Hava. "That's why they vote against zilfium use."

Arni's smile was sunny. When he spoke, it was in a manner Giddon was starting to recognize: the patient, deliberately reasonable tone he used when he was explaining something he thought foolish.

"She would say that," he said. "It's her obligation; it's the message that gets her family elected. The Varanas have voters because they touch a part of the popular imagination. Quona pretends to be unpolitical, but she's perfectly aware of what she represents. She communes with animals, you understand? From her house on her cliff above the sea, she forms relationships with silbercows, or so she says. I understand that silbercows are selective about whom they talk to, and we only have her word that they talk to her. She also makes her home a haven for stray cats. And so, people imagine her to be a protector, like a hero in the fairy tales. She symbolizes something idealistic a lot of people like, but fail to see the impracticality of. The reality is that Winterkeep will be left in the dust behind the zilfium engines of the other Torlan nations if we don't change our laws. And the other reality is something she's unlikely to let you see behind her carefully crafted image: Quona is a Varana. The Varanas are airship magnates. The only mode of transportation we *have* in Winterkeep besides horsepower is airships. We don't have trains like the rest of Torla. The Varanas have a monopoly on the production, leasing, and private sale of airships in Winterkeep; as such, they largely control the movement of the Mail and the Magistry; and they closely guard the secrets of airship technology. Naturally they don't want the zilfium laws to change. It would ruin their transportation monopoly. Quona wants to protect the environment because doing so protects her fortune."

It was remarkable, thought Giddon, how comfortable it was to sit beside this fire and listen to Arni's warm, gravelly voice deliver disillusionment and cynicism. He sounded perfectly sincere. Giddon sensed no falseness, and wondered whom to believe. No one? Everyone? He glanced across the room at Arni's big, stark desk, then decided Arni probably led all bank visitors to these armchairs near the crackling fireplace, even petitioners for loans. Even people who'd defaulted on their loans. Something about Arni's manner, gentle, polite, and certain, made Giddon think that he offered people warm drinks and a comfortable chair before telling them that they were bankrupt and the bank would be seizing all of their property.

"How are you feeling?" said Arni. "Warmer? Shall I show you the way to the Keep?"

ARNI LED THEM across town with an avuncular sort of concern for their tired feet, their level of warmth, their disorientation.

"See?" he said at one point, gesturing toward a simple, graceful iron archway, decorated with small lamps, over the entrance to a street. "That's a sign of an opening to an amble."

But the next amble opening they passed was different, a stone arch covered with ivy, and most of the arches they passed weren't openings to shopping areas at all. So Giddon gained no faith in these supposed signs.

"Mm-hm," murmured Hava, noticing his face. "You just have to know."

The last part of their route took them through the academy campus, which was like a small city of its own: white stone buildings set behind high stone walls; sweeping, well-kept yards and neat paths; gardens of flowers that even now, in this cold, pushed pink petals up through blankets of snow. Giddon's heart ached at the spaciousness and beauty of the Winterkeep Academy. He saw keenly that it was the kind of institution Bitterblue could only ever have dreamed of creating in Monsea, with or without the money she'd lost in the sales to the zilfium importers. Students crossed the paths together, laughing, shouting, not even looking around, as if their surroundings were nothing to them. Giddon hated them, then was ashamed for hating rich, self-centered children. He'd been that kind of child.

The campus was built on sloped land that rose to a place where a long stairway began, climbing steeply to the crest of a hill. Atop that hill sat a big white building with wide columns and a dome: the Keep, which had used to be the home of Winterkeep's monarchs. Flags flew to either side of the building's entrance, a deep blue sea below a sky of gold. At the bottom of the sea lurked a large purple shape, rather formless. On the water's surface, purple silbercows swam.

They stopped at the base of the steps. "I almost forgot," said Giddon, who hadn't forgotten at all, but wanted it to seem like an afterthought. "We saw you walking with someone I know, a woman from home named Trina."

A knowing light came into Arni's eyes. "Ah, yes," he said, "Trina. She's a well-known figure here, but one around whom we're all a bit awkward, I'm afraid. Of great use to many, yet few invite her into their homes. Or their banks," he said with a quick, rueful smile. "I have safety-deposit boxes, you see. And personal safes, and a vault. I'm charged not only with keeping my clients' possessions secure, but in some cases, with keeping their existence secret."

"You let me into your bank," said Hava, "not knowing what my Grace is."

Her directness seemed to surprise Arni, who glanced into Hava's face, almost involuntarily. Giddon wondered if he was seeking out her Graceling eyes.

"I asked your doctor, Coran, about your Grace at dinner last night," he admitted.

"I could use it to rob your bank," she said, which elicited another surprised glance, then a chuckle.

"I suppose so, yes," he said, "but that would be an unexpected occupation for a member of the Monsean delegation."

"But not unexpected for Trina?"

"I would never seriously imply such a thing," he said. "And I don't associate with her enough to know what she would do. But she's said to offer her location services for money, without much in the way of scruples."

"Scruples?" said Giddon, who didn't know the Keepish word.

"Ethical considerations," said Arni. "And I'm afraid that whenever something goes missing, people talk of her. You'll think us terribly rude, even backward. We're unaccustomed to Gracelings, you see."

"Gracelings are accustomed to backward attitudes," said Hava. She spoke without apparent offense, but also without sympathy, and Arni didn't seem to know how to respond. It was interesting, Giddon thought, to watch his discomfiture at standing in the truth of his own discourtesy. Hava, of course, showed no discomfiture whatsoever.

"Do many things go missing in Ledra?" asked Giddon.

Arni seemed grateful for the distraction of the question. "Not from my bank, I can promise you. But a few friends have misplaced important objects in their homes recently."

"If you tell us what they are," said Hava, "we'll keep an eye out for them."

"They aren't objects you're likely to stumble across," he said, with perfect equanimity. "Now, do you know your way around the Keep?"

"We do, thank you," said Giddon, who knew nothing about the Keep aside from what he could see as he looked up at it from the bottom of the steps.

"Then I'll leave you to it," said Arni. "I hope you'll let me know if your business in Monsea, or perhaps with that Council of yours, ever puts you in need of a foreign bank." He smiled at Giddon's carefully blank face. "We have privacy laws here that often surprise and delight foreigners, especially those with secrets. I'll go find my son now. Good day to you."

And he was off, gliding along a path that led down into the academy campus.

"He just offered to help us manage the funding for any illegal activities we're a part of," Giddon said, relieved to return to Lingian. Speaking Keepish was tiring. "You did hear that, didn't you?"

"Whatever," said Hava. "How many foxes do you see watching us?"

"None," said Giddon, whose mind was still consumed with Arni's outrageous offer. "How much do you think he knows about the Council? I'm not surprised he's heard of it, but don't you think he implied greater knowledge? Is it a bluff?"

"I'm sure Winterkeep has spies on the Royal Continent. Do you see the teeny little doors set into the big doors of the Keep? Do you think foxes can go wherever they want?"

"What if Trina's the one who told the Keepish importers about Monsea's zilfium in the first place?" said Giddon. "And the Council is how she got into Monsea—what if she's told the Keepish about the Council too? Secrets like that leave Monsea vulnerable. And it sounds like she has a price."

Hava started up the steps.

"Hava!" said Giddon, the name bursting out of his mouth for the fourth time today.

"Oh, who cares?" she cried out, spinning back to him. "Who cares anymore if Estill declares war on Monsea?"

"Bitterblue would care, deeply!"

"Bitterblue is dead!"

"She would want us to care about her people!"

"Well, I don't care about them. I care about *her*."

"I don't believe you don't care," said Giddon stubbornly.

"Well, good for you, for being so big and noble and sanctimonious," she said, throwing the words like daggers. Turning back, she ran up the stairs.

Sanctimonious? thought Giddon, following her.

CHAPTER TWELVE

BITTERBLUE WOKE TO a shriek that frightened her, then resolved into wind.

She also woke to a strange thought: It would be best not to tell anyone about the fox.

"What?" she said blearily, fighting against confusion, trying to figure out why so many things were happening. It was still daytime; the small rectangle of blue in the window had grown brighter. Paper crinkled under her. The paper with the drawing of Bitterblue City with Estillan and Keepish flags that she'd carried back to the bed.

Someone declares war on Monsea and you fall asleep? she said to herself. *Well done.*

Across the room, near the baseboards, gold eyes flashed. Bitterblue yelped. Then a small, dark fox took shape, pressing itself into a corner.

Right, Bitterblue thought, remembering. *Winterkeep has telepathic foxes.* Her mind reached for the details she'd read in the reports Mikka had sent home. *They're called blue foxes, though only the kits are blue. It could be bonded to someone to whom it can talk telepathically. It might even be talking to that person now.*

"Are you my guard?" she asked the fox, with a hard stare. "My jailer?"

There was no response, of course.

"I know how to close my mind, you know," she added hotly. "I have more practice than you can possibly imagine."

She realized then that she was talking to this tiny, quivering animal as if it were her father, the monster king, who'd ruined a kingdom with the power of his mind. She relented, slightly. From what she remembered, blue foxes only read minds if they were bonded to a person, and once bonded, they were friendly and obedient. This fox might be guarding her on behalf of someone powerful and cruel, but the fox itself was probably not much of a villain.

Still, she knew how to close her mind—she'd had a lot of practice with Gracelings—and she did so now. It was a force of habit.

Ignoring the fox—ignoring too the pain in her hands and feet, and the new, more frightening pain of hunger in her abdomen, the swollen dryness of her mouth and tongue—Bitterblue set herself to thinking about war.

It was something she'd thought about more and more recently. Monsea had the natural protection of treacherous mountains to the north, east, and west, and a sea border to the south. Nonetheless, with an eye to her warlike neighbors, Bitterblue had increased the size of her army in the last few years. With the guidance and example of her uncle, King Ror of Lienid, whose navy was the finest in the world, she'd transformed her small, disorganized fleet of ships into a still small, but competent and focused, navy. She'd also fostered a relationship with the Dells, her neighbor to the east, which had the world's largest and most powerful army. Every nation knew that Monsea, though weakened by its own recent history, was not necessarily alone. Monsea had soldiers with swords and bows, Monsea had ships, and Monsea had friends.

But it seemed that Estill also had friends. Why would Winterkeep, of all places, ally itself with Estill in a war? Unlike the Royal Continent, Torla was not a land of warlike nations. Its geography, with isthmuses, mountains, and ice separating its nations from each other, its difficult seas, made war costly and unproductive. Winterkeep didn't have much of an army, nor much of a navy to transport that army across the Brumal Sea. Airships couldn't cross an entire ocean. And even if they could, the Dells was positioned between Monsea and Winterkeep. There was no way for a Keepish soldier to reach Monsea without passing through the Dells. And Bitterblue highly doubted that old King Nash of the Dells would sit back and let an entire Keepish army through.

Did Winterkeep have some capability Bitterblue didn't know of?

Also, what did they want? Monsea's zilfium? Was *this* what Mikka had wanted to tell her? Was this why he'd died?

More immediately—now that the Keepish had her, what were they planning to do with her? Ransom her? Hand her over to Estill as a political prisoner? Kill her? Keep her hidden, letting everyone think she'd died, and wait for Monsea to fall apart?

Monsea would not fall apart. Before leaving for Winterkeep, Bitterblue had created small teams to handle each task in her absence. She'd made it plain that while each team might have a leader, no one person was to have more power than everyone else. No one was to become monarch in her stead. And if for any reason she didn't return, her teams were to continue with the temporary power structure she'd created, and bring in the Council. The Council was to help the Monsean government make as smooth a transition as possible to an independently functioning republic.

When her shocked advisers had begged her to keep this plan secret, she'd relented, because she'd understood the ways in which such an intention might advertise more political instability in Monsea than actually existed. But she'd put it in writing and sent copies to her uncle, the King of Lienid, and her friends in the Council. Bitterblue saw no use in pretending that Monsea's monarchy, as it stood, wasn't facing a crisis. Bitterblue's mother's family was Lienid royalty, not Monsean. Her father had had no known family and one of his early acts after stealing the throne had been to eradicate anyone who might have a claim to that throne. "The world is changing," she'd said to her advisers, with a steel in her eyes so hard and sure that they'd finally relented, or at least pretended to. She guessed they wouldn't have, had they known what was going to happen.

Now her intentions would become public soon. How heartbroken Raffin, Bann, Katsa, Po, her aunt and uncle, her cousins, her advisers would be, and how overwhelmed. How sorry she was for going out to get some air.

But still—*There's something wrong with my kidnappers' plan,* she thought. *Even if I die—even if they ransom me—I can't see what Winterkeep has to offer Estill in a war with Monsea. Nor do I see Estill winning that war, no matter their allies.*

With the unsettling feeling that there must be something she was missing, Bitterblue fell asleep once more.

CHAPTER THIRTEEN

THE ENTRANCE HALL of the Keep was unlike any building Giddon had ever seen.

He and Hava passed through gigantic doors onto a broad marble floor, into a space so bright and tall that their eyes craned upward automatically. Some four or five stories up, a dome of glass made the room's ceiling.

The walls around were composed of stairways and balconies, full of moving people, all brown-skinned, dark-haired. Voices echoed. The floor displayed a disorienting pattern of dark stripes on white.

"I hate this place," said Hava.

A woman at a long desk near the entrance was staring at them with high eyebrows and a bored expression. "Hello," said Giddon in Keepish, approaching her. "Would you be able to tell us where we can find Periwinkle, the Lienid envoy?"

A few minutes later, they stood at a balcony that hung four stories above the Keep entrance hall. Behind them, an archway opened to a long corridor. A small, bronze placard on the wall said "Foreign Envoys" in Keepish.

Hava leaned on the railing, peering down. "See the monster on the floor?" she said.

Giddon glanced at the long drop below, thinking of how much Bitterblue would've hated their proximity to the railing. From this distance, he saw that the dark marble stripes on the floor formed tentacles, belonging to yet another representation of that sea monster from the Keepish fairy tales.

"I think he's called the Keeper," Giddon said, saying the word in Keepish.

"She," said Hava, with a small scowl.

"Okay, she. And this is the Keep, and the country is Winterkeep."

"Wow, Giddon," said Hava. "It's like you have an advanced degree in etymology."

"Not nearly as advanced as your degree in sarcasm," he said, pretending to be less piqued than he was.

"Is that you, Giddon?" said a voice behind them.

Spinning around, Giddon saw the Lienid envoy, dark-haired, gray-eyed, with pale brown skin like Bitterblue's, eyes like Bitterblue's. He flashed with Lienid gold. "Periwinkle," said Giddon.

"Call me Perry, please," the man said, then gestured toward the archway. "Come visit."

He led them down the corridor to a small, lamplit office, where he sat them before a fire and pressed hot drinks into their hands. Giddon was beginning to wonder if this was the custom for all meetings in Winterkeep, always. Reaching into the breast pocket of his coat, Giddon pulled out a folded piece of paper. Opening it, he braced himself against Bitterblue's small, dear handwriting.

"Perry," Giddon said, "we were hoping for your help identifying the people behind the company names on this list."

He handed the paper to Perry, who glanced at it briefly. "What is this for?"

"It's the Keepish importers who purchased rock detritus from Bitterblue's silver mines at almost no cost," said Giddon flatly, "tricking her out of her own zilfium."

"Ah," said Perry, his expression clearing. "I understand."

"You do?" said Giddon. "You knew about that?"

"In Ledra, you'd have to live under a rock not to know about that," he said, his eyes narrowing on the paper. "Though this is the first time I've seen a list. It's an interesting group of people. Balava Importing: That's Ada Balava. Yes, that's no surprise, since she has no conscience. Tima Importing is Mirni Tima, yes. Cavenda Shipping is Benni Cavenda, and naturally he would be on this list. I understand Benni's been growing his shipping business too fast, even running it into the ground, and the Cavenda mine has run out of zilfium. His financial troubles were no doubt eased by cheating Queen Bitterblue out of some of hers. Oh, now, this one is interesting," he said, glancing at Giddon over the paper. "Keepish Importers is a Varana company owned by Minta Varana. She imports precious metals used in airship production, but I didn't know she'd joined the zilfium bandwagon."

"Minta Varana!" said Giddon. "Our host at dinner last night!"

"And the sister of the cat lady we're staying with," said Hava, her face like ice. "Lovely."

"I ate her food," said Giddon, almost spitting. "I thanked her for her hospitality."

"Yes," said Perry, sounding regretful. "I'm afraid you did. What are you planning to do with these names? Are you hoping to sue them for dishonest business practices? You could, but it might be tricky. You would have to prove both that they knew the rock detritus contained zilfium and that they knew Queen Bitterblue *didn't* know."

Giddon considered Hava, who looked back at him with an uncertain expression. How much should they trust this man? "It surprised us," he said carefully, "when our men drowned in the Brumal Sea. Mikka and Brek. Maybe you knew them?"

It was plain from Perry's sudden bright eyes that he had. "They were my friends," he said. "We foreigners get to know each other. In fact, we were together often. Mikka had an adventurous spirit; he'd talk Brek and me into overnight hikes, which I suffered through tolerably, I suppose. Then I would convince him to do something civilized, like try a new restaurant."

"I'm sorry," said Giddon.

"It has been a heartbreaking year for boat travel," said Perry, touching his sleeve to his eyes. "But what do you mean? Surprised, how?"

"Was there anything unusual about the shipwreck?"

"Unusual?" said Perry. "The seas here aren't like our seas at home. I understand ships often run into trouble. But"—and here he shifted in his seat, his confusion deepening—"do you mean foul play?"

For a moment, Giddon was silent. Perry touched his sleeve again to his eyes, anxious and unhappy. He wore gold rings on every finger, like every Lienid Giddon had ever known. Giddon had a vision suddenly of Bitterblue's hands, glimmering with gold, on the floor of the Brumal Sea.

"Why would you think such a thing?" said Perry.

"Because Katu Cavenda apparently thought it," said Giddon. "Do you know Katu?"

"I do. But Katu has gone traveling," said Perry, a tone of protest in his voice, as if Katu's absence could make the rest of it untrue.

"Do you know where he went?" said Giddon.

"Only rumors," said Perry. "Kamassar, Borza."

"We're worried about Katu as well."

"For what reason?" said Perry, in a voice of growing alarm. "Giddon, what are you saying? What's going on?"

When Giddon glanced at Hava again, she shrugged, then said, "We may as well tell him. He'll connect the dots himself even if we don't." She turned to Perry. "We think someone drowned Mikka and Brek," she said. "Because they'd found out that Monsea had zilfium and that people were cheating Bitterblue out of it. We think they were silenced so the queen would never know."

"Oh, no," said Perry, straightening in his chair, speaking with certainty. "They would never have been killed for that."

"We had word that before they died, there was something they wanted to tell Bitterblue about zilfium," said Hava.

"And that may very well be the news they wanted to tell her," said Perry, "but I assure you, they would not have died for that information. Everyone here knew that certain families were taking advantage of the queen's ignorance to import Monsea's zilfium at shocking prices. Mikka and Brek wouldn't have been killed to prevent them telling her. It was no secret. Everyone knew the queen would figure it out eventually."

Giddon couldn't breathe around his indignation. "And why didn't anyone else write to her? Did everyone here find her ignorance so entertaining? Why didn't *you* write to her?"

"I did tell Mikka. Look, I understand your feelings," Perry said quietly. "I share them. But I do think it was less that people were actively upholding the deception and more that people were busy, and forgot about it, and failed to care. There's an attitude here that all's fair in business."

"That's disgusting," said Hava flatly.

"I agree," said Perry. "But I assure you that it does not extend to murdering people to prevent them communicating information that everyone knows."

Then why were they murdered? thought Giddon, suddenly, impossibly frustrated. *Maybe they weren't? Could Katu have been wrong?* No. Katu was no fool; if he'd believed there was something suspicious about the drowning of the *Seashell,* believed it enough to start diving for the wreck, he was probably right. And his subsequent disappearance supported the theory.

But if the deaths of Mikka and Brek had nothing to do with zilfium or the zilfium importers, where did that put Giddon and Hava? Exactly nowhere, for the importers had been their best lead. Their only lead, really.

Giddon was suddenly afraid he was going to start crying in Perry's office.

"Perry," said Hava, "how did everyone in Winterkeep learn that Monsea had zilfium?"

"A woman from Monsea," Perry said. "A Graceling named Trina. I understand she's one of your Estillan refugees?"

And now Giddon had a new person to kill. *We helped her.* "She showed the Keepish how to trick the Monsean queen," he said quietly, "*and* she's talked openly about escaping Estill to Monsea?"

"She has a price," said Perry, "and a reputation. In fact, her reputation has largely ruined her own business here, if the rumors are true. People want her help, but they don't want to work with her."

"Is that because she's unethical," said Hava, "or simply because she's a Graceling?"

Perry seemed startled, then unhappy, deflated. "It's probably both. Was the queen aware of the size of her zilfium stores?"

"No," said Giddon. "She began a survey before we left, but there wasn't much time."

Perry's eyes widened. "Perhaps I should tell you that Winterkeep believes Monsea's zilfium stores to be truly massive," he said. "More massive than any known Torlan source. The queen is sitting on a fortune that Torla can't match."

Before Giddon could respond to this, a knock sounded on the door. Flustered, Perry called, "Come in," then remembered himself and repeated the words in Keepish.

The man who entered had pale skin and reddish hair and was dressed in the plain style of home, no scarves, no bold colors. He was also familiar; Giddon thought he'd been at dinner last night, though at the other end of the table.

"Ah," cried Perry, jumping up. "Come in, Cobal. You know Giddon from dinner, and this is Hava, also from the Monsean delegation. Hava, this is Cobal, the envoy from Estill."

Giddon's mind sharpened, a pleasant mask descending upon his own face. Cobal, the Estillan envoy, was small, cheerful, and flushed with pink, holding a brisk hand out to Hava, expressing his sorrow for their loss with what sounded like sincere regret.

Giddon noticed that Perry was still visibly upset. "Where are you from in Estill, Cobal?" he asked, to distract the man.

"The southern forests," Cobal said, with a quick, conspiratorial grin. "I know who you work for, son, and what you've been up to. You don't need to pretend."

Alarmed by this openness—and annoyed at being called "son" by a man who seemed little older than he—Giddon rose, deciding it was time to put an end to this visit.

"I didn't mean to chase you away," said Cobal. "In fact, I hoped you would deliver a gift to your host on my behalf."

"To Quona Varana?" said Giddon, growing more confused.

"Indeed," said Cobal. "Quona and I share a passion." Then, from inside his jacket, he pulled out a long stick that had a pom-pom dangling by a string from the end.

"That appears to be a cat toy," said Giddon, who was beginning to wonder if the Estillan envoy was in his right mind.

"Yes," said Cobal, his grin transforming into something apologetic. "I'd like to claim pure generosity as my motive, but the truth is, I got stuck inside an amble today without a pass and had to buy something. You don't have to tell Quona that, though."

Taking the toy, Giddon nodded, his pleasant mask still in place. Inside, however, he was struggling to understand a man who would intrude upon grieving people the day after their loss, cheerfully importuning them to carry a silly-looking cat toy across the city.

"Tell me," said Cobal, an interesting glint in his eye. "Who's leading Monsea now that this terrible tragedy has occurred?"

And now Giddon was beginning to understand. So was Hava; in his peripheral vision, Giddon saw her flicker, once, into a sculpture of a ferocious girl. Cobal let out a small noise of apprehension and stepped back.

Giddon spoke calmly, with no intention of answering Cobal's question, though he knew the answer. In fact, he knew every detail of every aspect of the answer, because Bitterblue had asked for Giddon's presence at every meeting on the matter, and his opinion on every part of her plan to transition Monsea to a republic should she die.

"The Monsean court is prepared for this situation, of course," he said. "I'll let them unveil the news at their own pace. In the meantime, however, I can comfort any worries you or Estill might have that Monsea has been left leaderless. The queen put a great deal of thought into her successor."

"Oh, good," said Cobal.

"We have to go now," said Giddon.

"Don't forget your toy," said Cobal.

The cat toy that Giddon now held in one hand was meant to make him feel foolish. Giddon understood this now, but he didn't feel foolish. He felt instead that the Estillan envoy had the maturity of a twelve-year-old schoolboy. While he was deciding how to respond—cycling through options that included throwing the cat toy into the fire, shoving it down Cobal's throat, or bringing it home, because it was a shame to waste a perfectly good cat toy—Hava took it from him and held it out, dangling the pom-pom in front of Cobal's face. She swung it gently, so that it tapped Cobal on the nose.

"Boop," she said. "Good kitty."

At Cobal's outraged expression, Giddon, who was finding it hard not to laugh, walked quickly into the corridor, where his bubbling hysteria immediately threatened to turn into sobs. *I will not cry here.* Perry was fluttering around him. "He's really quite a friendly person usually," he was saying, overflowing with apology and concern. "I think some people just don't know how to behave around grief. You go back to Quona's, Giddon, and get some rest. Here, you should have this."

He placed a letter into Giddon's hands. When Giddon looked down, he saw a sealed envelope, addressed to Bitterblue in Prince Skye's handwriting.

DINNER THAT EVENING was much like breakfast. The advisers were depressed and quiet; Quona was forceful; Hava pulled herself into herself; and the room swarmed with cats. One of them lay down on Giddon's foot again and fell asleep. He peeked under the table. It was a small, pale gray tabby with its belly on one of his boots and its four legs stretched out flat on the floor like an X, as if anyone would ever want to sleep that way.

"Can I persuade you all to come look at the stars from the comfort of my upstairs sitting room?" said Quona brightly as dinner came to an end.

"I have letters to write," said Giddon, who hadn't had a moment to himself since they'd returned to the house. First, Coran had insisted on checking his vital signs. Then Froggatt had spent an hour impressing upon him a list of all the dinners and parties to which they were invited and at which he, Froggatt, expected Giddon to manage Hava's unpredictable behavior.

"In that case, you may sit at the desk," said Quona.

"I thought I'd work in my room," he said. But then Hava said, "I'll join you, Quona," with such graciousness that Giddon became too suspicious to refuse. If she was up to something, it was best to know.

The advisers excused themselves, claiming to have some planning to do. Of course, this annoyed Giddon. Why should they get to escape? He watched them go with a measure of irritability he worked hard to hide, then wondered if he was being sanctimonious.

Go upstairs and look at the stars, said Bitterblue gently. *Say something gracious occasionally. Then you can go to bed.*

The upstairs sitting room, which was on the third floor, had windows overlooking the sea. Giddon had been in this room before, because he'd walked through it on the way from the airship. A staircase in one corner led to the roof. The rug, he noticed now, was patterned with curving shapes that looked like tentacles. The Keeper again.

Above them came the sound of scurrying feet. "Some of the cats are in the attic," Quona said when she saw Giddon glancing at the ceiling. She indicated a second staircase, between two fireplaces, that led up to a closed door. Then she showed him to a desk near one of the fireplaces, brought Hava to the chairs by the windows, pulled a cat into her own lap, and rang a bell for tea. Another two cats tucked themselves against her feet.

Giddon did have letters to write, but first he had Skye's letter to decipher. He hoped the key was "bratty little brother," like before. Otherwise, this enterprise would be beyond him. He was not a cipher breaker.

In the window, Hava had pulled the cat toy from a pocket and was dangling its pom-pom before the nose of the cat in Quona's lap. The cat glared at it suspiciously, almost cross-eyed, but didn't react.

"How fun," Quona said.

"I bought it in the Flag Hill amble," Hava lied. "Quona, did you know that a number of Keepish importers were buying the rock detritus from Monsea's silver mines for almost no money, cheating Queen Bitterblue out of some of her zilfium?"

Giddon watched Quona while pretending not to. "I did not," she said, seeming unruffled. "That sounds like an underhanded thing to do. I hope you've put a stop to it."

"Of course," said Hava. "But it's strange that you don't know about it. According to the Lienid envoy, a person would have to live under a rock not to know."

"Hava," said Giddon warningly, though this time, he didn't mean it. Sometimes, it was just his role in their partnership: Hava asked nosy questions, while Giddon pretended to be the conciliator. They'd gathered a lot of information this way.

"Perhaps living in an isolated house is akin to being under a rock," said Quona.

"Maybe," said Hava. "Did you know that one of the importers was your sister Minta?"

"Hava!" said Giddon. "Siblings are not responsible for each other's behavior."

"Oh, it's all right," said Quona. "I didn't know, and I'm sorry to hear it."

"Nonetheless," said Giddon, "I apologize for our rudeness."

"Grieving people have a special dispensation to say what they like," said Quona, who seemed unoffended, but nonetheless stood abruptly, carrying the cat away from the cat toy, going to stand in the window. Behind her, Hava shot Giddon a dry grin. He kept his face impassive, in case Quona could see his reflection.

A moment later, the alphabet created with the key "bratty little brother" began to turn Skye's letter into recognizable words. Giddon worked steadily, separating meaningful letters from blanks, building sentences and ideas, scratching notes onto the page.

Welcome to Winterkeep, Cousin, it said. *We're having a wonder-*

ful time. You should see eastern Torla. Trains are terrifying and grand. However, we've passed through Kamassar and most of the Borzan coast and no one's seen or heard from Katu, which people say is strange. He's not a low-profile traveler. Maybe you should look into it more.

Until our departure from Winterkeep, Saf kept getting that image from silbercows of a house with many windows on a cliff, an airship above, and a disturbance. Silbercows are upset. I doubt it's relevant. But Saf asked me to tell you he thinks it's worth investigating.

At his desk, Giddon gripped his hair, intensely conscious of the room in which he sat, in a house with many windows on a cliff. He studied Quona, wondering how well she knew the Estillan envoy, and whether it mattered.

"Do you see many silbercows from this house?" he asked her.

She was still standing at the glass, gazing outward. "Sometimes," she said, turning to face him. Wind pushed against the big windows, gusting and straining. "I even talk to them now and then, from a balcony in the attic. But I don't see as many as I used to."

"Where did they go?" asked Giddon.

"I've asked them that," she said. "The answer they give is confusing." She had a strange light in her eyes, as if some part inside her mind was lit up and had her attention. She was looking at Giddon, but he didn't think she saw him.

Suddenly a young woman stepped into the room, tall, brown-skinned like Quona, short-haired, something tight and quiet in her face. She wore furs, but not like the sleek, graceful furs Arni Devret had worn. It was a coat made of more than one kind of animal hide.

She squared her feet, a tiny blue fox kit tucked into the crook of her arm. The kit had a bandage on its face. Its fur wasn't gray but actually blue, a deep, twilight blue. "Professor Varana?" she said. "You asked to see me?"

Quona's eyes seemed to clear. "Nev!" she said. "Meet Giddon and

Hava, who are members of the Monsean delegation. Giddon and Hava, meet Nev, who is one of my finest animal medicine students."

"Nice to meet you," said Nev, touching them with her dark eyes. Her expression was flat, closed. *But tired,* thought Giddon. *Wary. Why is she here so late?*

"Come upstairs, Nev," said Quona.

Then Quona led Nev up the stairs to the attic, still carrying the cat in her arms.

CHAPTER FOURTEEN

BITTERBLUE WOKE AGAIN to a sound like a burst of wind against wood and glass.

Opening her eyes to the light of the moon touching her face, she thought, for a moment, that she was on the ship.

She'd tracked a full cycle of the moon on the deck of the ship, piecemeal, with Giddon, who'd seemed to fall in love with the night sky above the Brumal Sea. There had been so many stars.

"I think I could love it too," Bitterblue had said, her body braced against Giddon's, sheltered from the wind, "if I didn't feel like I was spinning every time I looked up at it."

"Does it help if you imagine the earth under you, supporting you?"

"But it's water under us. Not earth."

"But the water is holding us up."

"No, it's trying to swallow us. And the sky is trying to smother us, like a blanket we can't breathe through."

"Hm," said Giddon doubtfully. "I see the problem. Maybe you should try yelling."

"What do you mean?" Bitterblue said.

"Just shake your fist at the sky and yell something."

Bitterblue giggled. "I'll wake everyone up."

Giddon had an impish grin sometimes that made him look eight years old. "You're the queen," he said. "It's your privilege to wake everyone up."

"That doesn't mean I should!"

"Want me to do it with you?" he said, then raised both arms above his head, punched the air with his fists, and shouted, "You can't get me!"

"Giddon!" she cried, half laughing. "Anyone who hears you will think you're being attacked."

"I can breathe just fine!" he yelled. "You can't knock me over!"

Giving up, Bitterblue raised a fist. "I'm not going to vomit anymore!" she yelled.

"No vomiting!" Giddon yelled.

"I won't drown!"

"No drowning!"

"I don't care what you do!" Bitterblue yelled. "I feel great! I'm stronger than you!"

"She feels great!" Giddon yelled. "She's stronger than you!"

"It's not true, of course," she said in a normal voice.

"What isn't?"

Bitterblue looked at the moon, motionless above her, while the ground moved under her feet. "That I'm stronger than the sea."

"Okay," he said. "But you're stronger than the way the sea makes you feel."

AWAKE IN HER strange prison with moonlight on her face, Bitterblue couldn't remember for a moment if the conversation with Giddon had been a memory or a dream. Wind pushed against the walls, sounding like the sea. She propped herself on her elbow, feeling pain in her hands and feet, the dryness of her nose, mouth, lips, the ache of hunger that was beginning to frighten her, badly. Had her captors forgotten about her? Did they mean her to starve?

A shadow moved on the other side of the room and Bitterblue gasped. Then realized, as gold eyes flashed, that of course it was just the fox again; then had another fright as more eyes flashed around it. Multiple foxes? *Is this a dream too?*

Suddenly the foxes swarmed across the room toward her, moving like a wave, then disappearing under the bed. She heard something vaguely metallic. Tiny fox feet, touching metal? Bitterblue didn't understand what was going on, but she was awake now, and she knew she wasn't on the ship.

A key turned in the lock and the door swung open. Bitterblue was so surprised that she cried out.

A woman stepped in—a girl?—young-looking, tall, short-haired, brown-skinned, balancing a tray. A lamp on the tray threw yellow light at Bitterblue, blinding her, but still, Bitterblue recognized her. This was the young woman who'd pulled her out of the sea.

When the woman placed her tray on the floor, Bitterblue smelled stew. "Who are you?" said Bitterblue, straining to remember her Keepish, mopping her tearing eyes. "And what do you imagine you're going to get out of this?"

The woman lifted a small pot from the tray and came to sit at the end of the bed, fishing under the blankets for Bitterblue's feet. Then, opening the pot, she began to apply a salve to Bitterblue's aching skin that was so glorious that Bitterblue had to fight the instinct to let out an ecstatic cry.

"I would like to import this excellent salve to Monsea," she said, "once we've concluded my kidnapping. What do you say?"

The woman ignored her.

"Who are you?" Bitterblue said again. "Why are you doing this?"

Silently, the woman began to unwrap Bitterblue's bandages and apply the salve to her frostbitten toes. The relief from pain was immediate, and consummate. It was also throwing Bitterblue's hunger into such sharp relief that she was almost nauseated. She was finding it difficult not to lean out of the bed and stare at the bowl of stew on the tray by the door. She hoped it was thick with meat. It smelled thick with meat.

She was trying to decide how much to say. Bitterblue seriously doubted that this woman, who was young, closed-faced, and avoiding her eyes, was in charge. Every time Bitterblue spoke, she looked more unhappy. "I want to know your plans for me," she said.

"We have one rule," the woman said.

Bitterblue was so startled to hear her finally speak that it took her a moment to be sure of the translation. "One rule?" she repeated.

"One rule you must follow," said the woman, her mouth tight with a misery that made her look very young indeed. *She hates this,* Bitterblue thought. *Could I turn her into an ally?*

"What's the rule?" she asked.

"If there's anything you want," said the woman, "you will ask for it. I gave you the salve without you requesting it this time, so you would know what it was, but if you want it again, you will ask. Understand?"

"Certainly," said Bitterblue, who was beginning to feel a quiet, low hum of panic. Her captors weren't going to give her whatever she asked for. This rule was a trick.

"There's nothing you want?" said the woman.

Bitterblue wanted so many things. She wanted her heartbroken friends to know she was alive. She wanted to know who was holding her here, and what their plans were. She wanted to know where Giddon, Hava, and her advisers were right now, and if they were safe. She wanted rescue or escape. She wanted to kill whoever was in charge. The pain was returning to her feet, so she wanted more salve, and most of all, she wanted the stew on the tray.

"There's nothing I want," she said.

"Very well," the woman said, standing, striding to the door. Bitterblue watched, aghast, as she returned the pot of salve to the tray, then lifted the tray in one hand. She reached for the doorknob.

"Wait," said Bitterblue.

The woman turned back. "I forgot to add," she said, voice flat, "that you should always ask politely."

Bitterblue took a breath. "Please," she said, "would you wait?"

The woman nodded. "Go on."

"Please," said Bitterblue, "may I have something to eat?"

The woman lifted the bowl from the tray and placed it on the rug beside her feet. Then she stood there, waiting.

"Thank you," said Bitterblue.

"I'll stay until you've eaten it," the woman said.

"Please, would you bring it to me?" Bitterblue said. "I'm in a lot of pain."

The woman flashed her teeth, less of a smile than an expression of frustration. At Bitterblue? Or at whoever was making her play this role?

"Don't you think you're getting greedy?" she said.

Bitterblue held her eyes for a moment, knowing that this woman probably guessed she couldn't walk; understanding that she'd placed the bowl on the floor to mimic feeding a pet.

Humiliation is just a feeling, she said to Giddon. *You've known humiliation. So has Po, and my mother, and practically everyone who's ever mattered to me. I can know humiliation too.*

Carefully, she got out of bed, doing her best to balance, managing a few steps. Finally falling, trying to land on her knees and elbows to spare her hands. Her breath came out in a small cry.

She crawled to the bowl. There was no spoon. It hurt to lift the bowl, but she managed, drinking messily at the woman's feet. The stew was full of meat and vegetables; it was delicious. But salty. When she'd finished, the woman bent, took the bowl from her, and left, closing and locking the door.

Curling up around her still-growling stomach, Bitterblue wished for a drink to quench her rising thirst.

SHE STAYED BY the door for a while, curled in a ball, caught up in a realization. That last time Giddon had gone to Estill, to smuggle people through the tunnels. He'd been away for weeks, then come home, fallen into bed. She'd woken him, read him Skye's letter, gone off to check her records of trade. Come back in a fury about her lost zilfium.

He'd comforted her, planned this trip with her, changed his entire Council schedule to come to Winterkeep with her. And it was a silly thing to realize suddenly, here in this room, ridiculous that it should mean everything suddenly, but—while Giddon was in those tunnels, his birthday had passed. He had an August birthday. It was now October. She'd forgotten all about it. She hadn't even wished him well.

Giddon, she thought. *I've been so self-centered. And you never are, ever. You're unhappy somewhere right now, and I can't help you.*

She forced herself to sit up.

I'm going to get out of this room, and wish you a happy birthday, she thought.

She pushed herself back to the bed.

IT WAS STRANGE, wasn't it, the way she kept falling asleep? Bitterblue began to wonder if she'd been drugged.

She woke yet again, to hunger, thirst, and another peculiar, fox-related thought: that she really, really, really shouldn't tell anyone about all the foxes she'd seen before.

A fuzzy, odd, not-quite-dreamlike feeling accompanied the thought. Saf had the Grace of giving people dreams. The dreams he'd given Bitterblue, back when they'd loved each other, had had a sort of edge, a border, that felt like *him* somehow, like his enclosing arms, rather than like something that sprang from inside herself. She'd learned to recognize the difference between dreams that were his gifts and dreams of her own.

This thought about the foxes felt like a gift dream. It also reminded Bitterblue of the thought she'd woken to previously, about how she shouldn't tell anyone about that first fox.

Bitterblue looked around, unsurprised when she saw a single pair of golden eyes glimmering at her from the corner. Blinking, staring, blinking.

Are you talking to me? she thought at the fox. *I thought you didn't do that, unless we were bonded. Are we bonded?*

When the fox gave no indication of having heard or understood her, she tried speaking the same message out loud, in Keepish, but that garnered no response either.

Oh well, Bitterblue thought. *You probably don't hear me. But I won't tell anyone about you, or your friends. If there's a hole in the wall under the bed, or something, that my captors don't know about, I don't want them to know.*

And then she became paranoid, wondering if the whole thing was a test; if her captors were filling her room with foxes, then pretending not to know about the foxes, to see if she reported them. To tell if she was trustworthy. To catch her on the day she tried to crawl out of her prison through a hole under the bed, and laugh, and tell her they knew it all along, and punish her, by depriving her of food or water.

This is what they want, she suddenly realized, remembering the drawing, the rule, the lack of information, the humiliation. *They want me anxious.*

When the gray dimness of morning began to turn pink, the fox scampered under the bed and disappeared.

Thinking, Bitterblue waited.

When the light came, Bitterblue crawled back to the door and peeked through the keyhole. She saw nothing but more light and decided she was looking into a room with large windows.

Once more, she crawled back to the bed, but this time she examined the space under it. She could make nothing out in the shadows; no visible escape hatch. She grabbed one of the bedposts and tried to shift the bed, but the pain left her gasping. She tried moving it with her shoulder too, but it wouldn't budge. She felt her weakness, her exhaustion.

I will do it, she told Giddon, knowing that he could have moved the bed with one hand, but refusing to be ashamed. *I will, as soon as I can. My hands will heal.*

Next she stood on the bed, forcing her aching feet to bear the weight of her body. *I'm good at this,* she said stubbornly, *because I'm small, so the weight on my feet is less.* But all she could see through the window was sky, and the tips of one tree whose leaves had turned gold. The wind was ferocious. Sometimes it slammed against the walls.

This was her inventory: her bed; its sheets, blankets, and pillows; the pajamas she wore, which were dark and soft; the bandages on her toes; the chamber pot; one piece of paper with a drawing on it; her thoughts; and her own body.

Her body ached with frostbite and thirst. Her body coursed with anxiety too, but she met it, battled it back, with long, steady breaths and determination. Irrationally, she wished more than ever for her mother's ring to hold on to, something hard and real.

The conversation with Giddon on the ship, under the moon, had also been real. *I'm not stronger than my captors,* she thought, trying to lick moisture into her dry mouth. Dreaming of a drink, and a peppermint, and a toothbrush. *They're stronger than me. But I'm stronger than the way they're trying to make me feel.*

Okay, she thought, sitting down again. *Let's think.*

CHAPTER FIFTEEN

ON THE SUNDAY following Lovisa's adventure with the house guard, she wasn't sure whether to expect her father's arrival for their weekly walk home to Sunday dinner. It was a bit of a tradition, one Lovisa treasured: half an hour spent alone with her kinder parent, talking about whatever they liked. But if her mother thought she was a dirty slut who kissed the guards, would she still be invited to Sunday dinner?

Then a knock came, as always. Sitting at her desk surrounded by papers and books, she called for her father to enter, then waited, a bit nervous, as nothing happened.

"Come in!" she called again impatiently, then crossed to the door and pulled it open.

Her father was talking with Mari Devret in the corridor, asking after his studies, his family. "Would you like to join us for dinner?" she heard Benni ask Mari, whose eyes brightened with quiet acknowledgment of Lovisa when he saw her. Mari was a tall boy with a fine-boned face, a thin gold scarf around his neck. Gold had always been Mari's favorite color; it suited his warm brown skin. Lovisa could remember him at four or five, asking his mother to knit him a soft gold hat. When she did, he wore it every day for two winters.

Lovisa mouthed *Yes, please* to him behind her father's back.

Mari twitched a smile at her. "I'm sorry, sir," he said. "I wish I could, but I have too much work to do."

"Your parents will be there," said Benni.

"Please tell them I'm sorry too," he said. When Lovisa scowled, his smile widened. "Don't look so grouchy, Lovisa," he said. "You get to meet the Monsean delegation tonight."

"Ah, there you are, Lovisa," said Benni, turning, leaning down to kiss her forehead. "Where's your coat?"

"Is the Monsean delegation coming to dinner, Papa?" said Lovisa.

"Yes."

"Including the Graceling?"

"They're all invited," said Benni. "We have no control over who comes. Go on, choose a coat. Such a smart boy, that Mari," he added idly as Mari disappeared down the corridor.

Hearing the change in his tone, Lovisa instantly understood that her father had invited Mari to dinner because Lovisa had been caught with a house guard. Mari Devret—wealthy, well-mannered, from a good Industrialist family—was the sort of person Benni wanted to dangle before her.

It made her inexpressibly tired, to think that her parents might start trying to put her friends forward for that purpose.

She found a coat. "I'm ready," she said.

"There's some news, sweetheart," Benni said as they walked through the city toward Flag Hill. "You should know it, in case you're seated near a Varana at dinner."

"Oh?" said Lovisa, intrigued. "Social news or political news?"

Benni flashed a quick smile that showed her something she hadn't noticed before—the strain of exhaustion in his face—and yet, it was hard to keep up with him today. As he turned onto a staircase, she had to reach a hand out to slow him down.

"Criminal news," he said.

"Criminal!" she said. "What happened?"

"Some engineering plans have disappeared from a safe in Minta Varana's house."

"You mean she was *robbed*?"

"Presumably, yes," said Benni. "Someone stole a few chemical formulas, including one for the reaction that extracts the gases used in varane from the atmosphere."

"Am I supposed to understand what that means?" said Lovisa dryly.

Benni grinned. "The mixture of gases that makes up varane is perfectly balanced. Without all the formulas for how to extract and combine all the parts, airships don't float, and they're also dangerous."

"Dangerous how?"

"With the wrong combination? Among other things, fire," said Benni. "The Kamassarians have been trying to duplicate airship technology for years, and I understand they've had a number of deadly fires. The Varanas too had a couple of dangerous explosions early on, while they were tinkering with the formula."

This sounded familiar. "Didn't a professor in the school of chemistry get fired for causing an explosion in one of the labs a few years ago?"

"Yes, but that was something to do with zilfium."

"Zilfium explodes too?"

Benni waved a dismissive hand. "I don't know anything about it, just that it was zilfium, not varane. Regardless, the Varanas figured out the right balance of gases for varane, and the solution is a big secret."

"Do you think someone stole the formulas to sell them to Kamassar?"

"Or Borza, or Tevare, or Mantiper," said Benni. "Everyone wants airships."

"Did the thief who stole the formulas break Minta's safe?"

"No. Apparently they opened it."

"Really? Will Minta be at dinner?"

"No, but the prime minister will."

"Are people blaming that Graceling who finds things?"

"Trina? There's talk, of course," said Benni. "But Minta has as many guards as anyone, and that woman has never once been invited into her home."

Lovisa wondered if Minta's guards were involved. Then, thinking of the valuable item her father was keeping protected in the attic room, she wondered if her father trusted his own guards. Maybe Benni was wise to be taking extra precautions. "Well," she said, obscurely excited by the news. Wishing she could tell Katu. "I won't provoke Sara Varana about it at dinner. Unless, of course, you want me to."

"My girl," he said, smiling absently. Then he pulled her close for a moment, kissing her on the top of the head, his lips touching her white streak, right there in the middle of the street.

ATOP THE CAVENDA house, Lovisa saw Quona Varana's airship docked alongside her parents'.

She inhaled, preparing to be patient. "You invited Quona too?" she asked. "Why?"

"We couldn't invite the Monsean delegation without inviting their host, could we?"

"Want to bet how many times she mentions cats?"

Benni pursed his lips. "I'll go with five."

"Then I choose six."

"What are the stakes?"

"Candy," said Lovisa nonchalantly. "Anything but samklavi."

"Ugh. The loser should have to eat samklavi," said Benni, wrinkling his nose but giving no indication that samklavi had any recent significance to him. The guards opened the door and Lovisa stepped into a crowded, noisy party. Glancing up the stairs, she saw Vikti, Erita, and Viri tucked behind the banisters, peering down with interest. They spotted her immediately. Viri called out her name, then someone must have caught sight of them, because all at once they went wide-eyed and bolted upstairs.

In the meantime, her father had abandoned her, so Lovisa did what she did best: found a dark corner, made herself small, and watched.

AT DINNER, LOVISA sat near one end of the long table, next to her father and Mara Devret, Mari's mother, mercifully removed from her own mother. The room was ablaze with silbercow oil lamps. Lovisa wondered how much this dinner cost, and which of the foxes darting around the room was her mother's.

To her delight, two of the Monsean delegates were seated right across from her, including the Graceling, Hava, who, it turned out, was just a girl. Lovisa had been expecting someone grown-up, flashy. Not this pale, plain girl who never talked.

"Are you studying Lingian in the school of politics and government, Lovisa?" said Mara Devret in Keepish, an obvious attempt to draw the Monseans graciously into conversation.

"Yes, though I'm afraid I'm not very good at it," said Lovisa, who was excellent at it.

"I wouldn't be surprised if your Lingian is better than my Keepish," said the pale, dark-bearded man across the table from Lovisa, politely. His name was Giddon, and he was working hard to be attentive. Every time he spoke, he seemed to pull the Keepish words out from a deep, dark well. Lovisa wondered if he was one of the people who'd jumped into the ocean looking for the queen.

"We could all use some Lingian practice, I'm sure," said Mara, switching into Lingian.

To Lovisa's astonishment, Giddon was suddenly blinking back tears. "You're very kind," he said.

The Graceling girl spoke then, with a randomness that made Lovisa think she was trying to distract them from her crying friend. "We're curious about the relationship between humans and silbercows," she said, continuing in Lingian. "Are these lamps burning silbercow oil?"

"Ah, yes," said Benni pleasantly. "If you don't know the nature of our relationship with our silbercows, it might seem odd. When a Keepish person dies, we bury them at sea, which is traditionally considered to be an offering to the silbercows, since glassfish eat human bodies, and silbercows eat glassfish. Similarly, when a silbercow dies, its family brings its body to land and presents it as an offering to humans. And though humans don't eat silbercow bodies or use their hides, we do use their oil, for it makes the finest golden light in Torla. It's highly regulated, though, and very rare. Very expensive. I believe you import the tiniest amount to Monsea. We burn it in our lamps today to do you honor, and to express our sympathy for your loss."

Lovisa wondered how the Monseans felt, now that they were imagining glassfish eating their queen's body. She thought Benni might've found a way around planting that image in their heads. "Do you know our fairy tales?" she said, to distract them further. "About the Keeper, the hero who lives in the ocean and defends the planet, supposedly? The stories come from the silbercows. The Keeper is their hero, really."

"Is Winterkeep named after the Keeper?" said Giddon.

"Doubtful," said Benni.

"But of course it is," said Quona Varana smartly, leaning in from several places away.

"Respectfully, Quona," said Benni, "many nations refer to their fortress or their safe place as a keep."

"Yet we don't have a fortress here in Winterkeep," said Quona. "Our Keep is no more than a castle, sitting beside a school. And our careful, balanced relationship with the sea, the animals, and our natural resources is what defends us from self-destruction."

"What a conscientious Scholar you are," Benni said, with a sharpness that startled Lovisa. Benni was not usually sarcastic to guests, even ones with visible cat hair streaking their gowns.

Embarrassed for him, she spoke quickly, calling out to Sara Varana nearby. "Are you ready for the gala, Prime Minister?"

Sara called back, smiling. "Not even slightly," she said. "But we will be. It's a party that takes place in the Keep," she added to Giddon, as explanation. "It happens this time every year to celebrate the first snows. I trust you've received your invitations?"

"I'm sure we have," said Giddon politely.

"We hope you'll make it," said Sara, "but of course we understand if you don't feel like coming to a party. If you do come, we promise it'll be a very *nice* party."

The conversation continued in its usual mundane, tedious way, no more sniping. Lovisa noticed that neither Varana sister seemed visibly upset about the theft from their sister Minta's safe. Giddon, she thought, had a nice smile, though it sat in an unhappy face. The Graceling's eyes were lowered. Lovisa wondered what a girl so young and inconsequential-looking did at the Monsean court. What was her role? She had a quiet way of avoiding the attention of others that Lovisa had been trying to put a finger on. It had to do with her plain, nondescript looks, her silence and her small movements, all of which Lovisa understood, but there was something else too. It was almost as if . . . no, that was impossible. Lovisa turned her head away from the girl, looked back again. Turned her head away again, in the other direction, and looked back.

Yes. There was a way in which the girl, whenever she was in Lovisa's peripheral vision, took on a fuzzy, blurry appearance, and almost disappeared.

The Royal Continent, Lovisa thought. *Magic.* Then she stared at the Graceling directly, with no attempt to be tactful. Hava was thin, with a long, narrow mouth. Her hair was pale, but dull. She was not pretty. Lovisa wanted to see her eyes, to see what colors they were, and she wanted to know what her Grace was.

She leaned toward Hava and spoke quietly, in Lingian. "How are you doing that?"

To her absolute shock, Hava flickered into a stone sculpture of a girl. An instant later, she looked like a real girl again. Lovisa gasped so hard that she began to cough.

Giddon paused in his speech, glancing at Hava once, then returning to his conversation with the prime minister. No one else at the table seemed to have noticed, and Lovisa was already doubting what she'd seen. The inside of her head felt like it was expanding with cold air.

Then Hava looked right at her and Lovisa was staring into a face that had one glimmering, copper eye and one that was red like blood.

"You're shocking," Lovisa said quietly, still speaking in Lingian.

"It's impolite to stare," said Hava, in perfect, barely accented Keepish.

Lovisa was surprised to receive a rebuke from a foreigner, and a guest. "Isn't it impolite for you to control our minds?" she asked dryly.

"I'm merely protecting myself from being stared at."

Lovisa understood such an instinct, though she couldn't imagine how anyone like Hava could hope not to be stared at. "If I could do what you do," she said, "I'd do it all the time. How are you doing it?"

Hava flicked those unmatching eyes at her again. "I change what people think they see."

"Is that a Grace a lot of people have?"

"No," said Hava, shortly.

"Can you teach me?"

"Could one of your foxes teach me to read minds?"

"Ah, so, is that what it's like?"

"I don't know what it's like. When I want it to happen, it happens."

"Of course you know what it's like."

"What's it like to have a beating heart?" Hava retorted. "What's it like to be alive? I guess you have a lot to say on those topics?"

Lovisa had plenty she could say on those topics. Being alive was like a game, a race. She was going to win. "What's your office?" she asked instead.

"Office?" said Hava, wrinkling her nose at the Keepish word.

"What is your role in the Monsean royal court?"

"Oh," said Hava, instantly seeming confused, and distressed, and fuzzier at the edges. "I—" She flickered into a sculpture and back again, while Lovisa watched, fascinated.

Giddon suddenly turned to face them and broke into their conversation, speaking quietly, in Keepish. "Hava is uniquely situated to aid the queen, in a broad range of situations," he said, polite, bland, and firm. "Do you hope to enter politics, Lovisa?"

Lovisa thought it was interesting how different he was now, talking to her. No tears or sadness; he spoke like a politician, using a lot of meaningless words to make her stop pushing. *Uniquely situated. Broad range of situations.* And in Keepish too, which he'd claimed not to speak well.

She also thought she understood suddenly why a person who could disappear in plain sight might be useful to a queen.

"Are you a spy?" she asked Hava. "Like a blue fox?"

"I'm not like a blue fox," said Hava, with a touch of scorn.

An argument erupted suddenly, halfway down the table. "We had him!" someone cried. "We bent over backward to get him! How did we lose him?"

"Dev Dimara is an opportunist, like all Scholars," someone else said in a disgusted and familiar voice—her professor Gorga Balava.

"Now, Gorga," said Lovisa's mother, in that particular tone of condescending forbearance that made one ashamed of one's outburst. "This is a dinner party."

"Papa?" Lovisa said, touching her father's arm, interrupting his conversation with Mara. "What are they fighting about?"

"Oh," said Benni lightly, that same strain in his face again, "the Industrialists convinced a Scholar in Parliament, Dev Dimara, to change sides and vote for zilfium. It involved a lot of promises and favors. Now he's gone and changed his mind back again. But," he added, "we'll find the votes we need by December. Don't worry, sweetheart." And Lovisa relaxed, because now she understood why her father was tired and short-tempered. Everything was always less stressful once Lovisa understood.

Hava leaned toward her again. "Where do you fall on the zilfium debate?" she asked.

"I don't," said Lovisa.

"Don't you think it's important? Won't it have consequences?"

Lovisa thought of Katu, who hated Ledra politics—who saw, as Lovisa saw, the self-interest that drove every conflict, and wanted no part of it. She wished her uncle were at this table. They could roll their eyes at each other, then they could talk about what really mattered about zilfium, and about varane too. They were fuels, to *leave*.

"Sure, there'll be consequences," said Lovisa. "Either way the vote goes, people who are already rich will get richer."

"Then no wonder you don't care," said Hava. "Isn't your mother a Scholar and your father an Industrialist? You'll get richer, whatever happens."

"I'm sure a queen's spy is also well-situated," said Lovisa sourly, "even without her queen."

All at once, grief flooded Hava's face. She turned into a sculpture, but this time, she stayed that way. When someone nearby saw the stone girl sitting at the table like a petrified dinner guest, he cried out. Then everyone at the table was looking, exclaiming, standing, shouting, and Lovisa knew she'd misstepped.

Immediately, Giddon crouched over Hava, creating a sort of wall around her with his body and arms. He was muttering into her marble ear; when someone demanded an explanation, he put up a hand and said, "Please. We'll explain later, but now we need space. Please, look away, and I'll take her into another room, and someone will explain, but please, give us space. She's lost her queen," he said heatedly, standing, making himself into a barrier. "She's lost her queen. Have pity."

Lovisa herself was struggling not to stare at the sculpture-Hava, partly with nausea, partly with the fascination of someone watching a thing that should be impossible. Hava was a beautiful sculpture, her face frozen with pain. But Lovisa understood that all the eyes in the room were making things worse. Unwinding her own scarf from her body, dark pink, long, and wide, she passed it to Giddon, who used it as a curtain to hide Hava. Giddon, still shielding her with the scarf and his arms, shuffled her out of the room. Everyone was still standing, shouting. No one seemed particularly touched by Giddon's plea, though she could hear her mother's acid voice importuning everyone to "calm down."

Lovisa left the table too, then slipped out of the room. She didn't want to be part of the questions and explanations, and she needed to think. In the corridor, she saw a table on which were staged plates of pastries and went to it, thinking to steal some for the boys. But then she saw the guard at the foot of the staircase in the foyer and stopped in her tracks.

It was the sister of the guard she'd done those things with. Cold and grim, the young woman stared at Lovisa with an expression that conveyed all the contempt Lovisa had no doubt she felt. She looked like her brother too. She was beautiful, tall, straight-shouldered, like Nev, like everything Lovisa wasn't.

Cowed, Lovisa turned and slipped into her father's library.

Chapter Sixteen

THE FOX WHO was bonded to Ferla Cavenda was having a very stressful evening, and it was the fault of four of his seven siblings. Because they came to the party, uninvited! They squeezed through the secret crack in the cellar foundations he wished he'd never told them about! He sensed their arrival during dinner. One of the other visiting foxes, who was bonded to a little man named Gorga Balava, sensed them too, and was absolutely incredulous.

I'll handle it, Ferla's fox told Gorga's fox. Then he ran downstairs to confront them.

What are you doing here? he yelled at them while they fell all over one another, popping through the opening. It was Rascal, Rumpus, Lark, and Pickle. *You're risking the secrets of foxkind! The house is full of people who think foxes do what they're told!*

We ARE doing what we were told! they said. *Our person told us to come!*

Oh, he said, startled by this. *But, why?*

To be on hand in case she needs us for anything! they said. *She's so fun! We'll split up. We'll spread out. Anyone who sees us will think we're you, or one of the invited foxes. Calm down, Ad!*

"Ad" was short for "Adventure," because his siblings, even if they never did what he said, at least acknowledged who he was. Their use of his chosen name placated him slightly, until they began to disperse in every direction.

Wait! he cried. *Don't move anything! Don't use my tools! Don't go into my heat ducts! Someone will see or hear you, and I'll never be able to explain about the heat ducts! It's one thing to obediently crash a party and another to reveal that foxes aren't always honest! That I'M not honest! That I'm a builder and a spy in my own house!*

It's not our fault that you've taken your dishonesty to such extremes, Ad, they said. *YOU'RE the one who's risking the secrets of foxkind, by lying to your human TOO MUCH!*

You all smell like cats, he said crossly, a terrible insult, but they only sniffed.

Oh, stop worrying! We'll be careful!

It was enough to turn his fur silver. Especially since there were Monseans at this dinner, and the fox had learned that Monseans paid more attention to blue foxes than the Keepish did. That strange-eyed Monsean girl, Hava, stared at him, trying to tell him apart from the others. And her mind was strong. The fox tried, at one point, to influence her mind with the idea that foxes weren't worth noticing, and immediately she peered at him harder. Monseans seemed to *notice* when foxes tried to plant messages in their minds, which was a thing all foxes could do, with any humans, but which was supposed to be a secret of foxkind. How were the Monseans noticing that? Humans never noticed that! The fox influenced Ferla's feelings all the time by touching her mind with ideas about how trustworthy he was. He influenced the cook, with a suggestion of benevolent generosity toward foxes, so that she was more likely to drop snacks onto the floor when he visited the kitchen. He was also working on Benni's mind with visions of how distinguished Benni would look flying in the airship with a fox at his side, because Benni was the one who took the airship out most of the time. So far, the fox wasn't making much progress on that, but sometimes it took a while.

The point was, the Keepish never noticed when foxes were in their minds. But Monseans apparently noticed. Their minds were harder to read too. *You should be extra careful around the Monseans!* he told his four siblings. *They can tell when you're trying to get into their minds!* When they pooh-poohed him, he went electric with alarm, like a lightning bolt. He screamed. *I cannot solely be responsible for keeping all the secrets of foxkind!*

You're one to talk about being more careful, they told him. *Do you EVER do anything your person tells you to do?*

They didn't even know the half of what he did. The fox thought it must be nice to be part of a herd. To have six other minds on hand to come up with solutions, explanations, plans. To be able to hide behind someone else, if anything bad happened. To be bonded to a person who lived to please foxes and wouldn't mind at all if she found hers in the heat ducts, instead of to Ferla, who lived only for herself, had eyes like whip ends, and hurt those the fox wished to protect.

Well? said Gorga Balava's fox when he returned to the dining room. *Why are they being so carelessly disobedient to their person?*

She told them to come, he said.

Oh, said Gorga's fox, interested. *She's a rather reckless human, isn't she?*

There's something wrong with her, that's for certain, the fox said. What kind of human bonded covertly—and illegally!—to multiple foxes, created a secret fox paradise for them inside her home, then disguised the fur, the smells, the noises, with a crowd of *cats*? Then imperiled her own secret by giving them risky adventures! Bonding was never allowed to be secret. A person wasn't supposed to bond to more than one fox. She could get into so much trouble, and for what? He couldn't quite get a paw on it, despite trying sometimes to get into Quona Varana's head. She wasn't even political. She seemed to do it for fun! And it was true that he might obey his person too little, but sometimes he worried that his siblings obeyed theirs too much. That they loved her too much. What if they got careless, trusted her too much, and *told* her too much? What if they let slip the secrets of foxkind?

He didn't elaborate on any of these thoughts to Gorga's fox now. She didn't seem like the type who would cope well with tales of risk-taking. She was the sort of fox who pretended to have a temperature regulation deficiency so that Gorga would dress her in little fur boo-ties and a coat whenever she went outside. Her chosen name was Earmuff.

THE FOX WAS in Benni Cavenda's library, arguing with one of his sisters, Rascal, when those Monseans Giddon and Hava stumbled in.

The fox bolted under a sofa and crouched there, but it was too late to hide Rascal. He just hoped Giddon and Hava hadn't been counting carefully.

Luckily, the Monseans were distracted by their own problems. They looked silly too, for Giddon had wrapped Hava up in one of Lovisa's scarfs. They were clearly distraught. And they were also astonishing, because the moment they entered the room, Hava threw off the scarf and began snooping! She looked in the drawers of side tables. She lifted the edge of one of the rugs!

Giddon was very anxious about it. "Hava!" he hissed. "What are you doing?"

"Prying," said Hava.

"What do you think you're going to find?"

"Clues!"

"To what? We have nothing on the Cavendas! We should go back in there and eavesdrop on the Estillan envoy!"

"All these families are equally insincere," she said. "Don't you feel it? And maybe there's some information about Katu in this house!"

Giddon was clutching his hair. Inside him, the fox could feel his surrender. "All right," he said, turning toward the door. "I'll stand guard."

Then Hava spun to Benni's big desk and began pulling on the top drawers. "There are hidden drawers in this desk," she said. "See those panels? I bet there's a latch here somewhere."

The fox was impressed, because Hava was right about the secret drawers. The fox knew how to find the hidden latch in Benni's desk and he knew what Benni kept hidden in those drawers. If Hava found it, big things would happen.

Suddenly the fox sensed that Lovisa was about to step into the room.

Chapter Seventeen

First Lovisa crashed into Giddon, who was making himself enormous in her father's doorway. "Ow!"

Then, at the sight of that Graceling rifling through her father's desk, Lovisa was blindsided by her own indignation.

"What do you think you're doing?" she practically shouted at Hava.

"I'm looking for a handkerchief," said Hava. "Calm down."

In fact, Lovisa *was* trying to calm down. She wasn't a yeller; she'd taken herself by surprise. "You're the one who stole those formulas from Minta Varana, aren't you?" she cried.

"What are you talking about?" said Hava. "What formulas?"

"Do you really expect me to believe that where you're from, it's considered polite to snoop in someone's desk for a handkerchief?"

"I'm not myself," said Hava. "Really, I'm sorry."

Lovisa saw then that Hava's face was wet with tears. Hava blotted at them with her sleeve and they disappeared. Lovisa felt a little sick, but not at all repentant for making Hava cry. She had the sense that she was somehow being tricked. "Weren't you at Minta's house for dinner the night you all arrived?" she said, focusing stubbornly on the theft from Minta's safe.

"Hava didn't attend that dinner," said Giddon tightly.

"Couldn't Hava sneak into a house without anyone knowing?" said Lovisa. "You could absolutely be the thief."

"Are you seriously suggesting that the night we were all in shock from losing our queen," said Giddon, "Hava robbed one of your neighbors?"

"Anyway, robbed her of what?" said Hava. "What formulas?"

"Varane," said Lovisa, with a dismissive gesture. "The airship gas. I don't believe you don't know."

"And I don't like your indignation about thieves," said Hava. "Your own father is one of the thieves who tricked Queen Bitterblue out of some of her zilfium."

Lovisa remembered that incident. Lots of people had done that, and her father was not a thief. "It's not his fault if his vendors don't know their own business," she said hotly.

"Sounds like your father doesn't know his business," said Hava. "We heard he's growing his shipping firm too fast, even running it into the ground."

And that was an outrageous lie. "Better than running a whole country into the ground," snapped Lovisa.

Immediately, three things happened. First, Hava surged toward her, white with fury. Second, Giddon stepped forward to block Hava. And third, the moment Giddon wrapped his arms around her, Hava turned into a sculpture again.

Then she changed into an enormous bird, then a bear, then a sculpture again; it was terrifying, impossible, and Lovisa cried out, bent herself over her own heaving stomach. But she also kept looking, unable to stop herself.

"We're going to leave now," Giddon said calmly, as if the transformation weren't taking place. "Would you be kind enough to let your parents and Quona Varana know we've gone?"

"Yes, all right," Lovisa gasped.

"One thing before you go," said Giddon. "Is that a real place?"

He nudged his chin toward a painting on the wall across the room.

Lovisa, still fixated on Hava, didn't even glance at the painting, which she knew showed a large house on a cliff above the sea. "Yes."

"Where is it?"

"It's the Cavenda estate in the north. My mother and my uncle Katu grew up there."

"Thank you," said Giddon. "Do a lot of people in Winterkeep have houses on cliffs?"

What a weird, stupid question. "Yes!" she said. "Why would you ask that?"

"No reason. I suggest you close your eyes and find your way out of the room."

Closing her eyes as an experiment, Lovisa was instantly less disoriented. She bumbled and groped her way to the door, peeking back at them once before she went out. Hava wasn't changing anymore. She'd frozen into a sculpture of an angry, rageful woman much older than herself, and though her mouth wasn't moving, Lovisa could hear her directing low, furious, indistinguishable words at her captor.

Lovisa left the room.

IN THE CORRIDOR, no guard was in sight, so Lovisa filled her pockets and hands with pastries. Then she snuck up the stairs to the nursery wing.

She found the boys tucked together on Vikti's bed, whispering to one another. Their eyes went wide with fright when she cracked the door open. Then, when they saw her, not to mention the treasures she carried, their faces transformed into the pure happiness that always made Lovisa feel that whenever she wasn't with them, she was abandoning them.

They waved her in, making a space for her on the bed. Then, for a while, they all gorged themselves on pastries, the boys asking excited questions with full mouths and shushing one another repeatedly, for the nannies were in the rooms nearby, and each boy was supposed to be asleep in his own bed. Was it true there was a Graceling at dinner? Did Lovisa get to sit near her? What was she like?

It was a question with too many confusing answers, so Lovisa kept it simple, explaining what Hava could do. The boys went rigid with amazement and delight at her description, like little sculptures of their own.

"And how have you been?" she asked them.

"Mother and Papa are angry at each other," Erita said.

"Really? What are they angry about?"

Vikti and Viri both shrugged, but Erita had more to report. "Papa was reckless and impulsive," he said.

Lovisa remembered what Hava had said about Benni's shipping firm. "You heard that?"

"I heard Mother whisper-yelling at Papa that he was reckless and impulsive."

"What does *reckless and impulsive* mean?" Viri asked, then instantly shrank, as if remembering what happened the last time he'd asked Lovisa what a word meant. "Never mind," he said quickly.

Lovisa needed a moment to swallow the sadness that rose into her throat. "I hope you'll always ask me what words mean, Viri," she said. "Always. *Reckless* means careless, not careful. Like, it would be reckless to jump out of a high window, or fly the airship too far from shore, where the wind is too strong. *Impulsive* means doing something suddenly without thinking it through. Like, you might impulsively eat too many pastries because they looked good, then regret it when you threw up, not that I know anyone who would do anything like that."

The boys thought this was the funniest joke they'd ever heard.

"Did Mother say why Papa was reckless and impulsive?" asked Lovisa.

"No, but now they're in an impossible situation," Erita said. "And Mother can't trust Papa to fix it, because he'll mess it up, so she's going to fix it herself, which is something someone as important as the president of Winterkeep should not have to do."

"Wow," said Lovisa. "You have really good ears."

"Erita is the best at snooping," Viri said proudly.

"I was in the stairway between Mother's study and Papa's library," Erita said, with solemn modesty. "I couldn't help hearing it! I think Mother forgot she put me in there."

"She put you in there?" said Lovisa, puzzled.

"She's renovating the attic room," said Erita.

"Oh, I see," said Lovisa, trying to decipher this. "So she put you in the staircase instead, so you could"—she pitched her voice low to sound like Ferla's—" 'think hard about what you've done'?"

"Yes," said Erita, giggling in delight. "But I didn't mind it at all. I just climbed down and sat at the door to Papa's library, where it was warm and I could hear Papa working. But I *pretended* to be upset when she finally let me out, so she'd do it again."

"I see," said Lovisa. "It doesn't seem like it would be very nice in there."

"It's dusty. But it's way more interesting than the attic room. Are you staying overnight, Lovisa?"

Guilt stabbed her. "No. I have to go back to the dorm."

"But why?"

"I have homework to do."

"Couldn't you do it here?"

"I didn't bring it."

"Could you go get it?"

"I don't have time," she said, knowing she could skip her homework, that the homework shouldn't matter more than her brothers; but also knowing that she couldn't stay overnight in this house, where at every moment she felt the darkness closing around her like a cold, lonely cave. Knowing that part of the reason she needed to go was to escape the sadness of these boys. *Selfish coward.*

She kissed their freckled noses before she left, told them to take care of one another. It was something Katu often said to them, when he took off on his adventures. "You kids take care of each other until I get back, all right?" It occurred to her to wonder—for the first time—if Katu left because he was excited about where he was going, or because he also felt the trap closing around him if he stayed.

Shutting Vikti's bedroom door, Lovisa snuck out of the nursery wing and made her way to the door at the base of the attic steps. She was curious about her mother's supposed renovations. When had these "renovations" started, exactly? Shouldn't there be signs of disarray? Paper on the floors to protect the rugs from workers' boots, or something like that? Lovisa knew better. Why all the secrecy about whatever Benni was keeping in the attic room?

Ferla's fox sat in front of the attic door. She was certain it was him; though foxes looked a lot alike, she recognized that malevolent gaze, and her mother's fox had a longish nose and jaunty ears. He was panting, and also guarding a pastry that sat on the rug at his feet. It was odd behavior, but it hardly mattered. What mattered were his glimmering eyes, resting on Lovisa's suspicious face.

Downstairs, dinner was breaking up, guests milling through the drawing rooms and the game room, teas in hand. Lovisa decided to let her parents and Quona figure out for themselves that Giddon and Hava had gone. Finding her coat, she slipped outside into the cold. She wanted to go around to the back of the house and look up at the attic room window—for a light? A sign? A clue? Of what? Something impulsive her father had done? Some way in which he was damaging his own business?

But the fox had already seen her. It wasn't worth the door guards seeing her too.

The house glowed with the light of silbercow oil as she headed toward campus.

WHEN SHE REACHED her dormitory, a boy named Nori Orfa was on his way out. He was a northerner like Nev, but two-named like the Cavendas, from one of Winterkeep's most prestigious tea manors in Torla's Neck. In fact, he was one of the many Keepish who lived in a house on a cliff above the sea. Lovisa didn't like Nori Orfa, at all. She knew a girl he'd hurt, with lies. And she wasn't surprised to see him visiting this dorm; she'd noticed him and Nev chatting outside recently, stupid grins on their faces, like they thought they had a secret.

He smiled at her in that unsubtle, flirtatious way he always had, then held the door open for her in a way that crowded her and felt more intimate than it needed to. Ignoring him, she trudged up the steps, then through the corridors. As she passed Nev's bedroom, she heard a scuffle inside, like someone was dragging the furniture. Then a yowl, then a laugh.

She knocked on the door. She couldn't help herself.

A moment later, Nev swung the door open sharply. When she saw Lovisa, her face went expressionless. "Yes?" she said.

Lovisa's eyes slid to Nev's bed, automatically looking for rumpled blankets, the kind of disarray that might mean she'd just been having sex with Nori Orfa. She saw nothing. The blankets were neatly folded and a steaming cup on the desk suggested that Nev was doing homework. Her stove was burning and her window was full of plants, as always. Nev was one of those people who knew one plant from another.

"I heard yelling," Lovisa said.

"Did you?"

There was a small movement under Nev's bed. A dark nose poked out and one yellow eye peered up at Lovisa.

"You have a fox kit now?" said Lovisa.

"As you see."

"Are you bonded?"

"Is that any of your business?"

"Do you know it's against the rules to live in an academy dorm with an unbonded fox?"

"I have an exception from a teacher," said Nev.

"You mean Quona Varana," said Lovisa, understanding. "She gave you that fox, didn't she."

"As you know perfectly well, people can't give people foxes," said Nev. "Foxes choose their companions. She needed surgery. I performed it. She decided to stay with me afterward. It seemed appropriate to Quona, because I'm an animal medicine student. Now I'm caring for her."

"Right. She's homework," Lovisa said as the kit emerged further, her enormous ears comical above her tiny, bandaged face. "What's her name?"

"I don't know what she calls herself. I call her Little Guy."

"Stupid name. She looks like a pirate. What happened to her?"

"I had to cut an aronworm from her face. It's a pale, bulbous, wormlike parasite," Nev said blandly, as if she were trying to be disgusting on purpose.

"She's cute," Lovisa said, startling Nev, and herself too. She pushed away from the doorframe, grasping for an insult. "So that's what you and Quona do together? Remove parasites? Do you go to her house and pet her cats? Does she take you with her when she communes with silbercows?"

Something closed in Nev's eyes. A curtain coming down, for Nev to hide something behind. It was interesting. "I've seen some injured silbercows recently," she said. "Did you know that? Some have come to shore with cuts and burns."

"So?"

"So?" Nev repeated, with so much contempt that Lovisa took a small step backward. "Silbercows are important. They understand things about the world that we can't. They rescue drowning people."

Lovisa had tried to talk to silbercows once, at her mother's house in Torla's Neck, when she was little. It hadn't worked. The purple blobs out at sea had offered no acknowledgment of her existence whatsoever. It had made her feel . . . insufficient. Like she wasn't important enough. And it had made her half suspect that anyone who said they talked to silbercows was lying.

"They haven't done such a good job rescuing drowning people lately," said Lovisa, thinking of the queen. "I think Quona's just trying to brainwash you into believing her family's party line so you'll vote for the Scholars."

"Why would I care about party lines?" said Nev. "I'm not political, I'm an animal doctor in training. And at least I'm that. You're not anything."

Tears stung Lovisa's throat. "Good night," she said, turning away so that Nev wouldn't see her expression.

"Good night," said Nev, sounding confused suddenly, as if she hadn't expected to drive Lovisa off with her words. And why should she? She was only being honest, as Nev always was.

In the hallway, a crowd of boys passed by, greeting Lovisa, moving on. The last boy in the group was Mari Devret, who turned to look into the room of his ex. In an instant, his unhappy eyes seemed to absorb everything: Nev's fox kit, Nev's tidy bed, the messy piles on Nev's desk, the plants in Nev's window, Nev herself. Lovisa watched his eyes flash across Nev's face, hurt, reproachful.

Sighing, she took his arm and pulled him away.

"What?" he said defensively.

"When are you going to stop being so pathetic?"

"When you stop being mean," he said, then canted his face, looking at Lovisa more closely. "Are you okay?"

"I'm fine," she said. "Shut up."

"Very convincing," he said. "How was dinner?"

"There was an incident with a Graceling."

"Really? What kind of Graceling?"

"She can change what you think you see when you look at her. She kept turning into a sculpture at the dinner table."

This seemed to cheer Mari up. "That's the best thing I've ever heard."

"Mari?" Lovisa said, slowing her pace, letting the other boys move on. Pari Parnin, Kep Gravla, boys she would never trust with anything precious.

"Yeah?" he said, pausing with her. Then, when she didn't speak, he searched her face again with his clear, perceptive eyes. "What's wrong, Lovisa?"

Mari was, for all intents, Lovisa's oldest friend, the friend who knew more of her childhood secrets than anyone. It had been a long time since she'd shared any secrets with him, or with anyone. But now she wanted to tell him about the snooping Monseans. Why had they been trying to get into her father's desk? What were they looking for in there? Also, the thing they'd said about Benni running his shipping firm into the ground. It had made her so angry. But could it be true? The bitter feud between her parents, who usually never directed their bitterness at each other. Benni's banker's box—and the renovations—in the attic room. Lovisa couldn't connect the dots, but Mari had an imagination. He might have ideas. She knew she could trust him to keep it to himself too.

She found herself hesitating, not knowing why. "Will you vote Industrialist when you're older?" she asked instead.

"I guess so," he said, not looking much interested. "You know I'm not political."

Yes, she knew that Mari had no interest in his mother's political career, nor in his father's bank. Mari wanted to be a doctor, as in, for humans; he always had, since they were little. His parents were proud of him, for wanting to do something different. He was in the school of medicine here at the academy.

"I'm thinking of changing schools," she said, only thinking of it as the words came out of her mouth.

"Really?" he said, surprised. "To what?"

Lovisa had no answer to that. She'd never questioned her school before and she didn't suppose she was truly questioning it now. She wasn't sure what she was questioning. "I'll tell you another time," she said.

"Yeah, okay. You're being weird, you know that?"

"I'm just tired. Good night, Mari."

"Okay, good night. You know where I am if you want to talk about this wonderful new plan to get disowned by both your parents," he said.

She smiled, despite herself, then left him at his door. Inside her own room, the glow of streetlamps illuminated a crystalline pattern of frost on her window. She knew without looking that her desk was still covered with work. She knew she faced a long night of reading papers that bored her, burning her small stove for heat, wrapping herself in furs and blankets. Maybe moving out to the chair by the fire in the foyer, where studying felt less lonely, less meaningless.

Why did she work so hard, when she cared so little? She'd never found politics difficult to follow, because every dispute was the same. People were motivated by money, power, idealism, fame. Usually money. What was the real reason the Scholars didn't want to legalize zilfium use in Winterkeep? In Parliament, Scholars yelled at Industrialists for not caring about the air and water pollution that would impact Keepish industries like fishing and farming. They yelled about Winterkeep's beauty. Sometimes they even yelled about fairy tales, as if they actually mattered: According to the oldest stories of the silbercows, humanity's most solemn promise was to help protect the planet. The Keeper was watching.

But how could Lovisa believe that the Varanas weren't motivated by the need to protect their own transportation monopoly? If they really wanted to protect the earth, wouldn't they be *throwing* their varane formulas at other nations, so other nations could have environmentally safe transportation too? And what about the Dimara family? They were Scholars, shippers who transported Keepish zilfium to Mantiper. If zilfium use became legal in Winterkeep, new laws would limit zilfium's exportation, and the Dimaras would never find anything Mantiper wanted as much. Lovisa's own mother co-owned the Cavenda mine in Torla's Neck with Katu. The mine was situated right at the base of the Winterkeep peninsula, where a narrow strip of land connected Winterkeep with Kamassar. The zilfium had already been mined out of that land, but silver remained. Lovisa guessed that if zilfium trains became legal in Winterkeep, the inevitable train connecting Winterkeep to Kamassar would cut through Ferla's land, compromising her ability to mine silver. Lovisa did not believe, for one iota of one second, that her mother cared about pollution. She was a miner! Mining was known to pollute the environment! What Ferla cared about was her ability to keep mining.

And of course the Industrialists had selfish reasons too; they were just slightly more honest about it. Slightly. They argued that the rest of Torla was growing mechanized while Winterkeep was left behind. In another twenty years, how would Winterkeep compete? What about the poor Keepish farmers who could increase their productivity with zilfium plows? What about the poor Keepish fishers who could trawl more with zilfium-driven boats? But the truth was that Industrialist families like the Balavas, or like Lovisa's own father, wanted zilfium boats for *themselves*. They were shippers, and an exciting new continent full of people eager to buy things existed to the west.

Self-interest, self-interest. It was probably why there were no political fights between her parents at home: They had no real political differences, just varying opinions on how to make the most money. Lovisa had a perfect understanding of Ledra politics. And one day before too long, she would graduate from the academy, then be expected to choose a party and an industry. Whatever she chose would become her identity, for the rest of her life.

Suddenly Lovisa couldn't bear it. No wonder Katu was always leaving! What if she went to the Royal Continent, where politics were surely no less corrupt, but at least they were simpler, because one person's greed decided everything for everybody? And more importantly, where she knew no one, and could do what she wanted. She could be like Katu, sweeping into a place, sweeping out again when she chose.

And then her mind returned to her own home, her brothers. She couldn't leave them, could she? Especially with the recent list of small, odd things that were happening, none of which would be so noteworthy on its own, but that, together, left her with a suspicious feeling. The air at home tasted wrong.

Lovisa decided that before she went anywhere, she would find out what Benni was keeping in the attic room.

CHAPTER EIGHTEEN

AFTER GIDDON FINISHED his morning ritual of tears, he forced himself up.

Cobal, he thought, *the Estillan envoy who antagonized us.*

Katu, who is missing.

A disturbance in the water, reported by silbercows, below a many-windowed house on a cliff.

Mikka and Brek, drowned in the sea.

These are the mysteries I'm going to solve, he thought to himself, *for Bitterblue.*

The morning after the Cavenda dinner party, Giddon found Quona alone at breakfast, or at any rate, as alone as a person could be in a room swarming with cats. At a quick glance, Giddon, who sneezed as he sat down, counted seven.

"What are you and Hava planning to do today?" Quona asked him pleasantly.

Giddon and Hava hadn't discussed any particular plan yet for today, for they'd walked home last night in seething silence. Hava, furious at Giddon for physically restraining her, had ignored every attempt Giddon had made to talk. Hava hated to be overpowered, especially by men. Giddon knew that. But she'd been about to attack a teenager! And they had a job, an agenda, and it was secret. They couldn't be drawing that kind of attention to themselves!

"We thought we'd go to the harbor and check in on our crew," Giddon said, improvising. In fact, he did want to go to the harbor, but to talk to the boating company that had leased the *Seashell* to Mikka and Brek.

"Good man," said Quona. "I'm going north today. I may be gone overnight."

"Oh?" said Giddon. "What's in the north?"

"My family has property," she said. "A house and a hangar. We like to check on it now and then. It's my turn."

"I see," said Giddon, then, as Quona stood abruptly, added, "Well, have a nice day."

"You too. My staff will care for your needs," Quona said, sweeping out of the room with two cats nestled in her arms.

Froggatt came in next, sat down, and informed Giddon that he, Barra, and Coran intended to travel to Kamassar.

"It was part of the queen's original plan for us," Froggatt said. "We may as well proceed. She'd hoped to establish a Monsean envoy there, in time."

"All right," said Giddon, who didn't care what the advisers did, but still felt oddly sad at the fracturing of the group.

"I hope that when we return, Giddon," said Froggatt stiffly, "it won't be to the news that you've done anything that would have embarrassed the queen."

And now Giddon was much less sorry to see Froggatt go. Bitterblue's advisers had never wanted Giddon on this trip. They'd never, not once, understood or appreciated his value to her, nor Bitterblue's delicate and courageous relationship with the Council.

"You mean embarrassed *you*," he said, then stood and left the table, though not as dramatically as he'd have liked, given that first he had to disengage his foot gently from that pale gray cat, who seemed to find his left boot irresistible. "Sorry," he said with his head under the table, then told Froggatt in a chilly voice, "I was apologizing to the cat, not you." The whole exchange lacked dignity.

Mere seconds after he'd returned to his room, Hava knocked on his door.

He was still flustered. "Hello," he said cautiously as she entered.

Hava stared at him with an implacable expression, but he knew it wasn't her real expression. She was changing her face. He decided not to comment on it.

"I think we should go to the harbor," she said. "See if anyone knows anything relevant about the day the *Seashell* went down."

"Yes, good idea," said Giddon. "In fact, I told Quona we were going to the harbor today."

"Without asking me if I wanted to go to the harbor?"

"You literally just said you did."

Hava snorted. "Well, what are you waiting for? Let's go."

As THEY WALKED along the path that led past the Cliff Farm, Giddon tried to decide what, if anything, to say to her about last night. When Hava had run at Lovisa, she'd lost not just her temper, but her judgment. It was unusual for her. Startled, Giddon had done what he did with any friend who surged off meaning to hurt someone: He'd grabbed her, held her, forced her to slow down. He would do the same thing again.

But she'd lashed out with words that had hurt, because they'd been a version of the truth. "So nice to be big," she'd said. "It gets you whatever you want, doesn't it? What a hero you are, Giddon. Sanctimonious. Righteous. Superior. Get your hands off me!"

Was there something he should say now? Should he apologize? Should *she* apologize? Where was the line between bullying Hava and consenting to be emotionally bullied by her?

I think it's a moving line, Bitterblue said to him as he walked. *It's complicated by your ages, positions, and histories, and the fact that you're a man. She's right that your size is an unfair advantage. That doesn't mean you shouldn't ever use it.*

I miss you, said Giddon, with a small laugh that was really a sob. *You've always told me what you think and feel and need. I've taken that for granted.*

"What?" said Hava sharply.

"What?" he responded, startled.

"You laughed."

"Oh. Private thoughts."

"Are you laughing at me?"

"Of course I am," he said, trying sarcasm. "Everything is about you, brat."

Perversely, this made Hava smile, with a warmth that communicated to Giddon that her emotional blockade was over. "Good dinner party, hm?" she said.

"Oh, wonderful. Especially the part where the host's daughter found you snooping in the host's desk and you almost attacked her."

"I bet she won't tell anyone. She doesn't seem to care about zilfium, or anything else that matters, so hopefully she'll just assume I have light fingers and a bad temper and leave it at that."

She was speaking in that non-caring tone that always impressed Giddon. He often pretended to be someone other than who he was in his Council work, but he almost always played someone likable. He had difficulty doing otherwise. Hava, in contrast, seemed to have no problem playing a role that left people thinking badly of her. Was it the shadows from his past that stopped him? Giddon had tortured a man for information once long ago, for King Randa, tied him up and hit him, and it hadn't been a role. He remembered every noise that man had made. The man was probably still alive somewhere, remembering that experience. The people who thought badly of Giddon had reasons.

Giddon, said Bitterblue, in the gentle voice that meant it was time for him to stop wallowing.

All right. Giddon tried to bring himself back to the present. He breathed deeply, noticing the tiny, sharp flakes of snow that dove at his face. They were approaching a sprawling city beach dotted with the impromptu camps of travelers and traders, their carts and horses braced against the wind. A giant bonfire rose into the sky, surrounded by people warming their hands and laughing. Beyond the beach, Giddon could see the beginnings of the long harbor, the spires of masts, and the hulls of colorful ships.

"Have you noticed that a fox is following us?" said Hava. "Again?"

Every time Giddon saw a blue fox, he got the feeling, like a crawling on his skin, that it was following him, but he knew this was irrational. "Are you sure? There are so many of them."

"This one keeps popping up, wherever we are," Hava said. "I saw it once back on the cliff path too, near the farm. They don't feel right to me. You know?"

"I find I'm always guarding my mind against them," he said. "The way we do with mind readers back home, or Dellian monsters. I know it's pointless, since they can't read our minds. But I guess my instinct is too strong."

Hava made a humphing noise. "I think I guard my mind against everyone and everything, always. Old habits."

Both Bitterblue and Hava had worked to develop that habit as children, to protect themselves from the Grace of their father. Remembering this, Giddon's mood softened. "They make me nervous," he admitted.

"So, where are we going?" said Hava. "What's the boating company that leased the *Seashell* called?"

"I have it here," Giddon said, reaching into his coat pocket for a piece of paper. Finding it, but not finding the other item that was meant to be in that pocket, a small envelope he always kept there. Alarmed, he began to search all his pockets. When Hava said, "Well? What's it called?" he ignored her, kept looking.

It was a thing he carried with him always, transferring it from pocket to pocket, like a talisman to remind him why he did the things he did. It contained a few small, ciphered notes. They were the notes Bitterblue wrote to him and left on her dinner table on the days when her responsibilities kept her from dinner, and Hava and Skye were elsewhere too. Instead of letting him arrive unexpectedly to an empty table, she always had his dinner served in her absence and left him a note to puzzle over. The cipher key would be something on the table, usually something she'd placed in an odd position. An upside-down fork meant "fork" was the key. A napkin folded into a glider meant "napkin" or "glider" was probably the key. Then the note would say something so typical that he would sit there laughing. It might say, "Apple cake on bookshelf," so he would search behind the books for his dessert. It might say, "Why didn't the bear wear socks? Answer hidden among rubies," which would send him to the crown, which sat on its own table in the room. There, he would find another ciphered note that said, "Because he had bear feet."

He'd kept every note she'd written him, and he kept his three or four favorites in the envelope in his pocket, always. And the envelope was gone. It was useless to keep looking. He'd been to so many places since the last time he'd checked for it: across the sky in the airship to the Cavenda house, the long walk back again, the journey this morning to the harbor. It could be anywhere.

"What's wrong?" said Hava, who was watching him with rising impatience.

What was wrong was that Giddon was realizing, with a bright

white clarity he'd never had before, that a person did not keep notes like that from a friend, carrying them around like something precious, like a treasure, for no reason. It wasn't normal, it wasn't a routine thing to do, and Giddon had never wanted to be Bitterblue's confidant and counselor as she searched for a husband. He'd loved her. He'd wanted to *be* her husband. And he'd never said a word, never even tried. Why? Because he was a coward. And now she was dead. She'd died not knowing how cherished she was. He'd done every part of it wrong and now she was dead.

The numbness of his shock made it easier for him to moderate his expression. "Nothing," he said, with supreme calm. "I lost something."

"Okay," said Hava. "Can I help you find it?"

"I expect it's gone forever," said Giddon stupidly.

"Giddon, seriously," said Hava, scowling up into his face. "Did someone stab you with a tranquilizer and I missed it?" When he didn't respond, she went so far as to wave a hand in front of his eyes.

"I can't do this right now," he said.

"You can't do *what*? Walk along the harbor?"

"Hava," he said. "I just can't."

Hava took him by both arms and nudged him, not exactly gently, backward. When his legs met the edge of a bench, Giddon sat. Hava sat beside him, studying his face. "What happened?"

Nearby, a blue fox was peering at them from behind a post, not even being subtle. When Giddon looked into Hava's face, her features blurred and he blotted his eyes with his sleeve.

"I'm sorry," he said. "I have a memento I keep in my pocket. I just realized it's gone. I'm upset about it."

"Of course you are. You're a sentimental goon."

"Wow, thanks."

"It was probably a locket shaped like a heart with a painting of Bitterblue as a wood nymph, smelling of ferns."

"I don't even know what a wood nymph is, brat."

"It's just like a bully to call me names when I'm being sympathetic."

Giddon's brain was returning a little more every time Hava made him smile. "Is the fox behind that post there the same one from earlier?"

"Yes," said Hava. "It has the same smug nose."

"Okay," said Giddon. "Who do you think is having us followed?"

"I haven't the foggiest," said Hava, then pursed her lips. "Have you looked closely at every one of Quona's cats? Are we sure she doesn't have a fox?"

"What?" said Giddon. "What are you talking about? Of course they're cats! They're bigger, fluffier, less creepy, and also, they're *cats*!"

"Wow, Giddon. You should join a debate team."

"Well, you should *not* join a debate team," said Giddon. "You can't just propound a theory with no evidence."

"I have evidence."

"I'm listening."

Hava crossed her arms. "I asked Quona how many cats she has. She said twelve."

"Yes?"

"The other night, when we were in the sitting room and we heard scurrying footsteps above, she said it was cats in the attic. But I counted. There were ten cats in the room."

"Well? Two cats can make a lot of noise, Hava. You should spend more time with Lovejoy."

"It sounded like more than two cats," said Hava stubbornly. "Or more than two *something*."

"Okay," said Giddon. "As evidence goes, this is pretty weak."

"Well, and then that Nev girl showed up with a fox kit and they both went up to the attic and shut the door behind them, like it was a big secret, and I don't know about you, I'm sure there are cultural differences, but it was late at night, they're supposed to have a teacher-student relationship, and I thought it was weird."

"I have no argument that Quona is weird," said Giddon. "But it sounds like now you're talking about something else entirely."

"I think," said Hava, "that I'd like to take a look at that attic."

"Okay," said Giddon. "I can agree to that."

"Now," said Hava, "are we *ever* going to talk to that boating company?"

"I told Quona we were going to the harbor to check in on our crew," said Giddon. "If you think we're being watched, whether by Quona or anyone, we should probably do that first."

Before the mask of Hava's Grace came down, Giddon saw alarm in her face, then longing. He thought he understood. Hava loved the ship and its people, but everyone on the ship was touched by the same sorrow.

"We should sail away and never come back," she said.

To where? Giddon wanted to ask. No matter where they went, Bitterblue wouldn't be there.

THE *MONSEA* BOBBED gently, her fat dock lines growing taut, then slackening with her movement. Snow sat on her furled sails. Linny, a Dellian sailor, and Ozul, a Keepish one, were in the rigging with long brooms, knocking off the snow.

The familiar elegance of the ship speared him, her teal hull bright against the gray water and her three slender masts reaching for the sky. She wasn't big compared to other ships in the harbor, but she was graceful, the shape of her hull sleek in the distinctly Royal Continent style. More often than not, he'd thought of the *Monsea* mostly as a floating house that was going to make Bitterblue sick. Her beauty now made him feel very far from home.

Most of the crew was nowhere to be found, but Bitterblue's guards, Mart and Ranin, who were staying on the ship with the sailors, came out to shake their hands, looking ashamed of themselves. These two big, broad-handed men would probably live the rest of their lives feeling ashamed of themselves, thought Giddon.

The captain, Annet, was in the wheelhouse, a fur hat pulled over her long, pale hair. When she saw them, her face went quiet. Annet had been among those who'd dragged Giddon out of the ocean.

"It's wonderful to see you," she said, holding out a hand to Giddon, then Hava.

"And you."

"What can I do for you?"

Hava always became respectful and almost shy around Annet, a remarkable transformation Giddon had noticed but couldn't begin to understand. Annet was Monsean, in her mid-thirties, with ruddy pink cheeks, hair she kept tied back, and wire glasses. As the ship's captain, she was steady, competent, commanding, but so were a lot of people in Hava's life, and only Annet seemed to have this effect.

"We were hoping you could provide cover for us as we do some sleuthing," Hava said. Then she proceeded to tell Annet, with perfect honesty, everything they knew and suspected about the sinking of the *Seashell*. Everything! Without even checking with him. Giddon trusted Annet, but that didn't mean he would've told her everything.

Annet listened with a crease between her eyebrows. "So, you need to ask these boat people questions, but you don't want to be witnessed doing so?"

"Exactly," said Hava.

"What boating company is it?"

"One called Ledrami."

"Ah," said Annet. "They're here now and then."

"Here on the *Monsea*?" said Giddon, surprised.

"Our Ozul is friends with some of that crew. She used to crew for a boating company in Ledra before she came to the Royal Continent. We all visit each other in the harbor here," said Annet, smiling. "We have a card game in the salon pretty often. There's always someone off watch." She pushed herself up from her stool, went to the wheelhouse door, and shouted up at the sky. "Ozul!"

When the Keepish girl came stamping into the wheelhouse a few minutes later, she smiled to see Giddon and Hava, her eyes filling with tears. She was brown-skinned and tall, broad, strong, a scarlet scarf at her throat and a fur hat pulled over her hair.

"Ozul," said Annet, switching into Keepish, "are any of your Ledrami friends coming over today?"

"I think so," she said.

"Can you come back in a few hours?" Annet asked Giddon and Hava.

AT THE HARBOR amble, where Hava and Giddon went to kill some time, the glassy eyes of fish stared up at them from tables. Children played jacks, sitting on uneven flagstones in alleys smelling of fish guts.

When a small rubber ball bounced sideways, Giddon caught it without even thinking, then dropped it into the waiting hand of a little girl who came marching over to glower up at him as if he were a thief. "Royal Continent?" she demanded in Keepish. "Where are you from?"

"We're from Monsea," said Giddon politely.

"We have a Monsean clock in our shop," said the girl, then pointed with her entire arm at a shop across the street that displayed a thousand small devices in the window. She was glaring at Giddon with outraged expectation.

"Lovely," said Giddon. "Thank you." Then he crossed to the shop.

"If I were six, would you do whatever I said?" asked Hava, following him.

Giddon had a sudden vision of a six-year-old Hava stomping her feet and bossing him around, stern, but full of earnest feeling. "Probably."

"You're hopeless."

But the shop, which was the sort where you found yourself wanting things you previously hadn't known existed, soon absorbed Hava's attention as thoroughly as it did Giddon's. Clocks, typewriters, microscopes, compasses, all scratched from use but polished to a high shine, were tucked among unfamiliar devices. He found something with a mother-of-pearl handle and spinning arms that looked like it might be an eggbeater, so pretty and so redolent of some history in a foreign house that he briefly wondered if he could find a use for it. Then he reached instead for a small, golden tube shaped like a spyglass, extended it, looked into it, and saw nothing but darkness.

"That's for making stars," the shopkeeper called, from her desk at the front. "Here, bring it to me. I'll show you."

At the desk, the shopkeeper demonstrated how to aim the tube toward a light source, then, with one's eye to the eyepiece, move it around. Pinpricks of light appeared and danced inside the eyepiece.

"Go stand in the doorway and aim it at a bright patch of sky," the woman said, then chuckled at the surprised noise Giddon made as bright stars moved and slid inside the tube. "It's a starmaker from Mantiper," she said. "You're looking at the actual night sky in there, every star in its proper place."

"What?" said Giddon, incredulous. "How?"

"It contains a compass and a level, so it knows which way you're pointing. There's a light filter inside that moves depending on where you point it, showing you a representation of the actual location of stars at midnight, in the Mantiperan capital, on the first day of the Mantiperan year. Not that I've ever tried to compare it to the night sky in Mantiper! I bought it from a Mantiperan ship captain."

Someone pushed past Giddon into the shop.

"Yes, of course, come right in," said the shopkeeper with an ironic sort of amiability that Giddon noticed, then dismissed. He was busy trying to find familiar constellations that would support or disavow what the shopkeeper had said about the starmaker.

Then he felt a soft hand tugging him back inside and submitted to it, letting Hava pull him into a hidden corner of the shop. When he raised inquiring eyebrows, Hava cocked her head toward the person who'd come in.

Peeking around a stand of shelves, Giddon saw a blond woman in a pale yellow coat, standing in the middle of the store with her chin high, hands raised, and eyes closed. Giddon recognized that stance, as if she were sensing the air with her fingers. And of course he recognized the woman.

Bile rose in his throat.

"What are you looking for this time, Graceling?" asked the shop-keeper dryly.

"A pocket watch," said Trina, not changing her position. She'd aged. Giddon remembered someone who'd seemed little older than he, but lines now crossed her pale skin, bunching around her eyes. She looked weary, actually, washed out, as she stood there with hands raised. Giddon hoped her every day was an exhausting slog.

"Whose pocket watch?" said the shopkeeper.

"A man named Stava."

"The fishmonger from two doors down?" said the shopkeeper, offended. "Did he send you in here particularly?"

"No. I'm just being thorough."

"Well," said the shopkeeper, somewhat mollified. "I know you have to earn your keep, but you'll find no stolen goods here. I bought every item, and at a fair price too."

Trina paused in her sensing and turned to the shopkeeper, one eye so dark it might be black, one pale yellow like her coat. She seemed about to speak. But then she noticed Giddon, standing straight and tall. Immediately something closed in her face.

"You recognize me," said Giddon.

"Yes," she said.

"You might've had some loyalty," he said, "for the people who helped you and the queen who took a risk to shelter you."

A small flare came alive in her mismatched eyes. "You'd be surprised by the number of people who think I owe them my loyalty," she said. "Everyone thinks they've done me a favor."

"A favor?" said Giddon. "Is that what I did for you?"

"You shuffled me from one place where people wanted to use me to another place where people wanted to use me."

"And so you decided to start using people yourself?"

"How would you know what it's like?" Trina said scornfully, looking Giddon up and down. "When in your life have you ever lacked anything you want or need? When have you ever had to mistrust why someone wants to be your friend? Everyone has something they want from me. Everyone fawns and pretends, because they think I'm the solution to some problem in their life. If they're Estillan, they think I owe them something because I was Estillan once. If they're Monsean, it's because I was Monsean. If they're Keepish, it's because they paid me for a job once and now they think we have some sort of understanding. I don't owe you anything." Her voice ended on the smallest sob.

Giddon was about to deliver a sharp retort. Then, unaccountably, Trina added, "I was sorry to hear about your queen." The statement confounded him, not just what she said, but the way she said it, as if she were a different person suddenly, tired, and sad, and truly sorry.

"I—thank you," he said.

"I believe she had a hard life," she said. "I believe she would have understood mine. I was sorry to hear about your envoy too. Mikka, the one who drowned with his friend Brek. He came to me once. He knew I was the one who'd told about the zilfium, but he didn't try to put the burden of what people did with that information onto my shoulders," she said, her voice suddenly hardening again, growing sharper. She paused, swallowed. "He wanted my help. He was both polite and generous. I would have helped him, if I could."

Beside Giddon, Hava stepped forward slightly. Caught and held Trina's mismatched eyes so Trina could see her own.

"May I ask what he wanted your help with?" said Hava.

Trina seemed to be considering Hava's face. She raised her chin, a slight defiance. "I never knew for sure," she said. "He and Brek had gone north and come back. There was something there they wanted me to see if I could find."

"Something they'd lost in the north?" said Hava.

"No. Something they'd found there. Something they wanted confirmation of. But before we met again so he could give me the details, they drowned."

"Where did they go in the north?" said Hava.

"I don't know," said Trina, her voice beginning to rise again. "You ask a lot of questions. I know who you are and I think you know what it's like to be used, but that doesn't mean you get to use me."

Trina took a step back. She glanced once at the shopkeeper, who'd quietly watched the entire exchange. Then she turned on her heel and exited the shop.

CHAPTER NINETEEN

Two of Ozul's friends who crewed for the Ledrami boating company came to the *Monsea* that afternoon to play cards. They were happy to sit with Giddon and Hava in the salon first, drinking tea as the room bounced lightly on the small swells of Ledra's harbor.

One was a Keepish woman named Sorit. The other, a man named Riz, was Kamassarian. Both had been working in the harbor the day the *Seashell* foundered. Both remembered that a new, Kamassarian-speaking crew of six sailors had sailed the *Seashell,* setting off practically the instant the Monseans arrived.

"It's not odd for a leasing party to hire their own crew," said Riz. "But I do remember thinking it was odd for anyone to hire a crew who didn't speak their own language!"

"I think Mikka spoke some Kamassarian," said Hava.

"Maybe that accounts for it," said Riz.

"And what do you know about the accident?" asked Giddon.

Riz and Sorit shared a blank look. "Nothing," Sorit said.

"Nothing?"

"The *Seashell* was never seen again," said Sorit. "Of course, a few people saw her entering open water, but after that, nothing. It's a big ocean. We did a full-scale search the next day and found no sign, but by then, we weren't expecting to. The sea takes everything."

"Isn't it strange that no one survived in the lifeboats?" said Giddon.

"There was only one lifeboat on board the *Seashell*," said Riz. "We don't know what made the ship sink. If it was fire, the lifeboat could've been damaged. Or, it could've capsized in a wind. The weather on the Brumal Sea can get violent very fast."

"How was the weather that day?" he asked.

"I'm not sure," said Sorit, squinting like she was trying to remember.

"Don't you remember what Katu Cavenda said when he came back ashore?" Riz said.

"Katu?" said Giddon, keeping his voice even. "He also sailed that day? What did he have to say?"

"He was out in this little yacht he has, this beautiful slender craft he travels and races in," said Riz. "Usually he handles her all by himself. You have to admire his skill. He came back laughing, said it was so blustery, he'd almost capsized."

"Now that you mention it," said Sorit, "wasn't that also the day a couple of fishing ships lost their nets? The waves tore them right off the ships."

"Yes," said Riz, "I remember that too. It's why we all got a little worried when it started to get dark and the *Seashell* wasn't back."

"Did Katu say anything else?" said Giddon. "I don't suppose he mentioned the *Seashell*?"

"We did talk about the *Seashell*, actually," said Riz, "because Katu asked if I'd seen an airship go by full of people speaking Kamassarian, heading north. We hadn't, but it was a funny coincidence, of course, so I told him about the crew of the *Seashell*."

"I don't understand," said Giddon. "Why would he ask you that? Would an airship full of Kamassarians be significant?"

"I don't know," said Riz, shrugging. "Katu has all kinds of friends. Maybe he thought he recognized them."

"I see," said Giddon. "I don't suppose you know anything about our Monsean men going north before they drowned?"

"I can tell you that if they went north, it wasn't in the *Seashell,*" said Riz. "I don't know anything beyond that."

HAVA AND GIDDON walked back to Quona's house in relative silence.

"Any foxes?" Giddon finally said.

"I haven't even been looking," said Hava. "My mind is with Mikka and Brek."

"Me too," said Giddon. *And Trina,* he didn't add, not quite ready to articulate all the reasons that exchange had upset him.

"That Trina's a touchy one, isn't she?" said Hava. "'O how I suffer,' and all that?"

Giddon began to laugh. "Is that how you'd describe it?"

"The shopkeeper told me that people in the harbor amble hire her to find their stolen treasures. She lives above a bait shop, two blocks away from that store."

"Does she?" said Giddon, who would've expected something more glamorous, had he considered it yesterday. Now he just felt lost and out of sorts. He'd bought that starmaker, because he hadn't been able to help himself. Bitterblue would have loved it; it was the sort of thing she would've kept close, as a treasure. It thumped in his pocket as he walked.

"Hava," he said, "do I use you?"

"Oh, *ugh,*" said Hava. "I knew this was coming."

"There was something in what Trina said."

"Okay then, do I use *you?*" said Hava. "When we're at a party and I let you do all the talking while I hide? Or let you carry everything with your big muscles? Or let you distract everyone by looking all handsome and stuffed with valor?"

"How do you manage to be so insulting while giving compliments?"

"She was feeling sorry for herself. Do you always take everything to heart?"

"Not everything."

"You don't use me," said Hava. "If you did, I'd be sure to let you know."

"That's true," said Giddon ruefully.

Now Hava was the one laughing. "Giddon," she said. "Could we please talk about what we've learned? We know our men went north. While they were there, it sounds like they found something, something they wanted Trina to confirm."

"A discovery they were probably killed for," said Giddon.

"Right," said Hava. "The day they were killed, someone hired them a Kamassarian crew. The crew scuttled the ship, then someone, probably whoever'd hired them, picked the crew up in an airship and carried them north."

"Right," said Giddon. "There are some holes and we're making some assumptions, but that sounds like the size of it."

"So," said Hava. "How can we discover what they found in the north?"

"We need to know where they went," said Giddon. "There's a lot of Winterkeep to the north." Ahead, the Cliff Farm came into view, cows spotting the hillside. Beyond it, the glass of Quona's windows glinted in the light from the sea.

"Quona went north today, incidentally," said Giddon. "Did she tell you?"

"I managed to avoid her this morning."

"The Varanas have some property somewhere. She said she might be gone overnight."

"Really," said Hava, squinting ahead at Quona's tall house. She seemed to be studying the roof. "In that case, it seems like the perfect day to check out her attic."

THE DOOR AT the top of the stairway in Quona's sitting room was locked, but Hava made short work of it with her lock picks while Giddon watched for Quona's staff.

Behind the door, they found a high, bright, enormous space with many windows. The rafters were visible above; a massive fireplace and a single closed door were set along one wall.

Hava crossed quickly to that door and tried it. Finding it locked, she knelt, examined the keyhole, then tried her lock picks again. "This one's more difficult," she said.

As Giddon's eyes adjusted to the brightness, the big attic space became stranger than it had first seemed. "Hava?" he said, staring. "What do you think of this room?" Colorful paintings covered the walls. In fact, the paintings weren't just on the walls; they extended onto the window moldings and the rafters, even parts of the floor, most of the ceiling. They were scenes of blue foxes having adventures. Jumping from one tree to another; flying with what looked like makeshift wings; sleeping on mounds of candy; sailing in boats and soaring in airships. Furthermore, though the room contained no furniture in the usual sense of the word, there were narrow, raised platforms built directly onto some of the walls. Like shelves, but with unusual orientations. Straight passageways, steps, hills, slopes, maybe crossing a wall, maybe creating a path over and around a window. A sort of jungle gym? For the world's most spoiled . . . cats? Did cats like paintings of blue foxes? Also, why weren't there any cats up here now? And why was the attic kept locked if it was just a cat playroom?

"There are seven tiny little beds in front of the fireplace," said Hava, who'd come to stand beside him.

"Seven?" said Giddon. "Not twelve?"

"Either the cats share," said Hava, "or they're not for the cats."

"Wait," said Giddon. "But, *seven*? Now we're thinking she doesn't just have one secret fox, but *seven*?"

"If she's breaking the rules by secretly bonding to a fox," said Hava, "why shouldn't she break them even more by bonding to several?"

"But why would she do it?" said Giddon. "She wouldn't just be breaking rules, Hava. She'd be breaking the law."

"On the axis of annoying to interesting," said Hava, "Quona is tipping further toward interesting." Then she frowned at a spot about waist-height on the wall, walked to it, and pushed. A little hinged door, like a cat door right there in the middle of the wall, swung forward and back again. Stairs led to it and the painting on the wall obscured it.

"Whoever this room is for," said Hava, "it looks like they have paths into the walls."

Remembering all the sounds of scurrying, Giddon suppressed a shudder. "Can you get into that locked room?"

"I'll try again."

"The wind is really something," said Giddon as it threw itself against the windows. "You'd think we'd be able to hear the ocean, in a house on a cliff above the sea." Then he noticed a doorknob-like handle on the edge of one of the tall windows. He went to it to investigate. The window was actually a glass door on a swinging frame.

Opening it, he stepped out onto a small, flat platform and found himself overlooking the sea. The wind slammed against him.

"Giddon," said Hava urgently, startling him, for he hadn't heard her join him. She pointed out to sea. He followed her finger with his gaze, but saw nothing.

Then, all at once, his eyes found the bulbous, purple-blue bodies, racing across the surface of the sea. "Silbercows," Giddon cried, which made them turn suddenly to reach their noses to the house, the balcony, though they couldn't possibly have heard Giddon's voice from that distance.

They feel us, he thought. *They see us.* He sensed their curiosity suddenly, like a whisper under his skin. Tentatively, he tried to talk to them, stretching his thoughts out across the water, not knowing how to make himself heard. *A house on a cliff?* he said. *An airship? A disturbance in the water? What does it mean?*

Suddenly, unbelievably, he felt their voices.

Who are you? they asked him. *How do you know our stories?* But it wasn't words; it was images and feelings, impressions rushing through Giddon, like the battering wind against his body. They showed him the house high on a cliff, indistinct, but with rows of shining windows. They showed him a dark oval in the sky, blocking the sun: an airship. Then he saw an explosion in the water, a massive flash of light, terrifying, obliterating the sea, and he had to hold hard to the rail, and remind himself it was a picture, not something real. He felt the silbercows' pain. It took his breath away.

Help us, they said. *Stop them.*

Stop them doing what? said Giddon. *What's happening?*

They showed him a new picture. A boat at the bottom of the sea, with a pale gray hull. Keepish markings on its side said "Seashell." Its hull was splintered. Its cabin door was closed, padlocked. Inside the boat's cabin, visible through a porthole, were two bodies.

Mikka! Giddon cried. *Brek!*

Mikka, Brek? the silbercows said, curious, but not understanding.

Our friends! Giddon said. *Those two bodies. Someone closed them in there! They were murdered! This is proof!*

Proof? said the silbercows. Then they showed him a new image: Outside the boat was a gigantic, many-legged, many-eyed creature. An impossible creature, like the Keeper. And now Giddon was confused about everything he was seeing, because maybe it was all just a fairy tale.

It's real, they told him. *Our friend is guarding your proof. But can you help us? Will you stop them?*

Yes! said Giddon. *We're trying! But we don't understand! Stop whom?*

And then the silbercows' messages faded, because they turned suddenly, streaking off to the north.

Wait! said Giddon. *Whom should we stop? What are they doing?*

"Did you hear what they said?" said Hava breathlessly, beside him.

"Yes. They want help," he said.

"Did you see the house, the airship, and the explosion? The boat with the bodies?"

"Yes. And an imaginary Keeper too, which was confusing."

"We need to get into that locked room," said Hava. "The house they showed us could be this house."

"Or any number of houses," said Giddon. "The Cavendas have a house on a cliff in the north. A lot of people have houses on cliffs."

"Sure, but we're literally standing in one right now, Giddon. A house with secrets, and a locked room."

Something was still wrenching inside Giddon at the loss of the silbercows. Something about them had made him want to understand them so badly, but now they were gone. He gripped the railing, frustrated. "I agree we should get into that room," he said. "But we have a lot of questions to answer. The answers won't all be in that room. Mikka and Brek found something in the north." Mikka and Brek. What a nightmare, to be locked inside a cabin while one's ship sank. What a horrible way to die.

"I'm going to avenge them," said Giddon. "For Bitterblue."

"Of course you are," said Hava. "I am too. But heads up, because that looks like Quona's airship." She pointed north, where a dot had appeared in the sky.

"I hope not," said Giddon. "She said she might be gone all night. It's barely afternoon."

"I think we should start paying more attention to what she says," said Hava, "and how well it matches up with what she does. Now, let's get inside before she sees us."

CHAPTER TWENTY

ON THE NIGHT of the prime minister's gala, a week after her parents' dinner party, Lovisa arrived at the Keep with two questions. First, had her mother brought her fox to the party, or left him at home? Second—if the fox was indeed at the party—whom could she use as a decoy, to sneak home?

The entrance hall was alive with noise and color. Above her, the glass dome of the Keep disappeared into darkness, making her wish for quiet, solitude, the stars.

In a fitted black dress, Lovisa stepped behind the cover of a gaggle of academy boys who apparently found themselves hilarious. Reaching into the collar of her dress, she touched the string on which hung the attic room key she'd had made in one of the ambles. It scratched against her skin, for the woman who'd crafted it had inexplicably added a fake red gemstone, made of cheap glass, to its top. "Turns it into something special," she'd said, with a crooked-toothed smile. Lovisa had been embarrassed for her.

From her hidden position, Lovisa looked around. She spotted her father pretty quickly on a staircase, raised above the crowd like an actor on a stage, conversing with the chief of the Ledra Magistry. Then Ta Varana walked by, radiant in a deep pink dress. Could Ta be her decoy? They'd kissed once. It had been fine, except that Ta had kept talking, and talking, and talking. Even the memory was tiresome.

A fox scurried past, racing up to the second-story gallery that stretched around the perimeter of the entrance hall. Sighing, Lovisa saw herself spending most of the night chasing foxes into corners, then struggling to decide if they were the one she was looking for. She watched her mother join her father, then descend with him to Arni and Mara Devret, Mari's parents. Ferla's mouth smiled stiffly and Lovisa wondered if she herself looked like that when she smiled. Like it hurt her face.

Nearby, Lovisa spotted Mari with a few of his friends, including Ta. As she approached, she was surprised to notice that Nev was among them. Her surprise faded as she got close enough to overhear the conversation.

"What do you want, Nev?" said Pari Parnin.

Nev shrugged. "You spoke to me first. You said, 'Nice party,' so I said, 'Yes.'"

"I didn't," said Pari.

"Okay. You're right. I just announced the word *yes* to the air for no reason."

"Didn't you used to scream that a lot?" said Pari. "When you were with Mari?"

Nev paused for a beat, looking into Pari's smirking, self-congratulatory face. "Mari is a nice person," she said flatly. "I don't think he'd tell you, or anyone, anything about what we used to do. Or what he does with anyone." She shrugged again. "And maybe he doesn't like you suggesting he would."

"You don't know what you're talking about," said Pari with a nasty smile.

Nev rested her eyes on Mari, who was frowning at the floor in misery and embarrassment. She glanced at the others in the group, who were twisting their mouths and tittering. Nev's eyes, cold and scornful, raked sharply across Lovisa, then she turned and walked away. She held her injured fox kit in one arm, tightly enough that she was squirming. The squirming fox was the only evidence that Nev was more upset than she pretended.

Lovisa wanted to lash Mari with shaming words, for standing there like a coward while Nev dealt with Pari on her own. But that would have to wait, because now Lovisa was readier than ever to confirm the location of her mother's fox, then sneak home. She'd wanted a decoy she could stomach touching and kissing, but now her need for a strong stomach had vanished. She was going to pop Pari Parnin's puffed-up sense of self-delusion. She would make him think she wanted to have sex with him, then she would lead him all the way to the attic of her house in Flag Hill, where she would refuse him. If he got in trouble with her parents for trying to seduce their daughter in their attic, all the better.

"Hi Pari," she said, moving closer to him. "When did you get so funny?"

"I thought you'd never notice," he said with a smirk. She got to work, laughing at his unclever jokes, stroking his arm. She complimented his golden-green scarves and touched her fingers to the orange jewels adorning his pockets. He began to respond, not with conversation, but with heavy hands, knowing smiles, body-to-body contact.

Then, with a promise to return, she excused herself briefly. Was her mother's fox here or not? Moving through the edges of the party, she watched the occasional fox whiz past like a spinning leaf in a stream. There wasn't much hope of recognizing a nose or an ear if none of them ever kept still.

Lovisa saw Nev in a corner, standing alone. Scanning the crowd, Lovisa saw someone else who'd spotted Nev in her corner: Nori Orfa, that northern boy, quick to smile, flirty, the one Lovisa didn't trust. Nori began to move toward Nev.

Half out of her own need and half out of an unexamined impulse to interrupt Nori, Lovisa pushed through the crowd to Nev.

"Hi," she said, bursting breathlessly into the space before the taller girl.

Nev looked down at Lovisa, not speaking, but conveying worlds with her contemptuous eyes. She wasn't holding the fox kit anymore. Lovisa could see her shirt, black and high-collared, with long, thin ribbons in every color that wrapped around her torso and seemed knotted together at arbitrary locations. On someone else, it would've looked like a failed attempt to simulate current Ledra fashions. On Nev, with her high chin and her straight shoulders, her humorless mouth, it was exactly right. She looked like a queen.

"Come to pick on me?" said Nev. "Or do you people only do that when you have an audience?"

"Have you forgotten all the times I've picked on you when we were alone?" said Lovisa. "I'm hurt."

"Ha, ha. What do you want, Lovisa?"

"Can you tell foxes apart?"

"Sometimes."

"I don't suppose you've ever noticed the one that belongs to my mother?"

"Not particularly," she said. "When would I? I don't exactly get invitations to your house."

"Oh," said Lovisa, disappointed. "Oh well."

"Also," said Nev, "why would I do you a favor?"

Lovisa hesitated, considering. Then she said, "For a complicated reason that includes punishing Pari Parnin."

This was met with a brief silence. Then Nev spoke. "How old is your mother's fox?"

Lovisa did a quick calculation. "Seven or eight, maybe?"

"Then it's probably one of the ones who's not flying around like it's intent on tripping people. The manic ones are usually the young ones."

"Oh. I haven't seen any keeping still."

"They're less noticeable. They're mostly either standing with their person, or watching the party from the edges of the stairs. Excuse me," said Nev, slipping away. A moment later, Lovisa saw her joining Nori, the two of them grinning at each other in the shadow of an archway. When Nev grinned, it transformed her face, lighting her up with joy and mischief. It made Lovisa wonder if Nev ever kissed girls. It also made her feel sharply alone.

Whatever. Lovisa turned to examine the edge of the nearest staircase. Immediately she saw what Nev meant, for foxes crowded the spaces between the banisters, just like her little brothers did at home during dinner parties. One of them suddenly sprang to the floor from an alarming height—one Lovisa recognized, by her smallness and the bandage on her face. That was Nev's fox, Little Guy. Lovisa could see her bolting between people's feet toward Nev, and wondered if they were bonded yet. *Tell her not to hook up with that rotten loser!* Lovisa shouted at the fox, uselessly, of course.

Then a fox watching Lovisa from the steps caught her attention, and held it. She recognized that long-nosed profile, those perky ears. For a moment, the fox held her gaze with his flashing eyes. Then he stood and slunk away, but not before confirming what Lovisa now knew. Her mother's fox was here.

WHEN THE FOX who was bonded to Ferla Cavenda saw Lovisa glaring up at him on the staircase, he understood, instantly, what she was planning to do.

And now the entire calamity of what was likely to transpire was playing out in his mind, for he knew something Lovisa didn't know: Ferla, who had one of her stress headaches, was planning to leave the party early and go home.

The fox had never before experienced the level of anxiety he'd been experiencing lately. It was too much. He could not keep everyone safe all by himself! And his siblings, all of whom were present at this party, were as useless as ever. All they wanted to do was play

Trounce Each Other, with occasional forays into Catch the Falling Food. As if they were kits! They had no interest in helping him with any of his dilemmas. How could he foil Ferla's plans?

He could delay her departure home, maybe. Distract her from her headache. Then he could try to be on hand to help Lovisa.

The fox set out to find Ferla, composing a lie about having snuck into the inner Keep, then having seen someone trying to break into the president's office. That would delay her, while he came up with the next lie.

IT WAS EASY for Lovisa to convince Pari to leave the party.

"Come help me get my coat, Pari," she said.

"Are you leaving?" he said with a small pout.

"Aren't we both leaving?"

Outside, though, a light snow was falling, and he balked at the idea of going all the way to Flag Hill. "We live in the same dorm," he said. "No one would know."

She didn't respond, just kissed and rubbed up against him. Then, when they reached a place where the footpath diverged, she turned toward a staircase that led away from the dorms.

"What are you doing?" he said. "It's this way."

"Shut up, Pari," she said. "I have a better plan."

"The dorm is right here."

"If you want this," she said, "then you'll have to come back to my house."

"But, why? It's freezing out here!"

She took hold of his hand and put it inside her fur coat, thanking the cold for her hard nipples. She gave him a minute to touch her, kiss her throat. It wasn't terrible, actually. It was even a little bit exciting.

"Come on," she said. "Just come with me."

With a ragged breath, he followed.

Chapter Twenty-one

Leading Pari home was a little like trying to take a walk with an oversexed dog. He kept slowing their progress by stopping Lovisa, groping her.

"Won't your guards rat on you to your parents?" he said during one of these interludes. "Maybe we should do it here in the trees."

It wasn't time yet to break it to Pari that they'd be sidestepping the guards by climbing a wall, then a tree, then a trellis, then entering through a third-story window.

"I have a way around the guards," she said. "An arrangement."

"An arrangement with your guards? What kind?" he demanded, then smirked. "*That* kind?"

"Don't be disgusting. It's not an arrangement *with* the guards."

"It *is* that kind of arrangement," he said. "You'll have sex with anything, won't you?"

"What's that say about you, if it's true?"

"Whatever," he said. "Why shouldn't I benefit, if others do?"

It was easy to justify using him, when he talked like that. Maybe she should choose someone like him from now on. Snow was falling and the cold made Lovisa jumpy. When he grabbed her and pushed her against a stone wall, her heart began to hammer. The wall bruising her was the wall of the Devret estate, which meant they were getting close to her house. And he was grabbing her hard, manhandling her as he hadn't before. She couldn't push him off. It hurt.

"Let me go," she said.

He shoved her harder, pressing down on her shoulders. "Get down," he said.

"I won't," she said, beginning to panic, but making herself sound disgusted and brave. "Don't think I won't turn you in if you make me."

"No one would believe you."

"You think my mother and father won't believe me when I show them bruises on my back from you shoving me against the Devrets' wall?"

"No one even knows I'm here. You can't prove it was me."

"I told Mari I was bringing you here," she lied. "You know he'd defend me before he ever defended you."

Pari suddenly laughed. He released her. "Fine," he said. "This had better be one good screw."

PARI'S COMPLAINTS STRUCK a new tone, furious and mean, when they got to the Cavenda wall and he understood Lovisa's plan for entering the house through a high window.

New criterion, Lovisa thought to herself. *Someone less pushy, and scary, and whiny, and horrible.* "Just get over the wall, Pari," she said, beginning to wonder how she was going to hold him off once they were in the house. All this, just to figure out what her father was storing in that room? It had better be worth it. "Your screw is on the other side of the wall."

The pokey rocks were slippery in a snowfall, especially for someone unused to them, like Pari. By the time he landed on the other side, he had mud streaks on his coat and scrapes on his hands. "We could just do it here," he said, with a tone in his voice that said something else too. That he was done with patience, and they *would* do it here.

Electrified with a refusal to lose control over this situation, Lovisa set out quickly across the grounds and around the house, hoping he would follow, and then, when she heard his footsteps behind her, feeling chased. At the tree that led to the trellis, she reached one foot to a knot and, with all her speed, began to climb. She'd dressed for this, with her dark coat and with narrow skirts that were actually divided into pants.

Pari was in the tree now too, climbing slowly, swearing. Lovisa reached the trellis while he was still fumbling through low branches. As she climbed it to the window, it occurred to her for the first time that the trellis might not hold Pari's weight. It was designed for holding ivy, after all, not humans, and he was a lot bigger than she was.

Now Lovisa had an image stuck in her head: Pari lying on the lawn with a broken neck. He probably deserved it. But her life, if it happened, would become a disaster.

Moving as quickly as she could, she climbed back into the tree and scurried partway down. "Pari," she whispered. "The trellis might not hold your weight. Be careful when you get to that part."

All at once, Pari's frustrated noises transformed into laughter again. The laughter became hysterical.

"Shh!" whispered Lovisa, alarmed. "The guards!"

"Lovisa," he said. "Admit it: This is an elaborate prank. Right? Look at me. I'm stuck in a tree outside your house in the snow, with a deathtrap of a trellis above me. I don't even *want* to have sex with you anymore."

"I'm insulted," said Lovisa, matching his tone. "I planned such a nice night for us."

"You're a piece of work," he said, with a fondness in his voice that swung her sharply into a kind of guilt. *I still don't like him,* she reminded herself. *And he could still hurt me.*

"Come on. It'll be fun," she said, pretending to mean it, then scuttling up the tree to the trellis again. The window with the broken lock opened easily. With a small burst of pride, Lovisa climbed into the dark, empty bedroom.

While Pari continued to heave himself from branch to branch below, she tiptoed across the room to the desk. Pulling the drawers out, she fumbled for anything that could be used as a weapon. Her fingers closed on something long and sharp—a letter opener.

She returned to the window just as Pari climbed in. Fell in, really. He landed on the bedroom floor, then rolled onto his back. It was dark enough that she wasn't sure how to read him, until she heard him chuckling.

"What's next?" he said. "I assume we're in an isolated room with a big bed and fluffy pillows, but you want us to do this somewhere more challenging? Maybe on the ridgepole of the roof?"

"We only have to climb a few stairs," she said, relieved to find him less aggressive.

"I can hear you smiling," he said. "These stairs are guarded by bears."

"Get up," she said, "and take my hand."

Pari got up and took more than her hand. He kissed her, pressed against her, still laughing a little, his nose cold but his mouth warm and soft. For the sake of encouraging him, Lovisa held the letter opener out of his reach and kissed him back. It began to feel good, which made her unhappy. She wasn't going to do this again. She was too torn between the confusion of physically wanting someone who was awful; manipulating someone, yet feeling guilty about it; controlling someone, yet sensing that her control could spiral away at any moment he chose, because he was stronger, and volatile.

"Come on," she whispered. Feeling forward with her letter-opener hand, she led him out of the room.

THEY PASSED NO guards and, considering that most of their route was pitch-dark, made very little noise. Lovisa picked up a lamp from a table. "You carry that," she whispered to Pari, passing it to him.

"I don't suppose you'd consider lighting the stupid thing?" he whispered back.

"Soon," she said.

They reached the door to the attic stairs, which creaked as it opened. Climbing the stairs and passing through the second door, they stepped into the cavernous attic, made of darkness and shadows. Lovisa closed the door behind them and felt safer suddenly, hidden from the rest of the house.

"We're almost there," she said, tugging at the string around her neck that held the key. He crossed the floor with her, his breath quickening audibly. Lovisa reached out and felt for the door to the little room, finding the keyhole, while Pari pressed against her and gave his hands free rein. His hands were everywhere on her body. No, not everywhere, for he still hadn't discovered the letter opener. *A boy in the dark doesn't care about my hands. I can hide things in my hands,* she thought, filing it away for later, even though she was never going to do this again.

The lock clicked. "Okay, Pari," she said, "you just wait out here for a second while I get the room ready."

"I'm sure it's ready."

"Sometimes my brothers have sleepovers in this room," she said. "You want them to see us like this? Let me make sure it's empty and safe. Here, hand me that lamp."

He shoved the lamp at her. "Be quick."

"How about you count to a hundred? Okay? Think how good

it'll feel after you count to a hundred." She kissed him, then started counting, slowly. "One, two . . ."

While he gritted his teeth and counted, she disentangled herself, pushed into the room, shut the door quickly, found the keyhole, and locked it closed from the inside.

"Hey!" she heard him yell. "You're going to let me in, right?"

"Of course!" she said. "Be quiet! The guards will hear!"

Then a voice spoke inside the room, soft and vague, as if its speaker were half-asleep.

"Hello?" it said, in Lingian. "Giddon?"

Lovisa stood frozen. She felt as if her head were swelling up like a balloon. "Hello?" she responded in Lingian, not even knowing what she was saying.

"Who's there?" the voice said, stronger now, more alert, switching into Keepish. "Hello?"

The room was as dark as all the punishments Lovisa remembered from her childhood, and it smelled the same too, cold and thick, like a chamber pot. Shaking, she crouched down to set the lamp on the floor, so she could light it.

A spark. Lovisa raised the unsteady, growing flame.

A young woman in a bed looked back at Lovisa. She was small like Lovisa, dark-haired and plain like Lovisa, with big, wary eyes and a stubborn, determined set to her mouth. Her skin was browner than Hava's or Giddon's, but paler than Lovisa's. She looked like . . . she looked like the Lienid prince who'd had the Graceling boyfriend. Prince Skye.

"Who are you?" the woman demanded of Lovisa, in nearly unaccented Keepish. She glared, expecting an answer. Lovisa stared back, unbreathing, unbelieving, because this could only be one person, imprisoned here in her family's attic.

"Have you come to help me escape?" the woman asked, pushing

her blankets back and swinging her feet to the ground, standing, facing Lovisa. She was Lovisa's same height and she was wearing one of Lovisa's favorite pairs of pajamas.

Staring at this vision, Lovisa understood a number of things at once. Why her mother had left class early the day the Monseans had arrived, then been late for an important dinner. Why her parents were fighting, because of course Benni would never stand for this. Why it no longer mattered what her father had been planning to store in this room. How serious this was, for this was a capital crime. It was the kind of crime that could start a war.

She also understood that now she, Lovisa, was responsible for the Queen of Monsea. And she couldn't help this queen escape, because Pari Parnin was waiting outside the door. She couldn't help this queen escape, because, where would she take her? She couldn't help this queen escape, because her family would be ruined. Her parents imprisoned, maybe even executed, their wealth confiscated by the Keepish government, and Lovisa's name, her brothers' names, infamous, synonymous with scandal and shame, not just in Winterkeep but across Torla, and on the Royal Continent too.

My mother ruined our lives, she thought.

"Well?" said Queen Bitterblue. "Are you freeing me?"

Lovisa needed a plan. "Yes," she said, improvising. "But not right now."

"When?" said the queen, stepping forward. "Where am I? Who are you?"

Pari Parnin knocked on the door. His voice was a whine. "Let me in, Lovisa."

"Who's that?" said the queen sharply.

"I'll get rid of him," said Lovisa, moving toward the door. "Then I'll come back."

"Will you?" said the queen, following her. Then she said, in a voice that was certain, and more imposing than the tiny person who spoke it, "Why don't I believe you?"

Stricken with confusion, Lovisa spun back to her. "Please," she said, a bit wildly. "Don't tell my mother I saw you."

"Your mother!" said the queen. "Who is your mother?"

"I'll come back," Lovisa lied, "but don't tell anyone."

"Is this a private home?" asked the queen. "Am I in Ledra?"

"I'll explain everything later."

"Are you allied with the fox?"

"What? No! Of course not! He's bonded to my mother!"

"But you're allied with me?"

"Yes. I'll come back for you!"

Queen Bitterblue stared into Lovisa's face fiercely, not believing her. Lovisa knew it, and was ashamed. "Take this," she said desperately, shoving the letter opener into the queen's hands, as a sort of bribe. Then she rushed to the door, turned the key, pulled the latch. The queen followed, standing close. On the other side of the door, Pari pushed.

"Wait!" cried Lovisa. "I'm coming out."

Pari thrust the door so sharply that Lovisa stumbled and almost dropped the lamp. Pari surged into the room with a grunt of frustration. Then he stared wide-eyed at the queen, who stood before him in bare feet and pajamas, brandishing a letter opener.

"Who are you?" he asked in bewilderment.

"No one," said Lovisa quickly. "A cousin from the north. We're disturbing her. Let's go to my bedroom, Pari."

"She doesn't look like a northerner," said Pari, in the same moment footsteps sounded outside the door. A young woman, that guard who hated Lovisa, pushed into the room.

Ferla stepped in behind her.

———————

LOVISA'S MIND SPUN frantically.

"Who is that girl, Mother?" she said, in the blankest voice she could muster. "Why is she here?"

Ferla only stared at Pari with an expression more agitated, more crazed than Lovisa could ever remember seeing; and desperate too. And something else. Ferla looked sorry.

"Lovisa, give me that lamp and go wait in your father's library," she said.

"Mother?" said Lovisa. "I just came here with Pari Parnin, for some privacy. You said I could sleep with whatever academy student I wanted."

Ferla's fox was zipping around the room without pause, like he'd gone haywire. "Give me that lamp, then go to your father's library, right now, Lovisa," Ferla said, her voice so strange, almost a cry. Lovisa relinquished the lamp, then spun to the doorway, not understanding the emotion in her mother's voice. Pari turned to follow her.

"Pari," Ferla said in that same voice, "you stay here."

"Mother?" said Lovisa, in sudden anxiety. Then that guard shoved her through the door and slammed it shut behind her. Lovisa was left alone, in darkness.

Think, she told herself, numb, stupid, not understanding what was going on. Moving away from the door into the darker depths of the room, she sat against a far wall, where she wouldn't be seen. Wrapping her arms around her legs, shivering hard, she tried to comprehend this, but her brain was shutting down, turning her thoughts to cement.

The door opened suddenly. That guard came rushing out, shut the door, moved quickly to the stairs, and started down, in the dark.

After a moment, Lovisa crept after the guard, keeping her distance. She followed the guard along the lower corridor carefully, staying in the shadows, pausing at each corner to give the woman time to create some distance between them. When the guard began to approach one of the main staircases, Lovisa had to stop, because lamps lit this part of the house and she knew she would be seen; but before giving up, she did manage to overhear a conversation between the guard and someone else, presumably another guard. The first guard ordered the second guard to run to the Keep and summon Benni, for Ferla desired his presence, immediately. "It's an emergency," the guard said.

Quickly, Lovisa turned and ran back to the attic. Creeping up the stairs again, feeling her way to the far wall, she tucked herself into her corner, under one of the huge, sloping windows. Snowflakes tapped against the glass.

The guard returned, this time with a blanket slung over one shoulder and a steaming drink in one hand. She knocked on the door and was allowed inside. Briefly, Lovisa heard Ferla's harsh voice, and the queen responding. Pari saying something next, in a whiny, confused voice. Then the guard shut the door.

For a long time, nothing. Silence, interrupted only by the scrape of snowflakes on glass and the occasional push of wind. Cold radiated from the windows. Lovisa was glad for her fur coat. Gladder still that her father was coming, for certainly sense would return when he arrived, wouldn't it? None of this could be real, none of it could be so terrible, once Benni had arrived. Pari would come out. Her father would explain, and the explanation would make sense.

Finally, footsteps, hard and fast, and Benni came running up the stairs. Lovisa had never seen her father run, ever. He crossed the room and pounded on the door. When it opened, Lovisa heard Pari's voice, high-pitched. Then Benni went in and the door slammed. She heard his voice, urgently raised, but couldn't make out his words. Then she thought she heard her mother screaming back, in fury. She thought she heard the word "No!"

Lovisa's mind was still stupid and slow. She focused on the story she would tell her parents: She was in love with Pari Parnin. What was wrong with that? He was rich, from a good, Ledra family. She'd brought him up here because it was the most private place she could think of. She had no idea who the girl in the room was. A guest, maybe? Sleeping up here because she was ill, perhaps? In quarantine?

Lovisa grasped her hair, knowing, even in her numb state, that her parents wouldn't believe any part of that story.

The door opened again. Ferla stepped out with her fox, holding the lamp, followed by Benni and the guard. Benni and the guard carried something long and heavy and sagging, wrapped in a blanket.

It was a body. Of course Lovisa understood it was a body. She even understood, from its height and girth, that it was Pari's body. She saw it; it was unmistakable; and yet it was impossible. Her mind rejected utterly what her eyes saw.

Ferla locked the door, her every movement stiff, deliberate, angry. The figures carried their burden not to the stairs that led down to the house, but to the stairs that led up to the roof and the airship. They ascended the steps together, an awkward parade, while Lovisa crouched in the corner, incredulous, beginning to shake. The fox brought up the rear. Once, he swung his head to Lovisa, eyes gleaming, staring at the corner where she was losing her mind.

Benni was struggling with his grip. His hand slipped and a golden-green scarf Lovisa recognized emerged from the blanket. Ferla made an impatient noise.

"Maybe you'd like to carry it," Benni snapped at Ferla.

"Maybe I'd like to carry it?" Ferla repeated, her voice falling into the room like icicles crashing onto the ground. "Maybe *I'd* like to carry it? Have I wanted *any* of this? *You* did this. *You* created this situation, and every nightmare before it, with your precious ambitions. Or should I call them delusions? Can you not see that if you'd just rescued her, like a normal human being, then you'd be the hero who worked with the silbercows to rescue the Queen of Monsea? No one would've blinked twice at anything you did after that! My own brother, Benni. *My own brother!*"

"But now we have her!" said Benni. "It changes the game, don't you see? We have so many options! Monsea will pay for her. Estill will too!"

"We don't need ransom money!" Ferla almost screamed. "We never needed to hurt anyone! We were going to do everything legally! I was going to give you your zilfium vote! You never would have had to break a single law! *We had a plan!*"

Their voices became muffled as they rose. Then the heavy trapdoor on the roof closed behind them, and Lovisa could hear no more.

Shivering in the attic, Lovisa kept trying to push her mind to a place of understanding, but it was like her thoughts were made of smoke.

Her hands were wet and she realized she was crying. Then she was sobbing, gasping for breath, shoving her fur sleeve into her mouth to muffle the sound. Sobbing like Viri, like she was five years old. Like she'd gone running to Benni and Benni had knocked her down, slammed his library door in her face.

How could she revise her comprehension of—she couldn't hold on to the words—of someone she'd trusted, always. Someone she loved.

After a while, she made herself stop crying. She thought she could hear her parents' angry voices above her, still arguing on the roof. *Listen,* she told herself, but then she became afraid of what would happen if she learned more things. She didn't want to know any more things.

She heard her mother's voice more clearly, then the creak of the trapdoor. Springing to her feet, groping her way down the stairs, Lovisa fled to the room with the broken window lock and climbed out, lowering herself onto the trellis, then the tree. Her hands were numb and sore, clumsy. The snow had turned icy and sharp, stinging her cheeks.

She forced herself to run back to campus, pushing her legs through fatigue. There was no curfew on the night of the prime minister's party, so she didn't need a pass.

In her dorm room, she kicked off her shoes and climbed into bed. Then she waited for sleep to take all of it away.

PART THREE

The Keeper

The silbercows brought a gift to the creature.

It was the corpse of a boy, to add to her treasures. The boy was wrapped in a blanket from which a beautiful golden-green scarf had escaped, billowing around his head like the filaments of a forest fish. He had heavy metal chains around his ankles.

Thank you, said the creature, startled and touched by the gift, but also worried, because the silbercows looked worried. She positioned the boy on the deck of her Storyworld, admiring him. He had deep, gray-brown skin and a thatch of dark hair, but she knew that in time, his skull would turn white and wonderfully ghoulish.

Then she waited while the silbercows rested. They'd approached from a great distance, balancing the boy on their noses and their backs. The body had kept slipping off because of the weight of the metal around his ankles. She'd watched them struggling, their injured bodies bobbing unevenly toward her, her big, beating heart surging with happiness. Whenever they were gone for a long time, she'd start to feel anxious about whether they were safe.

Time stretched out, and still they didn't speak.

Thank you for this treasure, she finally said.

You're welcome, they told her. *How is your missing tentacle?*

It hurts less than the last time I saw you, she said, which was true, but it still hurt a lot.

The silbercows continued to float there, looking pensive.

How are your injuries? she asked.

The silbercows told her that their injuries were fine today.

Are they? she said. *Because I'm getting the impression that something's wrong.*

They told her that it was just their usual worries, then nudged their noses toward her new treasure. *We couldn't save him,* they said.

Oh dear! she said. *Do you mean you had to watch him die?*

They explained that no, he was already dead when they found him. Some humans had dropped his body out of an airship.

Oh! she said. *I saw some humans drop out of an airship that time, and steal that other human from the sea.*

Yes. The silbercows said they remembered. And of course they did; the massacre of their friends had happened that night. The creature was sorry for reminding them. *The metal eggs full of fire also drop into the sea from airships,* the silbercows reminded her, for they'd told her this before. People threw the metal eggs out of airships into the sea, then there was a moment of quiet, then there was an explosion. If the silbercows didn't get away fast enough, terrible things happened.

The creature went quiet, because she found herself formulating a brilliant idea. She puffed herself up a little, making her tentacles long and eye-stems alert, because she was proud of herself.

I have an idea, she announced.

The silbercows all wanted to know her idea immediately.

Airships are bad, she said.

The silbercows were not as staggered by her idea as she'd expected them to be. They looked at one another with knowing expressions, then told her that sometimes airships could be good, with people in them who cared about silbercows and wanted to hear their stories. Some humans in airships told them stories too, stories about humans. Sometimes, the silbercows and the humans could put their stories together and make sense of what was happening on land and in the sea. They asked her, *Do you remember the stories we've told you?*

Yes. You don't need to tell me again, said the creature hastily, then hummed a little, to discourage them. Since the day she'd lost her tentacle, they'd told her many of the stories behind her own treasures, and stories of other things too, happening in other parts of the ocean she hadn't seen. Some were stories about accidents, like a storm breaking a ship apart. Others were stories about humans hurting each other. She reached her limit very fast.

The silbercows told her that there was something they wanted to ask her, related to stories.

What is it? she said, suddenly nervous, for they were looking at one another in a particular way, with that shine they got in their big, dark eyes whenever they talked about the Keeper.

We spoke with some new humans, they said. *We learned something about one of your treasures.*

So? said the creature, not knowing where this was going, but definitely not liking it.

Do you remember that time you were a hero? they asked.

CHAPTER TWENTY-TWO

LOVISA HARDLY SLEPT on the night she discovered the Queen of Monsea in the attic.

Her muscles ached every time she moved; her head throbbed. The key, still hanging on its string around her neck, felt like it was imprinting itself into her chest.

Before light touched her window, she scrabbled upright and found her shoes, then the door. She was still wearing her party dress. Outside, that northern boy, Nori Orfa, was in the corridor, leaving Nev's room. He twisted his mouth at Lovisa when he saw her, cocky, interrogative.

"Morning," he said, in a manner she recognized. He was flirting with her, in the act of leaving another girl's room.

She summoned some strategy from somewhere. "If you're lying to Nev," she said to him, "you're going to regret it."

His eyebrows shot up with humor. "Oh? What are you going to do?" he said, with barely a northern lilt. Pretending to be Ledran.

"Write a letter to your girlfriend back home, for starters."

"I don't have a girlfriend back home," he said, looking a little uncomfortable.

"Oh, Sibra Liona isn't your girlfriend?" said Lovisa. Then, as his face turned nasty, she pulled her door shut again, because she didn't have the energy for this right now. She didn't know who Sibra Liona was. It was only a name she'd heard, sobbed by a girl Lovisa knew who'd been involved with Nori. Some girlfriend back home Nori had lied about. But Lovisa would write to her, if Nori pushed her. What a letter that would be. "Hi. I'm not sure who you are and you've never heard of me, but if you're Nori's girlfriend, did you know he lies about you and has sex with everything that moves? You can trust me, because I know his type." *Because I* am *his type,* she thought to herself, understanding, with a sudden avalanche of shame, that it was true. *I use people for sex too. I destroy lives.*

She stood in the dark, waiting. Then, after she'd given him enough time to clear off, she crept downstairs to Pari's bedroom. When no one answered her tap, she opened the door and stuck her head in. Of course the room was empty. She'd known it would be.

Moments later, she pushed out into the cold morning, pulling her coat closed and avoiding the streetlamps. The ambles opened just before sunrise on Sundays, and there was something Lovisa needed before the rest of the world woke.

SOMETIME LATER, BACK in the dormitory, her expression flat, her hair and clothing neat as they always were for breakfast, she went down to the dining room. There, she joined Mari Devret, who was at a small table by himself.

He was musing over a cup of tea. "Did you have a good time at the gala?" he asked her.

"Yes," she responded automatically. "You?"

"All right," he said. "I came back early. Got bored."

"You studied, didn't you."

He smiled over his tea. "Possibly."

"Predictable."

"Everyone else thinks I snuck away to do something more thrilling with people more popular, so don't tell."

"I never would."

"I saw you sneak out," said Mari casually, leaving it hanging. It was a mild question. He would never ask directly.

"Pari and I eventually went our separate ways," she said, after a moment's deliberation. "It didn't come to much."

"Ah. I'll admit I was a little surprised. At you," he added, when she raised an eyebrow. "Not your type."

"Oh? What's my type?"

"Someone who doesn't talk about it afterward." He poured himself another cup from the pot on the table. "Want some?"

"I've ordered my own," said Lovisa, knowing that Mari still drank the northern, grassy brew that was Nev's favorite, as an act of self-indulgent gloominess. Lovisa preferred the stronger, sharper teas popular in Ledra.

Nev came into the dining room then, her fox kit scampering around her feet. Almost imperceptibly, Mari stiffened.

Lovisa studied him for one tired moment, then decided he was better off knowing. "I saw a boy coming out of her room early this morning," she said. "I'm sorry, Mari."

"Who was it?" he asked sharply.

"I didn't see," she lied.

He snorted, trying to keep his expression nonchalant, but Lovisa saw the hurt sitting there. "I appreciate you telling me."

"She never appreciated you," said Lovisa, meaning it.

Mari snorted again. "That's not true, but whatever. I should probably stop moping."

"And stop drinking that disgusting cow-feed tea. You're a Ledra boy. Act like one."

His smile was genuine. He set his cup down onto the table, then, a moment later, got up and left, probably to comfort himself with more studying. Mari's grades were especially good when he was depressed.

Nev sat at a table by herself, on the other side of the hall. Her little kit leaned against her ankles as she ate, staring rather disconcertingly at Lovisa, who felt she'd had enough attention from foxes to last a lifetime.

What would Nev do if she knew the Queen of Monsea was imprisoned in the Cavenda attic?

Lovisa imagined Nev rescuing Queen Bitterblue dramatically, with fierce eyes and straight shoulders and a righteous dignity that made Lovisa feel like a coward for leaving the queen to suffer, for running away. Whatever. It was easy for Nev. She didn't have Ferla for a mother. *Or,* thought Lovisa, *Benni for a father.*

At that moment, Benni appeared in the dining room doorway. He stood tall and handsome as usual, sleek in a dark fur coat, a father to be proud of, a warm expression on his face as he glanced around the room. When he saw Lovisa, he motioned for her to come.

Punctured by her own shame, Lovisa stood and followed him.

THEY CLIMBED TO her room, Lovisa fighting off a strange panic.

Once inside, he spoke gently. "Sit down, Lovisa," he said.

He pointed to the bed, but she went to the desk chair. Its hardness made her feel less insubstantial. He sat on the bed across from her, very low to the floor, his hands on his high knees. He looked silly, actually. It was confusing.

"I'm not sure what you think you saw last night, Lovisa," he said. "But it's nothing you need to worry yourself about, because it's no longer an issue."

"What do you mean, it's no longer an issue?" she said, incredulous.

"The person you think you saw," he said, "is no longer in our care."

He means the queen is dead, thought Lovisa, with a sudden shock of understanding. *Because I found her, and saw her, they decided they had to kill her.*

A wave of bleakness broke against her. "It was never an issue for me," she said, hearing her own dull voice telling the lie. "Whatever you're doing, I'm on your side."

"That's certainly good to hear," he said. "Your mother and I both love you very much, Lovisa. But your recent behavior has made us wonder. I'm afraid your mother is quite angry. I think it's fair to say that your brothers are taking the brunt of it this morning."

Lovisa was choking on tears, that her father should say that so casually. "But they shouldn't be punished for something I did."

He shrugged. "Well, you know your mother. You might have expected it. Why did you go into the attic room last night, Lovisa?"

"It's a room with privacy," she started, but he held up a hand. Shook his head.

"I'm afraid that act won't work on us again, Lovisa. Not after last night. You used that poor boy, didn't you?"

"Where is he?" asked Lovisa, her voice cracking. "What did you do with him?"

"Pari Parnin took it into his head to leave school and travel," said Benni.

Lovisa cried out in disbelief, but Benni's face was smooth and calm as he continued. "We asked him where he meant to go, but he wouldn't say. Impulsive boy, isn't he? You'll be hearing the rumors soon. I think you understand how your mother will feel if you contradict those rumors in any way, Lovisa? She's already disappointed in your behavior. As am I, I'm afraid."

Lovisa couldn't answer. Her mind was whirling with new, bewildered thoughts of Katu. *"My own brother!"* Ferla had cried last night, blaming Benni for things Lovisa hadn't understood. Katu had also supposedly taken it into his head to travel, leaving no word, saying no goodbyes. Her father had been the one to tell her so. What if he'd lied about Katu, the way he was lying about Pari? But hadn't Katu been cashing checks in Kamassar and Borza? Arni Devret, who was Katu's banker, had mentioned it once. Lovisa was almost certain. So then, why had Ferla yelled *"My own brother"*?

"How did you get a key to the attic room?" asked Benni.

"I've had it since I was a child," Lovisa whispered, making up a likely story. "I stole it from Mother years ago and had a copy made. I was scared she would put me in there and forget about me."

"So you've been lying to us for years," he said. "And sneaking, and stealing. And now we're all faced with the consequences. Give me the key."

"I don't have it."

"Your mother told me to come home with that key," said Benni. "If I don't, I expect your brothers will be the ones to suffer for it. I also expect she'll come to you herself, looking for it."

Lovisa knew this was meant to frighten and shame her into acquiescence. It was also probably true. She reached into her shirt, pulled the string over her head, and held the attic key, its glass gemstone sparkling, out to him. Benni rose, took it from her, and looked down at her for a moment with a grave and mournful expression.

"Your mother and I love you, Lovisa," he said again.

Then he left the room.

ALONE, LOVISA LAY on her bed, curled into a ball.

The queen was dead. Pari was dead. Katu was "traveling," and Lovisa found herself unable to prod that thought any further for the moment. Her father was a stranger. Lovisa's mind was blank, her body empty of instinct or feeling.

After a while, she got up and lit her stove. A soporific tea would make her sleep.

The tea didn't help much. For a few hours, she passed back and forth from sleep to waking, but was afraid that drinking more of it would make her sick. It was Sunday. Sunday dinner at home was impossible; she couldn't go home. She doubted her father would come to collect her. Just in case he did, Lovisa got up and went to knock on Mari's door.

Mari's room was full of boys lounging on the floor and bed, all of them reading or writing, all snacking idly on cakes from an expensive Flag Hill bakery.

Lovisa needed something physical, something to tire her out and distract her. "Anyone want to go to the ambles?" she said. "I'm bored."

"I'll go, when I finish this page," said Kep Gravla, probably the last person in the room Lovisa would've chosen, because he was self-centered and insecure and never shut up. His family's house was next door to Lovisa's in Flag Hill and she'd spent her childhood avoiding him.

"Mari?" she said, because the most annoying people were more tolerable if Mari was there too. "You want to join us?"

"Which amble are you going to?"

"Any. I want some hot salted caramel. And maybe there's some good music," she added, knowing that Mari had a weakness for both of those things.

He gave her a look, and a smirk, because Mari knew what Lovisa thought of Kep Gravla. "I guess I could take a little break," he said.

"Good. Anyone else?" said Lovisa, not really waiting for a reply. "I'll get my coat."

It was Lovisa's second trip to an amble that day, but vastly different from her first. Once Mari agreed to go, most of the others did too, so that an uproar of obnoxious boys descended upon the nearest shopping area. The purveyors of certain shops—sweets, games, books—perked up at the sight of them, while other faces closed. Lovisa saw a man who sold fresh flowers drop a pile of roses with a glare in their direction as a woman who'd been dithering over them left, driven off by the raucous laughter of the boys buying hot drinks at the store next door.

"What's on your mind, Lovisa?" Mari asked her, peeking over a steaming cup of salted caramel. "You're standing there with your arms crossed like an angry professor."

"Does Kep know that his crass mouth drove all the shoppers away from the flower shop?"

"Probably," said Mari. "He's probably happy about it."

"Why are you even his friend, Mari?"

"You're his friend too."

"But you actually *like* him."

"Doesn't that make it more excusable that I'm his friend?"

"It makes me question your taste in human beings."

With a quiet lift of his eyebrows, Mari went to the flower shop, still sipping his caramel. He was there for some time, while the boys continue to shout, then shove one another until one of them inevitably dumped his caramel onto another. Lovisa rubbed her aching head, hating this, but knowing that nothing better awaited her anywhere else. She wondered, briefly, what Nev was doing. Probably rescuing a needy animal from some needy animal fate, and feeling good about herself.

When Mari came back, his arms were full of lilies, pansies, and violets. "He grows them in a glass greenhouse he built himself, on the roof of the shop," he said. "In winter, he pours water onto hot coals to make steam. Isn't that interesting?"

He handed a bunch of flowers to Lovisa. Then he moved among his friends, passing a small bouquet to each boy in turn. Of course they found this hilarious, stuck them in their buttonholes and wound them into one another's hair. One of them tucked a pansy behind Mari's ear and kissed him. Some of the flowers fell, getting trampled and ground into the dirty snow. Lovisa understood that Mari had bought them as an apology to the flower vendor. She could see the flower vendor's face, though, carefully blank, and she wondered if Mari understood that he might not enjoy watching a herd of rich boys destroying the flowers he'd grown, by turning winter into summer, with great care, in the glass greenhouse he'd built himself.

Without saying goodbye to the boys, she slipped away and went back to the dorm. She put her own flowers into a vase that she set beside a drawing she kept above her desk, one of Viri's representations of the Keeper. Reaching into a drawer, she found a somewhat linty piece of samklavi candy someone had pressed on her a few days ago, sniffed it cautiously, then tried to eat it, thinking it might connect her to her uncle or at least shock her into a different state of mind. It was so vile that she spit it out, gagging.

Again, she tried to sleep. Again, it didn't work. Every time she closed her eyes, she saw her father and that guard carrying Pari's body in a blanket. She heard her mother saying, "*You* created this situation, and every nightmare before it." Every nightmare before it. How many nightmares were there? "*We had a plan!*" her mother had screamed.

What was their plan?

That night, in her soft pajamas and fur-collared robe, she snuck down the corridor and tapped on Mari Devret's door.

He opened it immediately, a pen in hand, yawning and bleary-eyed, but awake. "Come in," he said, returning to his desk and sitting down, not seeming particularly surprised. "You've had something on your mind today. Out with it."

"I need a favor."

"Okay, I'm listening."

"Sleep with me," she said.

Now he *was* surprised, his eyebrows shooting up. "Do you mean, have sex with you?"

"Yes."

"As a *favor*?"

"I can't sleep. I'm stressed out beyond anything. I can't get my mind to stop spinning—"

"Why do I feel like this isn't how you seduce other people?" he said indignantly.

"There's nothing I can do," she said. "I need a distraction. You don't have to worry, I won't confuse what it means. We can do it, maybe we'll both like it, and maybe my mind will stop, and afterward I'll sleep. I mean, I'm not assuming you want to. But if it sounds okay, would you please sleep with me?"

"Lovisa," he said, his face still taut with surprise. "It's a bad idea. We've been friends forever."

"So? That's why I came to you."

"I want to keep being friends forever," he said. "I don't want to complicate things."

"It's not complicated," she said. "I know you're in love with Nev. You know I'm not in love with you. What's complicated?"

"But I don't want to change things!"

"If I don't sleep," Lovisa said, "I'm going to lose my mind."

Mari studied Lovisa for a moment, like he was trying to diagnose a complicated case. He'd always played doctor when they were little, loved to treat stomachaches or headaches or remove a splinter from her foot with great ceremony, as if it were a dangerous operation. She'd always liked it too, though she'd never admitted it to him. Mari was gentle, careful. It was nice to feel focused on, cared for.

Then he went to a chest at the foot of his bed and fumbled around inside it for a while. His hands emerged with a large wooden box. Sitting on the rug, he pulled a number of folded wooden boards from the box. Unfolded, they hooked together to make a carved map of city blocks, some containing ambles, some containing school buildings, some with government buildings, some with residences, hospitals, a dock area, and so on.

"Play City with me," he said. "If you can't sleep after that, we'll talk about it."

"You still have your City board?"

Dropping to the floor beside him, she fingered the pile of small, brightly clothed figurines that represented different kinds of people: shopkeepers, professors, sailors, guards, house staff, scientists, society figures, Parliamentary representatives, and so on. Their bodies were made of wood stained brown like her hands, their faces carefully carved, but their clothing was real fabric, their hair dark patches of felted wool. There was also a pile of carved wooden foxes.

"These are the same pieces we played with when we were six," she said, fingering the worn silk suit of a society man.

"I'm sentimental, okay?"

"I don't remember all the rules."

"You want a straight, uninterrupted line of five of the right kind of person on the right kind of street," he said. "You try to build your lines and interrupt my lines. Merchants, sailors, society people, and students can be shopping. House staff, foxes, and Parliament reps can go anywhere. Professors, students, and—"

"I remember all that," said Lovisa.

"If one of us manages a line of five," said Mari, "that person wins. But if you're certain you're losing, then it's better to let me win, because if no one wins, then we're not taking care of the earth and the Keeper rises up and crushes us all."

"I never got that part," said Lovisa. "If I'm going to lose, why shouldn't you be crushed?"

"Cavenda family motto?" said Mari.

Lovisa tried hard for an amused expression. She didn't think she succeeded, and she was pretty sure Mari noticed. But he said nothing, just divided the figurines between them. The foxes were plain wooden carvings with no fur or clothing, but tiny yellow gemstones made their eyes. One had a downturned nose and a quizzical expression and was stained darker than the others. Lovisa had always liked that one best in Mari's set. She also favored one of the sailors who wore a bright pink shirt with a red scarf and one of the wealthy ladies who had a perfect tiny amethyst at her throat. But she wasn't going to ask Mari for them. She wasn't six anymore.

He remembered and gave them to her anyway.

"You want to start?" he asked.

"This is a weird alternative to sex."

"Let's just play, okay? And tell me why you're so stressed out. Is it about Pari? I heard a rumor."

Lovisa took a breath. "What rumor?"

"That he's left for the Royal Continent," said Mari. "He was failing a couple of his classes and decided he'd rather leave than fail out. A spontaneous adventure."

"Without saying goodbye to anyone?" Lovisa said, because it seemed like what she would say, were this news to her.

"Yeah. Did he mention any of this last night?"

Lovisa focused on placing her pieces on the board. "There wasn't a lot of talking."

"Ew," said Mari. "And again, you came here to seduce me? Your technique needs work."

"I wouldn't try to seduce you, Mari," she said sharply. "If we have sex, it won't be because I lie."

"Seduction doesn't necessitate lying, you know."

"Whatever. Do you really like Pari?"

"He's had a hard go of it. You know that. His mother is dead, his father is always abroad, and when he's not abroad he isn't a nice person."

"Pari is a spoiled, rich, arrogant Ledra boy," Lovisa said.

"So am I," said Mari, with a small smile.

"But he's mean."

"Maybe I would be mean, if I had an unkind father."

A tear was suddenly rolling down Lovisa's face, fueled by exhaustion, confusion, and now, resentment at the ease with which Mari always inhabited kindness. His parents were kind. His life had been kind to him. He was handsome, and smart, and big, and popular, and everyone trusted and liked him. He had no ambition beyond what was expected of him, and what was expected of him was that he do what he liked. It cost him nothing to think kindly of mean people; it was instinctive for him. And his kindness made Lovisa feel like the lowest possible type of person, the kind of person who came from parents like hers. And now it was her fault that people were dead.

"Lovisa?" said Mari. "What did I say?"

"Nothing."

"You're crying. You never cry."

"I'm not crying," she lied. "I'm just tired. Leave me alone, Mari."

"You never told me why you're so anxious."

How good it would feel to tell him everything, make him share her problems. But she couldn't. There were no solutions, and even hints would endanger him. Pari was dead.

"Tell me what's going on," he said.

"Shut up, Mari," she snapped. "Just back off." The tears were making her furious, but they were also making her sleepy. She could feel herself sagging.

"Why don't you get into my bed?" he said. "See if you can sleep. And I'm not having sex with you, if you think that's what I mean."

Lovisa was far too tired to have sex with anyone now, especially someone she resented for his perfect life and his perfect behavior, his perfect heart. Clutching her favorite fox and her amethyst lady in one hand, she climbed into Mari's bed. Her other hand felt for the new attic-room key she'd had made in the nearest amble early that morning, guessing that her parents would confiscate hers. She'd decided to keep it on a string inside her clothing always, hanging low between her breasts, where she could control who found it. Of course, it was basically useless now, and sweaty against her skin. This one had a fake purple gemstone, even sharper and scratchier than the last stupid key.

A thought touched her. If the queen was dead, why had her father wanted the key back so urgently?

"Do you need anything?" said Mari. "A drink? Do you have enough blankets?"

"Stop fussing!"

She heard him snort. Then she heard him stand and start to walk away.

"Mari?" she said, frightened.

His voice came from the other side of the room. "Hm?"

"You're not leaving, are you?"

"I'm just getting you another blanket," he said, returning to her, unceremoniously dumping something warm and soft onto her back. "I'll be right here. Go to sleep."

CHAPTER TWENTY-THREE

LOVISA WOKE THE next morning needing proof that the queen was dead.

She bumbled through her classes, carefully avoiding her mother in the halls, trying to decide what to do. She couldn't search the house during the day because her father's schedule was unpredictable. A nighttime search was out of the question, because of her mother's fox.

Monday, Tuesday, Wednesday night that week, she ran home after dark, snuck onto the property, and watched the attic window for signs of life. More guards were on duty than usual outside the house. If the queen was dead, why would the house need more guards? But though she hid behind a tree, shivered in her fur coats, and never shifted her gaze from the window, nothing ever happened. No movement, no light. This didn't prove anything, of course. The window was too high to access from inside, and the queen, if she lived, certainly had no lamp or candles.

Could she get to that window? It was possible to climb partly up the outer face of the house, in theory. She and Mari had mapped it as children, identifying a stone's sharp edge where a toe could balance, a crack where some fingers could brace. Protrusions of windowsills, areas of slanting roof, et cetera. They'd never tried it, of course, just as they'd never tried the tree-to-trellis route. The climbing route stopped a floor below the window, where the face of the house became perfectly smooth.

What if there was a way to climb partly up, then do something with a rope?

It was when Lovisa found herself thinking along these lines that she would scramble over the wall again and push back to the dorm, fighting with herself, sometimes almost crying in frustration, over her wish to stop caring about whether the queen was alive or not. What did it matter? If she was alive, what could Lovisa do?

Every night, she tried to sleep in her own room; then gave up and tapped on Mari's door. They played City, or did homework together. Then she slept in his bed, a beautiful, deep night's sleep that her body only ever surrendered to if she was in this room, with Mari near. She woke in the morning when pink light touched her face, then opened her eyes to the sight of Mari on the rug, wrapped in blankets threaded with gold, his brown face slack and peaceful, snoring gently. In the morning light, his freckles were more noticeable.

"Okay," she'd say, dropping her feet to the floor. "You can have your bed back. See you later."

With a sigh and grumble, Mari would awaken. "When I'll destroy you at City?" he'd say, smiling, his eyes still closed.

"Whatever," she'd say, seeing the little boy with big ears and bone-thin face in that smile, the boy who'd been like a brother to her once, or like a brother was supposed to be, if brothers were allowed to be happy. Sometimes she knelt and kissed his cheek as she left the room, surprised by her rush of fondness, which felt an awful lot like sadness.

She could sleep in his room because Mari was safe. He wasn't going to turn into a different person with no warning. Sometimes she woke in the confusion of a fading nightmare. The sight of him at his desk lit by a single lamp, the sound of his pen scratching, calmed her panic. Listening to him working, she fell asleep again.

They talked about sex sometimes, but only as a concept. They'd decided together that it wasn't something they would do, at least not until they'd talked about it more.

"Do you remember that time at that party, when we were little?" he asked her once, grinning. "Listening to the women?"

Yes, she remembered. It had been one of the Varana parties, this one at Minta Varana's house, maybe Ta's sixth or seventh birthday. Mari, seeking Lovisa out, had found her in a dark library far away from the other children, where she'd been snooping on the mothers in the next room. They'd been talking about the sex they had with their husbands and wives, "and also *not* with their husbands and wives," she'd whispered to Mari in a fascinated voice. "Put your ear to this wall."

"Okay," Mari had said, reluctantly interested, as he always was when Lovisa snooped. The acts the women had described had sounded improbable. It had seemed unbelievable, really, that grown-ups would want to do those things to each other. The children had had to run into another room before their gasps and laughter gave them away.

Mari thought the memory was funny, because of how his understanding of sex had changed. But Lovisa was more caught up on the cheating, the lying, and how childish the memory made her feel. She had the unsettled feeling that Mari's attitudes about sex were normal and hers weren't. Why didn't she feel attracted to him, like a normal person would? She wanted to have sex with him as a distraction, to force her body to feel something different from what it always felt. But she knew that when Mari talked about it, he was talking about something tempting, something delicious he thought they should resist. He was talking about pleasure. And everyone on campus talked about how attractive Mari was, his fine face, his height, his popularity.

But all Lovisa's body had room for right now was this fear, screaming from her core to her skin, making her certain that something terrible was going to happen. That Ferla wanted to silence her. That Benni had done worse things than she knew. That the Queen of Monsea might be dead or in the attic needing her help. Pleasure? She couldn't imagine it. She also didn't deserve it, nor did she deserve the comfort of a warm body in bed beside her, helping her sleep.

On her way to the privy late one night, she almost ran into Nev rounding a corner. Nev wore her coat; she'd only just come in. That little fox was prancing around her feet and she smelled like sweat and cold.

"Where do you always go so late?" Lovisa snapped at her.

"Why do you care?" Nev said, in a voice rough with exhaustion. Lovisa studied her curiously, wondering if Nev was wearing herself thin. No. She saw now that Nev had straw in her hair and a face that glowed with the kind of insuppressible joy Lovisa knew how to read. Nev was spending her nights in a stable or a kennel somewhere, maybe pretending to do animal medicine work, but really having sex with Nori Orfa. For pleasure, like a normal person. For an instant, Lovisa was on fire with jealousy.

She rubbed her hair, tried to rub away her intense feelings. "Just, don't get in trouble for missing curfew," she said.

"Why shouldn't I?" Nev demanded, bristling in irritation.

Because I couldn't bear it if you got expelled, and left me, Lovisa wanted to say, but didn't. Like Mari, Nev made her feel safe. She couldn't understand it, but she knew it was true.

On Friday night, Lovisa climbed the pokey rocks as usual and hid behind a tree, gazing up at the house.

The uselessness of this grueling daily endeavor was making her resentful, as she'd never been before, of this house. She'd always liked it unthinkingly, been proud of its grandeur, of the airship on its roof. But it was a prison; it was the prison her little brothers would become men in.

And then something happened, up near the roof, that made her feel like her lungs were trying to climb out of her body. A clattering noise, faint, but eventually repeated. Then repeated again, and again. She waited and listened a long time, holding her breath in agony whenever the guards circled by. Sometimes it was more of a tap or a scrape; other times, it was as if glass rang like a bell; and Lovisa was pretty sure it was coming from the attic window. What did it mean?

Half out of her mind, she began the climb up the face of the house.

She didn't get far, not even past the first story, before logic returned and she saw it was too dangerous and difficult. But she got high enough that she could hear it more clearly, and confirm for herself that it came from the attic window. It sounded like something small and hard crashing against the window glass, over and over.

The letter opener, Lovisa thought. *She's trying to break the window with the letter opener.* And, *Oh, I wish she would stop, because they'll hear her, and then they'll kill her.*

She's alive, she thought, dropping back down to the ground, rubbing her painful fingers against her coat, almost sobbing. *She's alive. What do I do?*

CHAPTER TWENTY-FOUR

BITTERBLUE WASN'T COPING well in her attic room.

It was a kind of torture to have little to do but think. Was this what it was like for the prisoners in her jails, all the time? When Bitterblue got home, she was going to learn more about her jails.

That young woman, that guard, visited most days with a bowl of soup or stew, but rarely brought water. When she did bring water, she put it in a shallow bowl on the floor by the door, just like she did with the food, except that it was an even more deliberate effort to cast Bitterblue as a pet, or a fox. As if Bitterblue should mind sharing the behavior of a fox. Of all the Keepish people Bitterblue had met since her arrival, the fox who visited her regularly was easily the one she liked and respected most. He kept her company. And he brought her things. One night when she was feeling more hopeless than usual, he'd brought her a pastry.

Bitterblue had come to think of that fox as *her* fox. He wasn't the only fox who visited. Sometimes she woke to several foxes blinking at her with incurious gold eyes. But her fox was different from the others. He had a long nose and particularly large and perky ears, and he *felt* different. She thought—she was almost sure—he might be touching her mind sometimes. That girl who'd burst in—Lovisa— had said that the fox was bonded to her mother, but then, why did the fox feel like he was trying to help? Did blue foxes ever defy their humans?

She'd found the vent in the wall behind her bed and the heat duct it served, pulling the bed from the wall with hurting hands. But the vent was too small for her to climb into. She'd cried for a few seconds about that discovery, for sometimes she allowed herself a brief burst of tears, to relieve some of her pent-up tension. She never let herself cry for more than a few seconds, though, because she couldn't afford to dehydrate herself.

Investigating the grate with stinging fingers, she'd discovered that amazingly, improbably, it swung outward on hinges made of a soft, fine yarn. If Lovisa's mother wanted the fox to enter and leave this room by the heat duct, wouldn't she just use wire, or actual hinges? Bitterblue had turned and stared at the fox, who'd been watching her quietly from the corner.

Then with her small, tired shoulders, she'd pushed the bed back to the wall. She'd climbed under the covers and curled herself around her aching hands.

BITTERBLUE WAS GOOD at thinking. She had plenty of experience focusing her thoughts, like tiny, sharp beams of light, through a frightening darkness. And the more she thought, the more convinced she became that she was missing a piece of the puzzle.

On the day that girl, Lovisa, had burst in on her, followed by the tall boy, then the guard, and then the small, frantic woman, Bitterblue had learned that she was probably in the attic of a private Ledra home and that Lovisa's father might be a politician, for the woman had told the guard to have him fetched immediately from the Keep.

She'd also guessed, though it seemed extraordinary, that the woman might be the current president of Winterkeep. She and Lovisa looked *so much* like Katu Cavenda, even down to that white streak in their hair. Bitterblue knew Katu had a niece and a few nephews; he'd talked about them, though she couldn't remember their names. And Katu's sister, Ferla, was the Keepish president. So—the president of Winterkeep had given her a map of Monsea showing Keepish and Estillan flags. Why would Winterkeep and Estill imagine they could win a war against Monsea? Why would Estill ally with Winterkeep? Bitterblue kept reaching the same unsettling conclusion. Winterkeep must have some military advantage of which she knew nothing. She was missing something—something big.

Bitterblue had tried to prevent that boy from becoming a sacrifice that night. In fact, she'd introduced herself to him as a Lienid visitor named Goldie, using the name of her own prison master back home. Lovisa's mother had stared at Bitterblue, gobsmacked, and indeed, it had been a silly, useless attempt at saving the life of a boy who, according to Lovisa's rushed words, was only there to have sex with Lovisa.

Then the guard had left, come back, and handed her a drink. A warm, delicious, steaming drink, in a mug! Parched, Bitterblue had taken a sip, then realized that of course it was a trick. Her head had gone fuzzy and stupid and confused. The next thing she knew, she'd woken in daylight to a room empty of everyone and everything, except her, of course, and the fox.

She had cried, briefly, for the fate of that boy. She'd cried about Katu as well, because she couldn't understand what it meant for him if his family was involved. Was he traveling, far away, ignorant, safe? Or was Katu also in danger? Bitterblue realized that she hadn't thought much about Katu, here in her prison. It made her feel obscurely guilty.

ON THE DAYS the guard brought water, she did not bring food. On the days she brought food, no water. Bitterblue took to making jokes with herself: It was lucky she had so many years of experience needing to function intelligently while in states of dire distress, or she'd never be able to think her way through this thing at all. Ha, ha. Giddon would've thought it was funny. *I am stronger than the way this is making me feel.*

Oh, Giddon. How I wish I could hear those words in your voice. My own voice is wearing thin.

BITTERBLUE HAD DEVELOPED a daily exercise regimen, as much to prevent herself from losing her mind as from her concerns about weakening. Her fingers and toes were healing well and she'd removed her bandages. She did stretches, as Katsa had taught her, and ran in place. She did push-ups and sit-ups and tried not to mind how quickly she became breathless and dizzy. She kept Katsa close in her mind, for Katsa, who'd taught her to fight, knew about conserving energy. Katsa was an expert at pushing her students, but never too far. And Bitterblue was frightened to push her exercise regimen too far, given how little food and water she was consuming.

One evening in the dark, she did a few parries and attacks, using her letter opener as a sword. She'd taken to thinking about killing the guard with the letter opener. Not because she wanted to think about it, but because she *had* to think about it.

Giddon? she thought. *No one is going to rescue me.*

She began to cry again, painful, tearless crying. Her lack of tears frightened her and she cried harder just to prove to herself that she could make tears. Then, for a brief moment, she lost hold of her judgment. With a vague idea of making a sheet rope to climb out the window like she'd done once with her mother to escape her father, she began to throw the letter opener against the glass.

A few minutes later, the fox came bursting through the vent and ran back and forth, yipping, yowling, throwing himself around the room. When the letter opener clattered down beside his frantic body, he leaped onto it, grasping it between his teeth. He stood before Bitterblue, the blade in his mouth, his limbs braced and trembling, his ears high, his eyes glowing gold, and Bitterblue stared back at him.

"Yes," she said, returning to herself. "I gather you think escape through the window is a bad idea." She touched her own face gently, touched her own neck, as if reminding herself of her own frontiers. "And maybe that's because you're on Lovisa's mother's side," she said. "But maybe it's because you don't want me to fall to my death."

Bitterblue, who hated heights, shuddered. "All right," she said. "I lost it there for a minute. I promise it won't happen again. From now on I'll only do wise things, like think about murdering the guard." Then she started laughing. "Oh," she said, sitting on the edge of her cot and rubbing her greasy, hurting braids with her greasy, sore fingers. "How I want a drink, and cake, and some cream puffs, and a toothbrush, and a bath."

And she thought of Giddon, shirtless and muddy, disappearing into his bathing room and splashing water around, while Lovejoy the cat climbed into her lap. And then he'd come out and sat in the chair with them. She'd leaned against him. And even with the anxiety of Skye's unread letter in her fist, she'd been happy.

She wondered, what would he say if he were here now? He would say something perceptive that would help her understand her situation better. And he would be funny, and make her giggle and take herself less seriously. Giddon had a special gift for conversations when she was discouraged. All conversations, really. She went to him sometimes feeling like the cleverest person, excited to talk about some new, clever thing she'd thought of, and see his face light up, and make him laugh. And sometimes, when they were talking, he said things that showed her hidden parts of him, and those moments were like stumbling upon unexpected treasure.

When this ordeal ended and they all got home again, surely the Council wouldn't take Giddon away from her right away, would they? Katsa and Po, Raffin and Bann would understand that she needed him, right?

Bitterblue didn't know why she was crying. But she knew she had to stop, because she couldn't afford to lose the water.

CHAPTER TWENTY-FIVE

FERLA CAVENDA WAS making new plans, and they were terrifying. Every time the fox dipped into her mind, her plans turned his body into a rigid sculpture of alarm.

Ferla had cared once about not getting people killed. She'd wanted a perfect life, one that would have made her father proud: the perfect Ledra house, all the money in the world. The perfect family: children to raise as she'd been raised, who would go off into the world and reflect their successes upon her, and a husband she loved, who shared her ambitions and cunning.

Then Benni had struck that boy down right in front of her eyes.

What was Ferla to do, if Benni kept making decisions that shattered her plans beyond any ability to recover them? How could he not see that everything they'd planned for was impossible now? And what came next? Was Ferla supposed to end up in *prison*? The Queen of Monsea could not be in her attic. It was an obstacle that had to be removed.

And Lovisa? Her own daughter! Lovisa knew too much, Lovisa was unpredictable. What was Ferla to *do*?

The fox did not entirely understand the roots of all these thoughts. He couldn't comprehend the details of what messes Benni had made. But he could feel and understand Ferla's feelings about them, as clear as if they were his own, and he had some ideas of things Ferla might do.

That night, after Benni had returned from dumping that boy into the sea, they'd fought, viciously. Ferla had always had a terrible temper, but Benni's could be fearsome too, when things got bad enough: slow, methodical, and not always smart. Benni's temper had been getting worse lately. His shipping business was losing money, and he was scared.

They hadn't stopped fighting until bedtime, when they'd turned toward each other with that focus that always, briefly, made the hard, sharp, inexhaustible ambitions of Ferla's nature drop away. Usually, after sex, Ferla let herself fall asleep. This time, she'd waited for Benni to fall asleep, then she'd risen from bed. She'd gone to her study.

At her desk, she'd sat with her back straight as a poker, surrounded by golden silbercow light, a strange, almost jubilant look on her face. She'd felt like . . . too many things. She'd felt like the end of something, and the beginning of something new, as if a limb were tearing away from her body while a different thing grew in its place, a distorted growth that would allow Ferla to do things she hadn't thought of before. Unnatural, wrong things.

I might go to sleep now, the fox said to her, shaking with his memories of that boy crashing down, a trickle of blood on his face, *if you don't need me.*

All right, Fox, said Ferla calmly, while that lumpy, raw scar tissue grew over the way she'd used to be.

THE LITTLE QUEEN was having a hard time of it. She was alive, and her hands and feet were healing. She was exercising, trying to stay strong. But she also spent a lot of time on her bed, curled in a ball of hunger, pain, and fear.

Or, thought the fox, tapping gently on her mind, maybe it would be more accurate to call it a ball of toughness. It was hard to get into her mind. She was like those other Monseans, Giddon and Hava, who lived in Quona Varana's house with his siblings: She often closed her mind, made a wall he couldn't push through.

Other times, though, she opened her mind, and he could feel the person she was. A hundred times a day, she told herself, *I'm stronger than the way they make me feel.* Then she would sit there, stubborn and fierce, trying to think her way out of her prison. The fox was trying to think her way out of the prison too, but it was a frustratingly fruitless exercise. Humans were not as easy to manipulate as he'd been led to believe as a kit, not when they were humans like Ferla or Benni.

The queen had figured out a lot, considering her isolation. She'd guessed that Ferla was careful, logical, the kind of person who might decide to kill her as the result of sound deduction. But she hadn't seen Benni; she'd been asleep by the time he arrived. So she hadn't seen him strike Pari. She couldn't know that there was a man involved who could kill her in an impulsive moment of deciding it was the best next step in a haphazard plan.

She'd also guessed too much about the fox. This was due partly to her sharp, stabby mind and partly to his own limitations when it came to watching her starve. The food deprivation was so distressing. It made the fox feel empty too, as if the hunger of this little stubborn queen made a hole inside him, beside his own well-fed tummy. He couldn't sneak her a water bowl, not without spilling it everywhere. But the night the Monseans had come to dinner, he'd brought her a pastry. She'd gobbled most of it down while he'd sat in a corner pretending not to care, then had a bad hour while her confused stomach tried to force it back up again. She'd done something surprising and clever: crawled under the bed and tucked the pastry remains inside the heat duct, to finish later. Then she'd said, "Thank you, fox," and gone back to thinking hard, tucked into the far corner of her bed.

She hadn't guessed that the two people she thought of most often, Giddon and Hava, had been downstairs, eating dinner, snooping.

Not even knowing she was alive. How close Giddon and Hava had come to finding the queen's rings, which Benni kept in the secret drawers of his desk. Then they would have known, and something would have happened to put an end to this torture.

THE NIGHT THE queen started throwing her letter opener against the window, a Friday, the fox was in his bed, feeling it happen. It frightened him to pieces. He strained to hold all the minds in the house and sense whether anyone overheard. At one point, that poor, miserable guard started up the steps to the attic and the fox went so far as to shout an undisguised command in her mind for her to run downstairs again. The guard had no idea where the sudden, urgent, panicked instinct came from, but she ran downstairs, which got her away from the noise.

Then the fox went to the attic room himself to put an end to it. He sprang upon the letter opener and held it in his mouth until the queen got her senses back. Her mind was more open than usual afterward; open, aching, unhappy, and vulnerable. She was thinking about that big, pale Monsean man, the one called Giddon.

Should I? thought the fox. *Shouldn't I?*

It was the question he'd recently started asking himself: Should he, shouldn't he, talk to her? Openly, no longer pretending? Since she suspected so much already?

Why did he want this so badly?

He decided he wouldn't. He'd do something else instead: Bring her the small envelope that had fallen from Giddon's pocket in Benni's library.

The fox brought the queen the envelope to make her happy. To comfort her while she thought about Giddon. But once she opened the envelope and stared at the notes inside, a horror overtook her. She began to gasp, sob. He suddenly understood, with a flash of impatience at his own stupidity for not anticipating this, that she thought it meant Giddon was dead. That her captors had learned something about him, killed him, and, in this very house, emptied his pockets. It was the first time the fox had ever known the queen to be flooded with despair and it was intolerable, it was the opposite of what he'd meant her to feel.

And so he overwhelmed her with a different feeling, trying to make it seem like it was coming from inside herself, rather than from him: a clear, singing sense that Giddon was safe. That the envelope was a gift, not a message of anything bad. A treasure. Didn't humans like treasures?

She calmed down after that. She dried her tears and looked at the little papers differently, with new questions, with wonder at Giddon for keeping them in a tiny envelope like this. She held them to her face as if they were precious. She tucked them back into their envelope, and tucked the envelope into the heat duct.

Then she stared hard at the fox, for a long time.

The fox wondered, as he wondered more and more lately, how any fox who cared about any human ever managed to keep the secrets of foxkind.

His seven siblings didn't have a lot of sympathy for his plight.

Very, very late on the same night he'd brought the small envelope to the queen, he sensed his siblings entering the Cavenda house, then making their way to Benni's library. All seven of them: Rascal, Rumpus, Lark, Gladly, Sophie (short for Sophisticated), Pickle, and Genius.

With a heavy sigh, the fox dragged himself out of bed again. In the library he found them perched together on Benni's desk, gathered around the little drawers.

What is it this time? he asked them wearily. *What can you possibly be doing?*

We're curious about these secret drawers, they said. *Is there a hidden latch?*

Why would you need to know if there's a hidden latch? he said. *Did Quona Varana send you here to steal?*

No, they said loftily. *Just to poke around.*

He didn't believe them. *Why?*

She didn't say! Just for fun!

You should tell her you won't! Humans aren't supposed to ask their foxes to trespass!

You are NO fun, they said. *You should've bonded to Quona, like we did. You could do it now, if you faked your own death. You know she lets us ride in her airship, don't you?*

He did know that, though he always tried to forget it. *So?*

So, our lives are much less stressful than yours! We never have to worry about sad humans in our attic who are dying or going insane.

That's great, he told them, pretty sure they weren't picking up on his sarcasm. *Congratulations. Have you told Quona about the queen in my attic?*

No.

I'm relieved you don't just tell her everything, by default.

She hasn't asked us about the queen in your attic, they said.

Wait, but if she did, you would?

Why not?

Well, how would you explain that you knew? Would you tell her about my heat ducts?

Oh, we'd find some innocent way, they said. *Calm down, Ad.*

If she asked, would you tell her I'm disloyal to my human?

Of course not!

HAVE YOU TOLD HER THE SECRETS OF FOXKIND?

OF COURSE NOT!

Are you sure she hasn't figured them out on her own?

Listen, they said. *Even if she had, it would be safe.*

WHAT?!

She's safe! they said. *She's not like your human! She's not a danger to foxes! You're the one who should be more careful!*

She's completely bewitched you! he said. *She has you here, poking at a desk for no reason she cares to explain! And if she knows our secrets, then she's a danger! Don't you know the kinds of things foxes have done to humans in the past? Humans who know too much?* He was referring to the stories of foxes who'd killed humans who'd learned the secrets of foxkind. All foxes knew those stories.

Those stories are apocryphal, they said. *How could a fox ever kill a human? And anyway, NOW what are you suggesting? That we should kill the human we love most? That we're capable of murder? What do you take us for?*

He took them for a bunch of sloppy kits who were possibly drunk on too much love and happiness, and consequently capable of anything, but there was no point in saying so. They wouldn't be able to see it.

Even if Quona spoiled me night and day, he contented himself with saying, *I wouldn't want to live in her house.*

We don't all, you know, they said.

Don't all what?

Live in her house. She has more foxes than us seven.

What?!

She has one who lives at the Cliff Farm, they said. *One who lives at the Keep. One who lives at the Varanas' airship hangar. One who lives in the dormitories.*

Why does she have a fox who lives in the dormitories?

Because she worries about some of the students. Especially one named Nev. Also her niece, Ta Varana. Also Lovisa Cavenda. The fox keeps an eye on them all.

What?! said the fox. *Quona is especially spying on Lovisa Cavenda?*

Yes.

The fox didn't like this, not at all. *Why?*

Maybe because Quona is a student of human nature, they said airily.

But not just any human's nature? Lovisa's specifically?

Well, aren't you also a student of Lovisa's nature specifically?

That's because I'm trying to keep her alive! he said. *I have a reason! Will the fox in the dorms talk to me?*

She's a kit, they said dismissively.

The fox didn't know what that was supposed to mean, but he'd sensed Lovisa creeping onto the Cavenda grounds these past few nights. He knew Lovisa suspected the queen was alive. What he didn't know was if she appreciated how much danger she was in.

He told his siblings that the hidden drawers in Benni's desk contained nothing but boring love letters from Ferla. It was a lie, of course, but he didn't trust them with the truth that they contained the queen's rings. Then he waited for them to leave the house. After that, even though it went against every part of his nature to scamper across an icy city in the dark, the fox visited Quona's kit in the dorms.

THE KIT LIVED with a girl named Nev, who was an animal medicine student.

The fox stood on the pavement outside. *Did you see Lovisa Cavenda today?* he asked, while the kit perched in Nev's window, bouncing, knocking things over, excitedly peeking out at him.

Yes!

How is she?

Worried! Depressed! Gloomy! Wait! There's a bug!

Then the fox had to wait while the kit disappeared, presumably having it out with the bug. He stood, shivering, with the tired pads of his feet in the snow. He could just barely feel Lovisa in a different part of the building, if he strained his mind. But she was asleep. That was good, at least, that she was able to sleep. The fox himself wasn't getting much sleep these days.

I'm back! yelled the kit.

Could you tell me what Lovisa has been worrying about? he asked.

No, but can you believe that Nev has sex with a boy I don't like? Almost every night! At the Cliff Farm! I don't know why she likes him!

I'm sorry, said the fox. *Humans can be very aggravating.*

I wish he would get impaled by an icicle! said the kit. *I wish he would get trampled by a horse! I wish someone would bite off his penis while he's sleeping!*

You're not . . . going to do that, are you? said the fox, briefly diverted from his purpose.

Of course not, said the kit. *I'm not supposed to know what's going on. It would be a betrayal of the secrets of foxkind.*

Indeed, it would.

I tried to convince a goose at the Cliff Farm to do it, but she was too stupid.

The fox, who considered a disinterest in biting off a human penis to be a mark of intelligence, tried to refocus the conversation. *Is there nothing you can tell me about Lovisa?*

Nothing really! Wait! I smell a biscuit!

Wait! Wait a moment. Why does Quona want you to keep an eye on Lovisa?

Mostly she asks me about Nev, said the kit. *I'm supposed to report whenever I can and tell her if Nev is safe. But I also tell her if others are safe, including Lovisa.*

Why would she care if Lovisa is safe?

I don't think she likes Lovisa's parents. She doesn't like a lot of the students' parents.

Is Lovisa safe?

How would I know? said the kit. *At least she's not having sex with a horrible boy!*

This was a waste of time. The fox ran back home on numb paws, the journey long and cold. He climbed into his bed again, relieved to find the house quiet, no fox visitors, no new dramas. Ferla lay twisted in her blankets, stilled by the effects of a soporific tea that brought unconsciousness, but not true rest. She would wake with a spinning mind, trying to find her way out of the trap she found herself in, thinking confused thoughts about her husband, her daughter. Grasping at her options for eliminating the problem of the queen.

The fox shivered, unable to sleep. Like everyone else, he didn't know what he was going to do. And he had the sense that he was running out of time.

CHAPTER TWENTY-SIX

GIDDON WAS GOING to jump out of his own skin.

Every moment he spent neither talking to silbercows nor getting clear, hard answers to any of his questions was torture. Quona had returned before he and Hava were able to get into the locked room in her attic. They needed to know what Mikka and Brek had discovered in the north. But Quona never seemed to leave the house when they were home, and no matter how many parties or dinners they went to—no matter how much they hinted or nudged—no one seemed to have anything relevant to share.

The night of Sara Varana's party in the Keep, it was impossible to step into the entrance hall and not look straight up at the glass dome above. Impossible not to admire it.

"Do you suppose that if all the lights were out," Giddon said, "one could lie on the floor and watch the stars move across the sky?"

"Whatever," Hava said. "There's Arni Devret. I'm going to see what he knows about the north." And she stumped off, leaving Giddon unaccountably grateful for her roughness, because it kept him from feeling too much. His star question had been the sort of thing he would've asked Bitterblue. He'd said it without thinking, and he'd broken his own heart with it.

From Arni, Hava learned that more than a dozen prominent Ledran families had property in the north and maybe half of them had houses on cliffs above the sea. Giddon learned from Periwinkle that Mikka and Brek had gone north on foot. It had been one of Mikka's exploratory adventures.

"Mikka invited me to join them," said Perry, beginning to tear up again. "Of course I declined. I went out with them often enough to know how it would be: no clear agenda; no concern about the existence—or lack—of inns; climbing and slipping and sliding and all manner of nonsense. Oh, how I miss that fool," he said, mopping his face.

"Do you know where they went, exactly?" asked Giddon, tactfully handing him a handkerchief.

"I do not."

"Do you know what sights they saw?"

"Probably every rock between here and Kamassar," said Perry, blowing his nose.

Suppressing a sigh, Giddon moved off to talk to Quona as soon as he politely could, not because he wanted to talk to Quona, but because Quona was talking to the Estillan envoy, Cobal. Not that Giddon wanted to talk to Cobal either, but he knew he should be curious about what they discussed when they were together.

"A poodle!" exclaimed Quona as he joined them. "Hello, Giddon! Having fun?"

"So much fun. What's a poodle?" asked Giddon, who didn't know the Keepish word.

"A mid-sized, good-natured, fluffy dog," said Quona. "Cobal is trying to decide what kind of Keepish dog to send home to his children in Estill." Then Quona went on to enumerate all the advantages and disadvantages of poodles relative to other breeds of dog, while Cobal smirked at Giddon as if enjoying the impatience he suspected Giddon felt.

It was that kind of night. And it was followed by that kind of week, for in the hopes of hearing the right clue from the right person, they accepted one dinner invitation after another. They got a lot of exercise, tromping around the city in the dark.

On Friday night, after an unilluminating party at the house of a Scholar rep named Dev Dimara, Giddon and Hava walked home together. It was late, and cold. Their route took them through Flag Hill, where the houses stood like small castles behind heavy gates. Lights atop some of the roofs cast a pale glow over oblong balloons.

"Fox report?" said Giddon.

"It's a little confusing," said Hava, "because I think a couple are taking turns."

"Like a tag team of small, fuzzy stalkers?"

"Yes, exactly. For a while, we were being followed by this little one who hides dramatically behind tufts of grass, then leaps out and races madly to the next tuft. Then I didn't see any for a bit, until we rounded that last corner, and then I saw old Smug Nose. Wait," she said abruptly, her voice a quick breath and her hand catching his arm, pulling him off the road and into a stand of trees. He saw what she saw, a small form shooting down a staircase and onto the road ahead of them, but he didn't understand.

Then the person glanced around. The hood of her coat dropped to reveal twists of hair and the flash of a worried expression in a dark face. It was that Cavenda girl, Lovisa, who'd found them snooping in her father's library.

She ran off like a mouse.

"Why are we hiding?" asked Giddon. "Haven't you decided she's harmless?"

"I don't know. It was something in the way she moved. She didn't want to be seen."

"Any idea where she's headed? Isn't that the way to her own house?"

"Yes. But it's Friday night and she lives in the academy dormitories, so I don't know why she'd be sneaking home in the dark."

"Maybe she's the thief who stole the varane formulas," said Giddon.

"Ha," said Hava. "I wouldn't put it past her."

The darkness grew heavier, the sky pressing closer as they walked. When Giddon felt moisture touching his face, he looked up at the soft, drifting snow and remembered a night, maybe five years ago, when he'd convinced Bitterblue to go sledding outside her castle ramparts. How much Bitterblue had been suffering in those days, from all the damage her father had done. How his mood had lightened when the sledding had made her smile, even shriek with laughter. Giddon had wanted more happiness for Bitterblue before she died. He'd wanted her to grow old and have the time to heal from the nightmare of her childhood, the time to help Monsea heal in all the ways she hoped it would. He would have helped her, with all his heart.

As they reached the last stretch of the path to Quona's house, the Estillan envoy appeared before them, crunching through the light covering of snow.

His face brightened at the sight of them, with a cheerfulness that didn't quite match the touch of sarcasm in his voice. "Good night to you, Giddon," he said. "Good night, Hava."

"Good night, Cobal," said Giddon. "Have you had a nice visit with Quona?"

"Always," said Cobal, continuing past them toward the Cliff Farm.

"Why are those two so chummy?" asked Hava in a low voice.

"Poodles, supposedly," said Giddon.

"What?"

"A kind of dog."

"Right."

As they stepped into Quona's foyer, Quona, who was ascending the steps to the second floor, turned to greet them.

"Welcome home," she said. "Was it a nice party?"

"Very," said Giddon. "We just met the Estillan envoy on the path."

"I invited him to dinner," said Quona. "He loves my cats. I want to hear all about your party, but I'm so tired, I'm dropping. We'll talk at breakfast."

But when Quona joined them for breakfast the next morning, Saturday, she seemed to have forgotten her curiosity, along with her manners. Barely acknowledging them, she sat, then pulled a cat into her lap, which she didn't usually do at meals. She began to eat with bleary distraction.

"Did you sleep well?" asked Giddon.

"Terribly, I'm afraid," she admitted. "I'm going north again today, so please make yourselves comfortable. My staff will see that you're well taken care of."

Though Hava said nothing, Giddon could feel the change in her energy. Today they would get into that attic room.

HAVA HAD MEMORIZED the schedules of Quona's staff members, but still, she made Giddon stand lookout in the sitting room below while she worked in the attic with the lock picks.

"If anyone comes by, look noble and innocent, then have a loud coughing fit," she said.

The only person who came by was that pale gray cat, who tugged at Giddon's heart by jumping into his lap and cuddling against him in a way that reminded him of sitting with Bitterblue and Lovejoy in his big chair at home. She was soft and warm. "I still don't know your name," Giddon said.

Above him, Hava tapped on the floor—his ceiling—three times, which was his signal to come upstairs.

HE FOUND HER standing triumphantly inside the small room.

"Good work," he said.

Aside from a large desk and its chair, the room was empty, uncarpeted. The walls and floor were built of wood, finished but unadorned. It looked like a tiny, stark office. Hava was leaning over the desk under a single, high window.

"No foxes?" he said. "Or severed heads or sacks of money?"

"Just a desk with a million drawers," said Hava, who was pulling on each drawer, peering inside. "Containing millions of papers." When she got to a locked drawer, she pursed her lips in interest. "This would be a useful time to have Trina's Grace," she muttered.

"Except we don't know what we're looking for," said Giddon. "Can you pick it?"

"The lock is very small," she said, "but I guess I'll have to try."

It took her a long time, much longer than the door had done. While she worked delicately with her smallest lock picks, Giddon lit the lamp on the desk and began to look more closely at the papers in the drawers.

"Records of airship sales," he reported. "Records of—" He paused, then raised a paper closer to the light. "Hava," he said, "do you think it's odd that Quona should have letters written to people who aren't her?"

"Like who?" said Hava.

"Like Ada Balava," he said. "Do you remember that name? She's one of the importers who was cheating Bitterblue out of zilfium. In fact," he said, skimming the page before him, "this seems to be a letter on that very topic." He read aloud in Keepish. "'You'll find the queen to be selling her rock detritus at an advantageous price, to put it mildly. We suspect this price will last only as long as the queen's ignorance, so we should buy now while we can.' It's from Ada Balava's director of foreign operations."

"Weaselbugger," muttered Hava. Then there was a click and she made a satisfied noise. Sliding the drawer open, she began to rifle through it.

Suddenly, she cried out, "Giddon!"

"What?"

She was flipping through a small notebook. "Are these the scientific formulas for varane?"

"I'm not much of a scientist," said Giddon, looking over her shoulder.

" 'Proprietary property of Minta Varana'!" Hava cried, speaking the words in Keepish. " 'Varane'! It says it right here! Oh," she said, grabbing her own hair. "I'm so stupid. I should've guessed this. Look, the cover of this notebook has little dents in the edges!"

"Dents?" said Giddon in bewilderment.

"Tooth dents!" she said. "Her secret foxes steal this stuff for her!"

"Well, this is unexpected," said a voice behind them. "Isn't it, my darlings?"

IN THE DOORWAY, Quona stood watching them with an aspect of absolute amazement.

She wore a long, white fur coat, cold radiated from her body, and blue foxes were perched all over her person. One balanced on her shoulder. Two peered curiously out of her hood. One watched Giddon and Hava from her pocket, and two more stood on the floor at her feet.

"Where's the seventh?" said Hava, staring back at her coldly. An instant later, the seventh fox trotted into the room, shining golden eyes up at them.

"Aren't you clever, Hava," said Quona, sounding like she meant it.

"Why are you back?" demanded Hava.

"I changed my mind," said Quona simply.

"Or you lied," said Hava, "so you could catch us snooping."

"Indeed," said Quona, with a warmth to her voice that almost sounded like laughter, "I would never have known to try to catch you snooping. You've taken me entirely by surprise. How did you guess?"

"That you're secretly bonded to seven foxes? That you're the formula thief? We're not stupid," Hava shot back.

Giddon raised a hand. "I'm stupid, actually," he said. "Hava figured it out."

"You've had your foxes following us since day one," said Hava. "Haven't you? What else are you responsible for? How much do you know about our two drowned men?"

Quona was watching Hava now with a new expression, quiet and grave. "I'd like to sit down," she said. "Will you come downstairs to talk about this?"

"I'd rather stay near this desk," said Hava, crossing her arms. "This desk interests me."

"Yes, all right," said Quona, whose exhaustion was showing plainly in her face. Then one of the foxes at her feet began climbing directly up her coat, working its way to her empty pocket. Another followed, scrambling the distance to her available shoulder. When the last remaining fox made a move as if to climb, Quona said heavily, "That will have to be all, darlings," and Giddon took pity. Pulling out the desk chair, he set it before her.

"Thank you," she said, practically collapsing into the chair. The foxes on her shoulders almost toppled, but caught themselves, rebalancing. She took a breath or two, rubbing at her forehead, looking like a human fox-perch. "It's hard to know where to start."

"Why don't you start by telling us why you stole formulas from your own sister?" said Hava.

"Yes," said Quona. "All right. That's fairly simple. There's a Scholar in Parliament who recently decided to change sides on the zilfium vote and vote with the Industrialists to legalize zilfium use. I stole the varane formulas to bribe him back."

"Bribe him back!" Hava repeated incredulously. "Is this the man we heard people fighting about at the Cavenda dinner party?"

"I'm not going to tell you everything," said Quona, with an interesting, tired resolve in her voice. "You already have the power to ruin me, but I want this deal to go through. The Scholar in question has a friend in Kamassar who will pay him a fortune for the varane formulas. In return, the Scholar will switch his vote back, vote against zilfium, and help to ensure that zilfium use does not begin to pollute Winterkeep. Simultaneously, Kamassar will develop workable airship technology, reducing their dependence on zilfium."

"And that's so important to you?" asked Hava. "You would break the law, steal from your own sister, even ruin your own family's transportation monopoly, to ensure that zilfium remains illegal and Kamassar gets airships?"

"Yes," said Quona, shooting the word out. "It's so important to me."

"Why?" demanded Hava.

"Because it's our duty to care for the environment. We are bound by a promise to protect the earth and the sea. What happens if we don't? And people know it," she said wearily. "They know it matters, but they have other priorities. I nudge their priorities back into place."

"By stealing," said Hava.

"A big rule follower, are you?" said Quona sharply.

"What about all this other stuff?" said Hava, who seemed almost cheerful in the face of Quona's antagonism. She nudged her head at the open drawers in the desk, at the papers Giddon had been going through. "Letters to Ada Balava, and who knows what else?"

"My foxes bring me many things," said Quona. "They visit many homes, go through many desks, fireplaces, and garbage bins. I can't be sure what they'll bring back, but I keep everything in case it becomes useful later. In fact, that letter to Ada Balava might indeed be useful someday, to *you*. If you can demonstrate that the importers who cheated your queen out of her zilfium knew they were cheating her, you'll win a lawsuit in the Keepish courts."

"So, you *did* know about the importers," said Hava.

"Of course I did," said Quona. "Everyone in the Ledra elite knew about the importers. But I know more. I have more eyes than anyone else, and it's good that I do, because there aren't many people here who can be trusted to remember what matters."

A moment of silence passed. This was a new, unsettled version of Quona Varana, and Giddon would decide what he thought about it later. For now, the things she was talking about were not, in fact, the things that mattered to him.

"In the course of reviewing the papers your foxes have brought to you," he said, "have you ever stumbled upon anything that might explain why the Monsean envoy and a Monsean adviser to the queen were trapped in the cabin of their boat, then deliberately drowned?"

Quona turned dark eyes to him that were suddenly worried and serious. "I'm afraid that relates to my reasons for going north today," she said.

"Seeing as you were gone about five minutes, you can't have gotten very far north," said Hava sarcastically.

"You're right, I didn't," she said. "Almost immediately upon leaving, I saw the Cavenda airship, riding the winds north ahead of me. When Benni Cavenda flies north, he goes to his wife's property in Torla's Neck. That's where I was trying to go too. But I can't very well spy on Benni's house from my airship if he's there too, can I? So I shifted course, pretending to be en route somewhere else. As soon as he was out of my sight, I turned back home."

"So you think Benni Cavenda's house has something to do with our two drowned men?" said Giddon.

"Oh, I don't know," said Quona, suddenly frustrated. "But I think Benni himself may have something to do with them, and some house somewhere has something to do with something."

"How illuminating," said Hava.

"The silbercows talk to me," said Quona, ignoring Hava's sarcasm. "They tell me stories that contain a certain amount of fantasy. But there are always parts that seem real. I can tell when they feel actual distress, for example, and sometimes they show me details I doubt they could know if the image weren't true. When the silbercows show me things I suspect to be true, I can use my foxes to search for more evidence.

"Lately," she said, "the silbercows have been showing me some sort of . . . thing that explodes. Some weapon someone is testing, or some terrible toy, some *mistake,* being thrown from an airship into the sea near a house on a cliff. Silbercows have come to me with burns, crying, not understanding their own injuries. You don't look surprised, or even particularly moved," she said, studying their faces.

"Silbercows have shown us the explosions too," said Giddon.

"They talk to you?" she said, quietly. "They don't talk to everyone, you know. Have they shown you the sunken boat?"

"Yes," said Giddon. "With two people trapped inside. That's what I was talking about: It's the *Seashell,* the boat in which our comrades Mikka and Brek were murdered. That's why we came to Winterkeep in the first place. Not because we'd seen that image," he added when she looked surprised. "But because we'd started gathering hints that the drowning of our men wasn't an accident."

"I see," said Quona. "Well, they've been showing me the explosions for a while, but the boat is a new image. I didn't connect it to the boat that went down with your envoy, because I didn't know that boat's name. I've been focused on the explosions instead, trying to identify the house on the cliff. It's why I keep flying north: I've been studying the coast to see if any of the houses look right.

"But then, the last time I talked to the silbercows, they suddenly seemed to have more information about the boat. They knew the names of your men, Mikka and Brek. They also seemed to know that those men had been murdered. I'm guessing now that they got that information from you?"

"Yes," said Giddon grimly.

"Well," said Quona. "Last night something sparked in my memory. A letter my foxes brought me from the Cavenda house here in Ledra a long time ago. It's the reason I didn't sleep; it's the reason I tried to go north again today, to the Cavenda property in Torla's Neck."

"Well?" said Giddon. "What is it?"

"I suppose I should just show it to you," said Quona.

She stood up quickly, not seeming to worry about the foxes on her person. Giddon had the impression that they were accustomed to shifting around, maintaining their balance on a moving planet. At the desk, she shuffled through some papers, finally pulling out a crumpled letter, which she passed to them both.

Hava read out loud, in Keepish.

"'Note: Today, during my visit from the Estillan envoy Cobal, we were startled by a visit from the Monsean envoy Mikka, who is on a northern tour with a friend. The guards, knowing I was expecting a visitor but not knowing he was already with me, mistook Mikka for that visitor and brought him to the storehouse. They let him in at the back door. Cobal and I did not hear him enter. I believe Mikka overheard a great deal of our conversation before his presence became known to us. If you would kindly come north and honor us with a visit, I will furnish you with more details. Yours, LM.'"

Giddon's nails were digging into his own palms. "Benni Cavenda had Mikka and Brek murdered."

"Yes," said Hava. "Because Benni and Cobal are planning some-thing and Mikka found out. But what are they planning?"

"I don't know," said Quona. "I was up practically all night going through my papers, looking for clues. I sent my foxes out too, but they found nothing."

"It was signed 'LM.' Who's LM?" asked Giddon.

"No idea."

"What were you going to do today once you got to the Cavenda property?"

Quona threw her hands in the air, rocking the foxes, whose eyes flashed as they clung to her. "Compare their house to the one the silbercows have shown me?" she said. "Hope to find some connec-tion between the explosions and this letter? Find some clue of what Mikka learned? I don't know. I'm not cut out for this kind of intrigue. Murder is far beyond what I ever expected when I decided to . . ." She flapped a hand again.

"Interfere?" said Hava helpfully.

"I only ever meant to interfere with Parliament," she said. "With the zilfium vote in December."

"It's all right," said Giddon. "Hava and I *are* cut out for this kind of thing, and we have two choices. Either we stay here and try to wring information out of Benni and Cobal, or we go north, sneak onto the Cavenda property, and figure out what's going on."

"You know I like the second option better," said Hava. "It's what my Grace is made for."

"Yes," said Giddon. "And we'll be better able to wring whatever we need out of Benni and Cobal *after* we have a sense of what we're dealing with. Quona, why on earth are you friends with Cobal?"

"I am not his friend," said Quona.

"You invited him to dinner last night!"

"So that I could get him out of his house!" she said. "And send my foxes in to snoop! Why do you think I ever invite anyone anywhere? Unfortunately, my foxes found nothing useful, either at his house or the Cavendas'."

"We need to go to Torla's Neck," said Giddon. "Quona, who else knows what you know?"

A peculiar, guilty expression crossed Quona's face. "I can get you an airship as soon as tomorrow, which is Sunday," she said. "And there is someone else who knows some of what I know. It's someone who may be able to provide you with a discreet place to stay."

Chapter Twenty-seven

Lovisa spent all of Saturday remembering the tinny sound of the letter opener clattering against the attic window. The Queen of Monsea was alive. What should she do?

On Saturday night, she knocked on Mari's door with purpose.

When he saw her, he grinned. "City?"

"No. I need a serious distraction," she said.

"Okay," he said, going with it. "Why?"

"I just do."

"Oh, come on, Lovisa," he said. "Something's been going on for a while now. When are you going to tell me?"

"I can't tell you," she said. "Please stop asking."

"Is someone blackmailing you or something?" he said, sounding like it was a joke, a ridiculous notion.

"No."

"Threatening to hurt you?"

"No." But Lovisa hesitated.

With a new kind of understanding, Mari became indignant. "Who is it? I'll hurt them first."

"That's exactly why I'd never tell you! You'd rush off to do something stupid, and ruin everything. Good night. I'm going somewhere else."

She tried to pull the door shut, but Mari caught it. "I promise," he said. "I won't do anything you don't want, if you'll just tell me what's going on. I swear it, Lovisa. Please? You can't even sleep! I've never seen you like this!"

Lovisa was wiping sudden, infuriating tears from her cheeks. She knew Mari kept his promises, but it didn't matter. "I can't," she said. "If I did, it would endanger us both. And I wish I could, so it kills me when you ask. So will you please, please stop badgering me about it, and just let me be stressed out, and help distract me?"

"Are you protecting me from something?" he asked, incredulously.

"Shut up!"

He pulled her into the room, shut the door, and put his arms around her.

"What are you doing?" she cried, startled.

"I'm hugging you!" he said. "You're scaring me!"

"Are you seducing me? For sex?"

"Oh, for the love of the Keeper, Lovisa," he said, beginning to laugh. "No. I'm hugging you for comfort. Only you would ask that."

"Why shouldn't I ask about it directly?" she said. "Would it be so terrible for everyone to say what they mean when they do things, and what they want, and why? Wouldn't it make things simpler, and create fewer disasters?"

"Lovisa," he said, "*now* what's going on?"

"I hate everyone who's normal," she said, humiliated by the tears that were soaking into his shirt.

Mari began to rock her back and forth with his hug. She buried her face in his chest, heard his heart beating. When was the last time anyone had hugged her? When did anyone ever hug anybody? Her arms reached up to hug him back and his grip on her tightened.

"What a relief I'm not normal," he said, which made her snort with sudden laughter. No one was more normal than Mari, but it was true that she didn't hate him. And she told herself it was a friendly hug, fond, not sexual. But her body was telling her something else too, wanting to press against him, wanting to make his body respond, because that would feel different.

"Mari?" she said.

"Yes?"

She lifted her face to his, her mouth very close. "What if we reconsidered?"

He hesitated, understanding. Then he kissed her, once, tentatively. Yes, that was better. She kissed him back.

He pulled away. "Wait. We've talked about this. We're not thinking."

But Lovisa was thinking. "I know you're not in love with me," she said. "You know I'm not in love with you. We've been through it a hundred times. There's no confusion here. And I'm dying for a distraction."

He let out a big sigh. "Okay."

She took him to his bed.

It was nice. Interesting. Not tantalizing, but she liked being close to Mari, she liked burying her face in his neck, she liked moving with him and filling her mind with him. She trusted him. And he was attentive and patient, but also wanted her. It made her feel . . . important. It was such a strange feeling.

"It's fine," she told him, when he worried about her. "I'm not going to finish. It's okay."

Then, right about the time he was finishing, her body started wanting it. He gasped out his joy, then dropped into sleep, like someone had put a sheet over a birdcage.

"Hey," she said, poking his shoulder, frustrated.

"What?" he said, waking up with a start, looking around in blurry confusion.

"I didn't finish."

"I thought you weren't going to."

"Well. I was indifferent at first. Now I want to."

"Okay," he said. And to her vast surprise, he disappeared under the covers, positioned her legs just so, and began to apply his tongue to her, so gently that her body sang out in wonderment. Wow. When did Mari get so good at these things? Who knew?

The pleasure rose slowly, became almost overwhelming, then became shattering. When it was over, she started to cry again. She hid the tears from him, confused about whether she was happy or sad.

Mari fell asleep with his face buried in her neck. Lovisa lay awake for a while, sniffling quietly, thinking, released from the grip of worry about the queen, if briefly. She wondered if they'd do it again tomorrow.

In the early morning, she woke to him murmuring happily and planting tiny kisses behind her ear. When she turned to him, she saw starlight in his eyes.

"Wait," she said, immediately alarmed. "Why did you change your mind?"

"What?"

"About sex."

"I guess because I trust you."

"But you're not in love with me?"

"I've known you all my life," he said. "We're still friends, right?"

"Yes," she said carefully. "But maybe we shouldn't do that again."

"Didn't you like it?"

"It was very, very nice," she said. "But now I'm afraid of you falling in love with me."

"Because I was kissing you just now?"

"Yes."

"Maybe I just want to have more sex with you."

"Oh," said Lovisa, who hadn't thought of that. "Okay. But listen, Mari, will you promise me that you'll be honest with me, about all your feelings about this?"

He considered the question, with that sleepy morning dopiness that made her remember that she'd known him when he was five. "Would that be a one-way promise," he said, "or are you going to be honest with me too?"

"About my feelings about sex, yes," she said. "Not about the stuff I can't tell you."

"Okay. I promise."

"Also, when we stop having sex, promise you won't try to isolate me socially."

He propped himself up on his elbow and stared at her, hard. "What kind of question is that?"

"Like you did with Nev," she said, shrugging.

"I did not!" he said. "I never did any such thing!"

"Okay, but everyone else isolated her, as a matter of course."

"But I didn't tell them to do that!"

"You didn't tell them *not* to do it either. You saw it happening, and you could've stopped it with a word, but you didn't. I need a promise you won't do that to me. You know I'd have to retaliate, right? It would make a huge mess of everything."

Mari was staring mulishly at the bedsheets, thinking. Lovisa knew how slow he was to offense, how hard he considered everything, sometimes tortuously, before deciding what he thought. Unlike her. She was a little ashamed of herself.

"I'm sorry," she said. "I mean, I've isolated her too."

He sighed, still looking confused. "Regardless of whether you're right about her, I won't do that to you," he said. "I never would. I promise."

"Okay then," she said. "And I won't retaliate."

Mari rolled his eyes. "What a lovely future we've planned for ourselves."

"We've promised each other friendship, haven't we?"

"Yes, I guess we have."

"Why do you trust me, anyway?"

"I don't trust you with everything," he said, with a small smile. "But I do with this."

WHEN LOVISA WOKE again, her stomach hurt with emptiness and anxiety.

Tea, she thought, remembering the preventative tea against pregnancy. And then she remembered that she didn't have any. She tried to keep it on hand, it was easy to get from the academy infirmary, but the last time she'd been anywhere near the infirmary, it had been snowing, slippery, windy. Lovisa had spent too much time shivering outside in the cold lately.

She knew a lot of girls who'd have the tea on hand, but they were gossips.

Finding her robe, she left Mari's room, slipped through the corridors, and tapped on Nev's door.

When nothing happened, she tapped again and kept on tapping. Finally, the door opened a crack and Nev peered out, looking annoyed and rumpled. Lovisa remembered that it was Sunday morning.

"What do you want?" Nev said.

"Preventative tea," said Lovisa. "I'm out. Do you have any?"

Nev groaned, opened the door fully, then climbed back into bed. "In the window. It's that bushy one on the right that looks like the leaves are dying."

The room was dark, the pink glow of sunrise beginning to illuminate frost on the windowpanes. Lovisa couldn't tell the plants apart. "Seriously? You have it growing in your window?"

"Like I said."

"*Are* the leaves dying?"

"No, that's just how it grows."

"What do I do?" said Lovisa, not moving from the doorway.

"What do you mean?"

"I've never picked leaves from a plant before."

Sighing deeply, then rubbing her face, Nev muttered, "Ledra people." She rolled out of bed again, this time bringing a blanket with her as a cape. "Here," she said, lighting both a lamp and her little stove, then dipping a small, bashed-up tin pot into her basin of water. "We'll have some together." Then she went to the windowsill and picked a few small leaves from the plant.

"Is that enough?" Lovisa asked. "For both of us?"

"More than enough," said Nev. "People use ten times more than they need."

"I follow the instructions on the packet."

"The instructions are written by a merchant who wants you to buy ten times more than you need."

"Huh," said Lovisa, with a flash of appreciation for the merchant.

Nev dropped the leaves into a little metal strainer shaped like a silbercow that screwed closed at its middle.

"That's cute," said Lovisa. "Where'd you get it?"

"A woman at home makes them," said Nev, lowering the strainer into the pot, then going back to bed. The room was freezing. Standing awkwardly, Lovisa pulled the fur collar of her robe tightly around her throat. From the bed, gold eyes peered out at her.

"Are you bonded yet?" she asked.

"No," said Nev shortly.

I never say the right thing, Lovisa thought, then, suddenly exhausted, went to the bed and sat at Nev's feet, not asking permission. She wondered what Nev would think if she knew Mari Devret was the reason Lovisa needed the tea. Or that Lovisa had slept with him because the Queen of Monsea was trapped in her parents' attic, and she didn't know what to do.

The water began to bubble, a low, comforting whisper that made her want to lie down, curl up, and fall asleep at the foot of Nev's bed. *I could sleep in Nev's room too,* she thought, with a blip of surprise. *Even with her right there, annoyed at me.*

Nev pushed herself up in bed with her eyes closed, back propped against the wall. When the fox kit crept out of the blankets and edged closer to Lovisa, then pressed her small side against Lovisa's furry robe, Lovisa stiffened. It was strange to be making contact with someone's fox.

"Would it bother you if the person I had sex with was Mari Devret?" she asked, suddenly too curious to help herself.

Nev's eyes popped open. "No," she said, then said nothing more, which was frustrating. Lovisa wanted to understand.

"Is that because northerners never get jealous?"

"No! Why would you think that?"

Lovisa shrugged. "Most people wouldn't want me sleeping with their ex. I wondered if northerners cared less about those things."

Nev looked incredulous. "Do you think we're all the same?"

"No," protested Lovisa.

"Isn't your own mother a northerner? Doesn't she get jealous?"

Lovisa suspected there was no angry, twisted feeling of which Ferla was incapable. But Ferla was a different kind of northerner; she was rich. "Probably."

"Well," said Nev, her voice still frosty. "It's true that the people I know from home might have some different attitudes. For example, we'd never pay a fortune for a month's worth of preventative tea. We'd never buy cut flowers when they grow beside our roads."

She thinks she's superior, thought Lovisa.

"But we have normal feelings," she said. "Including jealousy."

"Do you get jealous?" Lovisa asked.

"Sometimes," Nev said, then added, almost indignantly, "Of course I do."

The tea was bubbling in earnest now. With an expression of disgust, Nev got up and leaned over the pot, stirred it, then mixed a spoonful of some congealed amber thing from a glass jar into the concoction. She pulled two cups from a shelf and carefully poured. She handed one to Lovisa.

Lovisa sipped cautiously, her stomach still roiling. "It tastes different from what I'm used to," she said. *Much less disgusting,* she didn't say aloud.

"I added some honey for sweetness, and some ginger syrup so it's not as hard on an empty stomach. The chemicals that prevent pregnancy can hurt the stomach wall."

"Oh," said Lovisa, then cursed herself for sounding interested. *You make me feel like a child,* she thought, still jumpy from the strange pressure of Nev's purring fox against her leg.

The two girls sipped their drinks, not looking at each other. Lovisa didn't know why Nev should matter to her—when Pari was dead and her parents were monsters; when the Queen of Monsea was imprisoned in the attic; when she didn't know how to think, or what to do, or why she was always such a consummate coward. Nor did she know why she cared whether Nev minded about Mari. *And why I'm always crying,* she thought, furiously blinking back tears.

"What makes you jealous?" she asked.

Nev sighed. "I can get jealous if I have feelings for someone."

"So, if you're sleeping with someone but you don't have feelings, you don't get jealous?"

"I don't know. I've never had sex with anyone I didn't have feelings for."

"Do you have feelings for Nori Orfa?" Lovisa asked, suddenly concerned.

"Nori *Orfa*," Nev repeated, as if she didn't understand the name.

"I heard a rumor," Lovisa said, not mentioning that she herself had seen Nori leaving Nev's room. "That you have a thing with him."

"With Nori *Orfa*," Nev said flatly.

"Yes," said Lovisa, growing impatient. "That's his family name. The tea manor boy from your own province up north. I mean, you're drinking that tea for some reason, aren't you?"

Nev's head went back and her shoulders straightened, almost imperceptibly. "That's a nosy question," Nev said.

"True," said Lovisa.

"Do you have feelings for Mari?"

"No."

"He's extremely decent," Nev said, "as long as you don't mind someone with a compulsive need to be good at everything."

Lovisa was outraged. What was wrong with wanting to be good at things? It was amazing, how good Mari was at things! Including sex! "Why did you break up with him, anyway?" she shot back.

"You're asking a lot of nosy questions."

"So are you!"

Nev took a few sips of tea, then stared into her cup, her expression impenetrable. "It's hard to explain," she finally said. "Mari thought I was always right about everything. He would've done anything I asked."

"He loved you," said Lovisa, feeling sick and mean.

"He couldn't even see me clearly," said Nev, "so, no, not really. And he was such a pushover that I always felt like I was controlling him. It was uneven. I was smothering in his adulation."

"Sounds terrible," Lovisa said viciously.

"You don't need to be jealous," Nev said. "He knows now that I'm not perfect."

"I'm not jealous!"

"Good," said Nev. "It's probably different with you, more healthy. He could adore you, but he's not going to forget who you are, right? He's known you all his life."

"He doesn't adore me," Lovisa said. "We don't have feelings. I've been having trouble sleeping and last night he helped me fall asleep."

"Well, that's good."

Lovisa jumped up from the bed, gratified when the fox kit yelped and went sprawling. She marched to the window and glared through the glass at silhouettes of trees and buildings, lined with the pink and gold of the rising sun. She couldn't believe they were even having this stupid conversation. How did Nev get her to reveal such personal things?

"Nori never told me he had two names," Nev said.

"What?" said Lovisa, turning back in surprise.

Nev was staring hard into her cup. Her voice was even, but low. "Especially not that his family name was Orfa," she said. "I know plenty of people at home who work for the Orfas."

Instantly, Lovisa understood. Nori Orfa, the wealthy tea manor boy, had pretended to be plain-old, one-named Nori from home, poor like Nev, humble like Nev, as part of his tactical pursuit of her. That was how he'd ingratiated himself. He'd probably emphasized his northern accent with her to hook her, make her feel like he was the kind of boy she'd known all her life. He'd probably talked of places in Torla's Neck they both knew, while leaving out the names of his particular friends. It was what she would've done too, if she'd had Nori's resources and her goal had been to take Nev in. There were traveling actors in Winterkeep, especially outside of Ledra, dancers, players, magicians who went from town to town, looking for audiences. Some of them were impersonators—of the Governor of Mantiper, or the richest lady in Borza, or a king from the Royal Continent.

Nori was a player too, impersonating a human who wasn't a piece of garbage.

She understood him perfectly and she wanted to scratch his face off. "There's more," she said, clearing her throat uncomfortably. "I think he has a girlfriend at home."

Nev had pressed herself into the corner of the bed, head bent. She looked as small as one of Lovisa's little brothers.

"I'm sorry," Lovisa said. "I think I know her name. I was considering writing her a letter about her boyfriend. Do you want her name too?"

"No," Nev whispered.

"Okay," said Lovisa. "I won't write to her if you don't want me to."

"I don't mind," said Nev. "But don't use my name or describe me. For all I know, she's my neighbor and she'll call on me one day to doctor her horse or something."

"Right," said Lovisa. "Of course." She didn't know what else to say. *I'm sorry I didn't tell you sooner. If I'd realized you were a normal person with normal feelings, I would have. But I've always thought you were on a plane above me.*

"What will you do?" she asked.

"I'm going home," said Nev.

"What do you mean?" said Lovisa, instantly worried. "In the middle of the term? Don't let him ruin your studies, Nev!"

"It was decided yesterday," said Nev. "I'm taking a leave of absence. There are—I've been—it's best if I go home for a bit. I'm leaving today."

"Oh. How sudden," said Lovisa, crushed by this, not understanding. "But, why?"

Nev took a moment to study her own hands. Then she raised a face to Lovisa that contained both uncertainty and defiance. "Apparently I've learned some things," she said. "Apparently they're dangerous."

"Oh!" said Lovisa, suddenly dismayed. "What things?"

"Well, obviously I'm not going to tell you, if they're dangerous!" said Nev. "But I talk to the silbercows sometimes; I always have. We grow up talking to them in the north. And they tell me things. They tell me and Quona Varana. And Quona says that now I have to keep quiet, and go. I don't even trust Quona!" she said. "But she's convinced me to go."

Lovisa was now fighting to breathe. What might the silbercows know, what might they be saying? "Who else have you told about this besides me?"

"No one. Why? What's wrong?"

Lovisa was deeply, intensely relieved that Nev was going home, if Nev had learned any of the things Lovisa knew. Maybe she'd be safe at home. "Nev," she said, "don't tell anyone else about any of it. Will you promise me you won't tell anyone else?"

"Lovisa!" said Nev, staring at her with new alarm. "What's going on? What do you know?"

Lovisa realized then that she was holding her cup so hard that it was shaking. How she must look. She breathed, then breathed again. "I can't explain," she said. "I can't tell you any more than you can tell me. And I'm sorry. But it's not safe for you to talk about any of it right now. Quona is right to swear you to silence and send you away. Do you trust me? I mean, of course you don't trust me. I understand that." She forced herself to take a sip from her cup. "But will you promise me not to tell anyone?"

"I don't know," said Nev. "Why should I do that?"

"Because it will keep you alive," said Lovisa.

Nev stood suddenly, sweeping her blanket over her shoulders, crossing the room to stand with Lovisa in the window. On the way, she bent down and lifted the fox kit into her arms. Together, they looked out through the glass, not talking. Nev held the fox kit close, her blanket cape brushing against Lovisa's shoulder. She was so tall. Lovisa wanted to lean into her.

"I don't know what's going on around me," Nev said. "Quona won't explain any of it to me. You won't tell me. Nori has been lying to me all along. The truth is that I want to go home and never come back. Home is so different from Ledra. Here, everything is stuck, spinning in place. Everyone is trapped in some role and no one stops to think about why they're doing what they do. *Why* they want the best grades, or the most friends, or the most information. Everyone lies and competes. Even some of the streets are traps, if you aren't rich enough or connected enough to have some cowshit pass. I hate it here," she said, in a voice that was composed almost entirely of contemptuous breath. "At home, you can see across the mountains. You can measure how much the glacier moves every year. You can breathe."

Lovisa wasn't sure if she'd ever been someplace where she could breathe. "Why *are* you here?" she asked, not as a challenge; just out of curiosity.

"Because my grandfather raised me to be an animal doctor," she said. "Because I want to take care of animals. The academy can teach me things I can't learn anywhere else on earth."

Lovisa knew her next question was selfish, but she couldn't help herself. "So you'll come back?" she said. "When all this is over?"

"I guess so," said Nev. "Whenever that is."

"Will you tell anyone else that you have dangerous knowledge?"

Nev paused. "No," she said. "I won't tell, until I understand better what's going on."

Lovisa's eyes filled with tears. "Thank you," she whispered. "What time do you leave today?"

"Early."

That was good. The sooner Nev went away, the fewer people Lovisa would have to worry about. "Thanks for the tea," she said.

"Thanks for telling me the truth about Nori," said Nev.

The light was changing, shifting. Lovisa perceived the slightest movement on the footpath below Nev's window. Then, suddenly, she saw a pair of blinking gold eyes. Then more: three pairs, four. As Lovisa's eyes adjusted, she kept seeing more foxes.

"How creepy," she said. "Why are there so many? Whose are they?"

"I have a guess," said Nev, sounding disgusted.

Then Lovisa saw a fox that was sitting right in the middle of the group, staring up at her. It had a malevolent gleam in its eyes, a familiar long nose, and jaunty ears.

"Oh," she said. *My mother's fox.*

"What?"

"Nothing."

It hit her first as despair. *That one, at least, is here for me. I'm never alone, I'm always watched. I can't get away from it.*

I'll never be free.

Then, to her surprise, a tiny seed dropped down and took root, somewhere inside her. It was a realization. It began to grow into something certain, and sad.

If I'm not free, then I have nothing to lose.

So I may as well do something drastic.

CHAPTER TWENTY-EIGHT

ON SUNDAY MORNING, after he got home from Lovisa's dormitory, the fox who was bonded to Ferla Cavenda sat in the corner of the attic room, peeking at the queen surreptitiously, worrying.

Should I talk to her? he wondered. *Shouldn't I?*

For there was something the fox was beginning to fear, almost as deeply as he feared his favorite humans not surviving. The queen suspected so many of the secrets of foxkind. What if she survived, then told someone else all the things the fox had done?

Around noon, while a weak light shone through the window and snowflakes softly fell, he stood. She was lying on her back in the bed, rubbing her head and reminding herself that she was stronger than the way her captors made her feel.

Excuse me, he said.

She stilled in her bed. Then she sat up, resting her clear gray eyes upon him.

"Did you just talk to me, directly?" she said. "On purpose?"

The fox blinked at her. *May I ask you for a favor?* he said.

"Does this mean we're bonded?" she said. "I thought you were bonded to that angry woman."

I am, he said. *But that's what I wanted to talk to you about.*

"Do you know my friends?" she said. "Giddon and Hava? Are they safe?"

I know of them, he said. *I think they're safe. They're leaving for the north today.* His siblings had told him that this very morning.

She breathed one long, slow sob. "What's in the north?"

Many, many things, he said, *but could we talk about that later?*

"They're in good health?"

Yes.

"Okay," she said, pulling herself together, focusing on him. "You said you wanted a favor? Certainly I owe you a great many favors. But I thought foxes couldn't talk to people unless they were bonded."

The fox blinked again. Then he burst out with it, because he had to.

Humans are supposed to think that, he said. *It's one of the fallacies we propagate, to protect the secrets of foxkind. I'm not supposed to be talking to you.*

The queen seemed struck by this. Her face was frozen with surprise. Then she wiped her eyes. "Have I lost my mind?"

No. I've been breaking a lot of the rules with you, because of not knowing how to help you. And also because I want to be honest with you. So badly! That's why I need a favor.

"What favor?"

Something is going to happen, said the fox.

"What?"

I don't know, he said, remembering the feeling of Lovisa that morning. *I'm not sure. But I think a human is going to try to help you.*

Another small sob escaped her. She waved at him to continue. "Please, go on."

When the thing happens that's going to happen, the fox said, *and for all the time afterward, will you promise never to tell any other human or fox that a fox who wasn't bonded to you talked to you? That he defied his bonded human? That he brought you food? That he snuck in and out of the walls? That he was able to read your thoughts, and tried to manipulate your mind?*

The queen was silent. The fox tapped on her heart and mind. She was astonished, processing rapidly his every word. She was a smart one; she understood what he'd done and what his request meant for Winterkeep.

She lifted her chin. "There are people in my life I don't lie to," she said. "One person in particular. I can't make a promise to you that would break a promise to him."

That was an interesting dilemma. The fox considered it. *Could you tell him, then swear him to secrecy?*

"I think so," she said. "But what if something in his conscience compels him to tell someone someday?"

The fox had never studied mathematics specifically, but he understood the meaning of *exponential.* This was the problem with secrets and lies, even among trustworthy people like this queen. And his heart was sinking, because he'd broken too many of the rules, and now he would never be safe. Nor would foxkind. *Yes,* he said. *I see.*

"But I also see the position you're in," she said. "And you're my friend. You've made this imprisonment bearable for me. You've even kept me safe, like that time with the letter opener. You have been honorable, helpful, and true. I can promise that I'll never tell anyone I don't need to, and that I'll do all I can to protect your secret. I'll also make every effort to consult you first, before I tell anyone new. Is that good enough?"

IT WAS STRANGE, how much better the fox felt after that. And how desperate he was for her to survive. She looked ferocious and grand whenever she parried with the letter opener as if it were a sword. She was completely unlike any human he'd ever known; she was wondrous. *She called me honorable, helpful, and true,* he thought.

Honorable, helpful, and true. Can that really be, when I've betrayed my kind?

But what was I supposed to do? Let her starve? I couldn't let her starve. Nor could I leave her feeling alone and helpless. I HAD to betray foxkind! Why are the rules what they are?!

He knew why, of course. Humans had the power to change everything in the world, including laws about the lives of foxes. Foxes needed to protect themselves. Keeping secrets and telling lies, letting humans believe that humans were in charge while foxes manipulated them, was a necessary protection for foxes.

But it didn't always make sense. Not when some humans were worth protecting from other humans, and some humans weren't worth protecting at all.

This queen can't be a wrong person to protect, he thought. *I can feel the rightness of her heart. She must survive. And I'm going to help.*

HE WASN'T SURE how much time he had before Lovisa came. Immediately, he began to bring things to the queen.

First, her own gold rings, because the fox knew that humans treasured things like that. He was familiar with the hidden lever that opened the secret drawers in Benni's desk, but one of them opened with terrible squeaks, so he had to wait till no one was anywhere near. And he could only carry two rings at a time, so he did a lot of running.

"My rings," the queen said in astonishment, the first time he burst into the room with two of them clenched in his mouth.

Hide them in the heat duct, he said. *I'll go get more.*

"I will, of course," she said, putting them on her fingers first, holding them up to the cold starlight. One had a large white stone that sparkled against her pale brown skin. The other had two inset stones, one gold, one silver. "But please don't risk your safety for my rings."

I can bring you Katu Cavenda's ruby ring too, he said. *And some of his other things. I know where they are, his papers and his traveling things. I suppose I should leave some of them where they are, though,* he said, suddenly imagining what Benni might think if he opened his secret desk drawers and found everything gone. Maybe he should leave all of Katu's things. Maybe he shouldn't have given the queen her rings!

Then he realized that the queen had stilled her body. She'd turned to him with wide, frightened eyes. "Katu Cavenda?" she said.

Oh, yes, the fox said. *He's Ferla's brother. Ferla Cavenda is the angry woman I'm bonded to.*

The queen sat down slowly on the floor, right where she was, and hugged herself tight. "I knew it," she said. "They looked so much like him. Their faces, the white streaks in their hair. But why would his sister have taken his things?"

It was Benni Cavenda who took his things, said the fox. *So that no one would find them and realize Katu wasn't really traveling.*

"Oh, no," said the queen. "Oh, poor Katu. What's happened to him? Please tell me he's not dead."

I don't know what's happened to him, said the fox.

Do you know about two Monsean men who drowned?

A little, said the fox. *Not much. I know Ferla is angry about it. I'm better with feelings and intentions, and with things that happen nearby.*

What do you know? said the queen. *How much time do we have? I want to know as much as you can tell me.*

CHAPTER TWENTY-NINE

THAT SUNDAY AFTERNOON, no knock sounded on Lovisa's bedroom door.

Funny how your parents murdering your friend can ruin a family tradition, Lovisa thought to herself. Then she burst into laughter, then curled up on her bed feeling sick.

Vikti, Erita, and Viri will begin to wonder what's become of me.

After a failed attempt to escape into sleep, she got up and found her coat. Lovisa had decided, with a premonition that set her nerves humming, that she was going home for Sunday dinner.

THE WALK TO Flag Hill was more slippery than usual, the sun low and blinding. Lovisa's mind was unconnected to her feet. She lost her footing at the top of an icy staircase and might have cracked her skull if a passing woman hadn't shot a hand out and grabbed her arm.

"Thank you," said Lovisa breathlessly.

"No worries," said the woman in a friendly voice. Then she looked into Lovisa's face and her expression changed into one of resentful politeness. Lovisa recognized her from the dormitory kitchen. She was the young one Lovisa had eavesdropped on the day Queen Bitterblue had fallen into the sea.

I'm just a spoiled, bossy student to her, thought Lovisa, surprised at how much it stung. Everything stung her lately. Her hide was peeling away, revealing something soft and baffling, and weak.

At home, Viri was standing in the entrance foyer at the bottom of the stairs, his feet bare. At the sight of him, she felt a mute kind of panic. Why was she here? What was she going to do? And how could she keep whatever she did from hurting her brothers?

"Lovisa!" Viri cried, shivering from the blast of cold air as she pushed in. "Lovisa! Are you staying overnight? Because Vikti built a telescope!"

"How exciting," she said. "I might stay overnight, I'm not sure. Where are Mother and Papa?"

"Mother's in her study and Papa's in bed."

"Why is he in bed?"

"I don't know. He was gone overnight in the airship, then came home, then went to bed. They don't talk to each other anymore and they get angry if we ask questions. Are you staying for dinner?"

"Yes. I'm going to do some homework in Papa's library. Then I'll come play."

"When?"

"Soon. What are you doing, anyway? Are you waiting for someone?"

"I have to stand in this square," he said, pointing down at the pale marble tile beneath his bare feet.

"Why?"

"Because I was bouncing a ball against a ceiling I didn't realize was Mother's floor."

"So you have to stand on that square?" Lovisa said, not understanding.

"It's cold in here," he said. "The air swoops down the staircase and under the door. Every time someone comes in, it's freezing."

Lovisa noticed the way he was shivering, hunching his shoulders to his ears. Looking up the stairs, she saw the fox, his eyes glinting through the banister, serving as Viri's guard. If she or anyone brought Viri warm clothing or socks, he would end up with an even harsher punishment.

Something inside Lovisa went hard and certain. "I'm going to check on you," she said, "soon."

Then, a little frightened of her own fury, she turned toward her father's library.

INSIDE THE LIBRARY, Lovisa stood like a girl made of electric confusion. She hardly saw the room around her. She only saw Viri on his square, and the queen trapped in the attic room. She touched the key tucked against her breast.

Lovisa understood that she was here to get the queen out of her prison.

But how? What could she do? Make a scene at dinner? It might've worked at the dinner with the Monsean delegation, but it was too late for that now.

What, then? The fox knew she was home, which meant that her parents knew too, and would be hypervigilant about keeping her away from the attic. Should she try to incapacitate her mother some-how while her father was in bed, then run for the attic? No. What was she going to do, attack her own mother?

Lovisa went to her father's desk and began yanking the top draw-ers open, looking for some clue that would make sense of everything and tell her what to do. What had those Monseans been looking for? She found pieces of graphite, pens, envelopes, a button, a neat little pile of unpaid bills. Another neat pile of Keepish cash. No clues.

When she reached the few small panels that she knew were the fronts of secret drawers, she focused on a childhood memory. She'd pretended to fall asleep in Benni's big armchair once, then peeked through her eyelashes as he'd felt around inside one of the top drawers with a deliberation that had interested her. As she'd watched, another, handleless drawer had popped open nearby.

Lovisa took a careful breath. After a minute or so of gentle fiddling inside the top drawers, a click sounded. One of the panels sprang forward, just enough for Lovisa to slip a finger inside. Quite satisfied with herself, she pulled the hidden drawer open, then cringed in horror as it made a terrible screeching sound. Quickly, she peeked into the drawer, saw that it contained some papers and jewelry, swept everything out, and shoved it into her pocket. She slid the noisy drawer closed and ran to the armchair, where she sat with her legs curled up around her, trying to look young and calm and innocent.

After a minute passed during which no one came, Lovisa reached into her pocket and pooled the things in her lap. A ring with a large red stone was familiar, and looked like her father's style. The rest were Benni's identification book and his checkbook. She opened the identification book idly, wishing for a clue for what to do.

Katu Cavenda's name stared back at her. It wasn't Benni's identification book; it was Katu's.

With the feeling draining out of her body, she opened the checkbook and found that it was Katu's too.

And now, of course, she remembered why she recognized the ring. She'd never once seen her uncle without it. She supposed she would never see her uncle again.

Lovisa's mind was working now. She knew what she was going to do.

FIRST SHE TOOK care of her brothers.

Running back to the foyer, she glanced up the stairs and saw that the fox was gone.

"Viri," she said to the little boy whose freckled face lit up at the sight of her. "Where are Erita and Vikti?"

"In the schoolroom, I think," he said. "Mother punished them too."

"Listen, I want you to do something naughty. I can't promise that you won't get in trouble, though. Will you do it anyway?"

Viri tilted his head at her, like a curious fox. "Is it for you?" he asked, his eyes glowing at her like dark stars.

"Yes."

"You look kind of wild, Lovisa."

"Yes," she said forcefully. "I want you to leave your punishment square and run up to get your brothers. Then I want all three of you to grab your coats, sneak outside, and wait there, someplace where no one will notice you. Stay outside, all right? And keep staying outside. Don't go back inside, any of you, for at least an hour. And put on some shoes!"

"What's going to happen?" he asked.

"You'll see," she said, then thought of Viri's games and books, of his small, grim life; inexplicably, of the special pieces she loved from Mari's City board. "On your way out, fill your pockets with your favorite things, okay?"

"You mean like snacks?"

"No, like your favorite treasures," she said, ashamed when her voice choked up. "And your favorite Keeper drawings. Tell Vikti to bring his new telescope. But hurry."

Viri stared at her in astonishment. "Are we all running away together?"

"Something like that," she said. "Go now, okay? Don't let anyone see you!"

He stepped out of his square and scampered up the stairs with an expression of thrilled determination, his bare feet slapping against marble.

Please, thought Lovisa. *Let me do this right.*

Then she returned to the library, jammed a chair under the doorknob, and got started.

It was a library, which meant that it was full of tinder. It was also connected to her mother's study by the narrow flight of stairs that started behind the swinging bookcase, and Ferla's study was full of silbercow oil. If Lovisa was going to start a small, distracting fire, the staircase was probably a good location.

She ran to the shelves near the swinging bookcase and began pulling books down at random, opening them, tearing out pages and crumpling them, but quietly. Then she began carrying things up the steps on tiptoe and piling them gently, soundlessly, outside her mother's door: the crumpled paper, the logs and tinder stacked beside the fire, every lamp in the room. There were so many lamps; it took several trips. She poured some of the lamp oil over her mountain of torn pages and logs, and some onto the floor. She tried to cast oil across her mother's door, but it was hard to know where it landed. Lovisa was shaking with the desperation of having no idea what she was doing. She'd never lit a fire before, not even in a fireplace. Also, she could hear her parents' muffled voices, arguing in Ferla's study.

"Why are you here?" said Ferla. "Get out of my study. Go back to bed!"

"The Estillan envoy is coming to dinner," said Benni. "I want my banker's box."

"Oh, no you don't," said Ferla. "You'll leave that banker's box here until he comes. I don't trust you with it. Get out. Get out!"

Lovisa heard a door slam and fled downstairs again, worrying that her father would come to his library next. That stupid banker's box had been the primary mystery of her life once. Now she didn't care what was inside it. In the library, she went to the fire, took the ash shovel in one hand and the tongs in the other. Digging into the base of the fire, she scooped bright embers onto the shovel. Then she chose the most boisterously burning log from the fire and grabbed it with her tongs. It was too heavy to lift with one hand. Awkwardly, she supported it with the same hand holding the shovel.

The journey back up the staircase with a flaming log and a shovelful of burning embers was not Lovisa's best or proudest moment. Focused intently on the log, which was trying to slip out of the tongs, she kept forgetting to hold the shovel straight. Embers slid onto the staircase as she climbed, landing on her own shoes and the edges of her coat. Lovisa had never appreciated the efficacy of a flue before. The stairway became so thick with smoke that she was choking by the time she reached the top, where she had no time to make a careful choice about positioning. She poured the embers haphazardly onto a pile of crumpled paper, placed the log somewhere on the mess, turned, and ran down the stairs again. She heard a sharp sizzle behind her as a flame touched oil. There was a roar, like a wind. Then she burst back into the library, gasping, nose pouring, eyes streaming, and remembered that in an earlier life, ten minutes ago, she'd had the idea to cover her nose and mouth with a wet cloth before lighting the house on fire, then forgotten.

It was done now. She closed the swinging bookcase, wanting to cut off the smoke—then cracked it open, remembering that fires needed air. She tried to peek into the stairwell, heard snaps and hisses and growls above. Saw light. The fire seemed to be growing. The library, dark now with only the fireplace to illuminate it, hung with a haze of smoke. Lovisa ran to the main library door and listened there too, waiting to hear anything out in the corridor: shouts, cries of alarm, any sign that anyone had noticed that the second floor of the house was burning. *Be outside,* she thought to her brothers. *Be outside.* Then she thought of the guards, the attendants and maids, the cooking staff; then turned that part of her brain off. There were many ways out of the house and she'd lit the fire in a place that wouldn't trap anyone. Everyone could get out, except the queen. Everyone *would* get out, and stay out, or else they would crowd around her mother's study trying to extinguish the fire. Both possibilities would give Lovisa time to get to the queen.

It seemed to take forever. Wasn't Ferla still in her study? Mustn't there be smoke streaming under her door? Lovisa was coughing badly. With sudden forethought, she went to the desk and shoved the Keepish cash into her pockets, next to Katu's papers and ring.

Then, instantly, everything happened at once. A cry came from somewhere upstairs, then more cries. Ferla's voice, the shouts of guards. People running, doors slamming. A guard downstairs began yelling.

And then, somewhere above, there was an explosion. It was stunning. The whole house shook; plaster rained down on Lovisa from the ceiling. A moment later, a strange, metallic smell filled the air.

Lovisa didn't understand it, but it didn't matter. Grabbing the ash shovel, she ran to the window farthest from the front of the house. The shovel was solid and heavy in her hands. She raised it like a cudgel and smashed it through a windowpane, unconcerned about the guards. No one was going to investigate a tinkle of glass while the house was exploding.

As she brushed the jagged edges of glass away from the window grilles, someone—her father—tried the main library door and called her name. In a panic, she stuck one leg through the grille, then the other, then pushed, let go, dropped to the ground. The cold was shocking after the fire, the air so pure that she felt herself almost drowning in it. She ran, circling the back of the house. The house did not look right. Part of the second floor—the place where her mother's study had been—was a black, gaping hole. She couldn't think about it now; she kept running. When she reached the tree on the house's other side, she threw her shovel down. Bark scraped skin from her hands but she climbed fast and hard, thinking of Queen Bitterblue and the need not to think about anything else. The trellis was easier to scale than the tree. The window opened smoothly. Lovisa dropped inside.

In the house's warmth, she raced down corridors, straining her ears, wondering if it was only her imagination that the air here, far from the source of the fire, was smoky. She'd inhaled so much smoke already that it was hard to tell. Far away, she heard more shouts. Something else too, something she would have dismissed as wind in the eaves if she hadn't had a horrifying suspicion that it was the crackle and roar of a house on fire.

Small fire, she thought, almost crying. *I wanted a small, distracting fire!*

No one met her as she ran to the attic stairs. No guards had been dispatched to this part of the house to rescue the queen. What must it be like to be trapped in that dark, smelly room, hungry and weak, as the walls grew hot and the air filled with smoke? Her parents had chosen that fate for another human being.

At the top of the attic steps, Lovisa opened the door and burst across the cavernous space, reaching into her shirt for the key. Her hands shaking hard, she unlocked the queen's door, then pushed into the room to find the queen standing there before her, as if waiting. Queen Bitterblue wielded the letter opener in one hand like a sword, a calm, ferocious expression on her face.

"You," said the queen, in Keepish. "I didn't think you were coming."

Lovisa tried to say something in response, but began coughing uncontrollably. She grabbed the queen's arm and pulled her out of the room and down the stairs. In the third-floor corridor, the smoke stung the back of Lovisa's throat and the distant roar was louder.

"Did you do this?" asked Bitterblue.

"I had to," said Lovisa, almost sobbing, pulling Bitterblue along corridors and around corners, stumbling, rushing. Both of them were coughing now. "Are you strong enough to climb?"

"If climbing is necessary," said the queen, "I can climb."

Lovisa pulled the queen into the room with the broken lock. "We have to get you out that window, down a trellis, down a tree, then over a wall." She dragged the window open. "I should probably go first, so I can stand guard while you follow. Okay?"

"Okay," said the queen, tucking her letter opener into one of the pockets of her pajamas. Her pockets hung heavily and her feet were bare. Lovisa couldn't worry about that now. Scrambling through the window, down the trellis, down the tree, she landed solidly on both feet, right beside the shovel. Grabbing it, she held it tight, feeling strong suddenly, and desperate, and determined. Then she looked up to measure the progress of the queen, who was climbing out of the window more slowly than anyone had ever climbed out of a window.

"Hurry!" she called in a whispering kind of yell, then set her mind to figuring out the next step. Where should they go? Whom could she trust? Who would even believe that her parents were kidnappers and murderers?

Her mother's fox rounded the house and ran across Lovisa's feet.

Newly terrified, Lovisa spun around and saw Ferla bearing down on her, fists hard, eyes enormous. Somehow, Lovisa maintained the presence of mind not to glance upward and betray the location of the queen.

"Lovisa!" her mother cried, reaching out to her. "Come away from there!" Ferla tried to grab at Lovisa with hands like claws and Lovisa took a mighty swing with the shovel.

Ferla slumped to the ground. Blood seeped from her temple, black in the light from the flaming house. Then suddenly, a phenomenal explosion above lit up the sky like the sun.

The airship, Lovisa thought leadenly, craning her neck, understanding. *I destroyed the airship.* Fire from the explosion shot across the sky. Disbelieving, Lovisa heard another explosion in the distance, saw another ball of light, and understood that she'd just destroyed the Gravlas' airship too. She'd probably set Kep Gravla's house on fire. *I killed my mother,* she thought. *I destroyed everything. It was supposed to be a small fire!* Then, with dawning comprehension, *I'm going to prison for the rest of my life.*

Bitterblue was beside her now, saying something urgently, holding on to Lovisa, supporting Lovisa as Lovisa stumbled. The queen smelled terrible up close. It woke Lovisa up.

"I killed my mother," Lovisa said.

Bitterblue reached down, putting her fingers to the pulse at Ferla's throat. "Her heart is beating," she said.

A terrible relief crashed against Lovisa, followed by certainty. "If she's alive, she's going to look for us."

"Where can we go?" said Bitterblue. "Whom do you trust?"

"I don't know!" Mari flashed across Lovisa's mind. Then Nev, but Nev was already gone. "I trust two people," Lovisa said. "One, I refuse to endanger. The other went north today."

"I want to go north," said the queen firmly.

"North?" Lovisa repeated dumbly. "No. We need to bring you somewhere safe and make an announcement that you're alive in front of lots of people. Then I need to run."

"If it would make *you* safe for us to announce my safety, then that's certainly what we should do," said the queen. "But you've destroyed a lot of property and hurt your mother, and I'm not inclined to trust anyone either. I've learned—from an informant—that my friends have gone north. I think our next move would benefit from some strategic thought, someplace out of the way. I'm inclined to go north." The queen was speaking calmly, patting her pockets to check on her possessions. "Do you suppose I should take your mother's coat, and her shoes?" she added. "She won't freeze, will she?"

Tears were running down Lovisa's face. "Her fox will find her soon," she said, bending down and beginning the unpleasant task of stripping things from Ferla's insensate body, which was heavy, and seemed dead even if it wasn't. When she began to sob at how awful the job was, the queen took over, pulling off Ferla's shoes and coat, bundling herself into them. They fit her well.

"Give me that," said Bitterblue, for Lovisa still carried the ash shovel in one tight fist, as if it were an extension of her arm. It didn't seem possible to put it down. The queen wrenched it from her grip, inspected its edge. Walked to a nearby window bright with flames, used it to stab through the window glass, then threw the shovel inside.

"Have you decided what's best for us to do?" she said as she came back. "Lovisa Cavenda," she added more gently, taking the girl's arm. "That's your name, right? You're Katu's niece. We have to move."

Katu. Lovisa couldn't bear the reminder of Katu. "I have a friend in the north," she said numbly. "I miss her."

"We'll go to her," said Bitterblue. "Please, lead the way."

As Lovisa led the queen to the easy rocks at the back of the property, she could hardly believe she was leaving her own mother like that, crumpled on the ground. At the wall, she showed the queen where to put her hands and feet. The queen took forever to climb. Finally, Lovisa started up behind her, then froze in alarm as that guard, the sister of the one she'd hurt, came running around the corner of the house. The guard stopped. Gaped at Lovisa, gaped at the queen. The guard saw Ferla lying on the ground.

Then the guard looked over her shoulder, turned back, and made a sweeping motion with her hands that conveyed a clear message. *Go,* she was saying. *Run.*

With one last, heartbroken thought for her brothers, Lovisa scrambled over the wall behind the queen, jumped, and ran.

PART FOUR

THE KEEPER

WHEN THE FOUR silbercows explained to the creature what they wanted her to do, she was not impressed.

Why would I do that? she said. *How could I do that? It would draw the attention of everyone in the ocean, just when all the other silbercows are finally starting to forget about me.*

The silbercows told her that no one in the ocean was forgetting about her. All the silbercows talked about her, all the time. The only reason she didn't see them was that they were careful not to get too close to her singing range.

Good, said the creature, who actually found this to be terrible news. She started singing, putting all her refusal into it. It made her feel so brave. Once, long ago, she'd been happy. She'd had treasures and no one had come near them. She'd hid, and watched the water above, and loved her treasures. It had been all she'd wanted. Then one night, because of a terrible attack on the surface that hadn't been her fault, her life had changed, and now she had silbercow friends she missed when they were gone, and her tentacle hurt, and they wanted her to do things she didn't want to do.

When she finished her song, ruffled and triumphant, the silbercows sat silently, staring at her. She waited for them to agree amongst themselves that she was very different from the Keeper, therefore unsuited to heroics.

Instead, as they continued to stare at her, she began to notice the way their shoulders slumped and their whiskers drooped.

She felt her own body droop. *What's wrong?* she said. *Is it my singing?*

The silbercows told her that in fact, they were starting to get used to her singing. *This thing we need you to do will help humans,* they said. *And we need to help humans, because then maybe humans will remember silbercows and feel an obligation to help us. But you're the only one in the ocean big and strong enough to do what we need. We don't know what to do, if you won't help.*

The creature decided to pretend that the silbercows weren't there. She swung her eye-stems away from them and held her ring up to the light, admiring it. Then, anxiously, she pulled that tentacle close and tucked it away, because she remembered that the silbercows knew the human who'd lost the ring. She didn't want to give them ideas about "helping the humans" by returning it.

She sank down and put an eye to her Storyworld, where her two skeletons lay in their well-preserved clothing. *Mine,* she thought. *Mine.*

The silbercows were still looking at her sadly. It was setting off unhappy implosions inside her heart.

I'm scared, she said, bursting out with it suddenly. *What you're asking is scary.*

The silbercows stirred, curious and interested. They asked her why it was scary.

I've never gone far from home, she said. *I've never undone anything that was done. I've never done anything for anyone else. I've never had to give up a treasure.*

The silbercows asked her if there was anything they could do to make it easier for her to give up this treasure.

She sat with that question, circling her tentacles around her body and sinking her head down inside the cave they made. She tried to think of what would make her feel least like a hero.

Then she popped her head back up. *You could come with me and guard me from other silbercows so they don't talk to me,* she said. *You could sing with me while I go. And you could promise me that I can have my Storyworld back after the humans are done with it.*

The silbercows asked her, would she accept two out of three?

CHAPTER THIRTY

GIDDON AND HAVA flew to Torla's Neck in one of the airships that conveyed the Keepish Mail.

You would hate this, Giddon told Bitterblue as the Keepish landscape slid by below. *The rocking, and the feeling of being blown out of the sky whenever the wind hits. Hava loves it, of course. The rougher it gets, the louder she laughs. I wonder,* he thought, as another gust made him think he might dissolve into wind, *if this is how it feels to be a bird.*

Quona had arranged this conveyance for them. "It'll minimize attention," she'd said. "No one would ever expect you to fly with the Keepish Mail."

This was probably because it was so uncomfortable, the car cold and jammed with boxes and sacks, the crew working hard in the open air for most of the flight. The Mail airship was very unlike those sold to the Ledra elite, which were designed for the comfort of passengers, with warm stoves, glass windows, comfortable seats, tables for eating and drinking.

When they'd arrived at the Mail hangar that Sunday morning, only three people had been there, loading an airship car with sacks. When Hava had handed an envelope to one of them, the woman had barely glanced at it.

"From Quona Varana?" she'd said.

"Yes."

"Climb in," the woman had said. A moment later, that academy student Nev had arrived, her fox kit sleeping in a bag strapped across her front, its head craned back and its little nose sticking out. A moment after that, the Mail carriers had unhooked the dock lines and the ship had risen into the air.

The three passengers stood together, watching the coast of Winterkeep go by.

"Why exactly are you here?" Hava asked Nev.

Nev shrugged, her brown face expressionless. "Quona says I know things that put me in danger, though of course she hasn't seen fit to tell me what's actually going on."

"So she's exiling you to Torla's Neck?"

"My family is there," Nev said shortly. "I'm going home. You're welcome to stay with us."

"Oh. That's very kind, thank you," said Giddon.

"Do you know about Quona's foxes?" said Hava.

"Hava," said Giddon warningly, for they hadn't discussed how much they were going to say about that to other people.

There was a long pause, during which Nev stared down at the little fox kit sleeping against her chest. "I've suspected she might have secret foxes," she said. "Some of the fur on her clothing isn't cat fur."

"Really?" said Hava, surprised. "You can tell that?"

"She brings me to her attic sometimes, too," said Nev, "where she has a balcony for visiting the silbercows. Have you been up there?"

"Yes."

"Then I don't need to describe it. Sometimes when we arrive, the doors in the walls are flapping, as if someone just left."

"She has seven secret foxes," said Hava, which made Nev's eyebrows rise to her hairline and stay there for a while.

"So," said Giddon quietly to Hava, when Nev had moved away. "We're telling her everything, are we?"

"We're going to need her help once we're in Torla's Neck."

"How hard can it be to sneak into a house?"

"Listen, who's going to be doing most of the sneaking? You or me? I want her help."

Giddon couldn't dispute that, so he watched the landscape instead. The airship hugged the coast, passing over hills with cows grazing on their golden slopes. Idly, he counted buildings, fields, tiny bright dots in a tangle of vines that might be pumpkins. Then he lifted his eyes to the bank of clouds far out at sea, which seemed to be growing as the airship flew north, masses of gray blobs piling themselves up into mountains.

Giddon was about to ask Nev about the clouds when something astonishing came into view. He'd heard of glaciers, but he'd never seen one before. The glacier, if that's what it was, was gray and wrinkled, but shining white and blue from within, like the delicate insides of a shell, but massive, as if the earth were an animal with beautiful scales just under a translucent membrane. It flowed between mountain peaks all the way to the sea, where it dropped blue blocks of ice into the water.

On either side of the glacier, the land stretched up from the sea in dark, climbing steps that were cultivated with rows of some now-dead crop that Giddon guessed was tea. Beyond the tea stretched forests of fir trees; beyond those climbed mountain peaks with more glaciers flowing between.

He was about to ask Nev about the glaciers when Nev pointed out to sea. Giddon knew, before he even looked, what she was pointing at, for he felt them: silbercows, filling his mind with a touch as light as a soap bubble.

Hello! Giddon called out. *I hear you!* Then he saw them, racing across the surface of the water, trying to keep up with the fast-flying Mail airship.

You! they said, sending him the image of the house, the shadowy airship, and the terrible, heart-wrenching explosion. Then they sent him the *Seashell,* resting on the ocean floor beside the gigantic tentacles of the Keeper. *We will help you!*

Help me! said Giddon, surprised. *How will you help me?*

We'll bring you what you need!

What I need? said Giddon, his heart filling with Bitterblue, even though he knew that couldn't be their meaning.

In response, their own feelings changed to a kind of surprise and confusion. Tentatively, they began to show him a new story. A swimmer; a drowner. The impression of a small, cold, furious, determined, drowning person passed through Giddon like an arrow and his whole being cried out in anguish and need, because he recognized her.

Wait! he shouted, for the silbercows were turning away. A fjord reached out into the sea, cutting off their path; the airship swept on, but the silbercows had to go around. *Wait!* he screamed, running to the airship's stern, trying to hold fast to the thread connecting his mind to theirs. *Show me the rest!* he cried. *Show me the rest.* But the thread was broken. They were gone.

Giddon dropped to the floor of the deck, his face buried in his hands. When, a moment later, Hava lowered herself beside him, there was no way to pretend he wasn't sobbing.

She was quiet, waiting until he was over the worst of it.

"Did they show her to you?" he finally said when he was quieter, numb.

"Yes."

"What did it mean?"

"I don't know. It didn't mean anything, beyond what we saw. We can't even know if it's true."

"But it was her. They saw her! We need to find them and talk to them again," he said. "As soon as possible."

"Giddon," said Hava, in a low, heavy voice. "She was drowning. Do you really want the silbercows to show you the story of her drowning?"

"Yes," he said, his tears starting up again helplessly. "Because then we're there, witnessing it, and it's less like she was all alone."

LATER, AS THE light began to turn to pinks and golds, a long isthmus came into view far ahead. It formed a bridge to a spreading mass of forests that Giddon, remembering his maps, realized must be the beginning of the rest of the Torlan continent. He was looking across an isthmus at the nation of Kamassar.

"Torla's Neck," he said out loud, forming a new understanding of the name of the Keepish province that connected the continent's head to its body.

"Where's the Cavenda house?" Hava asked Nev. "Do you know?"

Nev flashed sudden, surprised eyes at Hava. "It's at the top of the isthmus," she said, "very near the border to Kamassar. We're too far away to see it from here."

"Have you been there?"

"No, I've never seen it, but Torla's Neck isn't big. Everyone knows where the rich people live. Why are you asking about the Cavenda house?"

"Have the silbercows shown you the picture of the explosion?" Hava said. "With the house?"

Nev was quiet for a beat, turning her face away so Giddon and Hava couldn't see. "Is the house in the silbercow image the Cavenda house?" she finally asked.

"We think it might be," said Hava.

"Is it their airship? Their doing?"

"We don't know. We think it might be."

"Mmph," Nev said, an obscure, but plainly dissatisfied, sound.

"What?" demanded Hava.

"I may have abandoned a friend in a time of need," she said.

———————————

THE MAIL CREW landed at an airship dock on a cliff above a rocky beach, near a cluster of buildings at the edge of a pine forest. A man came running from the closest building, waited for one of the flyers to shoot an anchor into the landing web, then fed them a dock line.

"The post office is here," one of the Mail crew said, lowering the ladder. "After we deliver our mail, we can drop you closer to where you live, if there's a dock."

"This is perfect, actually," Nev said. "I live here."

"That's lucky," said the woman.

But then, once they'd disembarked, Nev began to walk toward the cliff edge.

"Where are you going?" said Giddon.

"Home," she said.

"The houses are that way," Giddon said, pointing.

"I pretended I lived there," said Nev. "I don't need Quona Varana knowing exactly where I live. Come on, it's this way." Then, a small pack on her back and her fox still strapped to her front, she marched right off the cliff edge. Immediately it became apparent that there was a stair of rock where she'd stepped, but still, Giddon started forward in alarm.

Gathering himself, he stepped in behind her, Hava following.

THE BEACH BELOW was difficult, covered with loose, uneven rocks. Nev marched along it as if it were a smooth path through a grassy glade.

The gathering clouds on the horizon seemed closer, more menacing. "Is that a storm?" asked Giddon.

"Probably," said Nev, not even glancing at it. "They grow for days, then move in."

"That sounds ominous."

"We're used to it."

After another minute, Giddon tried again. "Are you missing classes to take this trip?"

"Yes," she said shortly, breaking off from the beach and beginning up a dirt path that climbed steeply into hills of golden grass.

"Will you be able to pick up where you stopped?" said Giddon, who usually left this nosiness to Hava, but today he was feeling unlike himself. Off-kilter, ever since the silbercows had shown him Bitterblue.

"I don't know," she said, then changed course again, leading them over the top of a hill and down onto the other side. "Shortcut," she said, at Giddon's puzzled noise.

"I wouldn't want to have to follow verbal directions," he said.

"I would never send a stranger this way."

On the other side of the hill was a low wooden door, built so neatly into the hill's slope that Giddon almost didn't notice it. "What is that?" said Giddon. "Does that open into the hill?"

"It's a sod hut," said Nev, "for if you get caught in a storm."

"But you have to know it's there for it to be useful," said Giddon. "Why is it hidden from the path?"

Nev hesitated, considering her own climbing feet. Then she said, "This is federally owned land. It's against the law for us to build on it or into it. But storms rise fast. One of my neighbors died once, when I was a kid. We do what we have to, but out of the way."

"But wouldn't Parliament understand the need for a survival hut in a place with sudden storms?"

"Parliament takes forever," said Nev. "And no. With the exception of our own few reps, they don't tend to understand anything about life in the north. They don't understand anything about anything, really. Why are they talking about legalizing zilfium use, for one, when Torla's running out of zilfium? Every time someone reminds them of that, they pretend not to hear. That's how they are. Why should we need the permission of one of their committees to do something that's common sense? We prefer to take care of ourselves without drawing their attention. None of which I would tell you if I thought you were unsympathetic, but you seem too interested in the silbercows' recent stories for that."

Giddon glanced at Hava. Hava considered him flatly, then said, "We think someone in Winterkeep drowned two Monsean diplomats because they learned a dangerous secret. We don't know if it's connected to the explosion in the silbercow stories, but we do know it connects to the Cavenda house in the north."

"I see," said Nev. "So you've come north to look at the Cavenda house?"

"Yes."

"And then what?"

Hava shrugged. "That'll depend on what we find."

"Can silbercows testify in court in Winterkeep?" asked Giddon.

"No," said Nev. "Their stories are too chaotic, and mixed with things they've imagined. Or anyway, that's what Parliament's decided."

"Have—have the silbercows shown you the story of the drowning of our queen?" asked Giddon, trying, and failing, to sound casual.

"No," said Nev. "I'm sorry."

"That's quite all right," said Giddon, sinking into disappointment. Falling behind the others, he climbed the red-gold hills, higher and higher, colder and windier, looking out at another wrinkled glacier ahead, at the whitecapped sea. This place was so different from Ledra. The views stretched on forever, vast and open, and the wind felt like it was blowing uninterrupted from the other side of the earth.

I feel like I've been sprung from a trap, he told Bitterblue, aching for her to be able to see this and feel that way too.

IT WOULD NOT have been possible to find Nev's house without her guidance, no matter if she'd given them the most detailed instructions. She continued to climb, fast and untiring, just as if she weren't carrying a pack on her back. It was beginning to grow dark.

In a part of the forest that smelled like sulfur, they wound their way among small, steaming pools of water.

"Those ones are boiling," Nev said. "Keep your distance. There's a bath behind our house that's warm and safe. We also have a barn that we use as a kind of inn for passing traders. I'm sure it's nothing like what you're accustomed to, but you're welcome to stay there. I'm afraid our house is too small to accommodate you," she added, in a voice that contained no apology, and the tiniest challenge.

"I've slept in plenty of haystacks," Hava said.

"I spent my last birthday sleeping in a wedge of wet rock while moldy water dripped on my head," Giddon said.

"Show-off," said Hava, switching into Lingian to deliver her insult.

"Brat."

"Bully."

Giddon was relieved to see Hava's grin. Hava had a way of peering out across the landscapes of Torla's Neck, eyes narrowed and calculating, that made him feel like she was planning escape routes. "You know we need you for the Cavenda house operation, right?"

Hava snorted. "Giddon, I *am* the Cavenda house operation."

A stone barn with a wood-shingled roof emerged through the trees, with a garden and a tiny stone house just beyond, smoke rising from its chimney.

A sob caught in Nev's throat, then she began to run.

NEV'S FATHER WAS the only person home, and he couldn't have been more astonished to see Nev. Or more happy. He embraced her, this steel-haired man named Davvi who was as big as Giddon, tears streaming down his brown face. Nev and Davvi looked very much alike, tall, straight-shouldered. "And a fox kit?" he asked wonderingly.

"We're not bonded," said Nev. "I'm just taking care of her. Papa, these are two of the Monsean delegates, Giddon and Hava. Have you heard the news of the Monsean delegates?"

"Yes, of course. I'm so sorry about your queen," Davvi said to them, with immediate and sincere feeling. "Have you eaten?" he asked next.

He ushered them to a tiny table in a corner of the tiny, dark room, not asking why they'd come, bringing them bowls of a soup of meat and potatoes and thick, delicious slices of buttered bread. Then he stared happily at his daughter while she tried to explain the odd circumstance of their arrival. The silbercows' stories, Quona Varana's worries for her safety, her companions' needs. "They have snooping to do," she said. "We'll have to organize a boat. There's more to tell, but I'll wait for Mama and Grandpa to get home."

Davvi waved this away almost with impatience, as if the Monseans' needs were beside the point. He was so happy. It amazed him that his daughter should have flown home in an airship. He seemed to attribute it to the importance of the Monsean guests, then was concerned at Nev's suggestion that Hava and Giddon sleep in the barn. He was the opposite of his daughter, his feelings always apparent, his doubts expressed with jumping eyebrows and cries of alarm.

When Nev stood and offered to show them to the barn, Giddon let her and Hava step out of the house ahead of him.

"Excuse me, sir," he said quietly to Davvi.

"Yes?"

Giddon was feeling as if he'd slid out of his own body and was watching a large, bearded actor talk mechanically to a kind man. He understood where the strangeness was coming from. He had a question, and he was terrified of the answer. It would be better if he didn't ask it.

It burst out.

"If silbercows see a person drowning," he said. "Do they let them drown?"

Davvi's face moved with sympathy. "Silbercows are known for

trying to save the lives of drowning humans. I don't believe they would ever just watch a human drown."

"Then—if they do save a human, where do they take them?"

"Wherever they can," said Davvi. "Land, a ship, an airship. There are many happy stories. Sad ones too, I'm afraid, for sometimes the water's too cold. Why do you ask?"

"I'm just curious," said Giddon.

THE BARN WAS not what he'd expected. No beds of straw, no chilly drafts through ill-fitting shutters. Instead, he stepped into a long, cavernous, tall-ceilinged space with smells and flickering lanterns that reminded him of the horse stables of his childhood in the Middluns. Under the incurious gaze of one of the tallest cows Giddon had ever seen, Nev directed him to a corner of the barn where four small rooms had been built, clearly for the comfort of travelers.

Giddon's room was barely big enough for its furniture, and dark. He suspected he wouldn't see any glass in Torla's Neck until he reached the Cavenda house. But the room was clean, and warm from the heat of the brazier Nev lit for him. The bed was comfortable, his blankets soft.

Lying down, Giddon watched the light his brazier threw against the even boards of the ceiling, listened to the rustle of the chickens whose coop was on the other side of the barn. He felt that his heart was being pulled apart.

What if the silbercows had been showing him the story of Bitterblue's rescue?

But how could that be, when she'd never turned up anywhere alive?

Bitterblue? he ventured, afraid of the thing he wanted more than anything. *What do I do? How do I find out? And how will I survive, if it's not true?*

Chapter Thirty-one

Lovisa woke to the sound of crashing waves, her body colder, her muscles achier than they'd ever been before.

She sat up, knocking sand out of the fur of her coat, then squinting at the glare of a bonfire that shot its flames into the sky. They'd followed the light of this bonfire last night, climbing up and down hills, keeping it in view. When they'd finally arrived, they'd found the beach already crowded with sleepers, huddled together in blankets. Beyond the fire, carts had been scattered across the sand, horses whickering softly, people moving among them. Lovisa hadn't wanted to walk onto the beach, once she'd seen its inhabitants.

But the Queen of Monsea had made a guess that a city beach like this one was populated by the continent's poorer travelers and other ragtag citizens at night, and that two girls at loose ends would go unnoticed and unharmed, as long as enough of the others on the beach were women too.

"We'll make a better plan tomorrow," she'd said, leading Lovisa to the fire. Well, now the sky was streaked with pink; it was morning. Lovisa hoped the queen would wake soon, with some ideas about that plan.

The Queen of Monsea kept sleeping, despite all the clamor around them of wind and water, protesting horses, the shouts of waking people. Lovisa finally gave her shoulder a heartless shove.

The queen pushed herself up sleepily, awkwardly. As she glanced around, her face to the light, Lovisa became aware of a new problem. The queen's light brown skin and pale gray eyes were going to arouse curiosity. No one would mistake her as Keepish.

"Where are you two from?" said a voice.

Lovisa kept her expression flat as she turned to assess the speaker. It was a Keepish-looking woman who sat alone on a stump before the fire, apparently tending it, for as she waited for their response, she lifted a log from a stack at her side, leaned forward, and threw it onto the flames.

Lovisa had never dealt with a woman like this before, rough and blunt, steel-colored hair jabbing its way out of her hat. She was wearing neither coat nor gloves as she handled the coarse, splintery wood. Her fingers looked like hard stubs.

"Where are *you* from?" Lovisa said, surprised by the hoarseness of her throat and her own ragged voice.

"I asked you first," said the woman, with an icy smile.

"And I need a sense of whether I can trust you before I answer."

The woman threw her head back and laughed. "Bold words for someone so little. Are you girls in trouble?"

"Why are you asking?"

The woman chuckled again. "Because I'm inclined to help girls in trouble. Of course, I can only help you to the extent you're willing to trust me. You'll have to decide that for yourselves."

Lovisa glanced at Bitterblue. The queen was gazing up at the city rising above the water, its hills, towers, and spires touched by the sun's glow.

"Beautiful," Bitterblue said. Then she pulled off one of her many gold rings—Lovisa couldn't remember seeing those rings on her fingers before, but she knew the Lienid tradition—and held it in the palm of her hand. "Do you know of a place where I could get a warm bath?" she asked the woman.

This made the woman laugh again, then look upon them with something that really did feel like kindness, without self-interest.

"I do, actually," she said. "Far from the eyes of your wealthy persecutors."

"Do we so obviously have wealthy persecutors?" asked Bitterblue.

"With your evasive answers, and those fine coats you're wearing? And those thick golden rings on your fingers? I hear your accent too, girl. You should take those rings off if you don't want rumors circulating about a wealthy Lienid girl on Trader's Beach."

Bitterblue pulled her hands inside her sleeves. "Rumors about me are fine," she said. "It's my friend we don't want people noticing."

"Interesting," said the woman. "What else do you need, besides a bath?"

"Nothing," said Lovisa, who needed so many things. She needed to know what rumors were being told of a fire last night in Flag Hill. She needed to know how to get to the north, without an airship and without being recognized. And she needed the queen to stop talking so much.

"Are you on the run?" asked the woman.

"No," said Lovisa, too quickly.

"Mm-hm," said the woman. "The proprietor of the bath I mentioned can help people on the run. Especially people who want to get far away, fast. Ask her about it, if you like, and show her your fancy rings. And don't delay, for there's a storm moving in."

How suspiciously easy, how amazing that this woman could provide every last thing they needed. "Why don't you just point us toward this bath," Lovisa said, with no real intention of visiting the bath, "and we'll go."

"You won't find it on your own," the woman said. "I'll provide someone to lead you."

"No," said Lovisa. "We prefer to manage alone."

"But," Bitterblue said to Lovisa, "do you know the route to your friend?"

Lovisa responded in Lingian so that the beach woman wouldn't understand. "How hard can it be? We follow the coast."

"Do you know the terrain?" asked Bitterblue, also in Lingian. "Do you know how to sleep outside in the cold?"

"We'll find hotels!"

"Do you know for a fact that there are hotels? Hotels where you won't be recognized, or our identities guessed? Won't your parents ask at the hotels? We need to get you away from here quickly, without leaving a trail."

"'Far away, fast' means airships," said Lovisa. "Airships mean the Varana family. What if this woman is trying to drop us into the lap of the Ledra elite?"

"Does she really look to you like someone in league with the Ledra elite?"

"Is this the better plan you promised?" said Lovisa hotly. "Trusting everyone we meet?"

"We're going to have to trust some people! At least occasionally!"

"You need to start being honest about who you are," Lovisa said. "People won't hurt you if they know you're the drowned queen."

"We need to get you someplace safe before we start throwing that truth around."

"Maybe do not assume that people you meet speak no Lingian," said the woman, in rough but coherent Lingian.

Lovisa looked up at her in slack surprise. The woman was studying Bitterblue with a dawning interest, but she spoke plainly. "This is Trader's Beach," she said, speaking Keepish again. "This is where the Royal Continent ships come in. We all understand a bit of every language that passes through. Just a tip, as you make your way up the coast."

"Ah," said Bitterblue. "Thank you."

"You're welcome," the woman said. "As far as whom to trust, I'm Ona, and I live on this beach. I'm known as the firekeeper. Everyone knows me; ask whomever you like about me. I'm not going to sell two frightened girls to the wolves, certainly not to the Varanas. Anyone will tell you so. And I think that after all," she said, flicking a glance at the ring Bitterblue still held in her palm, "I'm not going to take one of those rings, just for helping you find a bath."

It seemed to Lovisa that the part of her that decided things, always so clever and sharp and keen, was broken. She couldn't sense the air around this woman. She couldn't feel whether it was smart to trust her or not. But she knew they had to do something. She glared at Bitterblue, who was probably making bad, unsafe decisions from a place of impatience and desperation, and felt tears sliding down her cheeks.

Except that Bitterblue didn't look desperate or impatient. She looked confident and unruffled, curious. *Happy.* She reminded Lovisa of Mari, when he was telling her the latest thing he'd learned in one of his doctoring classes. And she reminded Lovisa of Nev, needing no one, sure of herself.

Angrily, Lovisa flicked her tears away. She couldn't trust Bitterblue, but she had no ideas of her own. She would trust the part of Bitterblue that reminded her of Mari and Nev.

A KEEPISH GIRL who wouldn't tell them her name led them to the bath, north along a seaside promenade. From there, Lovisa had a clear view of the clouds gathering on the horizon.

To their left were cliffs that dropped to the water. Sometimes the path turned into wooden footbridges that crossed deep ravines. It was plain that the queen didn't like the footbridges; she bolted across them, squeaking in alarm when they shifted or swung under her feet.

"They're designed to move with the wind," said their guide, who was as small as Lovisa and the queen. Lovisa wondered if Ona had chosen this girl on purpose, to make them feel safe. So they'd be more easily taken in?

"How much farther is it to the bath?" Lovisa asked.

"Maybe an hour," the girl said, "at this pace." She led them off the path and away from the water, uphill, into a grove of trees. She kept glancing with big eyes at Bitterblue, which meant that the gossip had already begun. Bitterblue was eating, for Ona had given them bread, fruit, nuts for their journey. In fact, Bitterblue hadn't stopped eating since the moment the food arrived. She chewed slowly, with a kind of reverence. *Because my parents starved her,* Lovisa thought.

Their route steepened. At a high break in the trees, Lovisa stopped and looked back, trying to catch sight of Flag Hill.

"What is it?" asked Bitterblue, stopping with her.

Lovisa shook her head, wanting, needing to be left alone as she tried to find the place where her house had burned, and the Gravla house too. Needing to see with her own eyes what she'd done. Wishing she could spot her brothers, which was absurd, of course. But all she saw were hints of peaked roofs and more trees. She couldn't find it.

"Are you all right?" said Bitterblue.

"Fine."

"We're almost to the bath," Bitterblue told her gently.

"Don't patronize me," said Lovisa.

LOVISA HAD BEEN to most parts of Ledra, usually transported in the Cavenda airship, which dropped her down exactly where she meant to go. She'd never been in the woods an hour's hike north of Ledra, in a grove of conifer trees with a floor of uneven stones. Nor had she ever been instructed to keep to the higher stones so as not to leave footprints.

It was foolhardy to follow a stranger into a forest, leaving no trace. But Lovisa had given up on sense. She'd given up on curiosity too. When the rocks turned to a visible path of packed snow, leading through the trees to a small, stone building with a neat wooden door,

Lovisa only felt impotent and tired. How little she knew about her own home.

They entered the building to find an elderly Keepish woman reading a book, surrounded by lamps and braziers, her feet propped on a desk. She narrowed her eyes at Bitterblue, then Lovisa, then flicked an inquiring glance at their guide.

"Ona says hello," the guide said.

"Hello, Ona," said the woman.

"She says these two want a bath, then a conversation with Vera."

The woman nudged her chin at Bitterblue. "This one has a Royal Continent look."

"Rumor has it she's the lost Queen of Monsea," said their guide, "which we're keeping to ourselves."

"You mean she's one of the impersonators," said the woman.

"Nope," said their guide, with a small flash of a smile. "The real thing."

The elderly woman raised her eyebrows, studying Bitterblue over her own extended legs. "I thought you drowned," she said, like an accusation.

"I didn't," said Bitterblue.

"Well, isn't that interesting," said the woman. "The bathhouse is that way. Put your fancy clothing and shoes in one of the cabinets and wear a tunic. Then follow the stone path that starts at the green door."

And that was it. No questions or demands, not even much in the way of surprise that the drowned Queen of Monsea should land on their doorstep. Who were these people?

Lovisa and the queen did as they were told, undressing in a strange, bare stone room with wooden cabinets lining the walls, pulling on brown, shapeless tunics that hung on hooks. Under Ferla's coat, the queen was still wearing Lovisa's pajamas. Lovisa tried not to stare at her pale, too-thin body as Bitterblue took the pajamas off, or cringe at how she smelled. *My parents did that to her, for almost three weeks,* she thought, trying to feel sorrow, or anger, or shame. But all she felt was numbness.

"What is it?" said Bitterblue.

"Nothing," said Lovisa. "Those are my pajamas."

Passing through a green door, they emerged into the shock of a freezing morning. A stone path, cold on their feet, led them away from the bathhouse. One of the queen's feet was bleeding. She left red spots on the stones and winced as she walked, but she was cradling a pear like it was her precious child, and she was glowing with happiness.

At the pool, pale blue and steaming, Lovisa found the stone steps and descended straight into the water, crouching low until her body was submerged to the neck. Then she closed her eyes, not caring what the queen did, because a perfect warmth hugged her, embracing her with comfort that she didn't deserve. She dipped her face below the surface so the queen wouldn't see her sudden, inexplicable tears. But she couldn't hide the noises she was making, gasping, blubbering, sobbing. Weak. *Stop it. Stop it!*

Quietly, with annoyingly perfect tact, the queen moved away into a different part of the pool, where she ate her pear and pretended not to mind Lovisa's hysterics. She set the pear core on the pool's edge. Submerging her head, she seemed to be pushing her hands roughly through her hair, loosening her braids, scrubbing her scalp with her fingers. Then she noticed one of the yellow clumps of soap that sat at the edge of the pool.

"Oh," she said in a voice of veneration, then spent some time using the soap, applying it carefully, wonderingly, the same way she ate her food. "This is one of the best and most-needed baths of my life," she said.

"One of?" said Lovisa, who was more under control now. "How many times have you been kidnapped before this?"

Bitterblue smiled. "My life hasn't always been soft."

"Is this your idea of a soft life? Bathing in a rough public pool in a scratchy tunic, with somebody's leftover soap?"

Bitterblue only smiled again, closed her eyes, and ducked under the water. Lovisa didn't know why she kept throwing sharp little stones, launching them with hot bursts of breath, but every time they failed to wound, it made her want to throw them harder. Because that's who she was: a girl who burned down her own house, attacked her own mother, abandoned her little brothers.

She stood abruptly, left the water, and marched back to the bathhouse. There, she made herself wait outside in the cold, shaking as the wind chilled the water on her skin, until she couldn't bear it anymore.

Weak, she thought to herself ferociously. Then she let herself inside.

SOMETIME LATER, LOVISA and Bitterblue met Vera in yet another stone room, tucked among trees down another winding path. Lovisa had been to public baths before. None of them were isolated like this, or empty of patrons, or peppered with tiny, hidden, chimneyless rooms, or cloaked in so much secrecy.

Vera was gray-haired, tough, and expressionless, as the firekeeper and the bath monitor had also been. "Are you all sisters?" Lovisa asked.

Vera ignored this. "I've been hearing some unlikely rumors," she said, peering with hard eyes at Bitterblue. "But there are plenty of dark-haired girls with Royal Continent looks on our roads, saying they're the lost Queen of Monsea."

"Really?" said Bitterblue, quite surprised. "Why would anyone do that?"

"She means impersonators," said Lovisa.

Bitterblue was astonished. "You mean impersonators of *me*?"

"Traveling actors," said Lovisa, shrugging. "They put on a show. Like, dancing or something."

"Dancing!" said the queen, her voice more delighted and more incredulous with every word. Then she laughed, like a sweet, clear bell. "The kind of dancing where you keep your clothes on, or take them off?"

"You two have quite a patter going," said Vera, unimpressed. "Where do you want to go?"

"We're not telling you that," said Lovisa, in the same moment the queen said, "North."

"How far north?" said Vera. "Hardippa? Torla's Neck? Kamassar?"

"Hardippa," said Lovisa in an attempt at misdirection, in the same moment the queen said, "Torla's Neck."

"You might want to consult with each other," said Vera, "before you start putting your money down for things. Though I understand you're the one likely to pay," she added, turning her eyes to the queen. Bitterblue handed her a ring, which she considered closely.

"I have cash," said Lovisa, hearing her own childish belligerence and not understanding it. Who cared where they went? Who cared who paid?

"Let's save it," said Bitterblue quietly, "until we really need it. My rings are replaceable."

Vera was now studying Bitterblue more closely, with a new, amused gleam in her eyes. "Besides," she said, "I think that after all, I'd like a ring or two. I have a feeling that someday, they'll be souvenirs of a very interesting story."

"Oh?" said Bitterblue. "You've changed your mind about whether I'm an act?"

"My colleagues are quick to believe stories," she said. "I believe gold. I know the difference between the rings worn by the Lienid commonfolk and the rings they don't ever wear. Though I suppose you could be a thief," she added, still peering at Bitterblue critically. "But that would also be an interesting story."

"What exactly are we paying for with these rings?" Lovisa said. "We're not boarding an airship leased from the Varanas."

"Indeed you're not," said Vera. "We'll leave as soon as the sky is dark, and have you in Torla's Neck by morning. Until our departure, you're welcome to enjoy the comfort of our baths again, or the bathhouse."

"The baths or the bathhouse? Nighttime is hours from now!"

"There's nothing I can do about that," said Vera. "No number of fine gold rings will make the earth turn faster."

BACK IN THE bathhouse, the queen began to strip off her coat.

"You're bathing again?" said Lovisa.

"My whole body hurts," Bitterblue said. "It hurts less in the bath."

"Where did you get all your rings?" said Lovisa, watching them flash as the queen undressed. "I'm sure you weren't wearing them the first time I saw you."

"I found them," said Bitterblue.

"In the attic room?" said Lovisa, surprised.

"Yes."

"Oh," said Lovisa, slipping her hand into her pocket, touching Katu's ring.

"May I ask," said Bitterblue, "if you know anything about my delegation? Hava, Coran, Barra, Froggatt? Giddon?"

"I heard that Coran, Barra, and Froggatt went to Kamassar," said Lovisa. "Giddon and Hava stayed in Ledra. They came to dinner at my house one night and I caught them snooping in my father's desk." How angry she'd been about that, once. "I didn't know you were in our attic then," she added defensively, not actually sure she would've told them if she'd known.

The queen only nodded. "Did they find anything?"

"Not that I know of."

"How much do you know about what's going on?"

Lovisa's fingers closed around her uncle's ring. It was a small, hard, sharp reminder of why she'd done all the things she'd done. She pulled it out and sat beside the queen.

"This is what Hava and Giddon would've found," she said, "had they known how to open the hidden drawers in my father's desk."

"Katu's ring," said Bitterblue.

Lovisa was astonished. "You know my uncle's ring?"

Bitterblue glanced once, thoughtfully, into Lovisa's face. "I know your uncle," she said. "He visited my court a while back, for rather a long time. The first time I saw you, in fact, I thought of him, because of your hair."

"Oh, of course," said Lovisa, remembering Katu's stories about visiting the Monsean queen. Irrationally resentful, suddenly, of their time together in a place Lovisa had never been. "His ring made that much of an impression on you?"

Bitterblue shrugged with one small shoulder. "Rings matter to the Lienid. Do you know what happened to him? Have you heard from him since he started traveling?"

"He hasn't written," said Lovisa, who no longer had any doubt about why. "And he's been drawing money from his bank using checks in places like Kamassar and Borza, but I also found these in the desk." She fished Katu's identification papers and checkbook from her coat pocket and passed them into the queen's hands.

The queen examined this new evidence soberly. "It doesn't look good."

"I'm sure he's dead," said Lovisa, her voice flat and hard.

"I'm holding out hope until we know for certain."

"Oh? And how exactly will we ever know? Do you think they erected a sign over his body or something?"

Bitterblue's eyes touched Lovisa's with a kind of gentleness that irritated Lovisa further. "I intend to learn every single detail of what's going on," said the queen. "I believe it's a story that touches my own kingdom, which means I *need* to know."

"Why should Katu's murder touch your kingdom?" said Lovisa, with a sudden, vicious stab of jealousy. "He's not *your* uncle."

"I think he was murdered because he knew about things that touch my kingdom."

"What things, then?"

The queen hesitated. "Lovisa," she said, "how much do you want to know?"

Lovisa's fingers closed so tightly over Katu's ring that it hurt her palm. "What you mean by that is that my parents have done even more bad things, besides kidnapping you, murdering Pari, and probably Katu."

"Yes," said Bitterblue.

Lovisa stared at her hand. At the way her knuckles showed a paler brown because of how hard she was holding Katu's ring. She'd heard them arguing, after all. Her parents had had some kind of plan. Her father had been hiding something important in a banker's box. The Estillan envoy had been involved.

"I'll have to know eventually," she said dully. "It's not like I can live my life never knowing."

"How about I promise to tell you what I know," said Bitterblue, "but not right now?"

Lovisa was thinking of the cave her mother had used to tell her about, where she and Katu had been sent when they were children, as a punishment. Lovisa imagined it vast and secret, with smooth, curved walls and high ceilings, far removed from regular life, a place to hide, and not so scary if Katu was there too. She wished she could live in that cave, alone, touched by nothing. "Yes," she whispered.

"Are you coming into the bath?" asked the queen.

"No," said Lovisa, who needed solitude.

"All right," said Bitterblue, removing her shoes, inspecting the burst blister on the bottom of her foot. Touching Lovisa with worried glances.

"I would like to return my uncle's ring to his body," Lovisa said.

"I understand that," said Bitterblue. "Things like that have meaning. I had one ring that was unique and irreplaceable, and more important than any others. It was one my mother wore, in honor of me." She held her palms open and examined them, as if she were looking for something there. "It slipped off while the silbercows were rescuing me," she said. "It's at the bottom of the Brumal Sea."

How nice to have a mother to mourn, instead of parents you wished were dead.

Lovisa shouldered her way out of the room and into the cold.

LOVISA HAD DONE a lot of sneaking in her life, poking where she didn't belong, but never in a forest.

She knew the path from the bathhouse to Vera's office, so she headed down that path now. She noticed that it wasn't the most direct route to Vera's office; rather, beginning with a scramble of high rock, it veered off the wrong way at first. For misdirection? The footprints and packed snow began again after the scramble of rock, but someone standing at the bathhouse wouldn't be able to see that. The path turned to high rocks again as she neared Vera's office. A stranger who found Vera's office first would likely not find the bath.

She didn't go into Vera's office. Instead she searched the office's perimeter for more groups of rocks that could make a footprint-free path. She saw two options: one easier path with high, flat boulders, the other with sharp, sloping rocks that lined the crest of a winding ridge.

Seeing no reason to make this harder than necessary, she chose the easier route. For three minutes or so, she stepped from boulder to boulder, sometimes needing to jump, once using an overhanging limb to swing herself across a gap. Eventually, the boulders petered out into untouched snow. This was a path to nowhere.

She turned back. When she reached Vera's office, Vera was standing there, watching her arrival.

Lovisa ignored her.

"You're an interesting one," Vera said.

"How are we getting to Torla's Neck?" Lovisa said.

"There's some news from the city," Vera said. "Two houses burnt down in Flag Hill."

Lovisa stopped. Said nothing, just looked at Vera with as much dispassionate boredom as she could muster.

"The fire was started by a suicidal girl named Lovisa Cavenda who lived in one of the houses," said Vera. "Then spread to the other house when an airship exploded. The mother of the girl, who happens to be President Ferla Cavenda, was injured by falling wood. The daughter is presumed dead. Sad story, isn't it?"

Lovisa swallowed. "Was anyone else hurt besides the president and the daughter?"

"No," said Vera.

Her brothers were safe.

"But there's talk of changing the laws about how airships are docked," Vera said, "now that we see what happens if the dock catches fire."

Her mother was alive and her brothers were safe. And her parents were using the fire as an opportunity to ruin her reputation and pretend she was dead.

Her brothers probably believed that story. Mari probably did too. Lovisa's voice was rough. "How much does it cost to send a signal message from Torla's Neck to the Magistry in Ledra?"

"That depends," said Vera. "If you're reporting some sort of crime, and if you have credible evidence of the crime, it doesn't cost anything."

"The Queen of Monsea is pretty credible evidence," said Lovisa.

"I expect you're right," said Vera, with a quick smile that looked more like a grimace. Then she said, "How old are you?"

"Sixteen," said Lovisa.

For the first time, a softness touched Vera's face. To avoid the way it made her start to feel things, Lovisa turned and began scaling the second rock path, the one that looked uneven and difficult. Once she was on it, she found that it had deceived her, for with every step, a clear, flat surface met her feet. It was designed to look more treacherous than it was.

"Don't you worry about what you find out there, Lovisa Cavenda," said Vera. "I don't know what brought you here with the Monsean queen, but we'll get you to Torla's Neck safe."

WHAT LOVISA FOUND was a trail of trampled snow that led to a clearing. An enormous white sheet was stretched across the clearing between the trees, like a high roof. Lovisa understood that it was meant to look like a snowy field to any airships passing above.

Below the sheet was something resembling a toy airship her brothers might have made out of junk they'd found around the neighborhood on garbage collection day. It was tiny. The passenger area, which was roofless, was smaller than the smallest rowboat Lovisa had ever seen. The balloon, made of patches of some unrecognizable fabric, was pitiful, as if a real airship had had a baby that now lay sleeping, dreaming it could fly. The entire thing, car, sails, balloon, mast, boom, lines, was painted black.

Lovisa climbed inside. She wanted to see the varane tank that supplied the balloon with gas. When she found it, she started to laugh. It looked like something built of cheap tin and battered under the hooves of horses.

It was strange, the way she couldn't feel fear anymore. It was as if a balloon of nothingness had replaced her insides. She didn't care if this illegal pseudo-airship fell out of the sky while they flew to Torla's Neck.

No. That wasn't quite true, because her brain was starting to work again, ever since hearing that her brothers were safe. Where were they? Who was caring for them? Maybe Viri, Erita, and Vikti would never forgive Lovisa for what she'd done. But she could still send a message to the Ledra Magistry. With the queen's help, she could get her parents put into prison, couldn't she? In prison, they would be far away from the boys. Surely that would be better. Someone would take care of them, right? Someone competent, who didn't ruin everything, the way she did. Lovisa wanted a different life for her brothers than the one she'd lived. She wanted more for them: more choice, less punishment, less fear. She didn't need to be able to feel her feelings to know that that was true.

CHAPTER THIRTY-TWO

BITTERBLUE COULDN'T STOP smelling her own skin.

It smelled like soap, and she was the Queen of Monsea again, and Giddon and Hava were out there somewhere—were they safe? Would she be able to find them? Her thoughts were tumbling over each other and she couldn't stop eating. In fact, all her appetites were returning.

She kept picturing Giddon answering the door of his rooms, shirtless, with mud streaking his chest. She'd always noticed Giddon's steadiness and size, she'd tucked herself against him and felt how attached he was to the earth, but she hadn't known about his muscled shoulders, his chest, his arms, about how he *looked* half-dressed, and now she kept flushing with heat as she sat in the bath, eating fruit and hugging herself like she was trying to establish her own borders. She shouldn't be thinking about this. The fox had told her that Benni Cavenda had murdered her two men. She should be making plans to avenge Mikka and Brek. Instead she was spinning like a ball on a string, unwinding from weeks of pent-up tension.

Calm down, she kept telling herself. *Calm down. You're safe now.*

When Lovisa told her they'd be flying to Torla's Neck in an illegal, unregistered, uninspected airship that looked like something one of her brothers would make, then clarified that none of her brothers was older than nine, Bitterblue went to Vera and asked if there was a dark room where she could lie down for a while. "I'm a little over-whelmed," she said, speaking a thousand times more calmly than she felt. "Also, I'm afraid of heights and I get seasick. I'm concerned about this flight."

"Queen Bitterblue," said Vera. It was the first time anyone had called her that since she'd fallen out of her royal ship into the sea, and it helped. It made her feel like a person contained in a body, rather than a ball of frantic fear unraveling all over Vera's office. "We have teas in Winterkeep to help you with those feelings."

"You do?"

"In particular, we have a tea called rauha. It helps with motion sickness, while creating a state of anxiety-free well-being."

"It sounds like magic," said Bitterblue suspiciously. "There must be something wrong with it."

Vera nodded. "Certainly. It'll turn you silly. You should perhaps not make any important decisions while under its influence. And it's addicting if you take it every day, so you must use it only occasion-ally. You're small," she said, cocking her head sideways, surveying Bitterblue. "Your dose will be low."

"Is it legal?"

"Yes, and regulated. That's how we can be sure of your dose. Would you like to try some before night comes, as an experiment?"

Bitterblue had the sense sometimes that her entire life was an exper-iment. Should she try this drug, being pushed upon her by a criminal smuggler? "Why do you operate illegal airships?" she demanded.

Vera's expression was as closed as ever. "Because a single power-ful family in Ledra shouldn't have a monopoly on an idea," she said. "Especially an idea for which they overcharge."

"How did you get the technology? Please tell me that you do, in fact, use known technology?"

"All you need is one genius who has a modest position as a chemist in a Varana factory, a few years to observe and experiment, and a disregard for the non-disclosure contracts she signs."

"I see."

"A single family shouldn't have a monopoly on an idea," Vera said again.

"So your reasons are socialist," Bitterblue said dryly. "And ideological."

A sudden, surprising smile broke across Vera's brown face. "Sure," she said. "Also, Kamassarian smugglers pay us a lot of money for them."

"You build them for Kamassarian smugglers?"

"Or anyone Kamassarian who can promise to fly them only at night," Vera said. "We sell to the occasional Borzan too. Now, how about it? Would you like to try our rauha? It, at least, is thoroughly legal."

She spoke with a pleasant sort of graciousness that made Bitterblue laugh suddenly, and want to trust her about the tea. *What should I do?* she thought. *Giddon?* And with that, the answer came to her easily, for if there was a tea that might comfort Bitterblue through some of the natural and unnatural terrors of her life, of course Giddon would want her to try it.

"I'll have the tea," she said.

"Good," said Vera.

Thus, Bitterblue floated peacefully across the nighttime sky, letting an ocean of stars sink into the backs of her eyes. It was a new moon. She found it, its orb in shadow, and wished she could point it out to Giddon. Remembering her dizzy nights on the ship watching the sky with Giddon, she examined her present feelings. *I'm stronger than the way anything makes me feel,* she told Giddon. *I miss you. I miss you. Stay alive, so I can tell you how much I miss you.*

Then one logical, important, terrifying thought tore her mind away from Giddon. *Lovisa.* The girl stood across from Bitterblue at the edge of the little car, leaning out and looking down. Bitterblue didn't like the tension in Lovisa's shoulders, or how far she was leaning.

Standing was too scary, so Bitterblue scooted across on the floor. "Lovisa?" she said, literally sitting at Lovisa's feet.

"What?" the girl said, in a voice like Bitterblue had woken her from a deep sleep.

"Would you come sit down here with me?" she said. "I'm scared."

"I don't believe you're scared," said Lovisa. "You drank rauha."

Bitterblue wondered if maybe rauha made you un-scared of being blown away or crashing or other imaginary terrors, but left you free to see the real, truly scary things that stood in front of your eyes. "Please?" she said. "I was also hoping you'd explain about . . ." She grasped for a topic. "The history of proprietary technology in Winterkeep."

Lovisa let out one long, irritated sigh. Then she slumped down beside Bitterblue like a rag doll, a girl stuffed with disappointments. For a while she said nothing. Eventually she began a monologue, expressed in a very bored voice, about Winterkeep's proprietary attitudes toward airship and other technologies. She had a lot of opinions. Mostly her opinions were that all politicians in Winterkeep, and probably everywhere else too, were contemptible deceivers, motivated by money.

It was fascinating to hear someone so young speak so knowledgeably, and so cynically, about Winterkeep's political parties. Eventually, Bitterblue forgot that she'd asked the question in order to keep Lovisa from jumping out.

IN EARLY MORNING, the airship landed in a field that looked like a piece of night sky as they descended, so thick was it with scattered lamps. Bitterblue didn't understand the landing process. It seemed to involve people in the airship shooting small hooks at nets positioned on the ground.

When it was time to disembark, she climbed down the ladder, stumbled into the snow, then fell.

"It's my land legs," she said as Lovisa and one of the flying team hauled her back up again. "And my intoxication." Then a random man appeared out of the darkness and made her jump.

"Which way to wherever we're going?" she asked him, in Lingian. "Oh, I'm sorry," she said, repeating the question in Keepish, then beginning to giggle.

"Well now, where are you going?" asked the man, who was broad-chested and deep-voiced, with glasses that glinted from the light of the lantern he carried. He seemed surprised to be accosted by a small, swaying woman.

"I have no idea," Bitterblue responded, patting his chest as she enunciated each syllable. "My, my. Your chest is nice."

"Thank you," he said, chuckling.

"Um," said Lovisa, hastily interjecting. "We're looking for the home of a girl named Nev who studies animal medicine at the Winterkeep Academy."

"And where does she live?"

"I don't know," said Lovisa, "beyond that she's in Torla's Neck. We left in a hurry."

"Okay," the man said doubtfully, then pointed toward pure darkness. "I recommend you go that way until you find a trodden path atop a cliff. Then head north—to the right on the path—until you reach a small town set against some trees. Ask someone to direct you to the Magistry office there. Maybe they can help you find your friend."

"You're very kind," said Bitterblue.

"Wait until the sun rises," he said. "A person who's been drinking whatever you've been drinking shouldn't try to find a cliff path in the dark."

"I'm terrified of heights, you see," said Bitterblue. "So I drank some rauha, to help me with the illegal airship. I'm the Queen of Monsea," she said, taking his hand and shaking it vigorously. "It's nice to meet you."

"And I'm the Lord of Lost Souls," he said with good-natured amusement, then found them a couple of rocks to sit on until there was more light to guide their way.

From her rock seat, Bitterblue watched with interest as the people on the ground did some sort of exchange with the flyers in the airship, passing them small crates and taking crates from them. More smuggling? Then the airship rose into the sky again, a glow of pink in the east making Bitterblue wonder how far they would get before daylight presumably grounded them.

Before the Lord of Lost Souls and his companions melted into the darkness, he put some bread and cheese into their hands and entrusted Lovisa with a flask of water. "I think your friend is coming down," he said to Lovisa, indicating Bitterblue, who'd pulled her coat tight against the cold that was becoming more noticeable to her, and was quietly weeping. "Keep her hydrated."

"I'm all right, you know," said Bitterblue. "I'm crying from happiness and relief."

"She really is the Queen of Monsea," said Lovisa.

"Sure she is," said the man. "Second one I've met this month. It should be light enough for cliff-walking in half an hour. Don't dawdle. There's a storm coming in, and houses are few and far between in these parts. You'll be walking well into the afternoon before you reach that town. Good luck."

Bitterblue turned a beatific smile upon him. "Good luck to you too," she said, "in your life of crime."

His grin flashed in the darkness. He turned to go, then turned back and called out. "If it starts to snow hard," he said, "explore the land inland from the path. There are hidden huts."

Then they were gone.

As THE SUN rose, Bitterblue felt more herself. But she was also bone tired, and thirsty. Her blistered foot smarted terribly.

She'd never seen a place so vast and dramatic as Torla's Neck. The cliff to their left dropped to a black sand beach with crashing waves that pounded so hard that sometimes she imagined the feeling of the impact in her legs. To the right, the land stretched out in hills that climbed to fir trees. Beyond the fir trees, mountain peaks alternated with strange, wrinkly formations that Bitterblue suspected were glaciers. She wanted to ask Giddon, tell Giddon. If he was truly in the north as the fox had said, had he seen those glaciers? Was he somewhere among these hills?

"Gorgeous," said Bitterblue. "Just unbelievably gorgeous. Will it be obvious when we reach the town? Or will it be mostly empty, like this?"

"I don't know," said Lovisa.

"What did you say your friend's name was?"

"Nev."

"Do you know her family's names?"

"She doesn't have a family name. Poor people in Winterkeep don't have family names."

"Yes, but do you know the names of her family members?"

"Oh," said Lovisa. "Hang on, let me think. My friend dated her for a while. Grandpa Saiet," she said, after another moment. "Mari was always making me listen to stories about Nev's stupid grandpa Saiet. And her father might be Davvi?"

"Okay, that's helpful. What are their professions?"

"Are you going to ask me questions endlessly, all morning long?"

"Oh, Lovisa," said Bitterblue, then held back her sigh, frightened of how close Lovisa walked to the cliff. Of the long looks Lovisa kept taking, down at the sea.

"Will you tell me about your brothers?" she said.

"What do you want to know about them?" demanded Lovisa.

"How many do you have? What are their names? How old are they? What do they like?"

"Viri is five. Erita is seven. Vikti is nine. And it hardly matters what they like, because no doubt everything they owned got burned in the fire I started."

"I'm sure they got out safely," Bitterblue said.

"I know they did," Lovisa snapped. "I *told* them to get out before I ever set it."

"They'll remember that you warned them, their whole lives," said Bitterblue, who had distinct memories of such moments from her own otherwise muddled childhood, memories of her mother, of attendants, even of her father's advisers, doing things, saying things, to protect her from her father. "They'll always be grateful to you."

"I guess you know everything about my family," said Lovisa viciously.

Bitterblue bit back on a sharp retort. "I know it'll hurt your brothers if they never get to see you again, and never get to hear an explanation from your lips," she said. And then she did something scary: She abandoned Lovisa to her thoughts and decisions, left her alone on the cliff, and climbed into the hills. Because it had started snowing, and the clouds at sea worried her. They were tall and dark and seemed to be growing closer. She thought it wouldn't hurt to follow the advice of the Lord of Lost Souls; she also wanted Lovisa to have a job to do.

"Where are you going?" Lovisa yelled after her.

"You see those clouds?" she said. "I'm looking for one of the huts that man told us about. My foot is killing me. Do you know anything about feet? I need you to look at my foot."

Grumbling, Lovisa joined her.

IT TOOK A great deal of scrambling on and off the path to find any sort of hut. By the time they did, it was snowing hard, sharp flakes whipped their cheeks, and Bitterblue was becoming truly frightened.

They might have found the hut sooner if it were actually a hut, rather than just a wooden door in the side of a hill. The door stuck too; both women had to push it together.

Inside, the walls were made of dirt, reinforced with wooden supports positioned close together. The floor and ceiling were wooden too, and fine, smooth. Posts stood upright all across the room, presumably bracing the ceiling, which held the weight of the hill above. A stack of firewood sat near a stove with a chimney, which surprised Bitterblue so much that she ran outside to find the capped metal pipe that popped out of the hill, perfectly visible once you knew it was there, but otherwise camouflaged among rocks.

More than that, the hut had two mattresses with pillows and blankets, a low table, a lamp full of oil, a small collection of books, plates and cutlery, and food. "Ship food," Bitterblue said with pleasure, looking through the containers of dried meat and fruits, nuts, and biscuits hard as rock. "Biscuits to dip into tea," she said, when the next tins produced dried, pungent leaves.

"It's useless without water," Lovisa said.

"Maybe they presume that if you're here in a storm, you can melt snow for water," said Bitterblue.

"You can do what you want," said Lovisa. "I don't drink snow-water tea in dirt rooms."

Briefly, Bitterblue lost her temper. She grabbed a pot, marched out of the hut, and plunked it onto the ground. She watched with screaming impatience as practically none of the fast-falling snow landed in the pot. Who did Lovisa think she was, trying to out-snob a queen? Did she imagine that Bitterblue *wanted* to spend this day in a claustrophobic hut in a hill, instead of looking for the friends who thought she was dead? Her own sister! And Giddon, Giddon!

"Balls!" she shouted, in Lingian.

Then she jumped as Lovisa's curious voice spoke behind her. "What does *balls* mean?"

"Balls," Bitterblue repeated in frustration, as if that were an explanation. Then she said the word in Keepish, but Lovisa was clearly unenlightened.

"Like, balls to play a game with?" said Lovisa. "Is that a swear word in Lingian?"

"No!" said Bitterblue. "Like a man's scrotum!"

"Oh! You call that balls?"

"Yes!"

"We call it kittens," said Lovisa. "Because they're so delicate."

This undid Bitterblue. She laughed so hard that she had to lean her hand on Lovisa's shoulder, gasping. "That's my favorite thing in Winterkeep," she finally said.

"That's fair," said Lovisa, "since mainly you've been trapped in an attic." Then she smiled, a smile that made her look so young suddenly, and so sad, that all Bitterblue could think was that she was going to help this girl, one way or another.

"What do you think?" she said, even though she'd already decided. "I badly want to go on. But it's snowing hard and I'm quite sure my foot is bleeding again."

"There are horror stories about people who get caught in storms in Torla's Neck," said Lovisa. "If you want us to stay in this hole till it stops, I don't care. Anyway, neither of us slept much last night."

"That's true," said Bitterblue, relieved.

Inside, Lovisa sat on one of the mattresses, her back propped against the wall, and watched as Bitterblue started the fire. Then Lovisa began to remove her shoes and socks.

"They don't smell good," she said, holding her socks out to the queen, "but you should wear them. Those shoes are rubbing your feet raw."

"If I take your socks away, the same will happen to your feet."

"I don't mind hurting," Lovisa said simply. Then she laid herself down.

THEY BOTH SLEPT, for a long time. There was little else to do.

Then, in the middle of the night, Bitterblue woke to a howling wind.

What if the chimney gets clogged with snow? she thought to herself. *And the smoke backs up into the room? And we can't escape, because snow is blocking the door?* She felt the weight of the hill above, imagined the hill collapsing, dirt clogging her nose and mouth. She imagined dying here, buried inside the ground. Her friends would never find her. They'd never know.

She threw her blankets off, crossed to the door, and pulled. It crashed open, cold air rushing in. When she stepped out and down, she understood suddenly that the door in the hill was positioned at the hill's steepest point, and partly up its slope, where snow was unlikely to accumulate. And then she remembered the long chimney, protected from snow by its chimney cap.

I should trust the locals, she thought, going back inside, shivering, crawling into her bed. *Giddon? I'm scared of me dying, or you dying, or Hava dying, now that I'm so close.*

I know, he said. *It isn't going to happen.*

Do you promise?

Yes, he said. *I promise.*

But no one can promise that, she cried, almost triumphantly, as if she'd caught him out in a lie.

I know, he said. *But I'm promising it anyway, and you should believe me. Who's more trustworthy, me or your anxiety?*

That made Bitterblue laugh a little. And then her mind started playing with ideas of Giddon again. Sitting with him in his chair, pressed against him. Touching his chest. Touching his beard, which was scratchy. Kissing his mouth. Being kissed back.

Kissing Giddon, Bitterblue fell asleep.

THE STORM LASTED the whole next day and night.

"The single good thing about it is that my foot is healing," Bitterblue said grumpily. The hut was beginning to feel like her attic prison all over again. Only her fear of encouraging Lovisa's gloom kept her from devolving into constant complaints. That and the books, which told amusingly heroic stories about the Keeper and showed pictures of her in many shapes and forms, sometimes with innumerable eyes and arms, sometimes more of a blob.

Lovisa wasn't interested in the books, actually scowled when Bitterblue showed her one of the drawings, and hardly spoke. She ate, drank the tiny cups of tea Bitterblue made from melted snow, slept, and stared at the ceiling. "When we get to the town," she said, "I'm going to send a signal message to the Ledra Magistry. Do you know what that means?"

"Only vaguely."

"It means that soon, all of Winterkeep will know what my parents did."

"*All* of Winterkeep?"

"Signal messages are passed from station to station. The message is spelled out in flashes of light and every station in range receives it.

Then those stations send it along to the stations in their range, and so on. It spreads out like a web. And it isn't just the stations. Anyone in range who sees the mirrors and knows the signal language will also know. A lot of amateurs keep signal stations and pass things to each other."

"I see," said Bitterblue. "It sounds messy."

"Messages do get garbled. We send them twice."

"What will you say?"

"For now, only the things we know for sure. That my parents kidnapped you. That they killed Pari Parnin. That my uncle is missing. And I *won't* mention where we are," Lovisa said shortly, then said little else for the rest of the night. Lovisa could stare at the ceiling for hours, various hard expressions crossing her face. It was obvious she was trying to work out some knot inside herself. Bitterblue wished her well with it, but said nothing, for she had a knot of her own. The knot was in the shape of Giddon.

And it wasn't a knot, really. It was an entire neat coil, like the ropes the sailors wound into loops and hung on pegs on the *Monsea*. It was the stars that wound themselves in ropes around the earth; or seemed to, for really it was the earth that turned, spinning inside the stars' grasp.

Bitterblue had been too preoccupied to look at something, so she'd ignored it. While she'd ignored it, it had spun along merrily on its own course. Now she was paying attention. Bitterblue was good at knowing the difference between her body and her heart. One, she gave; the other, she didn't. Pella had been right about that. But these feelings she'd been having about Giddon, the ones that flushed her with heat but also comforted her, weren't coming just from her body. Nor were they new, or even particularly surprising. Honestly, she was a little embarrassed at not having noticed them before.

Somehow or other, Bitterblue had missed the moment when she

should have started guarding herself against loving Giddon. She couldn't backtrack now. She loved him already. It was too late.

But what did it mean? What was going to happen? Nothing? All the things?

What if he didn't love her? What would she do, left alone with all this feeling?

Worse, what if he *did* love her, and, as always, she shied away? *I do not want to hurt him,* she thought. *He's my best friend. I have to do differently, or I'll lose him entirely.*

In the morning, they woke to silence. No wind, no falling ice.

"All right," said Bitterblue, pushing herself up almost with ferocity. "Let's go find someone who knows where Nev lives." For now that she could see the truth, she was ready. Bitterblue had ample experience of forcing herself to face terrifying things.

CHAPTER THIRTY-THREE

IF GIDDON SAW one more snowflake, he was going to lose his mind.

The storm blanketed Nev's home for two days. Two days of being stranded, getting no closer to the Cavenda house, making no progress toward learning what Mikka had learned; two days with nothing to distract him from his stupid hopes about the silbercows rescuing Bitterblue.

Hava had berated him about that, not gently. In the cold barn, with snow gusting through the windows and chickens squawking in the background, she'd thrown hot words at him. "Then where did the silbercows take her? Why haven't we heard from her?"

"I don't know," he said.

"Why are you assuming they showed us something they saw? Maybe it was a story some human told them, or something they made up. Maybe they looked into your heart and got the story from you! Did you think of that? Why are you making this worse, Giddon?"

"I—" His voice cracked. "I don't know."

"Well, stop it!" she shouted, then pushed out of the barn into the blinding whiteness, leaving him alone.

Giddon had this hope that could apparently live, even thrive, on almost no sustenance. He wondered if he'd always had it. He supposed it might be why he'd remained at Bitterblue's court for years, working in Estill but always basing himself at her castle, while she came to him over and over to tell him her feelings about whatever man was sharing her bed. Why had he subjected himself to that? It had been because of his dumb, stupid hope.

Nev had a grandfather, whose name was Saiet. He was a tall, slight man with bright eyes in a brown, wrinkled face. He was always making Giddon and Hava cups of tea, then going out into the storm and not coming back for hours. Nev would go with him sometimes, or sometimes go out on her own, for they were animal doctors, visiting the sick animals of their neighbors. Giddon, who found the short trek from the barn to the house harrowing and used the rope extended between the buildings to guide himself every time, was impressed by their storm hardiness.

Nev's mother, Nola, Saiet's daughter, was solid-looking with a no-nonsense expression and short, dark hair like Nev's. She went out often too, because she was a healer with her hands, through massage, and had patients who needed her. Davvi stayed home, for Davvi was a builder and no one wanted a builder in a storm. He sat in the cold, open area of the barn sometimes, sanding and hammering boards into a configuration that began to look like a dresser. Davvi had built the house, the guest rooms in the barn, all the furniture. His workmanship, when Giddon could see it in the light, was tidy, elegant, even beautiful. He had a bad knee, from a fall off a ladder long ago, but it didn't seem to slow him down. The members of this family were clearly good with their hands.

Giddon's hands, in contrast, were useless. There was nothing for him to do in the storm, beyond move firewood from the barn to the house, which took him all of seven minutes.

"We have some ideas about how to spy on the Cavenda house," Saiet would say over dinner, but all the ideas were dependent on getting advice from friends and neighbors who were unlikely to emerge until after the storm.

And the storm went on and on.

ON THURSDAY MORNING, Giddon woke to a bright blue sky, a bright white planet, and Saiet's bright face as he shoveled a path between the house and the barn. Giddon, joining in, shoveled for hours, steady and fast, too stir-crazy to take a break.

"Giddon," said Davvi, pausing in his own shoveling to watch Giddon decimate an icy wall of snow, "don't you tire?"

"I'm tired," said Giddon, not slowing down.

"You're strong as an ox," said Davvi, laughing. "Don't hurt yourself."

Giddon was trying to kill his hope, but there was no point explaining it to Davvi. When the house and the barn were shoveled out, he started on the path into the woods, but Davvi asked him to shovel a path to one of the hot pools instead.

"And then I want you to bathe in the pool," Davvi said. "Please, Giddon, before you strain a muscle. Something's driving you too hard."

Davvi was right, of course. And the pool, pleasant-smelling and impossibly warm, enclosed him in an embrace he hadn't known he needed. Maybe this water warming his skin and soothing his muscles was the answer he was looking for. Maybe the hope could run out of his body, to be swallowed by this pool.

He bathed for a long time, breathing, trying not to think. At one point, a blue fox passed through the trees nearby, its paws perched atop the snow, glinting curious gold eyes his way. They lived in the forests around here, apparently, or so Saiet said. They stayed close to human establishments because humans liked them, fed them, let them inside, sometimes spoiled them shamelessly, and occasionally one bonded to someone.

Giddon heard a rustle behind him, much too heavy for a fox. Glancing around, he observed Saiet making his way along the path.

"That was quick, wasn't it?" said Giddon, for Saiet had gone out to check on a pregnant pig and Giddon had understood it to be a fair walk away.

"I ran into some friends on the road," he said. "I think you should put your clothes on, son, and come into the house."

Finally, someone who could help them with their plan. "I'm coming," said Giddon, pushing himself up, drying and dressing quickly, for the cold air was a special kind of torture after the bliss of the hot pool. He stepped into his boots and clumped down the path, not bothering to fasten them, rubbing water out of his hair and his beard with his towel. He got to the house and opened the door.

And there she was. His Bitterblue, his queen. Standing right there, looking right back at him. Giddon's eyes blurred. He fell to his knees and began to cry. Bitterblue wrapped her arms around his shoulders. He held her, sobbing into her stomach, loving the silbercows, loving their stories. She was real. She was solid. She smelled like soap and she was stroking his hair and her voice was saying soft, comforting words. His vision was turning to stars. He couldn't breathe. He heard her giggling and felt himself falling. Then everything went black.

WHEN HE CAME to, he was lying on the floor with his head in Bitterblue's lap.

"I hope you know you're never going to hear the end of this," Bitterblue said.

"Yes, please," said Giddon, who wanted to be teased about this every day for the rest of his life. She was still stroking his hair.

Nev's family was bustling around them, preparing a meal. Hava, her pale face luminous and streaked with tears, was helping them. Saiet was setting out again for the pregnant pig. Giddon knew it was a small room, and he as a big, tall person was taking up much of the floor, but he didn't want to relinquish his position. He was afraid that if he stood and she stopped touching him, it would turn into a dream.

"What happened to you?" he said weakly.

"Silbercows rescued me," she said. "And then I'm afraid the Cavendas scooped me out of the sea."

"What?" cried Giddon, turning to look into her face.

"They kept me in their attic," she said.

Giddon was up, on his knees, holding her shoulders. He could not contain this information. "Did they hurt you? Are you okay?"

Bitterblue put a hand over his. "They didn't hurt me," she said, "beyond trying to scare and humiliate me and not giving me much food. I hardly saw them. Giddon," she said, in that firm, clear voice that always cut through whatever whirl his mind was in. "Look at me. I'm fine."

Giddon looked at her. Her eyes were clear and gray, her hair in disorder, but familiar, dear. She was far too thin. She was wearing dirty pajamas. The face she held upturned to his was tired, and so happy. He could see that she was fine, but he knew that she'd suffered.

"We were in that house," he said, wonderingly. "You were there?"

"I was. It's gone now. Lovisa burned it to the ground and rescued me."

"Lovisa Cavenda?"

"She's sleeping," Bitterblue said, indicating one of the family's small bedrooms. "On our way here, she sent a signal message to the Ledra Magistry accusing her parents of kidnapping me and killing one of her friends. I think it was a very, very hard thing to do."

"Lovisa Cavenda burned her house down and rescued you?" he repeated dumbly.

"Yes. She even destroyed two airships."

"When?"

"Sunday."

"Sunday!" Giddon cried. "That's the day we left."

"I know," said Bitterblue. "I came as fast as I could, but the storm slowed us down."

"How did you know where to find us?"

Her hand reached up again and touched the side of his face, once. "I have a lot to tell you, Giddon."

OVER DINNER, BITTERBLUE shared with them, quietly, the story of all that had happened to her.

It was painful to listen to her relate her suffering and not be able to hold her, comfort her. He didn't know if she felt that way too or simply sensed his feelings, but she found his hand under the table and gripped it tightly while she talked. He could tell she was doing the same with Hava on her other side.

"All right," he said finally, giving her hand back, not because he wanted to, but because, holding two hands, she couldn't eat. "Have your dinner, Bitterblue."

And so she did, quickly, eating a mountain of food with small, reverential sighs that made his heart ache with happiness. Then she took his hand again.

For a long time after dinner, Bitterblue, Hava, Giddon, and Nev's family spoke and planned, low-voiced because Lovisa had not yet emerged from the bedroom.

"Does Lovisa know what's going on in her family's northern house?" asked Giddon. "Should we ask her what Mikka might've overheard?"

"I don't think she knows," said Bitterblue, "though we should ask, later, when she's feeling better. Lovisa is overwhelmed. I haven't even told her yet that her father drowned our men. And I'm afraid she found Katu's ring and identification papers in her father's desk. She thinks he's dead."

As Bitterblue turned her own rings on her fingers, Giddon studied her troubled face, guessing what she must feel about that. "Surely not," he said quietly.

She lifted serious eyes to his. "We need to find out."

"We will."

"How soon can we get to that house?"

"It's a few hours by sea," said Saiet. "We can arrange a boat for you, and we should talk about how to get those of you with no particular magic onto the property," he said, with a deferential glance at Hava.

"I could appear at the gate under the guise of a traveling animal doctor," said Nev.

"There's a traveling everything, here in the north," said Davvi. "I could be a traveling builder."

Bitterblue was rubbing her braids the way she did when her tiredness was turning to achiness.

"Let's decide tomorrow," said Saiet, noticing. "Tonight is a night for going to bed early."

Of course, if Davvi had worried about the Monsean delegates sleeping in the barn, his objections to the Monsean queen doing so were all the more earnest. When Bitterblue insisted that she'd slept in haystacks before, Giddon and Hava both started laughing.

"What?" said Bitterblue. "I have! You wouldn't believe the places I slept with Katsa, when we were running away from my father. Katsa can balance herself on a plow blade and have a good night's sleep."

"You'll have a bed in the barn," Giddon said. "A very comfortable one."

"But it's true that it may not be fit for a queen," said Nola quietly.

"It's fit for me," said Bitterblue. "And I'll feel safest close to my friends."

IN HIS OWN tiny, warm room, Giddon lay in his bed, closed his eyes, and listened to the wind blowing fiercely around the barn. It muffled all other sounds, making him feel like he could be private with his thoughts. Of course, he began to cry.

This is who I am now, apparently, he thought to Bitterblue, who was in the room next door. He never had to pretend-talk to her again if he didn't want to. And he didn't want to. Should he speak to her? How could he, with Katu's fate unknown? He needed to let her recover and he needed to give himself time to come down from his own sense of overwhelm. He let his tears run, knowing that there was too much baffled happiness coursing through his veins for him to sleep anytime soon.

His door clicked open and closed. Light footsteps crossed the floor.

Startled, Giddon propped himself on an elbow, watching Bitterblue approach. The face she presented to him, gold in the brazier's light, was full of so many things. Fear. Uncertainty. Determination. "Giddon?" she whispered.

She sounded so frightened as she said his name that he held out his hand, confused. "Yes?"

She put her hand into his. It was small and cold.

"Bitterblue?" he said.

"I've been obtuse," she said.

"Obtuse?"

"Yes," she said. "For a very long time."

Giddon understood what was happening. He couldn't help understanding what was happening. But that didn't mean he could believe it. "I've been a coward," he said.

"Giddon," she said, "you're never a coward. I'm the coward!"

"I've been a coward for a very long time," he said, dropping every defense, pulling her closer. Showing her his tears, and bringing her hand to his lips.

She let out one small breath. Then she knelt by his bed and reached her hand to his face, turned her own face up to his, and he could not believe their lips were touching, that he was actually kissing her perfect, soft lips. "I may be about to faint again," he said.

"Well, I like your scratchy beard on my face," she said, then climbed into the bed with him and began nuzzling his throat. The blood was most definitely rushing away from Giddon's head. When he told her this, she said, "Where do you suppose it's rushing to?" which almost made him shout with laughter.

"Sh!" she said, giggling. "We have to be quiet! I don't want Hava to hate us in the morning."

"No, I don't want that either," he said, still laughing, kissing her. "I can be quiet. But, Bitterblue, slow down, just a little. We have all the time in the world." And really, truly, he was dizzy, and completely overwhelmed. A miracle was happening and he felt like he was missing it.

Out of nowhere, she burst into tears. Her tears turned to sobs and she clung to him, gasping. Instantly he sprang into action, holding her, soothing her, almost a little relieved, because this made sense to him.

"I love you," she said. "I'm scared of losing you."

"I know," he said. "You won't."

"You can't know what's going to happen! You can't know what I'm going to do!"

"Yes I can," he said. "You're going to be the friend to me that you've always been, and I'm going to show you that you're safe now. We are not going to lose each other. You're not alone with your fears, Bitterblue. We're a team now, you see?"

"Hold me very tight," she said, "please?"

That was easy. He wrapped his arms around her firmly. As her tears quieted, he kissed her hair, and thought a few things through.

"I think I'm a little shy of touching you," he finally said. "I mean, sex-touching. You know? You're my favorite person in the world, Bitterblue, and we've been friends for years. It's a lot all at once. Until a few hours ago, I didn't even know you were alive."

"I can understand that," she said, still sniffling a little, but calmer. "It's different for me, because I've been fantasizing about you for days."

"You have?" said Giddon, who found this very interesting.

"I have," she said, the corner of her mouth turning up. "I've got a lot of questions. For your body, I mean."

"Do you?" he said. "I have answers."

Bitterblue laughed, then hugged him in the familiar way. She smiled into his neck. "Do you know about kittens?"

She'd spoken the word in Keepish. "Kittens? As in, baby cats?"

"Sort of," she said. "No, not really. Not at all." She began to trace her hand down his neck and over his shoulder, down his arm, his hip, his thigh, creating pleasurable shivers all along his side. She did it again, as if she was petting him.

"When you do that," said Giddon, "I begin to feel less shy."

She did it again. "Do you?"

"Does this have something to do with kittens?"

"That depends," she said, beginning to add little kisses while she petted him, to his ear, his throat, the inside of his elbow. The inside of his thigh.

"What does it depend on?" he asked.

"On where you'd like me to touch you."

With the next little kiss, Giddon found himself reaching for her. Tugging gently at her pajama top, which kept slipping down her shoulder, revealing a soft place on the inside of her arm that he wanted to kiss.

"Tell me about kittens," he said roughly.

"I will."

"And tell me what you want."

"I will," she said, beginning to smile. "Still shy?"

"I've recovered," he said, which was almost entirely true. "And don't think I didn't notice it was your doing."

"I believe what you said before."

Giddon was having trouble remembering anything he'd said before, which was also her doing. "What did I say?"

She touched his face. Showed him her eyes, which contained some shyness of her own. He kissed the side of her nose, the place under her ear. He wanted to kiss the part of her neck that was hidden by her hair. He moved her hair aside, touched his mouth to her skin. The small noises she was making in response banished the last of his shyness.

"We're a team, Giddon," she whispered. "You and I."

CHAPTER THIRTY-FOUR

THE FOX WHO was bonded to Ferla Cavenda was pretending to be dead.

The Cavenda family was now living in the guest apartments at the top of a steep staircase in the Devret house, and the fox was too. He concealed himself under beds and inside walls. He collected tools for modifying grates and stored them in the Devrets' heat ducts. *You could be bonded to Quona too,* his siblings had said to him that time, *if you faked your own death,* and then the house had caught fire. The fox had seen his chance. Not to bond to Quona Varana, though: to hide.

He'd made his "death" dramatic too, concealing himself in the trees and sending Ferla agonizing death throes. He'd pretended to be trapped in the kitchen, where the fire had found so many oils and the flames were blazing so furiously that he thought it would make for a tragic and convincing death scene.

What he'd never imagined was that Ferla would try to rescue him—and unfortunately, she'd set out in the direction that intersected with Lovisa and the queen's escape. So the fox had run over Lovisa's feet to warn her and he'd yelled up at the queen to keep still, then he'd hidden again, and waited. He hadn't gotten to send Ferla the final gasp of his departing life, because Lovisa had clubbed Ferla on the head with a shovel and knocked her out.

But he'd done enough. When Ferla woke the next morning,

headachy and sick, she assumed her fox was gone. She was bitter about it too. She believed herself to have lost a tool that might have helped to carry her through the rough times she guessed were coming.

For Lovisa was alive somewhere, hiding, and Ferla knew it. Benni did too. Benni, who'd searched the burning house for Lovisa, was sick now from smoke inhalation; and though he cried with relief when Ferla told him Lovisa had survived, he wasn't happy not to know where she was. He needed her back. Especially since no human remains had been found in the ashes. The fire inspectors had made the assumption that the airship explosion—not to mention that other explosion Benni and Ferla were carefully not bringing to their attention—had been so destructive that Lovisa's body had been obliterated. But the fire inspectors didn't know about the queen. What if the queen had gotten away too?

The day after the fire, Monday, very late, Ferla crept down the stairs of the guest apartments, through the rest of the house, and outside, passing money to the Devrets' guards at the door.

"I just want to stretch my legs," she said to them. "No one needs to know."

Then, headachy and ill, she set off down the road, the fur wrap Mara Devret had lent her pulled tight around her small shoulders, Mara's shoes on her feet. Mara was a tall woman, so the wrap was far too big and the shoes almost comical. Ferla looked like a tiny, unbalanced clown.

The fox had a way to exit the house through a crack between rotting stones in the cellar. He snuck out after Ferla, intensely curious. He had a sense of what she was up to, but her thoughts had been a little jumbled since her head injury, harder to read.

First she went to a faraway amble near the harbor that the fox had never heard of or visited, where the smells were wondrous, fish of every kind, breaded, fried, grilled, stewed, raw, rotting. It was a paradise! In a narrow, smelly street, Ferla tapped on a door until a pale woman opened it. Ferla spoke to the woman urgently. The woman, who had a closed mind with no cracks, like a heavy steel ball—like a Monsean—seemed offended, indignant. Ferla handed her money. The woman hesitated. Then she went inside, coming out again with her coat, which was the color of the moon, swinging around her shoulders like a cape.

Ferla led her all the way back to Flag Hill, then to the gate that stood before her own burnt and decimated house. She brought the woman right up to the edge of the house's stone foundations, then gestured across the pile of scorched rubble.

"Careful," Ferla said. "There's glass, nails, who knows what else."

"This is as close as I'm getting," said the woman. "You might've brought a lamp."

"The streetlamps will pick up anything sharp," said Ferla impatiently. "Now, will you look?"

"I need more details about what you're trying to find."

"Human remains," said Ferla. "No matter how small."

"Whose remains?" said the woman. "Keepish? Some other nationality? Male? Female? Young? Old? Where in the house are they most likely to be?"

"Can't you look everywhere?"

"Certainly, for more money."

"You're a vulture," said Ferla, sharp and disgusted. "You know perfectly well my own daughter is believed to have died in this fire."

"Am I looking for your daughter's remains, then? Knowing so will help my work."

"Why does it matter?" said Ferla. "Why must you make me talk about it? Is it necessary to be so heartless?"

"Given your reluctance to answer my simple question," said the woman, "I'm beginning to think you want me to look for the remains of someone other than your daughter."

It was interesting to watch Ferla make a mess of something. She had a painful and nauseating headache, which was obscuring her judgment and her ability to pretend to be heartbroken over a daughter she knew wasn't actually dead. Also, she was used to people doing what she told them to do. This foreign woman in the pale yellow coat was different. She wasn't scared of Ferla.

She spoke into Ferla's cold silence. "Well? Am I looking for someone else's remains?"

"Whose remains do you imagine you'd find here?" asked Ferla, her voice rising with outrage.

"I would vastly prefer to find no one's," said the woman in distaste.

"Listen," said Ferla. "I want to be sure no one was hurt. What if one of my children or a staff member had a visitor I was unaware of? My daughter was always sneaking around the house with lovers. I intend to pay you handsomely for your time." Then she stood with her palm to her throbbing head, sick and slightly swaying, while the woman, hard-mouthed, closed her eyes and raised her hands. She looked like she was trying to feel the parts of the air. She looked quite silly, actually, and Ferla lost patience with her long before she was done. Ferla also lost her dinner, staggering away and vomiting onto the base of a tree. Then she gave her own vomit a wide berth and timidly sat herself upon the ground. She put her head in her hands, because it hurt and because she couldn't bear the sight of the ravaged house. This too was a whole new Ferla, emotional, unwell.

The woman dropped her hands and turned. "I've found no remains," she said.

Inside her heart, Ferla cursed this news. "You're certain?"

The woman let out a short sigh. "Why don't you tell me whose body I'm looking for, President Cavenda? Then I could really help you."

Ferla raised her chin and looked into the woman's face. "Tell me," she said. "Is it true what they say, that you're the escaped property of the government of Estill?"

The woman cocked her head and studied Ferla. Her face was tired, her shoulders slumped, but her voice came out hard. "Why did you bring me here in the dead of the night to search for a body," she said, "and why are you disappointed I didn't find one?"

Ferla reached into her pockets, pulled out some money, and threw it on the ground between them. "I trust you'll find that satisfactory," she said. It was her chilliest voice. The fox, who recognized that voice, shivered.

The woman did something amazing. She picked a path carefully away from the house, walked toward Ferla, then stopped. For a moment, the woman's feelings were bright and visible to the fox: Anger. Discouragement. Shame.

Then, not even touching the money, she turned and walked out through the gate.

The fox badly wished the woman hadn't done that. Now he was afraid for her life.

FERLA AND BENNI worried constantly, but they did so in their own separate worlds. Each was trying to find a way out of the mess certain to ensue should Lovisa or the queen emerge somewhere and make accusations. Benni was trying to find a way out for the entire family, which, like most of his plans, was unrealistic. Benni was a romantic. He imagined success and glory for the Cavenda name. The fox tapped on his mind sometimes, puzzled by how someone with so much ambition could be so immature.

He was searching for Lovisa as discreetly as he could, but it was hard without his airship. To his friends who owned airships, he pretended to cling to the hope that since Lovisa's body hadn't been found, maybe she'd escaped the fire. Maybe she was out in the world somewhere, injured, muddled, confused. Would anyone be willing to lend an airship to Benni, so that he might have a look around for his child?

Benni went out in a borrowed airship most days, sad and apprehensive, unwell, then came back with nothing, slowly climbing the stairs. He took that guard with him when he flew, the young one with the dead eyes. The fox suspected that if that guard saw Lovisa or the queen from the airship, she might keep quiet about it. The fox suspected that Benni's chances of success were very low indeed. Still, the fox worried, anxiously waiting.

Ferla, in contrast, was trying to find a way out for *herself*. She didn't like that this essentially meant pinning everything on Benni, but she had little choice. And she couldn't figure out what to do should Lovisa show up alive. Ferla had tried to pull the girl away from the burning house and Lovisa, her own daughter, had attacked her with a shovel. Ferla wondered what her father would have done, a train of thought that was no comfort to the fox, since Ferla's father had basically been a sadist.

And Katu? Her baby brother, Katu, was where Ferla reached her rational limit. Ferla chose to stop seeing the truth about Katu, because it was too much. In their childhood, Katu had often been her charge, and always her ally. Her father had sent her into the cave alone for her punishments, until Katu had been old enough to understand; and then he'd sent them in together. And Ferla's terror had vanished. She'd had something to do in the cave, someone to comfort.

In her not-seeing, Ferla chose to exonerate herself from any part of Katu's fate. She talked to her dead father about it. *You understand, Father, don't you?* she said. *Benni made me. And you understand that sometimes people need to be punished, don't you? You punished Katu many times. Remember?* It was interesting, the way humans could decide not to see the truth when it made them too uncomfortable.

Sometimes Ferla took to flying into rages and breaking things. In the upstairs apartments, lifting ceramic statues, glass candle holders, or entire vases full of water and flowers from the tables, she slammed them against the stones of the hearth. Benni would stand there while she screamed, looking wary and far away in his thoughts. When members of the Devret family came to investigate the noise, he would rouse himself to say that he was terribly sorry, there'd been an accident.

"We dropped it," Benni would say, or "It slipped" or "It fell." One of these times, Mara crossed the room with a look of the deepest misgiving, took a portrait of her son, Mari, down from the wall, then carried the portrait away.

The Devrets believed, of course, that the Cavendas were mourning the death of a child. The fox liked to watch Mara and Arni Devret through the grate in their bedroom, where they spent a lot of time talking. Mara knitted in a chair, something pale and soft and blue that grew bigger in her lap every day, and he liked to steal loose pieces of the yarn. The Devrets had a warmth and an affection for each other, even in the midst of stressful houseguests, that the fox had never witnessed before, ever. They talked often about the little boys, who were trapped in grief. In fact, the boys' anguish for their sister was so uncontrolled, their confusion so inundating, that the fox had taken to avoiding them. Their pain set every hair of his body on edge and made him feel terribly helpless. The Devrets tried to comfort the boys, but the Devrets didn't understand what their lives had been. And anyway, what comfort was there for a sister gone?

Sometimes the fox watched Mara in her knitting chair when she was alone, tracking her feelings, her thoughts. She cried about her son, Mari, who was grieving Lovisa. Mara would hurt because Mari hurt, trying to think of some way to make him feel better. Deciding that there wasn't a way to make him feel better, and crying a little about that too. Then heaving a sigh and pushing her mind back to work. Mara was a politician, and her husband a banker. She was clever and cynical and sometimes she was hard. But she contained kindness too, in her thoughts, and toward the people around her. Whenever the fox touched upon her kindness, he poked at it, sniffed it, with something like hunger.

He wondered sometimes, now that he was free of Ferla Cavenda, if he needed to be so alone. What if news came through that Lovisa and the queen had gotten away someplace safe? What if Benni and Ferla were hauled off to jail and he didn't have to plot and plan and worry anymore? If he could know that Lovisa no longer needed his protection . . . did that mean he could go far away, to a place where no one knew or cared what a blue fox did? Could he go as far away as Monsea, and live with someone he didn't have to lie to? Could a blue fox be free?

THEN THE DAY came when Ledra's head magistrate arrived at the Devrets' front door. He had news: A person claiming to be Lovisa Cavenda had sent a signal message accusing Ferla and Benni Cavenda of kidnapping the Monsean queen and murdering an academy boy. The Monsean queen could confirm this, said the message. The queen was alive.

LOVISA WAS SAFE. The queen was safe. They were safe! The fox felt like his blood was made of light. Joy rushed in his ears. They were safe and this would all end soon. Ferla would go to jail, where she couldn't hurt anyone. He would find them. He would go away with the queen. Everything was going to change!

Then something agonizing happened: nothing. Nothing happened. The head magistrate didn't arrest Ferla or Benni. He didn't even bring them to the Magistry to ask them questions. He told them that his was a courtesy visit, to inform them of the situation, but that naturally the Magistry would need to confirm that the message really came from Lovisa, that Lovisa was of sound mind, and most of all, that the Queen of Monsea really was alive, and if so, what she had to say about it.

"Where are they?" Ferla demanded of the magistrate.

"We don't know yet," said the head magistrate. "The message didn't include the usual location marker."

"That certainly doesn't lend it credence," said Benni.

"Nothing lends it credence!" said Ferla. "Someone is trying to frame you for a monstrous crime, Benni!"

"Frame *me*?" said Benni.

"Frame both of you," the head magistrate corrected primly.

"It's absurd," said Ferla. "And the cruelty of it is stunning, when here we are, grieving our daughter's death."

"Indeed," said the head magistrate. "The entire thing is stunning. I'm sure you'll respond to our courtesy with courtesy of your own and stay in the Devret house until we have more information?"

Ferla put all of her vicious fury into her response. "Are you saying that we're under house arrest? The president of Winterkeep and a member of Parliament?"

"Certainly not," the head magistrate said, his eyes bulging with alarm. "It's just that we'll want to be certain of where to find you, should more information come to light."

"I'll be here, at one of my offices, or on our grounds sifting through our burnt possessions," Ferla said. "My husband will be here, at his office, on our grounds, or in an airship, searching for our missing child. When you've found the person responsible for these criminal accusations, we'll be happy for you to inform us of it anywhere, anytime, so that we can begin our own legal proceedings. Do you understand me?"

The head magistrate hesitated, swallowing. Parliament could

remove him from office just as swiftly as they'd placed him there. The fox felt him considering this. "Yes, of course," he said. "Thank you, I'm sure."

Then he scurried away, leaving the Cavendas and the Devrets together in the entrance hall. Mara and Arni stood quiet and unmoving. They weren't looking at each other and their faces were carefully composed, but the fox could feel the beginnings of their joint comprehension.

"Well," Mara said, with a deliberate attempt to soften herself. "This is a terrible thing. I'm so sorry, Ferla and Benni. Please let us know how we can help." Then, glancing once at her husband, she went away.

Arni grunted something agreeable and followed her. He wasn't trying as hard to put on an act, though the fox could feel that this was only because he was distracted. Arni was suddenly overwhelmed with concern for, and confusion about, the three small boys living under his roof. He went to seek them out in the guest apartments, invited them to his own library. For a while, he sat with them and read them stories, trying to assess, from some sign in their faces, how much they knew, how much of the magistrate's accusation was correct. He looked into their eyes, trying to see what their lives had been. He also sent a message to the academy, asking his son to come home, for he wanted to know what his son knew about what Lovisa's life had been.

But before that, still in the entranceway, Benni turned searching eyes upon his wife. "Frame *me*?" he repeated gently.

Ferla looked back at him, not speaking. The fox could feel the wall she'd built; Ferla was standing in another world. Her face was turned to Benni, but she couldn't even see him from where she was.

"My wife of twenty years," Benni said. "This is how you want it to end?"

Ferla walked away, climbed the narrow stairs to the guest apartments, barely hearing. She was plotting her escape.

THAT NIGHT, BENNI and Ferla planned separately.

Sort of. Benni was too bereft and bewildered by his new understanding of Ferla to make much of a plan, and anyway, planning a route through chaos had never been his strong suit. As far as the fox could tell, every time Ferla had ever blamed their dilemmas on Benni's decisions, Ferla had been right.

So Benni, under the pretense of planning, moped. He wished for his airship. If he only he had it, he could fly up north and make sure the house was free of incriminating evidence.

He climbed the stairs to the guest apartments, gripping the banister, not noticing that it was starting to come loose. He walked to his bedroom and stood numbly at the window, looking down onto the Devrets' dark, tree-filled grounds. He tried to figure out if this window faced the ruins of his own home, but couldn't remember, which made him feel stupid and impotent. Benni was usually good at things like directions.

Then Ferla came bursting into the room. He turned and watched her. She stared back, wound up with something Benni couldn't read. Then she crossed to him and began touching him roughly, kissing him. Her touches reached through his fog of grief and he grasped her, held her, cried against her, brought her to the bed and gave her the pleasure she wanted that made her even sharper and colder. Then Benni fell asleep. Ferla got up and dressed while the fox observed from the grate, trembling, wishing he'd never bonded to someone so manipulative and confusing.

When all of this is over, he thought to himself, *I want such a different life.* And he thought of Lovisa, hidden somewhere, bravely delivering messages; and the queen, the only being in the world to whom he'd ever told the truth.

When all of this is over, he thought to himself again, then stopped, because it *wasn't* over. And if Ferla did, somehow, manage to frame Benni for all that had happened, Lovisa would never be safe.

Should he? Shouldn't he?

But should he or shouldn't he *what*?

What could a fox do?

FERLA WAS UP all night. The fox plumbed her grasping mind, listening to her plans, trying to assess how realistic they were.

Ferla would claim that Benni had kidnapped the queen of his own volition, that Benni had killed Pari Parnin. That Ferla had objected, begged, pleaded against both crimes, but Benni had overpowered her. That he'd threatened her and the children should she ever expose him. Ferla was tiny. Benni was big. She would say it had always been that way in their relationship; she was afraid of him.

She would make the same claims if any of their other crimes were uncovered. She would say that Benni had done all of it without her knowledge. The business at the house in Torla's Neck, the scuttling of the *Seashell*, Katu. Especially Katu. Surely no one would believe Ferla would harm her own brother?

The terrifying thing about all these claims was that for the most part, they were true. Benni *had* done everything, every single thing, without her assent, and usually without her knowledge. He'd gone rogue with their careful plans, starting too soon, making dangerous decisions. He'd murdered the two Monseans without consulting her. He'd struck the blow to Pari's head while she'd tried to stop him. Katu. Katu! Ferla had known none of it—none of it!—until the day Benni had scooped the queen out of the sea, then told her all—with no regrets! As if he was proud of himself! As if he expected her to admire his initiative!

And Ferla *had* argued with Benni, berated him, pleaded for him to stop creating new problems. Had he bullied or intimidated her?

No, never. She was the bully. Had she ever hesitated to help conceal his crimes? Never once, not even with Katu. She had the brains. Would she be happy to benefit from the crimes, if they could only be sure of getting away with them? Of course. However, Benni couldn't prove any of that.

But what was the Magistry likely to believe? Ferla had a problem: She radiated power and strength. Everyone who worked with her knew this. Benni was the likable one. Ferla was the one who scared people. Could Ferla convince the Magistry that she'd been anyone's pawn?

In the drawing room of the Devrets' guest apartments, the fox watched Ferla sitting, standing, moving around, talking to herself, practicing looking believably bullied and scared. It was fascinating, because at first, she was terrible at it. She only knew how to open her eyes wide and throw her hands in the air; she couldn't cry, or show any subtle signs of fear. But she seemed to have enough self-awareness to realize that she was terrible at it, and she kept trying and trying.

She tried for two hours. Then she struck upon the notion of her own children. That made her sit back and consider. She stood and lifted the big mirror from the wall.

Things got eerie after that, for Ferla spent another hour imitating the expressions of her own bullied and frightened children in the mirror. And, quite naturally, she resembled her children; in particular, she had the facial features of her daughter. There was a certain combination of anger, hatred, fear, and sick resignation that came together in Lovisa's face sometimes. It was a complicated and believable expression and Ferla remembered it. Of course she did; she caused it. It was one of the trials of being the mother to such a girl.

Ferla searched her own face in the mirror, until she found it.

IN VERY EARLY morning, the fox scampered through the heat ducts up to the grate he'd converted in the Devrets' attic. He hadn't had much time in this house to convert grates yet. This was his one and only swinging grate, and his only access point to the paths inside the walls.

The fox stepped out onto the attic floor, trying to decide what it meant to be honorable and helpful and true.

Surely it didn't mean the plan he was about to execute?

The fox pattered down from the attic, past the room where Ferla lay sleeping beside Benni, then made his way to the guest apartment stairs. An unlit lamp sat on a table at the top of the steps, for the use of the Cavendas at nighttime. The fox, who had excellent night vision, jumped lightly onto the table and inspected the lamp. It had, as he'd hoped, a wick, a glass globe, and, most importantly, a deep, open well of oil.

Before he could second-guess himself, because really this was a terrible, threadbare, hopeless plan, the fox shoved the lamp off the table in the direction of the staircase. It soared through the air and landed with a thud about two steps down, then, with a tinkle of glass and a series of smaller thuds, bumped on down the steps. He could see the oil, slick and shiny, illuminating much of the top half of the staircase.

The fox reached out quickly to touch every mind in the sleeping house. No one had woken from the noise, but one of the guards who stood outside the front door thought he might've heard something. He was trying to decide whether to come inside and investigate. The fox knew his time was short.

Quickly, he leaped under the table and pressed himself against the wall. *Ferla Cavenda!* he cried, shouting into her sleeping mind. *Ferla Cavenda! Wake up! It's me! WAKE UP!*

Ferla started up in bed. Through her sleepy blur, she was astounded. *Fox?* she said. *Fox?*

It's me! yelled the fox. *Wake up!*

I'm awake! What's happening?

I'm alive!

Her mind was already spinning to determine what she could seize, if she had her fox at hand. *That's amazing!* she said. *That's wonderful! I tried to save you, Fox!*

I remember, he said. *I'm injured. I'm dying! I know important things about Lovisa and the queen! I know where they are and what they're planning to do!*

Ferla was electrified with excitement and alarm. *Where are you?*

I'm outside the front door! he said. *But it's cold, Ferla! I'm dying!*

Ferla pushed out of her bedroom and moved toward the stairs. She was still recovering from her head injury. He felt her dizziness. *Hurry!* he cried. *I'm fading!*

Ferla staggered through darkness. The fox waited in a panic, screaming at himself not to jump out too soon, for that would ruin everything. Then, as she neared the top step, he sprang into her path. Ferla's sharp foot stabbed into his side and he yelped, scrambled for purchase, pushed against her, trying to unbalance her. Ferla tripped and went flying. She hit the oil and slipped again. She tried to grab on to the banister and it wobbled, slipped out of her hands.

Crashing down the steps, she landed in a heap at the bottom.

The fox clambered down after Ferla, gasping at the pain in his side, realizing that now she knew what he'd done. If Ferla survived this, he would have to grovel, come up with excuses, pretend his mind had been injured in the fire, go through every kind of contortion to keep her from believing his disloyalty. For if he didn't, she would guess that foxes lied. And maybe there were some humans who could safely know the secrets of foxkind, but Ferla wasn't one of them. He wouldn't be able to leave her. He would have to stay, penitent and devoted, until he was sure she trusted him again. He would be hers.

At the bottom of the steps, he found her whimpering. In the dim light of the landing, he could tell that she was twisted oddly, one of her legs bent wrong and one of her arms trapped under her body. It was better luck than he'd dared to expect. *How could a fox ever kill a human?* his siblings had said.

Her head was arched back, her coat open at the top, exposing her throat. *Fox,* she shouted, vicious, furious, frightened. *Fox. I'm going to kill you.*

Quickly, the fox checked the house again for waking humans. He found none. Then, as if he were moving through a dream, he lifted the pads of his paws to the delicate part of Ferla's throat. Bracing his hind legs as hard as he could, he pressed. *What did I just do?* he said. *I thought I was outside in the cold. I'm so sorry! Did I hurt you?*

Something feels wrong, said Ferla. *I'm choking! Fox! Are you choking me?*

I don't know what I'm doing, said the fox, pressing harder. *I think my mind must have been injured in the fire. Where am I? Who are you?*

Ferla was trying to thrash, but she couldn't move her limbs. Something had broken inside her body when she fell. *Fox! Stop!*

I'm your fox, said the fox. *You can trust me.*

Then her terror faded away. Everything about Ferla's feelings faded away. The fox waited a moment, still pressing.

When he was sure she wasn't breathing anymore, he stepped down from her throat. Then, retreating slowly, he tucked himself against the wall. He was freezing, and old, and stiff. And Lovisa might be safe from her mother now, but he was pretty sure he had at least one broken rib. He felt like he had a broken soul.

That guard had decided to come inside after all. He was heading toward the source of the noise.

Pushing himself through pain, the fox ran.

Chapter Thirty-five

For Lovisa, everything was happening too fast.

Everyone else kept complaining that things were too slow. When the Ledra Magistry didn't arrest her parents right away, the Monseans were incredulous. When the local Magistry showed no interest in their evidence because part of it came from stories the silbercows told—the queen got angry.

"Why can't silbercows give evidence?" she demanded. "Why shouldn't their knowledge matter? People have been murdered!"

"They make things up, Lady Queen," the magistrate kept saying.

"But what about the things they *aren't* making up?"

"And how are we to know which is which?"

"By looking into it!" the queen almost shouted. "People make things up too, you know! Do you believe everything every human witness tells you just because they're human?"

"You aren't from here, Lady Queen," the magistrate kept saying dismissively.

But Nev and Nev's family *were* from here, and Lovisa could see the resolve strengthening in their faces during these conversations. Everyone around Lovisa, Keepish or Monsean, was determined to see this through, regardless of rules or laws. It might almost be inspiring—except that what they were striving for was the ruin of Lovisa's family. It was also the ruin of her own life.

She spent a lot of time sitting at the fireplace, watching people come and go, listening to the northern accent of Nev's family wash around her, remembering that she'd used to sit by the fire in the dormitory foyer, keeping tabs on everyone's business. It felt like a lifetime ago. It was literally last week. And she couldn't get a handle on any of these people; Lovisa had lost the clever person she'd used to be. She was hollow and dry, like a shell made of powder. If anyone touched her, she would collapse into dust.

The morning after their arrival, she sat by the fireplace watching Nev, who was talking with her grandfather. They were having the most extraordinary conversation, in the presence of everyone, for Nev had told her grandfather about Nori Orfa, then asked him if he'd ever felt sexual jealousy. Her grandfather! She'd asked him that! Lovisa had whipped her head up at the question, unable to pretend she wasn't startled.

"Of course I have," he said.

"You have?" said Nev. "Why?"

"Your grandmother had many lovers before me," Saiet said, at which point, Lovisa had to get up and go to her bedroom in the barn, because she didn't want to hear another word. The barn was a huge, empty space, cold, full of creepy shadows and noises at night, like the attic at home. When she entered, the cow looked up from her pen, staring at Lovisa with big brown eyes, chewing. Beyond the cow, the chickens' throaty noises were actually almost soothing.

This is how things have devolved, Lovisa thought, going to sit on some hay near the animals. *I socialize with cows and chickens.* Light caught floating motes of dust in the air. She sat and wrapped her arms around herself, shaking. Nev's life was small. Wasn't it? It was animals and dark, tiny houses; it was no one ever knowing her name. Why did the look on Nev's face while she was talking with her grandfather make Lovisa feel like Nev's life contained every-thing, everything?

LATER, BACK IN the house, Lovisa watched Giddon and Bitterblue working on the plan at the table. Everyone was obsessed with the plan.

Suddenly Giddon caught up Bitterblue's hands and examined her rings. "Bitterblue," he said in a voice of dismay. "Where's your mother's ring?"

The queen told Giddon about the ring falling into the sea. But first, she let him touch her hands with his own big, gentle, white hands, an expression on her face that instantly informed Lovisa that Giddon and the queen were sleeping together.

Two more normal people having sex for normal reasons. She hated them.

"Lovisa?" Bitterblue said then. "Will you help us?"

"With what?" she snapped.

"Well, with our plan," said Bitterblue. "You know the plan?"

Yes, Lovisa knew that everyone was planning to invade the house, *her* house, to find the answer to why her parents had drowned the Monsean envoy and a royal adviser. Because yes, apparently, on top of everything else they'd done, her parents—her father—had done that too.

This is why I'm so numb and stupid, Lovisa thought, struck through with an aching beam of clarity. *Because the only route to a place of intelligence passes through the land where I have to believe such things of my father.*

When will I? How will I? Am I a coward who refuses to believe what's plainly true? Didn't I see some of it with my own eyes?

She went to sit with Bitterblue and Giddon at the table, answer-ing their questions woodenly. Yes, she could draw a floor plan of the northern house and a map of the grounds. Yes, there would be caretakers at the house, and probably guards too, who might or might not recognize Lovisa. Yes, they'd probably heard her kidnapping accusations, because signal messages always generated rumors. Yes, she knew that someone with the initials LM had written a letter to her father about the Monsean envoy overhearing something in the storehouse, but she didn't know who LM was.

All the time, she ran an image through her head. Over and over, she forced herself to watch her father carrying Pari's body across the attic to the roof.

THE NEXT DAY, Saturday, Ledra's head magistrate arrived at the Magistry in Torla's Neck. Queen Bitterblue went to meet him and present her evidence. Hava and Giddon went too, because they were known Monsean delegates who could confirm that the queen was who she said she was.

Lovisa stayed behind. "I don't want the Ledra Magistry anywhere near you," Bitterblue said, "until I've made it clear to them that everything you did, you did to save my life."

To Lovisa, it felt like the beginning of the end. She'd burned two houses down. She'd attacked her mother. The Ledra Magistry wasn't going to brush that off.

She was sitting on the hay again, watching the moon move across the sky, when they returned. She heard their voices, the cheerful back-and-forth of three people still surprised to be returned to one another. How tired Lovisa was of their happy ending.

A few minutes later, Bitterblue came into the barn by herself and stood there before Lovisa, her hands folded over the handle of a lamp. It was funny, because even though she still wore Ferla's coat, Lovisa had come to think of those sleek furs as belonging to the queen.

"How'd it go?" Lovisa asked, not caring.

"You won't be charged with a crime," said Bitterblue.

Lovisa was stunned. "Are you sure?"

"The Magistry understands now what your parents did to me, Lovisa, and why you had to act."

"Thank you," she said weakly, surprised at how much lighter it made her feel.

"No need to thank me. My own court is forever in your debt." Then the queen was quiet, for longer than was normal. She stood there looking serious.

"What is it?" said Lovisa, suddenly understanding that there was more, and that it was bad. "Aren't they charging my parents?"

"When the head magistrate gets back to Ledra tomorrow, he'll charge your father."

"My father," Lovisa repeated, mystified. "Isn't my mother at least an accessory to his crimes?"

The queen took a small breath. "Your mother met with an accident Thursday night, Lovisa. She fell down a flight of stairs. They think she dropped a lamp and slipped on the oil, then hurt her neck and suffocated."

Lovisa was electric with disbelief. "Are you saying my mother is *dead*?"

"Yes."

"And she died in an *accident*?"

"Yes."

"I don't believe it," Lovisa said. "I don't believe it. How did she suffocate?"

"If you break a certain part of your neck," said Bitterblue, "you lose the ability to breathe. They think that's what happened."

"It can't be," said Lovisa.

"Apparently it's true. I'm so sorry, Lovisa."

Lovisa was grasping around with her hands but she couldn't find anything to hold, just pieces of straw. "Don't be silly. There's nothing to be sorry about. She didn't love me."

The queen said, "Lovisa—"

"Don't you tell me that she did," said Lovisa, her voice rising. "That was not love."

"I would never, ever tell you that," said the queen. "I believe you. But you are worthy of love."

"What does that have to do with anything?" Lovisa cried, then pushed herself up and stumbled to her bedroom. Her mother had tried to pull her away from the burning house. Lovisa had hit her with a shovel, as hard as she could. That was the last exchange Lovisa would ever have with her mother.

She crawled under her covers and stopped thinking.

DINNER WAS LATE because of the queen's visit to the Magistry. Lovisa ate hers in a chair by the fire because there wasn't enough room around the table and because she didn't like the careful, sympathetic looks people kept shooting at her, as if something terrible had happened to her and there was something she should be crushed about.

Suddenly, to her humiliation, tears began to roll down her face. Then she was sobbing, gasping for breath. She spilled hot tea in her lap and shouted as it scalded her skin.

The people in the room moved calmly and swiftly, as if her outburst were the most routine way for a person to behave. Someone— Nev—brought her into Nev's tiny room, checked her legs to make sure she wasn't burned, applied a salve. Someone else—Nev's grandfather, Saiet—tucked her into bed, pulling a soft, Nev-smelling blanket up to her chin. Someone else—Nev again—brought her unfinished dinner and a drink into the room and left them on the bedside table, in case she wanted them.

"Can my mother come to you later, Lovisa?" Nev asked. "She's a healer, you remember?"

"I'm not sick," Lovisa said.

"Can she come?" Nev said again, firm as always, but gentle too. Worried.

Oh, who cares? Lovisa thought. *More useless mothers.* "Fine," she said.

Sometime later, Nola came into the room, carrying a candle. A wind was moaning steadily outside. It made Lovisa feel like Torla's Neck was the end of the world.

"Lovisa?" she said.

Lovisa grunted, pretending to be more asleep than she was.

"How are you feeling?" said Nola. "Do any of your muscles feel tight?"

It was a hilarious question. Lovisa couldn't find a muscle in her body that didn't feel tight. The muscles of her shoulders, neck, and skull were trying to pop her head right off her body. "A little," she said.

A hand touched her shoulder. "May I?"

"I don't care," she said. "Do what you like."

"I need a yes or a no, Lovisa."

"Fine. Yes."

So Nev's mother massaged her back, shoulders, and neck with skilled strokes, finding the lines of tension, smoothing them. How unexpected, to be soothed by a stranger. Lovisa began to cry from the intensity of the comfort it gave her. When Nola found a necklace on Lovisa's neck, she moved carefully around it, because Lovisa wouldn't remove it. It was the cord that held the attic room key. The attic room no longer existed, but Lovisa couldn't let the key go. It was the only thing she had left that she understood.

The candle hissed. Puffs of wind pushed at the walls. Lovisa imagined that this was her home, her life. *But this is my life,* she realized; then, before she could get too confused about that, she fell asleep.

In the middle of the night, Bitterblue woke her with a soft "Lovisa?"

"Huh?" she said, coming awake to a pounding headache. She was still in Nev's bed. The queen stood beside her, wearing Ferla's furs and holding a glowing lamp. "What?"

"We're leaving for your house."

"Now? What time is it?"

"About four o'clock," Bitterblue said. "You don't have to come, but we didn't want to leave without giving you the choice."

"Can you do the plan without me?"

"We'll manage," said Bitterblue diplomatically.

In the dark blankness of her half-awake state, Lovisa's biggest truths arranged themselves starkly for her consideration. Her mother was dead. Her father was probably already in jail. Her brothers. Who was taking care of her brothers?

"Bitterblue?" she said in a breaking voice. "Is there some hope, do you think, for a better life for my brothers?"

"Oh, of course," said the queen. "I'm sure of it, Lovisa."

The queen's certainty annoyed her, and woke her up.

"There's hope for you too," the queen added. "Lovisa—"

"Oh, stop," said Lovisa. "I don't need any more inspiring slogans." The queen saw everything as flowers and sunshine, because she was in love.

"All right," said Bitterblue quietly. "I have to go, because the others are waiting. Nola and Saiet are staying behind if you need anything today."

How would her brothers ever be able to understand what was happening to their lives right now? Who could explain it, really, besides her? Who could ever understand what they were going through, besides her? And how could she understand it herself, if she was too afraid to look at the truth?

"Wait," she said. "It's my house. I'm coming."

Chapter Thirty-six

Divide and distract. That was the plan: Get as many of their team onto the Cavenda property as possible, then create distractions. Locate the storehouse. Find out how many people are on the grounds, how many are armed, and where they're situated. Convey that information, probably via Hava, to the people still waiting outside—Lovisa, Giddon, and the Queen of Monsea, the three of the party unlikely to be able to show up at the gate pretending to be someone else. Then, decide what to do next.

It was a flexible plan, adaptable. Giddon spent his life throwing himself into loose, open plans, then sorting out the details as he went along. This would be no different.

The walking path to the water at four in the morning went past a glacier, but all Giddon saw was a stretch of darkness that blotted out the stars.

The fastest and most discreet route to the Cavenda house was by boat. A friend of Nev's family, Saba, had a boat with black sails and knew how to navigate the route up the coast in the dark. Remembering that the route eventually led to Kamassar, Giddon tactfully asked no questions about Saba, who he guessed was a smuggler. "You can trust her discretion," Saiet said, which Giddon believed.

Saba would sail them to a cove with a cavern she knew. From the cavern, they could climb to a forest and walk to a road and head north. When a stone wall appeared on the left, that was the sign they'd reached the Cavenda property.

Hava would go over that wall, because Hava had the Grace to hide herself from anyone on the other side. Then, sometime later, Nev would arrive at the property gate, offering her services as a traveling animal doctor.

"I could poison the animals," Hava had offered, "so they're more likely to invite you in."

"No," Nev had said firmly.

"All right, well, at least I'll break some of the furniture," she'd said, since the next part of the plan involved Davvi appearing at the gate to offer his services as a traveling builder. Davvi had laughed at Hava's joke, but Giddon had been pretty sure she wasn't joking.

As they neared the water, Bitterblue turned and touched her hand to Giddon's chest. In the darkness, she traced a path all the way to his face and touched his beard gently, flushing him with heat, happiness, and that unshakable sense of disbelief that it was happening.

"Do you have the flask?" she said. "I think it's time."

"Yes," he said, then softly called to the group to wait. "Bitterblue's drinking her tea." For Bitterblue was going to drink some rauha, carefully brewed and flasked by Saiet, in preparation for a boat trip north that would otherwise make her sick. The right amount, Saiet had said, to help someone of her size just enough, then wear off in time in case she had to play a role in the sleuthing operation. He'd included enough for the trip back as well.

The group waited in darkness while Bitterblue drank. Nearby, a sharp crack, followed by a rumble, broke the silence: the glacier calving an iceberg into the sea.

"Did you hear it?" Giddon whispered, not wanting Bitterblue to miss anything beautiful.

Her hand found him again. "Yes." Then she turned him around, felt for the pack he was wearing, and slipped the flask back into it.

"Here's Saba," Nev called out quietly. "Is everyone ready?"

IT WAS A frigid trip north through a relentless wind, made somewhat warmer by the need to enclose Bitterblue in his arms to keep her from standing up in the boat and making announcements. They were very unpredictable announcements. One was about wanting to split her Ministry of Education into two parts, half for the education of children and half for adults. Another was a general inquiry about whether anyone had brought any pie. One time she just stood up and yelled, "Kittens!"

It wasn't the announcements that needed to stop, but the standing, because of the very real danger that in her rauha-induced state of silliness, she would fall out. It was intensely comforting, actually, to be in a boat with her, holding her tight in his arms so she wouldn't fall out. It felt like a redo from the last time. And she seemed to like it too, nestling against him, certainly the warmest person in the boat. He missed the announcements, though.

"Can I eat your nose?" she asked him, which would certainly have given their secret away if she hadn't already asked Hava, Lovisa, and Davvi if she could eat their noses.

"What's wrong with *my* nose?" Nev asked, a joke that sent Bitterblue into a peal of giggles that kept quieting, then resurfacing again.

Sometime later, they made land.

"Do you think you can walk?" Giddon asked Bitterblue as he and Hava helped her onto a pebbly beach. The stars were so thick and low here that he wanted to reach up and brush his fingers against them, then touch his starry hand to Bitterblue's face.

"She fell when we landed in the airship," Lovisa said, in her dull, faraway voice that made Giddon worry about the wisdom of including her in this mission.

"It's my land legs," Bitterblue said, then clung to Hava. "You remind me of Katsa."

"That's quite a compliment," Hava said. "I've got her," she added quietly to Giddon, who moved away, letting Hava help Bitterblue up the path to the trees. He was conscious of having monopolized Bitterblue since the miracle of her reappearance. And maybe Hava needed a redo too.

SITTING ON THE floor of Saba's cavern, surrounded by walls of stone that reached up to the sky, the group shivered in companionable silence until the sun rose. They snacked on bread, dried fruit, and cheese.

"What if I'm getting cavern dirt on my bottom?" Bitterblue asked. "And I end up having to approach the gate, announcing I'm the Queen of Monsea? Would a queen believably have a dirty bottom?"

"Are we sure she drank the right amount of rauha?" asked Lovisa, who kept rubbing her temples. "Isn't it supposed to be wearing off?"

"Saiet packed it for me," said Bitterblue. "I trust Saiet." Then she lay on her back and said "Saiet" several times at the ceiling to see if it made an echo.

"She does seem pretty far gone," said Nev. "Did she drink more than half?"

Giddon fished in his pack for the flask. The moment he touched it, he said, "Uh-oh."

"What is it?" said Nev.

"Bitterblue?" he said. "Did you drink the whole flask?"

"Of course," she said. "Why?"

"You were supposed to drink half."

"What!"

"And save half for the trip back."

"I thought he gave you two flasks!" she said. Then she sat up, put her hand to her mouth, and started giggling.

"Oh dear," said Nev.

Now Hava was laughing too, snorting and cackling, which wasn't helpful.

"Did she drink an unsafe amount?" asked Giddon anxiously.

"Not unsafe for her," said Nev. "Unsafe for our plan, though, if we need her."

"Don't worry," said Bitterblue, throwing a hand out and whacking Giddon's chest. "I can act so normal!"

"I doubt she's coming down for a long time," said Nev. "And even if she could act normal, she's not going to be able to hide pupils the size of plates."

"Okay," said Giddon, whose heart was sinking. "I'm afraid any part of the plan involving Bitterblue is out."

"Although . . ." said Hava.

The scheming look in Hava's eye made Giddon hopeful, but wary. "Yes?"

"Could she be someone else?" said Hava. "A traveler in need of medical assistance? I mean, in her current state," she said, pointing to Bitterblue, who was lying back again making very poor bird calls, "they'd never believe she was the Queen of Monsea anyway."

"Who, then?" said Giddon.

"She's obviously Lienid," said Lovisa.

"People in Torla's Neck aren't going to be primed to expect a Lienid traveler," said Hava, "are they?"

"They might be looking out for this very Lienid traveler, if they've been watching the signal messages," said Lovisa with a snort.

Bitterblue lifted both legs in the air and used them as leverage to swing herself up to a seated position. "Everybody," she said. "I know how to get me and Giddon into the house, and I think I could make it *very* distracting."

———————————

SOMETIME LATER, BITTERBLUE and Giddon trotted up to the Cavendas' front gate.

All had gone to plan so far. Hava had taken off first, then, sometime later, Nev. Davvi had followed Nev. Then, climbing out of their cavern under a pale pink sky, Bitterblue, Giddon, and Lovisa had stepped into the forest, passed through the trees, and found the road. The road had led them to the high stone wall.

"That's it," Lovisa had said. "I'll hang back and hide behind trees."

"All right," Giddon had said, still not liking Lovisa's uncertain role. The hope was to get her onto the property secretly somehow, so that her native knowledge would be available to the others, but she seemed so unfriendly and remote that Giddon didn't entirely trust her. Should they really be bringing the daughter of the house to the storming of the house? Mightn't she have her own agenda? "We'll be near," he added.

When Bitterblue and Giddon reached the gate, they found only one guard. Also, the gate he was guarding was open, which was going to make things much, much easier. The guard was tall, but slight. Giddon was taller.

"Hello!" Bitterblue cried, speaking in Lingian, then following her greeting with a strange bow that involved a lot of expansive arm movements. The guard, watching her with a puzzled and nonplussed expression, didn't respond. Giddon imagined he was getting pretty weary of random visitors showing up at his gate this morning.

"I am the Queen of Monsea!" Bitterblue almost shouted.

Something cleared in the guard's face. "Another one?" he said, in Keepish. "I met one last month."

"The others are imposters," Bitterblue cried in Lingian, bowing again. She swept a hand at Giddon. "This is my royal retainer!"

"And what's your act?" the guard asked, in Keepish.

"Not dancing!" she announced. "Not naughty dancing either!" which briefly startled Giddon. She held her hand out to the guard, fingers closed over something. "And now," she said, "are you ready for a little magic?"

Grinning, the guard held his palm open to her. She made a show of opening her hand, but when she did, it was empty. She shook the hand and glared at it, making frustrated noises at it as if it were malfunctioning.

"My magic is stuck at the moment," she said. "I'm sorry."

"I'm sure you're very good," said the guard kindly, still responding to her Lingian with Keepish, which was making Giddon a little dizzy. Behind him, Giddon heard the tiniest movement, which he guessed to be Lovisa slipping from tree to tree, so he made his shoulders big and tried to block the guard's view.

"What's wrong with her?" the guard asked next, for Bitterblue was now leaning both hands on the wall and resting her face sideways, gently, against the rock. She'd cleverly chosen the wall beyond the gate, which turned the guard's back to Lovisa. Her expression was familiar to Giddon, for she was plainly trying not to vomit, and as she blinked up at the guard, her pupils were as big as saucers.

"Oh," the guard said knowingly. "You should be careful with our teas, miss. Some of them are quite addicting."

"Might I rest inside your gates?" said Bitterblue. "Until I'm feeling better?"

"I'm afraid we don't have those kinds of facilities," the guard said.

"Not even for the Queen of Monsea?"

"I'm sure it seems cruel to someone of your magnificence," he said with a sympathetic grin.

"It's all right," Bitterblue said, pushing herself away from the wall. "Sincerely yours, Queen Glitterboo," she added thickly, as if she were signing a letter, then tried to sweep away, stumbled, and crashed to the ground.

In the ensuing hubbub, Giddon couldn't tell whether her collapse was real or not, which made his performance as a worried royal retainer even more convincing than it otherwise would have been. He shoved the guard aside and insisted on picking her up himself, relieved that the thing he wanted to do was the thing someone in his position would believably do.

"You can't leave us out here," Giddon said, in Keepish.

"I'm sorry—" began the guard.

"I'm bringing her in," Giddon said, taking full advantage of his height, his breadth, the combined volume of him and Bitterblue as he walked straight into the guard and pushed him back through the gate. "Get some water!" he shouted over the protests of the guard. "And a doctor! She has a heart condition!"

"A heart condition?" cried the guard in renewed alarm as Giddon bullied him along a path that wound through leafless trees. "What kind of heart condition? Would an animal doctor be sufficient?"

"Does she look like a poodle?" shouted Giddon, briefly proud of his Keepish. He could see the gray, weathered wood of the house through the trees ahead, then the place where the trees stopped, with nothing but air and light beyond. A rushing noise he'd mistaken for wind resolved itself into the sweep and pound of water against rock, reminding him that this house stood on a cliff. Behind him he heard nothing, but he knew Lovisa had had every opportunity to enter the property and begin to make her own way through the trees.

"It'll take a while to call a doctor," said the guard, who was no longer making any serious attempt to stop Giddon. His aspect was rather depressed, actually, and Giddon wondered if his failure to refuse them entrance was going to get him into trouble. "But there's an animal doctor on the property at present. That's why I suggested it."

"I'm sure he's busy with your animals," said Giddon.

"It's a woman."

"I don't care if it's the prime minister! We need a doctor." Then,

as the guard moved ahead up steps that led to an entranceway surrounded by late-blooming flowers, Giddon squeezed Bitterblue
harder. "Hey," he whispered. "You okay?"

She opened her eyes and shot him a mischievous, black-eyed look.
Then she closed her eyes and let her mouth hang open slightly.

Giddon relaxed.

Inside the house, rooms opened to left and right and a corridor
streaming with light extended straight ahead. A woman was marching
down this corridor toward them, her boot heels clomping like horse-
shoes on stone and a peeved expression on her brown face. Her white
hair, soft as a cloud, was pulled into a knot at the nape of her neck.

"What now?" she snapped at the guard, deep-voiced and annoyed.

"Traveling entertainers," said the guard, looking cowed before the
woman, despite his greater height. "Heart condition."

"I'm the Queen of Monsea," Bitterblue moaned, still tucked in
Giddon's arms.

"Of course you are," said the woman, glancing at Bitterblue's
bedraggled furs and the plain, overly large tunic and pants she wore
beneath it, borrowed from Nola. Her messy hair, her enormous black
eyes. "And who are you supposed to be?" the woman barked at Giddon.

"I'm Giddon," said Giddon.

"Yes, I've heard of you," she said sourly. "Very good. Big and loyal-
looking. You only need the Graceling and a few pasty men and your
act will be complete. Would you like to plop Her Majesty down on a
couch?" she said, extending an arm through an open doorway. "We
can rustle up a drink for you, but I'm afraid that then you'll have to
be on your way."

"We need a doctor," said Giddon firmly.

"We can direct you to the nearest doctor."

"My companion can't walk, as you can see."

"We'll lend you a horse," she said with finality, then turned and swept off. "No more guests!" she shouted for the benefit of the guard, who was still standing by, shoulders slumped, face tight with apprehension.

"I hope we haven't gotten you in trouble," Giddon said. "She's plainly upset about something."

The guard seemed unable to decide what to say. "I'll ask someone for water," he said, turning to go.

"I'll do some magic for you later, to thank you," Bitterblue moaned, which made him turn back once, half smiling. Then he left the room, leaving Giddon to tuck Bitterblue into a sofa with dark fluffy cushions and pillows into which her body sank, as if it were a bath.

Immediately Bitterblue popped her eyes open. "This sofa is eating me," she said, fighting with the upholstery in an attempt to rise, then holding her hand out to Giddon, fingers closed over something. "And now," she said, "are you ready for a little magic?"

"Always," said Giddon, opening his hand below hers, knowing where this was going. She dropped his own pocketknife into his palm. It explained why, a few minutes ago, while he'd been carrying her, she'd very obviously stuck her hand into his pockets and groped around.

"Remarkable sleight of hand," he said gravely.

Her giggles began again, then immediately turned into moans. When Giddon reached for her in alarm, she touched his face, patted his cheek. "It's okay," she said. "I have waves of feeling happy as pie, then waves of feeling like I ate too much pie. Too much poisonous pie," she said miserably. Then she checked herself, her expression changing as she looked at the doorway.

Giddon turned to see Lovisa standing there, staring in at them silently. He opened his mouth to say something cautionary or bossy, but Bitterblue tugged his arm to stop him.

Lovisa slipped away.

CHAPTER THIRTY-SEVEN

LOVISA WAS SO happy for the Queen of Monsea and her gigantic boyfriend, that they should be enjoying this invasion of her house so much. What a hilarious act, the queen's "are you ready for a little magic" bit. Especially while Hava snuck around somewhere, spying, interfering with things that weren't hers, all while employing *actual* magic. Lovisa had used to fantasize about the Royal Continent and its magic, but now she could see that that magic was really just another kind of lying. This was a game to them. Find the clues, solve the riddle, while Lovisa's life came apart.

The white-haired woman who'd received Bitterblue and Giddon was a disgraced academy professor named Linta Massera. LM. Lovisa had recognized her immediately. And a puzzle piece had settled, with a sickening click, into place, because Linta Massera was the chemistry professor who'd been kicked out of the academy a few years back because something had exploded in her lab. Lovisa had mentioned it to Benni, during their conversation about the explosive properties of varane. He'd responded that *that* particular explosion had had to do with zilfium.

"Zilfium explodes too?" Lovisa had said, and Benni had waved a dismissive hand. "I don't know anything about it," he'd said, but he must know something about Linta and her work if she was living here in the Cavenda house, giving orders to the Cavenda guards as if she were the queen. Linta had disappeared from Ledran society after the shame of leaving the academy. No one talked about her anymore. But she had to be the LM who'd written a warning letter to Benni.

Lovisa needed to get to the storehouse.

She heard a sound in a nearby room. Before someone stumbled upon her, she slipped through a narrow doorway that looked like a cupboard but was really a back stairway down to the kitchen.

FROM HER POSITION behind the kitchen door at the bottom of the steps, Lovisa could hear someone doing something with broken pieces of ceramic and glass. Sweeping them, possibly, across the slate floor? And someone else was hammering, and a woman who sounded like the cook, Liv, was yelling that it was nice to have a chat with new people.

Davvi's voice responded to Liv. Then a third voice, sweet and female, said, "The water's almost boiled."

Nev's voice responded. "I'm grateful."

"Is it a bad blockage?" said the sweet voice.

"I don't know yet," said Nev, "but these things can be quite straightforward, once you've got your hand in the right place."

"Poor thing's been off her food for days."

Liv said, "Here, Ella, you run this water upstairs to the sitting room and I'll bring Linta Massera her tea."

"Yes, ma'am," said the sweet voice. Footsteps shuffled away; doors opened and closed.

"What've you learned, Nev?" Davvi asked in a low, urgent voice.

"The white-haired woman works in the storehouse," said Nev. "I'm dealing with a constipated cow and I can see her marching to and from that building. I'm sure Hava's somewhere, but I haven't spotted her. How many people have you seen?"

"The white-haired woman," said Davvi. "Liv, Ella, and a man who seems like the housekeeper. There were two guards at the gate when I arrived this morning."

"Yes, me too," Nev said. "One of them's now watching me in the barn and at least four others have walked by the barn windows. Seems like they're doing some kind of regular patrol."

Lovisa pushed the door open. Both Davvi and Nev started in alarm, Nev joggling the cauldron-sized kettle she held with both hands.

"So, at least six guards total," said Lovisa. "That's a lot of guards for a mostly empty house. Have fun sticking your arm up a horse's butt," she added to Nev, who was carrying her kettle toward the outer door.

"It's a cow," said Nev, "don't you listen?" Then, with half a grin, she strode outside.

Lovisa surveyed the kitchen. The long row of cabinets that stretched along the upper wall was tilted at a funny angle and the strip of wood that formed the base seemed to have come disattached. A bin in a corner was full of the fragments of plates, bowls, and glassware.

"Hava did that?" she said, impressed.

"I don't even know how she managed it," said Davvi, "unless she carries a crowbar hidden inside her clothes."

Lovisa glanced around the kitchen and saw two or three implements that could double as an improvised crowbar, for an imaginative woman with personality problems. "I'll go check out the storehouse," she said.

SHE WAS NOT experienced in sneaking across yards in daylight, and she didn't have Hava's advantages. But she was a quick learner. Aiming for the barn, Lovisa slipped from tree to tree, diving behind a fallen trunk once as a guard strode by.

A moment later, peeking out from a corner of the barn, Lovisa assessed the storehouse. Unlike the house that was perched on the cliff, one whole side composed practically of glass, the storehouse, like the barn, was set back from the cliff and had few windows.

Inside, it resembled a stable, with open areas divided by low walls into sections that functioned as stalls for the storage of supplies. In Torla's Neck, you had to travel for supplies, buy in bulk; or you stocked up once a year as vendors passed through. The storehouse was full of *things*, spices and cheeses and sacks of flour that left a cloud of white dust on everything nearby; as a child, Lovisa had pretended it was the hold of a ship, a place she'd never been. She'd escape to the storehouse sometimes, tuck herself among the supplies, find a snack with which to comfort herself, then pretend she was going somewhere far away and different.

The storehouse had a large front entrance with big barn doors. Lovisa crept through the trees to the back and entered through the small back door, which gave straight into one of the storage stalls. She knew it would be dark back there, hidden from the open front of the building.

As she'd expected, she stepped into an unlit stall. It smelled faintly of firewood. She closed the door quickly, grateful for the distant roar of the ocean that muffled the sound.

Light shone from the front of the storehouse and she could see a moving shadow there. Slowly, crouching low, Lovisa worked her way forward from stall to stall.

When she got close enough to see the front of the storehouse, she folded herself against a wall and peeked out. In the slender open area before the big doors, Linta Massera sat at a table, facing Lovisa, making notes in a small notebook. The table was crowded with objects and implements, some, like a stove, oddly shaped glassware, a microscope, reminding Lovisa of the laboratories at the academy. Others seemed more like the detritus of life. A cup of tea; a tray with empty dishes and cutlery; papers and pens; a short stack of notebooks like the one Linta wrote in. Ropes hung on the wall behind her. A small, square trapdoor was set into the floor near the table. Lovisa had noticed it before but never tried it, for it had always been locked. It intrigued her now, because she could see the key in the lock, sticking out of the floor like a tiny spike.

A pot on the stove at Linta's left elbow bubbled gently. Linta turned toward it to check on it, and when she did, something moved against the wall to her right. When she turned back to her notebook, the movement stopped. A moment later, she reached for the pot again and the same thing happened. Lovisa watched, fascinated, as a sack of some foodstuff, positioned among other sacks of foodstuff, shifted closer to the table. A wave of nausea swept through Lovisa, heightening when she forced herself to stare at the sack and was able to discern in its rumples and folds, ever so slightly, the shape of a crouching girl. The sack was Hava. And Hava was trying to get closer to Linta's table.

What should she do? How could she help? Lovisa began hunting around her stall, looking for an answer. She found it: a sack of some dried thing—beans—with a tiny hole in its side. A bean lay on the floor beneath the hole. Lovisa stuck her finger into the hole, widening it. She caught the stream of beans that emerged. Then, the next time Linta seemed intent on her notebook, she hurled the beans to the side of the room opposite from where Hava was lurking.

They made more noise than she'd intended, crashing against the wall, pounding down onto barrels, bouncing across the floor. Linta jumped up, stared around, then left the table and walked to that corner, muttering to herself. Instantly, Hava mobilized, stretching into a clearly girl-shaped sack that crept to the table, snatched up Linta's notebooks, then shot down the narrow alleyway between the stalls. She dove into Lovisa's stall. Turning back into a girl, she grabbed Lovisa.

"Get down. I can hide you," she whispered.

Lovisa really thought she might vomit. The rapid transformations were so overwhelming. "How did you know I was here?"

"I saw the flight of whatever you threw. Sh!"

Together, they peeked out. Linta had found a few beans on the floor. She stood holding them in her hand, staring up at the wall and the ceiling, then, still muttering to herself, walking back to her table.

Instantly, she saw that her notebooks were missing. She froze, grabbing a knife that lay on the table, glaring out across the stalls. As Hava pressed Lovisa down, Linta's footsteps neared. Hava crouched over her, covering her with her own body.

Lovisa closed her eyes, needing not to see Hava's transformation, not to move, not to breathe. Linta's footsteps grew closer, padding toward their stall. Continued past it and receded; turned back and approached again. The footsteps returned to the table, where Linta could be heard swearing under her breath. Then the big front doors slammed and Linta's voice rose, shouting in the yard about stolen notebooks.

Hava moved, grabbed Lovisa's arm. "We need to find a better hiding place, quick," she whispered.

"There's no place to hide in here. They'll tear it apart," said Lovisa.

"What about that trapdoor?"

"I don't know what it leads to."

"Let's try it," Hava said, pulling Lovisa out of their stall—then, when the big doors burst open again, pushing her into a different stall. It was mostly empty, not packed tight with supplies as the others were. Terrible for hiding, containing only three wooden chests, stacked one behind the other. The chests were locked with padlocks.

At the front of the room, Linta was loudly explaining to someone what had happened.

"We have to get out of here!" Lovisa whispered.

"We're stuck in this stall for now," Hava muttered, reaching into her pockets and extracting some long metal sticks that attached to a ring. Lovisa watched in amazement as she began to insert various sticks into one of the padlocks and fiddle around. Lock picks? *Now?*

A click sounded. The padlock slid open. Linta's voice grew louder, heavy footsteps pacing, a man's voice asking a question, another man responding. Two guards? Carefully, grimacing with anticipation of creaks and squeaks, Hava opened the chest. It made no sound. With a grin at Lovisa—this girl was a maniac; what was she so happy about?—Hava reached inside and pulled out something Lovisa had never seen before: a metal, egg-shaped thing, about the size of a large potato, with a ring and pin at one end. Hava inspected it closely, holding it to the dim light, then bringing it to her own pale face. She turned it around, then turned it back again. All the while, Lovisa was staring at the thing with a growing sense of distress that she couldn't articulate. She wanted Hava to put the thing down, close it back inside the chest. She thought to herself, *Whatever Linta Massera is making here, it can't be good.* She thought to herself, *That would fit in a banker's box.* She thought to herself, *When the house was on fire, something exploded in my mother's study.*

"Put it back," Lovisa said sharply, not even caring if Linta heard her. "Put it back."

Hava, her eyebrows furrowed in curiosity, took hold of the ring at the end of the egg. And Lovisa knew; all at once, she understood what was going to happen. As Hava pulled the pin from the egg, Lovisa screamed. She snatched the egg from Hava and threw it as hard as she could, then grabbed Hava and knocked her down. She covered Hava's ears with her hands.

The world turned to sound and light.

CHAPTER THIRTY-EIGHT

THE ROAR OF the explosion shot Giddon to his feet. He felt the room shaking and thought, momentarily, that he must be losing his mind.

"What was that?" Bitterblue said thickly, the nausea plain in her face. He helped her up and they ran toward the sitting room door. In the corridor, when they encountered a guard who was also rushing to get outside, Giddon made a split decision.

"Sorry," he said, driving his fist into the astonished man's face. As the man struggled for balance, Giddon grabbed the sword at his belt, then cracked him across the temple with the hilt. The man crumpled to the ground, breathing shallowly.

Giddon spun to Bitterblue, expecting an appalled expression. She was already to the door, knives of her own in each hand. "Here comes another one," she said, pushing outside and marching unsteadily toward a guard who was running from the front gate.

What was she going to do, stab him? It was the nice guard, the one who'd been kind to Bitterblue about her magic. Gritting his teeth, Giddon burst after Bitterblue and ran at him. Instantly, the startled guard unsheathed his own sword, but Giddon was upon him, knocking him down, punching him, clipping his temple.

"I never knew you were so efficient," said Bitterblue.

"You take this," said Giddon, handing her the guard's sword.

"Should we be leaving these men alive?"

"It's a risk I'd prefer to take."

"All right. I'm in no state to make important decisions. Let's go," she said, setting off through the trees toward the noise of distant voices.

Their route led them away from the cliff, toward a barn. Rounding it, they came upon what must until recently have been the storehouse. At its back end, broken walls rose from rubble and dust billowed like fog. Its front end was gone, transformed into hills of detritus that circled a massive hole in the earth. The air smelled strange, metallic.

Giddon spotted a guard near the hole, overturning pieces of wall and roof. Noticing Nev near the building's broken walls, Giddon called, "Nev! How many guards are there?"

"At least six," Nev called back.

"Two are dead," came a voice, small and frightened, from somewhere inside.

"Lovisa?" said Nev, turning sharply at the sound. "Lovisa? Where are you?"

"I'm going to fall," said the voice, "so listen to me. If anyone sees a metal thing shaped like an egg, do not touch it."

"Lovisa!" cried Nev, trying to find a way over the broken walls.

"Nev, don't!" said Lovisa. "You stay there! The floor is caving in!"

"Nev, see if there's a back entrance!" shouted Bitterblue, and in that moment, the guard who was digging through the detritus cried out. His digging had unearthed the body of one of the dead guards. Looking around wildly, he spotted Giddon heading toward him with a sword. Unsheathing his own sword, the guard ran and attacked. Giddon had been carrying his sword in his right hand, a habit he'd picked up to hide his secret advantage of left-handedness. He waited until the guard was near. Then, switching sides, he surprised the man with a left-handed parry that gave him an opening for a punch.

Then Davvi was beside Giddon, helping him grapple the guard to the ground.

"We need something to bind them," said Giddon, who was getting tired of handing out concussions. "And there's at least one more guard."

Davvi grunted, distracted. He was staring across the hole in the ground, trying to make out what was happening at the other edge of the hole, where the broken walls of the storehouse began.

"Nev!" he shouted, then jumped up and ran around the hole, then around the storehouse, disappearing behind it. Giddon squinted, trying to see what Davvi had seen. Nev was on her knees on the storehouse's broken floor, crawling toward the edges of the hole. That's when Giddon saw Lovisa, clinging to the crater's edge.

"Bitterblue!" shouted Giddon, because the queen was there too, leaning over Nev, using her sword as a cane, trying to look into the hole. "Get back from that edge!" He thumped the poor guard on the head. Then he ran after Davvi, as fast as he could.

Inside the storehouse's back entrance, piles of rubble blocked his way. Giddon pushed through it, stepping into broken barrels, scratching himself on nails. By the time he reached the operation at the edge of the hole, Davvi was on his knees, anchoring Nev's legs.

"Bitterblue!" Giddon grabbed her, dragged her back from the crater. "You are not well enough for a rescue operation!"

"You're right," she said, tears running down her face. "But what about—"

"You stay there," he said, dropping beside Davvi onto a painful hill of splintered wood and taking one of Nev's legs. Nev had hold of Lovisa's arm, but Lovisa was gripping some sort of broken post, some pillar that had used to be part of the storehouse floor, with both hands. She wouldn't let go.

"You have to," said Nev. "Lovisa. You have to let go, or we can't pull you up."

"I'll fall in!"

"I will not let that happen," said Nev fiercely.

All at once, the lip of the crater began to break. Lovisa screamed, released her hold on the post. For one horrible moment, Lovisa dangled over empty space by one arm and Nev plunged in after her. Giddon and Davvi dragged on Nev's legs as hard as they could, harder, back, away from the edge, across a floor that snagged and cut them. Giddon got hold of Nev's shoulder, yanked. His hand closed around Lovisa's arm. He pulled. They all fell together, scrambling back as the crater continued to widen. Someone else had Lovisa. Giddon grabbed Bitterblue, who still hovered too close, trying to see into the hole. He spun her up and pushed himself over the rubble to the back door, burst out into the air with Bitterblue in his arms, running, putting distance between them and the storehouse.

In the yard, Lovisa dropped onto the ground, gasping, crying. Nev dropped beside her and wrapped the smaller girl in her arms.

"But what about Hava?" said Bitterblue. "Does anyone know where she is?"

"She fell in," said Lovisa. "She fell in."

THEIR SHOUTS YIELDED no response.

"Hava!" they repeated. "Hava!" Bitterblue's cries were the most piteous of all. She kept drifting toward the hole, crying "Hava" with tears running down her face, to the point that monitoring her safety became an exigency of the group. Someone was assigned to the intoxicated queen at all times.

It was impossible to approach the crater, impossible to get a good view inside or even contemplate trying to climb down. The ground was still crumbling at its edges. Even Giddon, who should have been able to muscle himself down into that hole and find her, find her!, was reduced to shouting.

He searched for rope in the barn, instead finding the sixth guard, trying to sneak out on a horse. Giddon, exhausted, worried, and hacking up dust, dragged the man down from his saddle, then did his best to knock him out without killing him. These things weren't exactly a science, after all, and it was getting harder to care, what with Hava inside the earth somewhere, not responding to their cries.

Finding no rope, he returned to the others. Bitterblue lay flat on the ground, too close to the rubble, ear to the dirt. At first the sight frightened him—she looked like she'd collapsed there—but then she turned her head, pressing her other ear flat to the ground.

She raised a hand. "Everyone," she said. "Silence."

Everyone went quiet, standing still, staring at the prostrate queen.

"I hear her," Bitterblue said. "She's calling my name."

HAVA'S ANKLE WAS trapped under a ladder. It was, by her estimation, sprained or worse, and her head hurt, but she insisted she was otherwise fine. She'd been knocked unconscious. As she came awake, her voice grew stronger. The group, gathering as near the crater as seemed safe, could hear her, and shout down questions.

"It's a cave," she told them. "With high, curving walls. There are even stalactites and stalagmites"—she spoke those words in Lingian—"though I can never remember which is which. I can't move this ladder. Both of its ends are trapped."

"Can you see any path down that looks steady?" called Giddon.

"No. And stuff keeps falling in and there are explosive eggs near me. Kindly don't drop more rubble down here and set them off."

"My mother told me of a cave," Lovisa said numbly, sitting farther away than the others, her back to a tree, shivering.

Giddon spun to her. "What did she say about it?"

"Her father sent her there for punishments," said Lovisa.

"Hava's cave doesn't sound like an accessible sort of cave," said Giddon.

"I saw a trapdoor in the floor of the storehouse," Lovisa said. "With a key sticking out of the lock."

"Well then," said Giddon, with rising impatience, "if that was the access point, it's gone now."

"She used to talk of being able to watch the sun set from the cave. She talked of being visited by birds," said Lovisa, speaking with the numbness of an automaton, as if she had a rote announcement about the cave and had to make it all the way through from start to finish before stopping. Meanwhile, Hava was trapped. Giddon wanted to shake anyone who wasn't helping.

"That means there's another access point," said Bitterblue, who was still lying with her ear to the ground.

"What?"

Bitterblue sat up. She turned big, black, unhappy eyes to Giddon. Then she pointed out across the yard, to the place where the trees gave way to nothing but sky.

"This property is on a cliff, Giddon," she said. "If Ferla could see the setting sun from her cave, it means there's an opening to the cave in the cliff wall."

THE DIM VOICE of Hava confirmed this theory.

"Yes," she called. "I see daylight, now that I'm looking for it, straight ahead. It seems small, and far away."

"The storehouse is built back from the cliff," said Giddon grimly.

"We need rope," said Bitterblue.

"I found no rope in the barn."

"The rope was kept in the storehouse," said Lovisa, in that same expressionless voice. "We exploded it."

And so, they collected every sheet in the house. The house staff—

a cook, a maid, and a housekeeper who all seemed so thunder-struck by the situation that Giddon was inclined to believe in their innocence—helped them, leading them to a spare pantry that even Lovisa didn't know about. The staff's eyes went huge whenever they glanced at Lovisa, who stayed against her tree, filthy, scratched, tat-tered, and crying. One of them brought her a cup of tea. Lovisa held it in her hands, unseeing.

While the others tied sheets together, Giddon rubbed grime out of his eyes, then experimentally stretched his arms. Like everyone else in the group, he was still coughing from dust, which filmed his eyes, nose, tongue, the back of his throat. His hands were stiff and bruised from punching guards. But he understood that the person who went over the edge to look for a route to Hava needed to climb down the cliff wall, then free her from that ladder, then probably carry her. That meant him.

The others—Davvi, Nev, Lovisa, the cook, the maid, and housekeeper—would arrange themselves in a line above the cliff, grasping the sheet rope's other end. They agreed on a system of shouts and tugs for communication, though Giddon wasn't sure how anyone would be able to hear anything over the crash of the water, or how he was supposed to tug on a sheet rope while clinging to a rock face.

Bitterblue was forbidden from helping, with anything. She was still too high. Nor was she allowed to remain near the hole by herself, where at least she could've comforted herself—and Hava—by talk-ing to Hava. She sat against a tree near the rope operation, rubbing her braids with shaking fingers and pretending to be fine.

A sheet rope tied tightly around his waist and groin, Giddon went to her.

"Bitterblue," he said, crouching before her, meeting her enor-mous, frightened eyes. "I'm just going down once. I'll find her and free her. Then we'll both come back up again. It'll be over in a few minutes. Okay?"

She whispered, "Okay."

"The rope is safe," he said. "We've checked and double-checked every knot, and I'll climb wherever I can to minimize the strain on it. Do you understand that?"

"No, but it comforts me that you do. Will you give me a math problem?"

He would've smiled if she hadn't looked so sick. "Square integers for me," he said. "When I come back, I want you to tell me how far you got. Okay?"

"You promise you'll come back?"

"I promise."

"Okay," she said.

He kissed her forehead. Then, returning to the others, he approached the cliff's edge, got down on the ground, and peeked over. The ocean was very, very far below. The water pounded against rock. Giddon saw no cave opening.

He checked with the rope team, swung himself over, and began to climb down.

THE CLIFF FACE was slippery. Cracks and knobby places abounded, but his cold fingers couldn't grasp slick rock. He slipped once, his full weight yanking down on the sheet halter, and the team above held on. Below him was the tiniest ledge.

I'll climb down to the ledge, he told himself. *I can make it to the ledge.*

After a few more minutes of wedging his fingers hard into cracks, he achieved it, his feet touching down. It wasn't much of a ledge, narrow, running sideways around an outward-curving bend to a part of the cliff wall Giddon couldn't see. But it held his weight while he breathed, refocused, and tried to examine his surroundings. He spotted no doorway to a cave.

Giddon took another, calmer breath, quieted his shaking, and looked harder. He saw one bird, then another, come from the sea and shoot straight toward the part of the cliff face he couldn't see, at a speed that was either suicidal or indicated that there was no wall to stop them.

Then he understood. That was the opening, on the other side of that bend. He began to move sideways along the ledge, trying not to think about how the rope would swing him like a pendulum if he slipped again. The route became smelly, and slimy with bird droppings, then with blood that seemed to be seeping from one of his hands. The ledge grew narrower, and still he saw no cave opening.

Suddenly birds exploded out of rock right beside him, launching themselves across the sea. He nearly lost his grip, it startled him so much, but he steeled himself and kept pushing sideways, knowing it must be near. He stretched, reached, wedged his bleeding fingers into cracks. Yes! He could see it now, a small, dark gap in the cliff! As he neared it, the ledge petered out. For a few terrifying steps, he had to balance his toes on any knobs he could find, straining not to slip.

Finally, excruciatingly, his boots reached the safety of the opening, where he could stand.

A hand grabbed his ankle.

CHAPTER THIRTY-NINE

GIDDON WOULD HAVE fallen if it weren't for the solid rock on which he stood.

As it was, he screamed. The others above heard the scream and, with natural misunderstanding, started pulling, so that Giddon was briefly stretched between the rope and the viselike grip on his ankle. But then he got his breath back and yelled up to them to stop. "I'm fine," he shouted. "I'm fine. Give me some slack, and shift to your right.

"Hava?" he said next to the hand on his ankle, even though he knew this couldn't possibly be Hava, who was far back in the cave, trapped under a ladder. Giddon had a wild, incredulous idea of who this must be. As the sheet rope loosened, he crouched down.

Another hand came out of the opening and grasped his wrist. Giddon saw a hunched form gray with dust and dirt, a scraggly, dark beard. "You're safe now," he said in Keepish, peering closer at a man who stared out of the hole with crazed eyes in a bone-thin face. He looked, and smelled, like the most misused, neglected human Giddon had ever seen, and Giddon realized his guess had been wrong. He'd never seen this man before.

"Giddon?" said the man. "Is that you?"

Giddon, stunned, searched the man's face. It couldn't be; he was too small, too old. But then a flicker of something flashed in those eyes, amusement, if that was possible, resolving the man's face into one Giddon recognized. Tears choked Giddon's throat. He was going to kill Benni Cavenda.

"Katu," he said.

"Am I hallucinating?" said Katu Cavenda, one of his hands letting go, his finger touching Giddon's shoulder with a tentative poke, as if he expected a ghost. *He* looked like a ghost.

"I'm real," Giddon said. "Let's get this rope on you and get you out of here."

"What's happening?" he said. "Why are you here?" His voice turned into a cry. "There was an explosion! The roof caved in! I've been hearing voices!"

"We know," said Giddon. "Everyone's all right. We can talk about it after we've gotten you out of here." Then he shuffled into the cave opening beside Katu and began to unwrap himself from the sheet rope, and Katu began to panic.

"What are you doing?" he cried, knocking Giddon's hands away from the halter.

"Tying you to this rope so my friends can pull you up," said Giddon.

"But you can't stay here!"

"They'll lower the rope for me after you're safe."

"You have to come with me! I'm not leaving you here!"

"Katu," Giddon said, grasping the man's shoulder. "There's not enough rope for us both and the weight would be too much. My friends aren't going to leave me down here! One of them is your niece, did you know that? Your niece is on the other end of this rope."

"My niece?" said Katu, in utter disbelief. "Lovisa?" Then his shoulders dropped and he began to sob.

"Let's get you attached," said Giddon, returning to his halter. "We don't want to waste time."

But Katu was too overwrought. Leaning into Giddon, he shook

and cried. So Giddon wrapped his arms around his smelly companion, waiting until he was ready.

KATU HAD NO strength to contribute to his own ascent. Imagining him tipping upside down and sliding out of his halter, Giddon triple-knotted the sheet rope around Katu's waist and groin and even passed it over Katu's shoulder once. He tried not to worry about what happened to sheets when dragged over rock with the full weight of a person at one end.

Next, Giddon tugged with the signal that meant "Pull!" Then he lay on his side in the cave opening with his feet braced and his arms and torso hanging over the ledge, so that should Katu fall, Giddon could grab for him. He knew it was unlikely to work, though. More likely, Katu, falling, would bring Giddon down with him. *I'm risking my life to save the life of my future wife's past lover,* he thought with a sigh.

Slowly but steadily, Katu rose; he even attempted alertness, grasping for handholds in the rock to keep himself from spinning. When Katu got to the top, the arms of Davvi reached down for him. Then, with a flailing of limbs, Katu was on solid ground. Giddon supposed everyone up there must be pretty surprised to see Katu Cavenda instead of Hava. And then he forgot about it, because he needed to get Hava out of there.

Carefully, he felt his way deeper into the cave. "Hava?" he called, his voice echoing.

"Here," she said, her voice echoing back to him from some distance. "Don't shout any more than you have to," she added calmly. "It makes the ceiling crumble. Walk slowly and watch for metal eggs."

The cave was huge, and curved and strange, like being inside the shell of a gigantic mollusk. There was the hole in the ceiling ahead where light filtered down from the place where the storehouse had used to be, illuminating streaks of floating dust. There were piles of rubble below, broken chests and barrels, glass jars and sacks. Then, part of a metal ladder. Hava's ladder. Giddon moved as quickly as he could with a light tread.

When he rounded a pile of debris and spotted her, tears began to make paths through the grime on his face, because of how nonchalant she looked. She'd propped herself up against a broken barrel with one leg tucked against her torso and the other extended, her ankle trapped under the ladder as she'd said. Blood was sliding down from a gash on her forehead and she blinked up at him, red and copper eyes, in a face white with dust. And she was reading. Calm as calm, with those dangerous metal orbs scattered around her, with the ceiling caving in and no certain rescue, with that heavy metal ladder pressing down so hard on her leg that Giddon, examining it more closely, became frightened that she might lose a foot, Hava had a notebook open before her and was reading.

But he could hear the quickness of her breath. She was in pain, and she was scared.

"Anything good in that book?" Giddon said quietly, grabbing the ladder to either side of her foot and heaving. Nothing happened. It was the longest ladder he'd ever seen—probably the means of entering the cave from the storehouse—and it was trapped under rubble at both ends. It was also slippery with dust.

"You sap," she responded, watching the tears run down his face. "Was that Katu Cavenda I heard you rescuing?"

"It was."

"And here I thought I was alone."

"He was pretty out of it." Giddon took his coat off, then, deciding it was too thick for his purposes, pulled his shirt over his head.

"I was hoping for a rescue too, not a striptease," she said, watching as he wrapped his bloody hands with the sleeves of his shirt, then used them as improvised gloves to grip the ladder. Giddon heaved again, muscles of his arms and shoulders straining. The gloves helped. But still, nothing.

"To the best of my ability to decipher these notes," said Hava conversationally, "the explosive eggs are made using zilfium and a byproduct of silver refining, among other things."

"Fascinating," said Giddon. There was nothing in the nearby debris strong enough to use as a lever to free her leg. There was no way to dig a cavity under it, because her leg rested on rock. He studied the rubble mountain at either end of the ladder, then chose the mountain that looked less formidable.

"It *is* fascinating," said Hava, "seeing as the world's richest known zilfium deposits belong to Bitterblue. Do you understand what she's sitting on, Giddon? The value of her mountains, economically and politically—militarily—if *this* is what she could do with them?"

The rubble at this end seemed to be mostly rocks and wood. No metal eggs. Giddon adjusted his improvised gloves, bent his knees, and grabbed the ladder. When he tried to lift it, it shifted, ever so slightly.

"Giddon," said Hava. "If you can't get me out of here, promise me you'll take these notebooks. I think they contain the plans to make the eggs."

"Hava, love," he said. "Get ready to move your foot. It's going to hurt, and I might not be able to lift this thing completely clear."

Hava looked across at him for one long moment. When a tear ran down her face, she let him see it. "Okay," she said. "I'm ready."

With all the strength in his body—with his legs, his back, his shoulders screaming, with his hands tearing and a roar bursting out of his throat, Giddon lifted the end of the ladder.

Shrieking from the pain, Hava pulled her foot through the tiny aperture he created.

When he saw that she was free, Giddon dropped the ladder, then bent over, coughing. Stones and dirt were falling from above, pinging onto the floor of the cave like a hailstorm.

"You okay?" he managed to say.

"Yeah. You?" Her voice was rough.

"Yeah."

"Let's get out of here."

"Yeah."

"Giddon?" she said as he made his way back to her.

"Yeah?"

She was crying, really crying, which Hava hardly ever did. But the eyes she turned up to him were glowing, with a kind of joy that seemed out of place. "You did good," she said, and Giddon understood that she hadn't been expecting to survive this.

Stiff, aching, he pulled his shirt and coat back on, then dropped to one knee beside her. "Did you think I was going to leave you down here, brat?" he said, lifting her into his arms.

IT WAS HARDER to send Hava up on the sheet rope than it had been with Katu, because she was in so much pain. He strapped her into the halter, then braced himself in the opening as he had during Katu's ascent. Every time her injured ankle jarred against the rocks, he felt it in his own body. Giddon was feeling everything in his own body. He couldn't remember ever having been so tired, sore, bruised, and cold.

Then Hava was safe on solid ground, and suddenly Giddon's heart started pounding. It was time for his own climb back up the cliff. What if now, after all he'd done, he made a mistake? What if, with the team's arms at their tiredest, the sheet rope at its most tattered and strained, and his own fingers bleeding and stiff with cold, he slipped, and fell? Giddon didn't want to die. He had work to do. He had happiness to feel. He was a baby; his life had begun anew only a few days ago.

Giddon turned and pushed himself up, walked back into the cave, to distract himself from these thoughts. There was no way to get back onto solid ground without passing through his fear. He would think about the others, who believed he was strong enough to climb back. One, in particular, who wanted him back badly. What a gift, that she wanted him back that way.

Giddon took in the cave one last time. A stalactite near him reached down toward a stalagmite, the two almost meeting in the middle to form a pillar. It was cold in this cavern, stark and strange. What had Lovisa said—that Ferla's father had used to send Ferla here for punishments? How long had Katu wasted away in here? It seemed impossible that such a place should exist, or that any person should ever discover it. Inhumane that anyone should use it to discipline children. From where he stood, he could see the broken barrels, jars, and chests that must have been stacked in the storehouse a few hours ago. How peculiar to see the results of an explosion from below. "Wow," he said. The word echoed back to him, soft and deep.

And then he saw a few of those metal eggs, scattered near the edges of the fallen supplies. He studied them; he committed them, and the damage they'd done, to memory. He knew that he was look-ing at a terrible evil. And though he hadn't responded to Hava earlier, he understood some things about what it meant. The exploding eggs were an invention that, once invented, couldn't be un-invented. They were made from a fuel that lived in Bitterblue's mountains. Hava possessed the plans to make them. And Bitterblue was a queen, with a kingdom to defend, surrounded by militaristic nations like Estill. What would happen to the world, once everyone knew what Benni Cavenda had made with zilfium?

Now Giddon knew he would get to the top of the cliff, because he wasn't going to leave Bitterblue to find the answer to that question alone.

THE CLIMB WAS exhausting. His fingers were senseless nubs and his arms heavy as iron mallets, and just as useful for climbing. He loved the sheet rope. It was the world's best friend to humanity. He wanted to bring it home, ragged and dirty as it was, and keep it in a chest at the foot of his bed. Was that strange?

Arms reached down out of nowhere and pulled him over the edge. He heard cheering. He heard himself gasping. Someone untied him and someone else wrapped a cloth around one of his bloody hands. He lay on his stomach above the cliff and hugged the ground.

Then he looked up and saw Bitterblue, still sitting against her tree, staring at him with enormous eyes.

Picking himself up, Giddon went to her.

CHAPTER FORTY

WHEN NEV AND DAVVI dragged that scraggly gray man up over the edge onto the ground beside her, Lovisa didn't recognize him. He was a shriveled, terrible-smelling rat and she recoiled, until he looked up into her face. When he saw her, he smiled.

"Katu," she cried.

"Lovisa," he said, his smile growing beatific.

Abandoning her rope, Lovisa threw off her coat and gave it to him. When he seemed confused by how a coat worked, she helped him with it, stuck his hands into the sleeves and pulled it over his shoulders, and then she was hugging him, crying, unable to hide how much his gauntness upset her. She couldn't find the white streak in his hair, then realized it was because his hair was so grimy.

"What did they do to you?" she cried.

"Well, my dear," he said lightly, resting a tentative hand on her shoulder, as if steadying himself. "I was attacked while I was diving. Next thing I knew, I woke up here."

"While you were diving! You mean, you were attacked underwater?"

"Yes. I was diving for the *Seashell*. You know the *Seashell*?"

"Yes, but how did you know about it?"

"I saw a strange thing at sea, through a glass, the very same day the *Seashell* disappeared," he said. "An airship lifting people out of a lifeboat."

"Is that so strange?" said Lovisa. "It sounds like a rescue."

"The last person who left the lifeboat took an ax to its bottom," said Katu.

"Oh," said Lovisa, her heart sinking.

"Then the airship passed close by me," Katu said. "I heard snatches of conversation in Kamassarian and I thought to myself, *This is a Kamassarian mystery.* They saw me. I tried to turn my craft so they couldn't read her name and figure out who I was. But then the balloon shifted in the light. I recognized it."

"It was my airship," said Lovisa.

"Well, your parents' airship," Katu said with a small smile. "I certainly didn't think to myself, *That Lovisa is up to something.*"

"My father."

"Or your mother," he said grimly.

"Your own sister?"

"My sister presumably trapped me in our childhood prison," he said, "alone, for months. Recently, they started feeding me more, and giving me my favorite candy."

"Your favorite candy!"

"Samklavi," he said.

"Samklavi!" said Lovisa, who heard herself repeating things stupidly but couldn't help it. A few weeks ago, she'd watched her furious mother hand her father a wallet of samklavi. "I think my mother sent you the samklavi, via my father!"

"Well," Katu said, with a noise like a snort. "Despite that act of magnanimity, I can't say I'm moved by ties of sibling loyalty just now."

"My mother is dead," said Lovisa.

Katu went still, all the light fading from his eyes. He tucked his chin to his chest, put his hands into the pockets of Lovisa's coat. Then, to his own patent amazement, he extracted his ruby ring. "What on earth?" he cried.

Suddenly Nev shouted at Lovisa to return to the sheet rope to haul Hava up. "I'll be a minute, Katu," she said. But once Hava was back on solid ground, she had to help with Giddon. By the time Lovisa returned to Katu, he'd curled himself into a shivering ball. When she touched his shoulder, he recoiled.

"Quick," she cried, alarmed at the transformation. "He's ill!"

Davvi, Liv the cook, and Ella the maid came running, Davvi lifting Katu into his arms like a child, carrying him toward the house. Behind them, Nev and Roni the housekeeper supported Hava between them, headed in the same direction. Giddon and the queen followed, so Lovisa tagged along too, alone, cold. Liv and Ella were in quite a state about Katu. They kept exclaiming their wonderment, unable to believe what had happened to him. When a guard came stumbling out of the barn, clearly dizzy and concussed, Liv turned on him, shrieking vitriol, accusing him of having known, of having perpetuated an outrage against the Cavenda family. Tears were practically flying from her face. Lovisa watched her with a kind of fascination, wondering what would happen if *she* started screaming and crying, flinging tears around at the outrage of it all. Would it make her feel different? More certain of what was true?

She'd thrown an egg and killed Linta Massera and two guards. That was true. She didn't want to think about it.

Giddon went into the barn, came out with horse tackle, and began binding the hands and feet of the guards, whose bodies, in various states of consciousness, seemed scattered across the grounds and house. Everyone else gathered in the sitting room, where Nev began to give orders about how to tend to Katu and Hava. Nev, an animal doctor, probably knew what she was doing. Maybe a human was like a tiny, upright, small-nosed, hairless horse?

Lovisa heard herself having these thoughts and tried to focus. Her body hurt, so much. The explosion had thrown her, then the crater had opened and she'd felt herself sliding, caught that pillar, clung to it forever, expecting at every moment for it to break off and plummet into the hole, bringing her with it. All the muscles in her arms and hands ached, her entire body felt like a giant bruise, and her ears were ringing. Her mouth tasted like blood.

Katu lay on a sofa near the big sitting room windows, shivering, but lucid. So Lovisa stood beside him, holding his hand. He'd put his ring back on. It slid back and forth on his skinny thumb. Lovisa tried to imagine refusing food to one of her own brothers. She couldn't. It was unimaginable.

Hava, on a sofa nearby, seemed in good spirits. Probably because Nev had told her she wasn't going to lose her foot. "Your ankle is broken," Nev said, "and so, I think, is one of your ribs," and Hava laughed, a strange laugh that turned into a high note of pain, but a laugh, nonetheless.

With small gasps, Hava told the story of how Lovisa had thrown the explosive egg. "You saved my life, Lovisa," she said flatly, and then everyone was looking at Lovisa, who didn't want the attention.

"I killed Linta Massera and two guards," she said.

"I'm the one who pulled the pin," said Hava. "I almost killed *you*." Then she went on to describe how Giddon had lifted the ladder away from her foot. "I was briefly confused when he started stripping," she said.

"He didn't strip for me," Katu mused, sounding hurt. The queen's giggles rang out like bells, then Bitterblue left Hava's side for a moment, coming to Katu. She leaned down and kissed his forehead.

"Welcome back, Katu," Bitterblue said quietly.

"I've never been gladder to see you," Katu said, giving her the gift of his warmest smile, which made Lovisa's heart hurt. When he did that, he looked like himself, and grief flooded her for all that had happened to him.

Bitterblue returned to Hava.

"The queen looks thin," said Katu. "Has she been ill?"

"It's a long story," said Lovisa.

"Is she all right?"

"She's high on rauha just now, but yes, she's fine. Wonderful, really," said Lovisa, with that familiar burst of resentment. "She's in love with Giddon. They're disgusting together."

Katu closed his eyes. He seemed to shrink, becoming distant and subdued. Every time he cut himself off like that, he left her alone with these foreigners who kept breaking into rapid Lingian when they spoke to one another, straining her tired mind.

"When I was in my attic prison," Bitterblue was saying, "I couldn't fathom why Estill would ally with Winterkeep in a war against Monsea, and why Estill would think they could win. Now we know. Benni Cavenda was going to sell them this weapon."

"Remember, in the beginning," said Hava, "Mikka wanted to tell you something about zilfium?"

Bitterblue's voice, when she responded, was terribly sad. "He wanted to tell me about this zilfium weapon. He wanted to warn me of how the world had changed."

"Lovisa," came Katu's voice again. "What does the queen mean by her 'attic prison'?"

Lovisa could not bear the burden of explaining these things to Katu. He was her uncle. He was the one who was supposed to explain the world to *her*. He was supposed to say, "I'm going to take care of you and your brothers now. It's all over, Lovisa. You're safe."

"Let me explain it to you later, Katu," she said, "please?"

"Lovisa?" he said. "Are you all right? You're all scratched up. What happened to *you*?"

Through the window, she caught sight of a dot in the sky, moving steadily between the trees. It took shape—balloon above, sails in the middle, car below. It was an airship, coming from the south. It was losing altitude, as if headed for the Cavenda house.

Lovisa dropped Katu's hand, stepped closer to the glass. She knew all the airships of the important Ledra families. This one was deep blue, covered with gold stars, which made it the Tima family airship. The Timas were Industrialists, friends of her father.

From Hava's sofa, Nev said, "Lovisa? What's wrong?"

Lovisa left the room, heading upstairs to the roof.

ON THE ROOF, the wind gusted, sending her sideways.

The airship hovered, buffeted to and fro, having some trouble docking, because no one was present to feed it a dock line. Lovisa knew she could come forward to help, but she didn't. There were two flyers. She squinted against the light, unable to make them out, but unsurprised when the ladder lowered and the person stepping down resolved into her father.

He was supposed to be in jail, but of course nothing happened as it was supposed to. Pushing her mucky mind back, she realized that the head magistrate's visit to Bitterblue had been only yesterday. Benni had probably left Ledra in a borrowed airship before the magistrate had ever returned.

When Benni spotted Lovisa, his footsteps faltered. She saw the surprise in his expression, and also a kind of relief. Then he found a careful mask, one she recognized. It was his Disappointed Father face.

"My darling!" he said. "I can't express how happy I am to see you. But what happened? You're a mess!"

"Don't come any closer!" said Lovisa.

"Darling!" said her father, continuing to move toward her. "What can you mean by that? Aren't you glad to see me?"

"We found the eggs!" she said.

He laughed. "Eggs, darling?"

"We found Katu!"

"Ah," he said, pausing in his advance, a flicker of uncertainty crossing his face. Then he stepped toward her again, so that Lovisa began to step back.

"Your mother is dead, Lovisa," he said. "Her tyranny is over. I can finally start to make amends."

"Amends!" cried Lovisa, alarm shifting into confusion. "What amends?"

"I'm so sorry," he said. "I never wanted any of this. You understand how it is to be under your mother's power, don't you? I came here to release Katu, now that your mother is dead. She can't hurt us anymore."

Lovisa wanted to believe the words he was saying. But she'd heard them fighting. She'd heard her mother accuse her father of doing something to Katu. She'd seen him carrying Pari's body.

Her back came up against the railing that made the roof's perimeter. "You're trying to trick me," she said.

"I can't believe you would think that of your father," he said, stepping forward and reaching for her arm.

A voice came sharply behind him. "Lovisa!"

Benni spun around.

"Lovisa?" said the Queen of Monsea, climbing through the trapdoor and starting toward them in Ferla's coat. Tiny, swaying, wincing at the wind. "What are you doing up here? Who is that?"

"It's my father," said Lovisa in utter confusion. "Don't you recognize him?"

"We never had the pleasure, not while I was conscious, anyway. Why aren't you in jail?" said Bitterblue, marching right up to Benni with no fear in her big, intoxicated eyes.

"Bitterblue," cried Lovisa. "Don't trust him."

"Of course I don't trust him," she said. "You're on the run, aren't you, Benni Cavenda? You came to see Katu killed, and to collect your weapons."

"Queen Bitterblue!" said Benni. "We finally meet!"

"Are you kidding me?" said Bitterblue.

"I'm here to make amends for the wrongs of my wife!" he said.

"Oh, please," said Bitterblue, rolling her eyes. "You know, I've had just about enough today. Lovisa, go downstairs. I'll deal with this kitten-head."

"Lovisa?" said Benni. "Is this really the Queen of Monsea? She seems a bit unhinged."

"I *am* unhinged!" said Bitterblue. "You took my hinges!"

Then Benni grabbed at Bitterblue and everything happened at once. The queen whipped a knife out of nowhere and stabbed Benni right through the hand he was grabbing her with. As Benni howled, the queen kneed him in the crotch, once, twice. As Benni began to fold, behind them, Giddon emerged through the trapdoor, Davvi behind him. "Bitterblue?" Giddon said, glancing around, squinting. "Where did you go?"

Benni struggled up, yelling some indiscernible command across the roof, to the flyer in the airship. Lovisa suddenly recognized the flyer—it was that same guard, the woman who'd motioned to Lovisa to flee from the house, the sister of the one Lovisa had seduced. The guard began running from tiller to lines, preparing the airship for departure.

Benni stumbled toward the airship, but Giddon and Davvi came forward, intercepting him easily. Lovisa heard a terrible crack and knew it was a fist in her father's face. Benni fell.

"Bullies!" Lovisa cried, rushing toward them. "Bullies! All of you, against one of him!" With a massive shove, she knocked Giddon away from her father. She dropped beside Benni, cradling his bleeding face in her hands. "Papa," she cried. "I'm sorry. Papa, I'm sorry."

He spoke to her through a broken mouth. He was weeping, tears making messy tracks down his bloody face. "My daughter," he said. "I'm sorry too."

Even that was a lie; she could tell it was a lie. How could he murder people, then say he was sorry? She didn't want his lies. She wanted forgiveness for her crimes.

Through the sound of her own sobbing, Lovisa heard the distinctive hiss of a varane tank. Glancing up at the airship, she saw the guard staring at Benni, who was crumpled on the ground. The guard looked once at Lovisa. Then, producing a blade, she cut her tether.

With a swing of the boom, the guard caught the wind and headed north toward Kamassar.

The journey back to Nev's house was horrible.

Benni wouldn't stop talking, and his words were always directed at her. Lovisa, exhausted, heartbroken, alone, was engaged in a battle inside herself, a battle to keep hold of reality.

"I never wanted any of this to happen."

"Your mother threatened to hurt you and your brothers if I didn't obey her."

"We can have a life together now. The courts will understand. We've lost a lot, but we'll have enough for the five of us."

The queen, who stayed near Lovisa, told her that they could gag him if it would help, but Lovisa couldn't give the order to gag her own father, especially not when his mouth was broken and bleeding like that.

Finally, she cried out to him. "Why do you have to make this worse for me? Isn't it bad enough already?"

He perked up at her response, eagerness surging in his voice. "But, Lovisa! I'm trying to make it better! Don't you see? We can be free of all this now!"

"I heard you," Lovisa said. "I heard your conversations with Mother. I know you're the one who kidnapped the queen. I know you killed Pari, not Mother. I know she didn't want any of that. I know you drowned the men on the *Seashell*! I know you trapped Katu in that cave, with that horrible scientist building explosive weapons above him!"

Benni sat with that for a while, in an injured sort of silence. The evening grew darker, and colder, as they sailed; Lovisa was grateful to be unable to see his face. But he could put so much into his voice. He'd always had that power. She supposed he was a consummate actor.

"That really hurts," he finally said. "You can't imagine how it hurts to hear those words from you, Lovisa. I'm your father. Are you forgetting everything I've done for you?"

She heard low, sharp voices telling Benni to shut his mouth, and became terrified that someone would hit him again. Finally, in desperation, she leaned herself against the queen. She let Bitterblue wrap her small, strong arms around her own shivering form. She let Bitterblue rub her back while she wept.

"I'll be held liable for the Gravla house, you know," Benni said, in a new voice. A voice of reproach, for a bad daughter. "And their airship, which is even more expensive. Probably the Tima airship as well."

"Let us gag him, Lovisa," Bitterblue begged, close to her ear. "Don't let him do this to you. He's bullying you!"

"I can't," she whispered, crying harder.

"It's absurd to imply that anyone drowned those men in the *Seashell,*" Benni added, in a voice that contained both reproach and a kind of fatherly chiding, for a daughter who was being silly. "There's been nothing to suggest that. Not a jot of evidence."

"I'm going to tell you all about the Royal Continent," said

Bitterblue in her ear. "More than you ever wanted to know. I'll tell you about every Graceling I've ever met. Okay?"

"Okay," said Lovisa.

"You're worthy of love, Lovisa," said the queen, whose voice was close enough to drown out Benni's voice, which had risen again. "You're stronger than the way he's making you feel."

"I'm not," she cried.

"Of course you are," said the queen. "Haven't you figured out that Hava would be dead if it weren't for your quick thinking? That we couldn't have rescued Katu or Hava without your knowledge of the cave? Don't you remember that you saved my life?"

To THE SOUND of the queen's chatter, Lovisa finally fell asleep.

When the boat reached land, she woke to the feeling of being carried. She cried out, needing to know where her father was.

"Our magistrate took him into custody," a gruff voice said. She could feel the voice vibrating right through her body. It came from Davvi, who was carrying her against his chest, like a child. "He's on his way to the Ledra Magistry now."

Lovisa thought of her father being pulled away from her, dragged across the sky, all the way to Ledra. She thought of her mother, dead. Katu had stayed behind at the house with the house staff, who were going to care for him, and keep the guards bound until the Magistry could come for them. "Where are my brothers?" she asked. "Who's taking care of my brothers?"

"We'll find out for you, Lovisa," said Davvi. "I promise. For now, you can let yourself sleep. We'll help you figure out the rest tomorrow."

She believed him. Did that mean she'd given up, if she trusted him? Was it safe?

Carried in the strong arms of Nev's father, Lovisa surrendered herself to sleep.

CHAPTER FORTY-ONE

IN EARLY MORNING, Lovisa woke in Nev's bed.

It was all done now. The mystery of the banker's box solved. Katu found. The criminals captured. The Monseans could go home; it was over.

But for Lovisa, there would never be an end.

Cautiously, she reached up, felt her face, her hair, her neck. She had a small bandage on her forehead, and a split lip. Everything hurt. Her body screamed with tender places when she moved, but when she tried, she was able to stand.

When she stepped into the house's tiny, main room, there was already a distinct sense of something new: departure. Giddon and Hava sat at the table, filling their mouths with stew and talking to Saiet. Hava didn't look like she should be sitting up. Purple bruises ringed her copper-colored eye, shocking against her pale skin. She also had a bandaged forehead, a plaster cast on her lower leg and foot, and she gasped whenever she moved. But she seemed cheerful.

"We'll go back to Ledra soon," Giddon was saying to Saiet. "Everyone's waiting for Bitterblue."

Saiet, noticing Lovisa, held out a hand to welcome her. "Lovisa," he said, and she braced herself against the questions she knew were coming. *What about you? When are you leaving? What are you going to do now, with the ruin of your life?*

"Where are my brothers?" she said.

"Our magistrate has sent a message to the Magistry in Torla's Neck, asking that question on your behalf," said Saiet. "We should know sometime today."

"Oh."

"Lovisa," said Saiet gently, studying her face. "Can I offer you something to eat?"

Lovisa didn't think her stomach could accept any food. Then Davvi bustled out of the other bedroom, Bitterblue came in from outside, and the room was far too crowded with people who had questions in their eyes.

"Is there somewhere I could go?" she said. "And sit, and be alone?"

"Yes, certainly," said Saiet. "I have cows to visit to the north. Would you like to come along? I'll deposit you in a nice, quiet place with a pretty view. Then I'll pick you up again on the way back."

So Lovisa set out with Saiet, wondering what had become of her life that she was a person setting out to sit and stare at nothing, while her companion, an old, creaky man who made no sense to her, visited cows.

She was terrified he would ask her questions as they walked. Or start talking about something ridiculous she didn't want to think about, like jealousy, or his wife's many lovers. Or Nev. Lovisa wouldn't be able to bear it if Saiet started talking about Nev, who had a life Lovisa could never have.

But he walked beside her quietly, then showed her to a hill with a rock shaped like a bench. Hidden from the path, she could see across rolling hills to the wrinkles of a glacier tucked between rises of land. Far, far away, so far it might be Kamassar, she saw mountains with white peaks. It was freezing on her bench. She pulled her fur coat more tightly against her neck.

"Now," he said. "I won't be long, but if you get too cold, do you remember the way home?"

"I'll wait for you," she said. She watched his tall, narrow form wind its way back to the path until he disappeared, then gazed across the hills to the glacier, the mountains. Nev had said once that in Ledra, everything was stuck, spinning in place. That in the north, she could breathe.

Lovisa stood, walking to a place where she could see the water. *Where do I belong?* she asked the ocean. *What do I do now? Go back to school? How do I do that?* She waited for the answers to come, but nothing came.

A movement out at sea caught her eye. Though they were very far away, she recognized the round, sleek, purplish forms of silbercows. With a small, unhappy thud, she remembered a part of the story she'd pushed aside. Her parents had hurt silbercows too. Hadn't they? Nev had talked of injured silbercows, coming to shore with cuts and burns.

She watched the silbercows turning in the sun. She'd never succeeded in talking to a silbercow before, and she knew she was too far away. But she cried out anyway, because it was part of the reckoning. *I'm sorry,* she cried to them. *I'm sorry.*

LATER THAT DAY, Nev found her, curled up in Nev's bed.

"Lovisa?" she said gently.

"Yes?" said Lovisa, not moving.

"Your brothers are safe," said Nev. "They're with the Devrets. The Devrets want to give them a home and take care of them. Even adopt them, if it comes to that."

So they can grow up like Mari, thought Lovisa, instantly, unexpectedly bereft.

"Lovisa?" said Nev. "Are you okay?"

Lovisa felt her brothers stretching away from her, to a place where she couldn't follow. "I'm fine," she said. She was the sister who'd burned their house down and left them. She'd ruined their family. They didn't need her and probably wouldn't want her.

Nola bustled into the tiny, cramped room. "Lovisa?" she said. "I finally have some time. How are your muscles?"

Lovisa didn't deserve a massage from Nola. She began to cry again, tears seeping quietly down her face.

"Let me help," Nola said.

"You're just pitying me," Lovisa said, trying to sound harsh and unfeeling, but knowing she only sounded pitiable.

"*Pitying* is definitely the wrong word," said Nola, sitting on the bed beside Lovisa, shooing Nev away, then finding the sore place where Lovisa's shoulders met her neck. "You don't have the sort of spirit that lends itself to pity."

Because I'm hard, like my mother, Lovisa thought. "Everyone is leaving," she said.

"Yes, everyone is leaving," said Nola, in a smooth, measured tone, fitting words into the rhythms of her strokes, reaching deep, to the places where Lovisa's sore muscles met bone. Had Nev grown up with this blessing too? Being touched, healed, by a mother? "Not right away," Nola said. "But everyone seems to have places to go. You may stay as long as you like, Lovisa," she added, "if you're not ready."

Lovisa swallowed. "Is Nev leaving?"

"Yes. Nev needs to get back to school."

Lovisa grieved those words. School had used to be her kingdom. The chair in the dorm foyer was her throne. Nev and Mari were her neighbors. They were her friends, weren't they? Could Lovisa have friends?

"What is your scholarly discipline, Lovisa?" asked Nola.

"Politics and government."

"What a great deal you could do with that," she said, "given everything you know and all you've seen."

"No one can do anything with politics and government," Lovisa said scornfully. "It's just two bickering sides who're exactly the same, pretending to fight about good sense and ideals when really it's all about money."

"Hm," said Nola. "Imagine if someone came along with intelligence, and passion, and experience. And deep insight into how our government works, and how it affects the land. Someone who actually *did* have good sense and ideals."

Lovisa didn't know what Nola was talking about, and saw no point in imagining it. No one would ever want to work that hard, while standing in opposition to such a force.

"Someone who was good at taking old power structures down," said Nola. "I wonder what someone like that could achieve."

THE NEXT DAY, she walked with Saiet again as he went on another farm visit.

"Have you ever visited a pig, Lovisa?" he asked.

"What do you think?" said Lovisa snappishly. "When would I ever have had occasion to visit a pig?"

"Exactly," he said. "This could be a once-in-a-lifetime opportunity."

"What is this? Do you want me to come with you?"

"Not if you're afraid of pigs."

"Oh, please. Why would anyone be afraid of pigs?"

"Then you're coming?"

"I didn't say that!"

"I dare you," said Saiet. "I dare you to come visit this pig."

"How old are you, nine?"

"Nine is quite mature," he said, "for a pig."

"Oh, kittens," Lovisa said, borrowing the queen's favorite expletive. Then, unable to hold it back, she laughed, a quick, exasperated breath. "What's wrong with this pig?"

THE PROBLEM WITH the pig was that an endless stream of piglets was popping out of it.

"That's the most disgusting thing I've ever seen," Lovisa said, watching Saiet wipe bloody sacs away from the mouths and noses of the little piglets, rub them with towels, tie off their umbilical cords. She couldn't believe she was here watching this, and she couldn't stop talking. How could he touch those things? "They look like slugs. They look like pink poops!"

"What, have you never seen a piglet before?" said the farmer who owned the pig, resting her heavy boot on a bucket, chewing on a piece of straw. "City people."

"Here, warm this one up," Saiet said, holding a teeny-tiny piglet out to Lovisa, then actually looking rather angry and stern when she cringed away. "Warm it!"

"All right," she said, "all right!"

She took the tiny thing in her hands, suddenly petrified she'd hurt it, drop it, squeeze it too hard. The piglet was wrapped in a soft towel. It wasn't very warm, so she brought it to her chest and tried to cradle it in her arms. Its eyes and mouth were tiny wrinkles and its miniature nose was the funniest, strangest thing she'd ever seen.

"Why do people like babies?" she demanded.

No one answered her, for Saiet and the farmer were busy with the other piglets, of which there were impossibly many. They just kept popping out, as if any pig had business being so pregnant. What if this one, out of all of them, was the one that didn't survive? What would it mean about the kind of person she was? She found a bench nearby and opened her coat, so the piglet could nestle into her body heat. She imagined a shield around this piglet. A shield made of her arms, and her iron will.

"All right," she whispered to it, very quietly, so no one else could hear. "It's you and me, piglet. Okay? You need to survive. Okay? Survive. You are worthy."

THAT AFTERNOON, WHEN Lovisa stepped back into Nev's house with a piglet in her arms, she fended off the curious looks, and especially the amused looks, with a chilly kind of hauteur.

"It's the runt," she said. "The farmer didn't want it."

"I see," said Giddon unperturbedly, for Giddon was the person she'd happened to be glaring at when she'd made her announcement. He was sitting at the table with Nev and the queen. Probably planning their departures.

"It's cute," said Nev.

Lovisa glanced at the fox kit Nev held in one arm and said caustically, "Yes. I like that it can't read my mind."

"Have you named it?" asked Bitterblue.

She had named it. In fact, she'd named it after the queen. "His name is Worthy," she said, then, before she started to cry again, went out to the barn.

Nev came looking for her later, without her fox.

"Lovisa?" she said, finding Lovisa in the semi-dark, where she was sitting on the hay beside the cow again. She was teaching Worthy to suckle on a milk-soaked cloth from Saiet that she twisted like a nipple.

I cannot believe this is my life, Lovisa thought as Nev approached her. "What?"

"An airship's coming tomorrow from Ledra," Nev said. "We're leaving the day after that."

Lovisa grunted. It was so soon. Too soon.

"Will you come with us?" Nev asked.

How confusing it was to hear Nev say that. "I—don't think I have anywhere to go," she said.

"The Devrets want you, if you like," Nev said. "You could live with your brothers. The academy also wants you back."

Lovisa snorted at that. "Says who?"

"Says every message coming through the signal stations."

"The people at the academy just want to be able to look at me and gossip," said Lovisa. "I can't go to Ledra. You know how it is there."

"Yes," Nev admitted. "I do."

"Anyway, how could I?" Lovisa said. "Everyone'll know who I am. They'll know what I did, and what my parents did."

Nev seemed to think about that for a minute. She stroked the cow's neck and the cow took on a blissful expression. Lovisa watched carefully while pretending not to. She'd wondered the safe way to touch that cow.

"It's true that I can't imagine what this is like for you, Lovisa," Nev finally said. "You've had to make harder choices than I ever have, harder than most people ever do. But I don't want you to think that you're alone." She paused. "I understand you might not consider me a friend."

"Don't be ridiculous," said Lovisa through rising tears.

"If you come back to school," said Nev, "you won't be alone." She paused again. "Okay? Just think about it."

She left for the house. Then, while Lovisa was thinking about it, Nev came out again, poked her head into the barn.

"Lovisa? Your uncle is here."

WHEN LOVISA ENTERED the house with Worthy in her arms, Katu was sitting in a chair by the fire. He was clean, his hair newly cut, but he was so small, so thin.

His eyes touched the piglet and he began to laugh, coming to

Lovisa, embracing her. They'd never really had an embracing sort of relationship, but something had changed. She hugged him back hard with her free arm.

"You look better," he said.

"You too."

"I'm all right," he said. "It's going to take me a while. I'm lucky I have brawny friends." He flashed a smile at Giddon that was rueful, and that included Bitterblue, who sat in a chair beside Giddon. There was something odd about the smile, something stiff, that made Lovisa watch Katu closely.

"Katu has some news, Lovisa," said Giddon.

Katu shot Giddon another stiff, sideways smile. "Yes. The guards got away."

"The guards?" said Lovisa, mystified. "At the house?"

"Yes. We were keeping them locked in a bedroom upstairs, but it was too much for the staff to watch them all the time, you understand? Not with caring for me, and dealing with the cleanup and all. Apparently one of them got out of his ties and freed the others. They hurt the girl Ella on their way out. Knocked her into a glass door. She'll be okay, but she's bruised up."

"Oh," said Lovisa, not really caring about the lost guards. "Oh, well."

"They might've served as witnesses," he said. "But I expect they're long gone now."

"Oh, well," she said again. There were going to be plenty of witnesses. The Queen of Monsea herself was a witness.

"Before the guards got away," Katu said, "one of them told the local magistrate something about Linta Massera yelling that her notebooks had gone missing, right before the explosion. If any of you know anything about that, be aware that the Magistry will probably want to know."

Giddon cleared his throat. "Noted. And the cleanup?"

"Yes. We're collecting the explosives," said Katu. "Very, very carefully."

"Who is?" said Giddon. "The cave was full of them!"

"The Magistry has climbers. And actual ropes," Katu said, with another smile directed vaguely at Giddon.

"Fancy," said Giddon, grinning back.

"But what will they do with them?" said Lovisa.

"For the moment, they're storing them in a locked box," said Katu. "And keeping them as evidence."

"Against my father?"

"Or your mother," said Katu.

"But is it safe to keep them?" said Lovisa. "Couldn't they explode them somewhere, so they're not dangerous anymore?"

"Where?" said Nev.

"I don't know," said Lovisa. "Underground? Underwater?"

"What?" cried Nev, glaring at her. "Don't you understand how many silbercows have already been hurt? People have tossed those eggs into the water to test how they explode! *And* they've murdered silbercows too, to get rid of witnesses!"

"But of course I meant not near silbercows! In some part of the water where nothing is!"

"And where's that?" cried Nev, still indignant. "What part of the ocean's ecosystem is expendable?"

"Well, I don't know!" said Lovisa, taking a few steps back, turning away. "I don't know anything about the ocean." And now Nev was angry with her and she couldn't bear it.

"Lovisa," said Nev quietly. "I'm sorry. I misunderstood. Of course you meant well."

But Lovisa didn't want Nev's apologies. She found a hard chair in a dark corner of the room and sat there, bending over Worthy, pretending he needed her attention.

"Katu," said Bitterblue. "What will you do now?"

Katu's neck, if possible, was even more stiff when he was talking to Bitterblue than to Giddon. "My doctor's told me to rest," he said, "for an absurdly long time. She says I've endured an extreme ordeal. But I feel fine, really. I just need to eat, and build some muscle."

"I'm sorry this happened because you were trying to figure out what became of my men," said Bitterblue.

"I'm sorry about what became of your men," said Katu, finally looking straight at Bitterblue, with an unhappy appeal in his face that solved the mystery of Katu's strange stiffness. Lovisa now understood why Bitterblue had recognized Katu's ring at a glance. And why Katu had been so concerned about the queen, the day of the rescue.

Lovisa searched inside herself for her own anger about Bitterblue and Katu, about everyone being lovers. About someone rejecting her uncle. She couldn't find it. She didn't care. People were stupid. Pigs were infinitely more worthwhile.

Then Katu stood up.

"Are you staying in Torla's Neck?" Lovisa called from her corner, in a voice that broke. "Or are you going back to Ledra? Or traveling again?"

He turned his bright eyes to her, stretching his arms above his head like a man who'd worked a hard day, and was tired, and needed a long sleep before the next adventure. He wore his ring; it slid along his thumb, like a bracelet on a very small wrist. "I'm sure I'll go back to Ledra before too long," he said, smiling. "Isn't that where you'll be?"

"I—we'll see," she said.

Then everyone was standing, moving toward each other, people saying their goodbyes to Katu.

When Nev stood up, she came to Lovisa. "Your uncle's hoping to see you in Ledra too," she said, looking down at Lovisa with quiet eyes.

"I'm sorry I said the ignorant thing about the silbercows," said Lovisa.

"It's all right," said Nev. "I'm sorry I snapped at you."

"I don't know anything about the ocean. I mean, really. I've never thought about it."

"Aren't the Scholars supposed to know about such things?" said Nev. "Isn't their entire party supposed to revolve around protecting the environment from zilfium engines, and mining slag, and—one would hope—anything that hurts silbercows?"

Lovisa wasn't certain what mining slag was, exactly. Shouldn't she know that, since her family owned a mine? "I'm pretty sure it's just about money," she said.

"Surely not for everyone?" said Nev. "Is it really that hopeless?"

"Yes. It's why I don't want to go into politics."

"But shouldn't we *want* people who care about something other than money to go into politics?"

"And do what?"

"Throw their weight around!" said Nev. "Get in other people's way!"

"I'm—very small," said Lovisa.

Nev smiled at her joke, slow and sweet. Lovisa found herself holding Worthy closer, warmed by that smile. She wondered how long she'd been walking through a world she knew nothing about. Her whole life? Was there a way to learn more than she'd been taught?

"You should come back to school," Nev said.

"I'm thinking about it," said Lovisa.

LOVISA DID THINK about it. She thought about it constantly, but she couldn't see what it would mean. Nev couldn't protect Lovisa from the nightmare she'd be walking through, once her feet hit the ground in Ledra.

The next day, she went to the hill with the rock seat Saiet had shown her. She had Worthy with her as usual, and a rag, and a flask of milk. He never, ever, seemed to stop eating. Lovisa was getting quite proficient at wrapping his little bottom in diapers, for what went in, later came out. *Who am I?* she asked herself, every time she performed a diaper change. *What would the girls in the dorm think of this? Would they think I'd turned into an eccentric, like Quona Varana?*

When, on her hill, she stood and walked to the place where she could see the water, then realized she was waiting, and hoping, for silbercows to appear, she wondered what her school friends would think of that too.

The problem, she thought as she stood there, was that she wasn't ready to go back, but it hurt, terribly, to be left behind. And as much as she was afraid that her brothers wouldn't want her, she wanted them; she wanted to hold them, keep them in her arms. Tell them she was sorry.

It was a problem with no solution. Whichever path she chose would be harder than she felt she could stand.

She caught sight of an airship in the distance, crawling north along the coast. That was it, then.

Then she saw another airship not far behind the first one. She started murmuring questions to Worthy. "What's that second one for, my piglet? Are we too many people for one airship? No," she decided, counting. "We can fit in one, even if I go." She didn't recognize either airship.

How strange it was, to feel curiosity pricking inside her. How long had it been since Lovisa had felt curious about anything? How strange too when her curiosity began to outshout her wish to be invisible and left alone.

She started back to Nev's. It was a longish walk, this path in the woods that only days ago had seemed arbitrary, not a path at all. As she neared the house, a voice sounded sharply ahead. It contained cheer, politeness, and something deeply familiar. If it weren't impossible, Lovisa would think she recognized that voice.

Disbelieving, she began to run, holding Worthy close, trying not to joggle him, then stopping cold at the sight of a person in a gold scarf. Mari, in the yard, talking to Grandpa Saiet. He was tall, and solid, and bright-eyed, and really there. He saw her and spread out his arms, shouted his joy. His parents were beside him. And suddenly her brothers appeared around him, her brothers. Vikti, Erita, Viri, alive, well, laughing. They shouted her name, ran at her, swarmed her with their sharp little knees and elbows, their wriggling, happy bodies. She had them in her arms.

She had everything now. It didn't matter if she stayed or went, it didn't matter where she was or what she did.

And they didn't seem angry with her. They weren't blaming her for anything. Surely it was a trick? "Lovisa!" said Erita. "Is that a *pig*?"

"It's a *pig*!" said Viri delightedly. "It's wearing a *diaper*! Arni! Mara! Mari! Look! Pig! Diaper!"

Lovisa stood shakily, confused, as Mari and his parents joined them. She didn't know how to see Mari again, after everything. When she looked up at him shyly, he hugged her. "Don't squash my pig," she said, which made him start laughing.

"Say hello to my parents," he said.

Lovisa had known Mari's parents all her life, but never like this. Never in a forest, with a pig, after she'd burned half of Flag Hill down and thrown an explosive egg and her father was a murderer.

"Lovisa Cavenda," said Mara, formally, but kindly. Lovisa had always felt like a mouse, or a mushroom, or at any rate, a child, beside Mara Devret.

"We're all hoping you'll come back with us," she said. "Won't you tell us that you will?"

I don't know, Lovisa wanted to say. *I can't decide yet. I'm scared.*

Then a small, sticky hand tucked itself inside hers, and Lovisa had her answer.

PART FIVE

THE KEEPER

THERE WAS NOTHING easy about carrying a ship across the ocean floor, especially now that the creature had a hurting nub in place of one of her tentacles.

The silbercows were surprised that her missing tentacle made such a difference, when she had so many other tentacles.

Only twelve, she said, beginning to wonder if silbercows thought everything was easy when one was big.

The silbercows asked her, given how hard it was, if it would conserve energy for her to stop singing so loudly as she went, but obviously that was a ridiculous suggestion. None of this would be possible if she weren't bellowing her heart out as she dragged herself across the ocean floor. The bellowing protected her from how sad she was, which also happened to be the topic of her song. She was sad about losing her Storyworld and her tentacle, and she was worried about the skeletons of the two humans as she moved along. The silbercows had told her the story of what it must have been like for those two humans to find themselves locked in a room while other humans chopped a hole in the bottom of their boat, then abandoned them. Now she didn't want them to be jostled. The thought of them suffering more than they'd already suffered was unbearable. That was the main thing she kept singing about.

The humans couldn't suffer, the silbercows told her, now that they were dead. But of course this didn't comfort her. Surely they hadn't wanted to die!

The silbercows told her that sometimes a human or a silbercow didn't have a choice, in a world of bullies.

I know! she said. *That's why I'm singing!*

It's also why the ocean needs heroes like the Keeper, said the silbercows significantly.

She could get very impatient when the silbercows started talking about the Keeper. The Keeper was silly, with her mesmerizing songs and her drawings that chased enemies away. And what about the part where the Keeper rose up and crushed the silbercows and humans if they didn't do what she wanted? *The Keeper sounds like a bully,* she said. *I think if you ever actually meet her, you should let me know, because I'm big, so I can stop her from bullying you.*

The silbercows kept their thoughts about that to themselves. As she had requested, they sang with her as best they could—her songs were unpredictable, so it was hard sometimes to prepare for the next verse—and, gently, they shooed away any curious silbercows who approached. *Not today,* they told the visitors. *Some other day. We'll tell you when.* It was interesting, how many silbercows tried to approach, for the singing today was especially powerful, and terrible in its sadness. But maybe the ocean was getting used to her singing. Maybe some were even drawn to its sadness, because it touched their own.

CHAPTER FORTY-TWO

UPON THEIR RETURN to Ledra, Bitterblue and her delegation moved into a hotel.

This wasn't customary for foreign dignitaries visiting Winterkeep, but Bitterblue was suing a few of the Ledra elite for openly lying to her in the course of trade, which made things awkward. She claimed that her evidence had been "mailed to her anonymously." Since everyone knew her accusations to be founded, no one seemed prone to interfere.

Bitterblue's advisers, who'd recently returned to Ledra, and her guards, who'd moved out of the ship to be with her, wandered around the hotel as if in a happy dream. Her advisers kept seeking Bitterblue out, then not knowing what to say. So she would invite them to eat cake with her, knowing that they just needed to sit with her for a while, looking at her, so that they could really believe that she was there. And she needed cake, so it served her purposes too.

They also accompanied her to dinners with the Ledra elite, who tried to one-up each other with how long she stayed at their tables and how much she liked their food. Or at least, that was the impression Bitterblue got. It surprised her, how much the elected leaders of this republic reminded her, at least superficially, of the nobility she contended with at home.

The delegation was renting the entire hotel. It made for empty, silent corridors and a slightly confused hotel staff, but Bitterblue needed the mental space it provided. Of course, it also meant that when a small fire broke out in the remote sitting room Hava used for herself, it took a while for anyone to respond to her calls.

When Bitterblue burst into the room, Giddon and several staff members on her heels, Hava was balanced on a crutch, trying to beat the flaming rug with a pillow.

"Hava!" cried Bitterblue. "Come away!"

"The notebooks!" Hava cried, resisting Bitterblue's attempts to pull her off. "Linta Massera's notebooks! They're burning!"

"What? All of them?"

"I removed a couple of pages yesterday," said Hava, beginning to cough violently. "The rest is gone."

Consequently, when the Ledra Magistry arrived a few mornings later to ask whether the Monseans knew anything about the location of Linta's missing notebooks, Hava handed them a bucket of burnt and sodden scraps, plus two perfectly preserved pages.

When the two pages turned out to be the instructions for mixing a chemical bath into which an egg could be submerged in order to degrade it, rendering it harmless, Bitterblue carefully avoided Giddon's eyes. The whole thing was suddenly far too convenient.

"I'm so sorry," Hava kept saying to the Magistry officers, using her Grace to make herself look fluttery and sweet.

"It's all right, miss, really. It can't be helped," the Magistry officers kept responding, never quite noticing that their disinterest in challenging her was coming from the power her Grace had to slide their attention away from her.

The Magistry officers stayed for lunch. When they left, Hava did too, clunking out of the dining room and down the corridor on her crutches with small gasps. She wasn't supposed to be relying so much on her crutches. It created a strain on her broken rib. But it was impossible to force Hava to keep still, impossible to impose any will upon her beside her own, so Bitterblue bit down on the words she wanted to say.

"Care to bet what Hava's been up to?" she said quietly to Giddon.

"I'm hoping we're about to find out," he said, spreading butter and honey onto a slice of bread with the focus and precision of an artist. Giddon did things like that when he was pondering something else. He did it with his touch too, when they were together, rubbing Bitterblue's shoulders or her neck unconsciously, but carefully, finding her tight, aching spots, while they talked or planned. It was definitely in her top ten favorite habits of his.

A few minutes later, they heard Hava's crutches approaching again. She entered the dining room, lowered herself back into her chair with a small grunt of pain. Reached into her shirt and pulled out a thick pile of papers, which she handed to the queen.

Wordlessly, Bitterblue flipped through the pages. They were written in Hava's handwriting, composed of diagrams and symbols Bitterblue didn't understand, interspersed with stretches of Keepish.

"I copied them exactly," Hava said. "Every picture, every page."

Bitterblue cleared her throat. "And then," she said, "you set the hotel on fire?"

"Hardly," said Hava. "Just the rug."

"You have a broken ankle and a broken rib. You stayed in that room, inhaling smoke, risking falling down—"

"You came when I knew you would."

"Hava! You could have told us the plan."

"I'm telling you now," said Hava. Then she pushed herself up again and left the room.

Bitterblue sighed, then gathered the papers together, rolling them into a tube. She didn't want them in her hands. They felt like a menace that might explode in her face. But they were hers now, and she was going to have to guard them, and decide what to do.

"Will I ever stop worrying about her?" she said, wishing that in addition to her criticisms of Hava, she'd remembered to say "Thank you."

"Unlikely," said Giddon, licking butter from his thumb.

"I keep secrets from her too," Bitterblue said. "Things she should probably know." For example, she hadn't told Hava that blue foxes could read everyone's minds and defied their bonded humans yet. She'd told Giddon, but was worried that telling Hava would break her promise to the fox. Nor did Hava know about Giddon, for the relationship was still so new, and so newly dear. Bitterblue didn't have the armor yet to hold up against Hava's sarcasm.

"You'll tell her, when it's time," said Giddon gently.

"Yes," said Bitterblue. "Speaking of which," she added, her expression turning into something rueful. She didn't want to do the next thing on their agenda today. "Should we go talk to Froggatt?"

THEY FOUND FROGGATT in the greenhouse on the hotel's roof, staring at a tall, slender, pink lily.

"Would you join us for some tea and cake, Froggatt? Here among the flowers?" said Bitterblue, a suggestion that seemed to make him rapturously happy.

They sat at a small garden table. "We're about to tell you something you must tell no one, Froggatt," said Bitterblue. "Not even other members of my staff."

Froggatt swelled at this honor. "Yes, Lady Queen?"

"Giddon and I are getting married."

Now Froggatt flushed. "But, Lady Queen!"

"I don't want to hear a word about him being a disinherited ex-lord from the Middluns," said Bitterblue.

"My concern, Lady Queen, is less that he's a disinherited ex-lord from the Middluns and more that the *reason* he's a disinherited ex-lord from the Middluns is that he spends his time crossing the seven kingdoms—"

"Seven Nations," Bitterblue corrected.

"Seven *Nations,* which are no longer the seven kingdoms precisely because your proposed future husband is a renegade who, along with his renegade friends, captures and deposes monarchs! *And you are a queen!*"

"Yes," said Bitterblue. "We agree it's awkward. But no relationship is without its challenges, Froggatt. This is going to happen. I've chosen you as our ally here at the beginning because someone in a queen's circle should know her marital intentions, and because we'll need support when we make the news public. Was I wrong to trust you?"

Whatever Froggatt had been going to say next, he swallowed it. "Of course not, Lady Queen."

"You understand that you have no license to try to talk me—or Giddon—out of it?"

"I understand that you've made up your mind, Lady Queen."

"Good."

"And I hope you'll both be very happy," he added belatedly, perhaps after noticing the twitch of Giddon's mouth across the table.

"Thank you," said Giddon gravely.

"Lady Queen," said Froggatt, suddenly anxious, "are you really all right? Your advisers can tell when you've been crying."

Bitterblue had, indeed, been allowing herself a lot of tears recently. "I'm recovering from an ordeal, Froggatt," she said, remembering the word Katu's doctor had used. "The last few weeks have reminded me of a lot of old things. Sad things. You understand?"

"Yes, of course I do, Lady Queen," said Froggatt, who'd worked in her father's court before he'd ever worked in hers.

"It's productive crying," she said. "I'm making progress. Though if I'm being honest, my head and neck ache from it."

"Have you been remembering to stretch before crying?" said Giddon.

Froggatt turned to regard Giddon with an indignant and incredulous expression.

"It's also good to do a little warm-up cry before you go all out," said Giddon, which sent Bitterblue into giggles and finally brought her up out of her chair, taking his hand and announcing she had things to do, because (she didn't announce this part) she wanted to get into bed with him.

Froggatt watched them together, a kind of aggrieved confusion on his face.

THE NEXT CHALLENGE surprised Bitterblue. She *wasn't* surprised that in her meetings with the Ledra elite, more than one Industrialist casually mentioned Benni's upstanding character, even expressing that it was hard to believe he would build an illegal weapon, imprison his own brother-in-law, kill a boy, or abduct a queen.

"And yet he did," she would respond calmly.

But she was surprised at what one person asked: "Did you ever see him, Lady Queen? According to the parts of his defense that I've heard, you never actually saw him."

"Certainly I saw him. Most recently, I saw him trying to hide evidence in Torla's Neck," Bitterblue replied.

But later that night, as she waited in her bedroom for Giddon to arrive, Bitterblue considered that in fact, she *hadn't* seen Benni hiding any evidence. She'd stabbed him before he'd had a chance. Nor had she seen him during her kidnapping. She'd been unconscious when his airship had snatched her out of the sea. She'd been unconscious from a drugged drink—given to her by Ferla's guard—when he'd murdered that poor boy. The fox had told her Benni was guilty, and she believed the fox. But the fox's involvement was a secret she'd sworn to keep. She had every intention of honoring her promise to uphold the secrets of foxkind.

The truth was that if she was asked to testify in court against Benni, there was little Bitterblue could honestly report, beyond inferences. And if Benni decided to claim that Ferla had coerced him, or threatened his children, her inferences couldn't contradict that.

The guards from Torla's Neck who might have served as witnesses against Benni had fled. The young woman who'd brought Bitterblue her food in the attic had escaped to Kamassar in the Tima airship. Linta Massera was dead. The Kamassarians who'd scuttled the *Seashell* were gone, and anyway, there was no hard evidence that the sinking of the *Seashell* had been anything but an accident. The Magistry wasn't considering it a crime.

Even Katu seemed content to think Ferla was his abductor. He knew from experience that Ferla could be ruthless, while Benni was a nice guy. And the Devret guards had reported that Ferla, not Benni, had gone out one night, bribing them to keep quiet. A Graceling named Trina, Graced with finding things, had come forward, claiming that Ferla had tried to hire her to locate human remains in the rubble of the burnt Cavenda house.

Bitterblue was gazing through the starmaker at the fire in her grate when Giddon snuck in.

"Hi," he said, closing the door with a quiet click.

"Hi," she said gloomily, swinging the starmaker to the lamp in his hands. Bitterblue loved the starmaker. It gave one part of her mind something nice to do while another part tried to solve problems.

Giddon set the lamp down and climbed under the covers. "What is it?" he said, pulling her against him and holding her in that way that always made her feel treasured, the same way using his gift, the starmaker, made her feel treasured.

"I don't want Lovisa to have to testify in court against her own father," she said. "I don't want that entire burden to fall to her. But she's the only reliable witness, even though we all know he's guilty. I know things the fox told me that it kills me I can't share."

He breathed evenly against her hair for a while, thinking about it. "Are you considering exposing the fox?"

"No! Of course not. I can't do that."

"Are you considering . . . something else?"

Now Bitterblue took a moment. "If I pretended to have heard or seen something while I was in their attic," she said, "I don't think anyone would doubt me."

Giddon's voice was unhappy. "I don't think so either."

Bitterblue was obscurely ashamed of her next question. "Giddon? How terrible would it be to use one's power as a queen to make up evidence in a foreign court? Evidence that everyone would believe?"

"Evidence of a crime that's punishable by death?"

"Yes. To spare a sixteen-year-old girl having to testify against her father?"

Giddon scooched down, brushed the stray hairs away from her forehead, and studied her expression. She knew he was going to advise her against it.

"Maybe my method for deciding if something is terrible is different from other people's," he said. "But as a rule, if *you're* doing something, it can't be terrible."

"Giddon," she said, almost frightened. "That's a dangerous attitude, when I'm a queen. I need to be able to depend on you to tell me if you think I'm doing wrong."

"I always will. I promise. We're a team, Bitterblue. But you're not making a careless, unconsidered decision here, and I see what you're trying to spare her."

There was another silence.

"Why don't you talk to Lovisa about it?" he said.

She rested her face against his chest. "Yes," she said. "All right. Maybe I will." His heart was thumping against her ear. "Your heart is beating fast."

"I wonder why," he said, in a teasing tone that made her bring her face to his, take his mouth with hers. It scared her sometimes, the easy way he could bring her tired, aching body back to happiness. She'd decided she wasn't going to spend every moment being afraid of losing him. Bitterblue was going to learn to look into his face and see not just the fragile bones under his skin, but *him*, Giddon, her husband, her support.

"Giddon?" she said, pulling back. "There are some really difficult decisions ahead, with my zilfium stores, and this new weapon."

"Yes," he said, kissing her, sliding his hand under her pajama top.

"I don't think it's going to be easy to be my spouse," she said. "Do you know how hard I'm going to lean on you?"

"I'm big and strong," he said. "Remember?"

Bitterblue did not get the sense that he was appreciating the gravity of her point. She sat up, a little annoyed. "Seriously, Giddon. There's so much to worry about. What if our children are horrid? They'll have to rule Monsea one day, you know, which means they'll have to be responsible, intelligent. Kind, yet forceful. Tireless. Wise. What if they're *not*?

"Giddon?" New waves of emotion were racing across his face. Hope, wonder. Joy. She realized that this was the first time either of them had broached the topic of children. "Giddon? You look like you're having an aneurysm."

"Our children will be perfect," he said, a tear running down his cheek. "I'm going to read them bedtime stories."

"Giddon," she said crisply. "We will love our children, no matter what they're like. They will be whoever they are. But it won't serve anyone, including our children, for us to be disattached from whatever the reality is. The world is changing! There's a great deal to think about!"

"Of course there is."

"Are you sure you're up for it!"

"Bitterblue," said Giddon, taking her chin in his hand. Looking into her eyes. "There's nothing I want more in the world than to be your person while you're being the Queen of Monsea. Everyone expects you to be their support. Well, I want to be yours."

Tears began to run down Bitterblue's face.

"With all our horrid children gathered around our knees," he added.

Now Bitterblue was laughing outright.

"How many should we have?" he went on hopefully.

"How about we take it one at a time?"

"We should probably get a dog," he said.

"Anything else?" said Bitterblue. "A bear? An otter?"

"I'll make a list."

"Do you know you're wearing too many clothes?"

"Am I?"

"Would you like my help?"

"Please."

Bitterblue loved the moment when Giddon's shirt fell away from his shoulders, his chest, his torso. She loved pulling his pants down over his hips.

"Oh. But wait," she said, sitting up again.

"Yes?" said Giddon, with infinite patience.

"I'm going to be your person too, you know."

"I accept."

"Tell me something you need emotional support for right now."

"I'm fine right now, sweetheart."

"Please? I'm trying to make a symbolic point here, Giddon."

It was very dear, the shyness that crept into Giddon's face as he considered her request. "Okay," he said. "May I have some extra points? For rescuing your ex-lover?"

Bitterblue hugged him, so hard. "Of course you may," she said. "Extra points, and rewards."

"Rewards?" he said, grinning.

"Are you ready for your rewards?"

"I've been ready for half an hour," he said. "You keep talking."

"Punishments for disrespect," said Bitterblue severely, then subsided into a happy silence under his mouth, his weight. Her worries fell away.

CHAPTER FORTY-THREE

THE NEXT DAY, Bitterblue visited Quona Varana.

Though Giddon and Hava had warned her, the cats were still alarming. Some eight or nine tagged along as she followed Quona up the stairs to the sitting room, zipping forward, dashing back, turning the steps into an obstacle course.

Quona sat Bitterblue near a massive window, in a chair with a view to the sea. It was lovely, especially when a man brought chocolate cake.

"I must thank you," said Bitterblue, cradling a plate in her lap, "for the letters that prove the guilt of some of the zilfium importers. I'm sorry my friends broke into your locked room."

"It was quite natural, in the circumstances," Quona said, in a brisk, no-nonsense manner. "I'm sorry I underestimated them."

"Yes, well. I know you're bonded to seven foxes secretly," said Bitterblue, "but I've no intention of telling anyone. Nor will my friends."

"In return for what, Lady Queen?" said Quona, with a smile that was grim and efficient, but not unfriendly. Bitterblue supposed she could picture this woman influencing the zilfium vote with bribery and blackmail. She was eating her cake like it was an enemy to be vanquished.

"Information," said Bitterblue. "Education. Knowledge."

Quona nodded. "Knowledge is power. Zilfium is also power. If the rumors about your zilfium stores are true, Lady Queen, you're going to be in a position to make important decisions on behalf of the entire world."

Bitterblue studied Quona for a moment, taking a few bites of cake, creamy and rich.

"The truth is that I don't entirely trust you," Bitterblue admitted. "But I'd like to have a correspondence with you, once I go. As you say, I have zilfium, and I believe that you know a lot about what having zilfium means. I need help understanding not just the political repercussions, but the environmental ones. I need recommendations for scientists and engineers. People to help me find a safe path, if one exists."

"I'd like a correspondence too, Lady Queen," said Quona flatly. "Your future decisions are liable to have an enormous impact on the things I treasure most."

"I'm wary of your methods," said Bitterblue. "But in fact, I think we're on the same side. Why would I want to develop a resource if doing so poisons the earth?"

Now Quona was the one studying Bitterblue, with pursed lips. "We have stories in Winterkeep that come from the silbercows," she said. "About a gigantic sea monster called the Keeper, who protects the planet for us. They're funny, scary stories."

"I've heard the stories," said Bitterblue. "I've wondered if anyone believes they're really true."

"I don't believe there's a character in a story who's going to take care of us," said Quona, with sudden, real scorn. "But I believe we should try to be the keepers of each other. If you mean what you say, Lady Queen, then I think you believe that too. I would want such a person to be the guardian of the world's biggest store of zilfium. I'm disposed to be honest with you."

"Thank you," said Bitterblue. "It would be a great help."

As they sat watching the ocean, Bitterblue looked for flashes of purple on its surface, remembering her time in that water almost as if it were a dream. A new cat, a little gray one with a sideways gait, entered the room, then came to rest against her foot. Giddon had told her about the little gray cat who loved feet. She reached down to touch it, to thank it for comforting Giddon.

"Tell me," she said, suddenly remembering. "Do you know what happened to that fox who was bonded to Ferla Cavenda?"

"According to Ferla," said Quona, "he died in the fire."

Bitterblue fought back the shock she felt, because by no means should she seem devastated that Ferla's fox was dead. But she was.

She left soon after, before it became too much to hide.

OUTSIDE, IT WAS snowing, a gentle but steady fall of big, thick flakes. Bitterblue had the sense that it had been snowing for months; it seemed impossible that it was still October. *Poor fox,* she thought. *It's hard to think we only knew each other for a couple weeks.*

She commanded her guards Ranin and Mart to give her some space, gently. They needed her kindness too.

Then she glided along the path above the sea. As she passed the Cliff Farm that was part of the academy, she wondered if she could turn existing institutions and industrial centers in Monsea into schools.

There was so much to think about.

Bitterblue dashed quickly across the wooden footbridges that appeared now and then in her path, then skirted Flag Hill, not wanting to go anywhere near the remains of her own prison. She took the route above the beach where she and Lovisa had slept, then through the harbor. Working her way up staircases and along narrow streets, she eventually reached a fork where she couldn't remember which way to go. People on this street were staring at her. She was small, good at hiding inside a hood, and she'd wanted to take this journey alone, or at least, as alone as she was ever allowed to be. Bitterblue wanted to prove to herself that she wasn't afraid of Ledra, or afraid to be alone. But it was probably too much to expect Ledrans not to guess who she was, especially with two large, pale foreigners dogging her steps.

Excuse me, said a small voice.

Bitterblue jumped.

Little queen? said the voice.

Bitterblue whirled in astonished circles trying to find him, because she knew that voice. *Fox?* she said. *Fox!* Then she saw his nose peeking out from behind the slender trunk of a tree beside a building. *Fox!*

Yes, he said. *Greetings. You should walk along normally and stop standing there gaping. People see you.*

Oh, right, said Bitterblue, picking up the pace again, trying to look like she knew where she was going. Swept along by happiness and relief. *But I'm confused. They told me you were dead!*

I faked my own death.

Oh! she said, understanding. *How clever of you! Do you happen to know which street I want? I'm going to a hotel called . . .* She couldn't remember what the hotel was called. *Where is my brain?*

I don't know the location of Hotel Where Is My Brain, but the street on the left will take you into an amble.

No, my, oh—never mind, said Bitterblue. *What's an amble?*

A shopping area.

Oh? Shopping sounds nice. I never go shopping.

It isn't nice for humans. You'll have to buy something.

What do you mean? There's nothing I need.

If you enter the amble, they won't let you out unless you buy something.

This sounded extraordinary to Bitterblue. *I think I have a coin,* she said, wrinkling her nose. *Is there anything you need?*

She asked because it was a practical thing to ask at that moment, but also because the fox seemed different. Oddly subdued. His tone was tentative, almost depressed, and she was trying to figure out what was wrong. She wondered where he lived now. On the street?

I am a bit peckish, he said.

All right, said Bitterblue, realizing that she herself was ravenous, with that sudden, almost violent onset of the feeling common to a person who's been recently underfed. She turned left. *Is everything all right?*

Certainly.

Oh, good. Do you know Quona Varana?

Yes.

Do you know about her seven secret foxes?

The fox didn't respond at first, just scampered on ahead, trying to keep a low profile behind signposts and under counters. But he sent her a tired kind of uneasiness.

What is it? she said.

They're my siblings, he said. *Rascal, Rumpus, Lark, Pickle, Gladly, Genius, and Sophie. Sophie is short for Sophisticated.*

Oh! she said. *Your siblings! What a coincidence. That's—nice, isn't it?*

She has more than seven secret foxes, the fox blurted out.

She does? said Bitterblue. *How many?*

I don't even know, the fox said, almost wailing. *She keeps them everywhere! At the academy, the Keep, the Cliff Farm, the Varanas' airship hangars. And they're all so obedient!*

Goodness, said Bitterblue. *She's more of a force than I realized. Well. Is that such a bad thing, for them to be obedient?*

Maybe it's not a bad thing if your person isn't a monster, the fox said gloomily. *It's a luxury I've never had.*

I expect Quona is much more compassionate to foxes than Ferla Cavenda was, said Bitterblue sympathetically. *And certainly more fun. You, my fox, have had to be a hero. That's much harder.*

There was a long pause, during which Bitterblue examined the street, bustling with shops and vendors and small, noisy children. It was quite a smelly place, really. Fishy.

Fox? she said, suddenly thinking of it. *If your siblings have names, does that mean you have a name too?*

Yes, he said.

What is it? May I call you by it?

There was a longer pause. *My name is Adventure Fox,* he said. *Adventure, for short. My siblings call me Ad.*

That's an excellent name, said Bitterblue. *Thank you.*

This was followed by the longest pause of all. Then the fox spoke in an almost inaudible voice. *I don't deserve to be called by my name. I'm not a hero.*

What? Whyever not?

Because I did something terrible.

She'd been right, then.

It was objectively terrible, he said. *You'll never think well of me again.*

Suddenly, instantly, Bitterblue guessed what was coming. She'd wondered about this, like the tiniest light paw touching her mind with curiosity, doubt. Now she took careful control of her thoughts and reactions so that the fox couldn't feel them. *Why don't you tell me what it is,* she said, *and let me decide?*

The fox had stopped. He was crouched under a short staircase that rose to a shop door and he was pressing himself to the wood siding of the shop, trembling. It was hard to resist the urge to crouch down, pull him out, sit on the stoop, and settle him into her lap, soothing him like a cat. This fox had comforted her when she'd been desperate. He'd risked his own safety to keep her safe.

. Instead, Bitterblue climbed the stairs to the shop, because that would look normal to passersby. She shot a glance at Mart and Ranin, warning them not to follow. Then, stepping inside, she pretended to muse over rows and rows of what turned out to be pastries.

Go on, she nudged.

His voice got even quieter. *I sort of, more or less, murdered Ferla Cavenda,* he said. *More, not less. I tripped her. Then I choked her. She was going to hurt you, and maybe Lovisa too.*

Well. That was it, then. And it was more awful to hear than she'd expected, because tripping and choking were no small thing to imagine him doing. They were violent. Shocking.

But how different were they, really, from framing someone in a court of law, if the results were the same? And what would she have done, if she'd been a fox?

Oh, it was all such a mess, the things people did to each other, and the decisions that had to be made.

Why did you decide to tell me? Bitterblue asked.

Because you think I'm honorable and helpful and true, he said in a voice like crying. *I want you to see who I really am, even if that's the most terrible fox in Winterkeep.*

The Cavenda house created the same illness in everyone, it seemed. *Adventure,* she said. *You're not terrible.*

How can you say that?

Because I know it's true.

How do you know?

She didn't have the words for it yet. This fox had been her friend in a desperate time. He'd broken his own rules because he cared for her.

She realized that she was staring, unseeing, at a pastry very much like the pastry the fox had brought her once in the attic. To the astonishment of the shopkeeper who'd been watching the Queen of Monsea bumble vaguely around her shop, she attempted to purchase two of them, discovered that the coin in her pocket wasn't enough money, tried to put one back, had both pastries pushed upon her by the shopkeeper who insisted that the queen could have everything in the shop for free if she liked, shamefacedly promised to send her guard in to pay, then turned to go.

"Wait! Your proof of purchase, Lady Queen!" the woman called, then handed her a slip of paper Bitterblue was sure she didn't deserve.

Kittens, Bitterblue said expressively to the fox as she left the shop. *The richest woman on earth is not the woman who should be getting her pastries for free.* She tromped across to Ranin to ask him to take care of it. Then she surreptitiously slipped one of the pastries into the hood of her fur coat, took a big bite of the other, and said to the fox, *Is there some dark corner somewhere where we could get you into my hood, so you can have a treat?*

The fox's voice sounded confused, and incredulous. *You want me to ride in your hood, and have a treat?*

Do you not want a treat in my hood? she said, then remembered that her coat had once belonged to Ferla. This fox had been in this hood many times. *Oh dear,* she said. *I forgot that I wear her coat. I'm so sorry. Of course you might not want—*

I want to ride in your hood, he said.

Oh. Good. Here, I'll sit on this rock under this droopy tree and pretend I'm fixing my shoe. Can you manage to sneak in?

A moment later, the fox was in Bitterblue's hood.

Is it tasty? Bitterblue said.

I—I'm afraid to eat it.

Why?

I don't understand what it means.

The pastry?

What any of it means, said the fox. *You really don't think I'm terrible?*

I think you did something terrible, said Bitterblue, *because you had to. I don't think you're terrible. It's not the same thing.*

It's not?

These matters are morally ambiguous, said Bitterblue with a sigh. *I've done terrible things too. I think we need to discuss it more. I'd like to include Giddon.*

I remember Giddon, said the fox. *He's the big one who wrapped Hava in a scarf.*

No doubt, said Bitterblue, who hadn't heard that story yet, but thought it sounded silly enough to be true. *He knows about you.*

I gave you his notes, said the fox.

Yes. He was very happy to see them again, said Bitterblue. *Those notes were helpful to me. They helped me with some important realizations. Oh!* she cried, remembering. *I still haven't told Giddon happy birthday!*

Is it Giddon's birthday?

His birthday was in August.

You're very late, the fox said frankly.

Yes.

I've been thinking, said the fox, *about what it'd be like to be bonded to someone I didn't lie to.*

Bitterblue had wondered if this topic would be forthcoming. *Adventure,* she said. *I'm not certain you comprehend what a queen is, or how complicated it would be for one to have a telepathic fox.*

Complicated sounds interesting.

I could not possibly lie about you to any of the people I trust. I'm afraid it would extend far beyond Giddon.

I've been thinking about that, said the fox. *You live in Monsea. There are no other blue foxes there. What if I began a brand-new culture of foxkind, with brand-new rules? Less lying!*

I admit, that's interesting, said Bitterblue, meaning it. Such a thing would be both complicated and interesting.

Do you have airships in Monsea? asked the fox primly.

No.

You really should.

Adventure, said Bitterblue. *Focus. I don't think you realize how many ground rules we'd have to have. For example, no reading people's minds.*

What? said the fox. *Ever?*

Maybe, if someone is an enemy. I don't know. We'd need to talk about it.

I'm not sure how not to read people's minds, the fox said, *if their minds are hanging wide open.*

Well, practice, said Bitterblue, feeling stern, and tired, and hopeful. *There are three dozen people on this street, all staring at me. Can you try reading none of their minds?*

W HEN B ITTERBLUE FINALLY reached the hotel, the hotel guards were closing the doors behind a pale, blond-haired woman in a yellow coat.

"Oh, hello," said Bitterblue, who'd never seen this woman before. She was so surprised to encounter someone from home that she almost forgot to speak Lingian.

The woman shrank at the sight of her. She shot Bitterblue one quick, searching look through black and yellow eyes. "Hello, Lady Queen," she said, then scampered away down the street.

Bitterblue found Giddon inside the doors, staring into the middle distance with a thoughtful and slightly grumpy expression. Since no one else was in the lobby and Ranin and Mart were still trailing behind, Bitterblue had the pleasure of admiring him for a moment, then going to him and kissing him.

"I have something to tell you," she said.

Happy birthday? suggested the fox, who was still hiding in her hood.

You be quiet! Bitterblue said. *And no mind reading!*

I'm not! he cried indignantly. *But you should ask him about that woman! I know her!*

"And I, you," said Giddon, the grouchy lines of his face smoothing as he returned her kiss. "Did you see that woman who just left?"

"I did."

"That's Trina."

"The Graceling who betrayed you?" said Bitterblue, surprised.

"And you," he reminded her.

"What did she want?"

"Believe it or not," said Giddon, "she claims she wants to know what it would mean to get involved with the Council."

"Oh," said Bitterblue, understanding. "Do you trust her?"

"That's always the question, isn't it?"

"Along those same lines," said Bitterblue, "before you say anything more, I have someone to introduce to you."

"Okay," he said. "Wait, what?" he said suddenly, groping at her coat, his voice changing. "Bitterblue? Is there a fox in your hood?"

"Yes," she said.

"Oh dear," he said, in a voice like he knew what was coming.

"Yes," she said. "Are you ready for the next big decision?"

CHAPTER FORTY-FOUR

LOVISA FACED AN awful choice.

Where was her father now? Suffering in a jail cell, with nothing to distract himself, nothing to read? *Good,* she kept telling herself. *That's where he belongs.* And her mind knew it was true, but her heart was with him in his cell, wondering if he was cold. If his face had healed, if his mouth hurt when he ate. If he was scared.

And then her heart would jump to that boat trip, sick and confused, as he lied and made excuses that eventually turned to threats.

If she testified against him, she was probably signing his death warrant. *Which is what he deserves,* she kept telling herself, but that was a place her heart could not go.

If she decided *not* to testify against him, he might actually get away with it. Maybe do some prison time for smaller offenses, as an accessory to someone else's crimes. Maybe lose a portion of his fortune. But then, be a free man. Be the father to her brothers. Raise them. Be her own father. Be part of Ledra society. Probably begin to rise, politically or commercially, again.

So then? Should she testify?

If she did, then it was as if they were standing together on the roof of the northern house again and she pushed him, her own father, off the edge.

WHEN AN ACADEMY messenger intercepted Lovisa on campus, handing her a sealed note that turned out to be an invitation to Saturday lunch with the Queen of Monsea, Lovisa was only half surprised.

After all, Lovisa was famous. Everyone wanted to have lunch with her. Strangers, acquaintances, family friends, lawyers—especially lawyers. So many people were trying to push themselves into Lovisa's life right now to "help" her with her family situation that it was hard to do her schoolwork, walk through campus to class, cross the city. People seemed to recognize her immediately. The white streak in her hair that marked her as Ferla's daughter turned her into a beacon for opportunists. A few of her friends—Nev, Mari, some of Mari's crowd, and even a few teachers, like Gorga Balava—had taken to offering their chaperonage, wherever she went. Lovisa had a feeling that some of them offered because they liked the association with a notorious celebrity. But some of them—Nev, Mari, Gorga—seemed actually concerned for her.

What surprised Lovisa about the invitation was that when she arrived at the queen's hotel and was ushered into the dining room, the queen was the only person in the room.

In fact, once Lovisa was seated, Bitterblue got up, pulled the door shut, then sat catty-corner to Lovisa at a table that would easily have accommodated twenty.

Lovisa was tired of fuss. She also had a lot of homework to get back to. "Bitterblue?" she said. "What's this about?"

"Have some duck, it's delicious," said the queen, whose plate was already full. "There was a soup, but I told them to bring it back later. I'm too hungry to be filling my stomach with water."

"My parents starved you," said Lovisa, with a small implosion of shame.

"I shouldn't have reminded you," said the queen more gently. "I'm sorry. *You* didn't starve me, Lovisa."

"It doesn't matter," said Lovisa. "Why are we having a secret meeting?"

"I'll get to the point," said the queen. "I've been wondering if it would help you if I were to pretend that *I* was the one who overheard your mother yelling at your father. That I was awake when your father struck Pari Parnin down, while your mother tried to stop him. That I, not you, saw him carry Pari to the airship."

The queen kept talking, but Lovisa hardly heard, because she'd entered a beautiful kind of shock.

"Why?" she heard herself saying. "Why? Bitterblue? Why would you do this?"

For the first time in the conversation, the queen looked uncertain.

No, Lovisa thought to herself, watching Bitterblue's quiet, steady face, her firm chin. The eyes that seemed to shine at Lovisa with unshed tears. *She's not uncertain.*

She sees me, Lovisa thought, falling into another, new surprise. *She understands.*

"It will cost me nothing," the queen said quietly.

"I can't quite believe that. My father will refute you, accuse you of lying. And you'll know he's right."

"It will cost me much less than testifying will cost you, Lovisa," she said. "And being able to help you will be my reward."

Lovisa reached her fork to the serving plate and took some duck. Sliced it, pushed it around. She wasn't hungry, but she needed something to do, while she tried to absorb the shock of this woman caring about her and her situation.

"Lovisa," the queen added. "Did you ever overhear your parents allude to the sinking of the *Seashell*?"

"No," said Lovisa. "Not specifically."

"I don't like the gap it leaves in the court case," the queen said. "My men were murdered. And Katu's suspicions, and his abduction, make little sense without it too. Ah well. Have you shared any of your evidence with the Magistry yet?"

"No," said Lovisa, thinking about the words her mother had yelled at Benni. "We never needed to hurt anyone! We were going to do everything legally! You never would have had to break a single law!" She'd told Mari her evidence. She'd told Nev. She'd shared it with her piglet, Worthy, cuddling him in a quiet corner of the Devret house, which was where Worthy was living these days, delighting her brothers, and apparently gaining a reputation as a genius. "We found him in the heat ducts," Arni had told her gravely, the last time she'd visited. "Wandering around inside the walls from room to room. No idea how he got in there. Seemed confused about it himself."

But she hadn't shared it with the Magistry. Lovisa's evidence lived inside herself, wandering around from head to heart to stomach, trying to decide where it belonged.

Maybe it could stay where it was?

"I'd like to think about this," Lovisa told the queen. "May I have a few days to think about it?"

"Of course," said Bitterblue. "As long as you need."

"I—have homework to do," Lovisa said. "Do you mind—"

She knew she was being rude. A queen had invited her to lunch. But just now, Lovisa needed to escape. She had a feeling Bitterblue would want her to escape, if that's what she needed.

"Go, and be well," said Bitterblue.

OUTSIDE, LOVISA'S FEET carried her to the Devret house. She wanted to visit her brothers.

She saw a lot of them now, bringing her homework to the Devrets' some nights, sleeping over on weekends. She and the boys had bedrooms of their own, in the part of the house where family slept. She would crowd with them on one of their beds and they'd all be talking and snacking and laughing, and she wouldn't be able to shake the sense that it wasn't safe. And then she'd remember that none of them were going to be punished if they were found together. Joy was no longer a thing they needed to steal.

Today she wished she could talk to Viri, Erita, and Vikti as their older selves, five, ten, twenty years from now. Find out how her decision about testifying would touch their lives. What would hurt them least? Her testimony, or the queen's?

It was an impossible question to answer. They weren't old enough. They were five, seven, and nine.

She did notice, as she walked, that her own question had changed. It had used to be: Should she testify or shouldn't she? Now it was: Who should testify, Lovisa or the queen?

That was a big change.

TODAY, SHE FOUND the boys crowded together on the Devrets' library floor, playing City with someone familiar.

"Katu," Lovisa said, always warming with relief and joy when she saw her uncle. From his position on his stomach, Katu shot her a smile.

"Lovisa!" the boys cried out. "Come play!"

"There's hardly room!" she said, laughing.

"I'm going to steal your sister for a minute, boys," Katu said, pushing himself up from the floor with creaks and groans. "Listen to me. You'd think I was sixty years old."

"You'll get younger as you recover," said Lovisa jokingly, hoping it was true. He did look and seem older, and it tugged at her heart.

He led her into the corridor, then around the corner to a small sitting room close to the staff stairs. It was Lovisa and Katu's unofficial meeting place at the Devret house, a room out of everyone else's way, where they could sit together and catch up. The Devrets had noticed.

The fire was always burning in here, whenever Katu came to visit.

"Erita told me something that touches upon one of our unsolved mysteries," Katu said.

"Oh, no," said Lovisa in dismay as she pulled a chair close to the fireplace. "Something he heard?" Erita kept randomly coming out with conversations he remembered having overheard between Benni and Ferla. It made Lovisa wonder what else was trapped inside these boys that they weren't telling her yet, either deliberately, or because they'd forgotten.

"Yes," said Katu grimly. "Apparently he heard Ferla yelling at Benni for not waiting until the zilfium vote before he started experimenting."

"Before he started experimenting—with the explosive weapon?"

"That's my guess."

"So, he was supposed to wait for the zilfium vote to start making the weapons. But he didn't. And that—ah," said Lovisa, understanding. "This explains a piece I hadn't fathomed before. Namely, how my mother ever imagined they could develop a zilfium weapon without breaking any laws. But she believed they could have done so, once zilfium use was legalized in Winterkeep. And she was planning to throw her vote," said Lovisa, remembering another piece she'd forgotten. "I heard her tell my father, 'I was going to give you your zilfium vote.' She was planning to go against her party with the tie-breaking vote to help the Industrialists legalize zilfium use."

"Yes."

"Does Erita understand it?"

"I don't think so. But it's hard to tell."

Erita was the boy who seemed to be coping best with all that was happening. Every time he mentioned some memory that piqued the interest of his sister or his uncle, he swelled with pride for being helpful. He didn't seem concerned with what any of his memories meant.

In contrast, Vikti, the oldest, seemed to shrink at Erita's announcements. He was so quiet. Too quiet, with something shuttered behind his eyes that made Lovisa's heart rise in her throat. She wished she could see in there, figure out what he needed.

Viri, the youngest, asked questions constantly. Details he wanted clarified about the night of the fire, the night she'd found the queen in the attic, or the days she'd spent in the north before they'd joined her. It choked her with tears, over and over, when Viri kept coming to the conclusion that she'd been a hero. She hadn't. She'd abandoned him. He kept asking, "Are you going to leave again, Lovisa?" And Vikti's eyes would rise to her face, watching her carefully while she answered.

"I can't promise you I'm never going to go anywhere ever," she would say, because she would not lie to them. "In our long lives, we're all going to visit lots of places. But I'm not going to disappear again, and I'm always going to be where you can find me, all right? I promise."

Now, before the fire, Katu was watching her.

"As much as I want a clearer idea of what my parents did," Lovisa said, "I hope for his own sake that Erita doesn't have too many more secrets to share."

Katu was silent for a moment, staring soberly into the fire. "I don't think it would be quite right to say that I ever understood my sister," he said. "But I saw her adolescence, and what my father subjected her to. I might be able to help you understand where some of her wrong ideas came from, Lovisa."

Lovisa considered that. She already knew a lot of those stories. "No, thank you," she said.

"Are you sure?"

"If I have children someday," said Lovisa, "I won't expect them to blame my parents for the wrongs I do to them. They get to blame me."

Katu studied her, a smile playing around his lips. "You're a good kid, Lovisa," he said. "Have you considered a career as a judge?"

Lovisa snorted. "Parliament appoints judges. Have you noticed the kind of person who gets elected to Parliament?"

"Become a judge," he said, "then throw Parliament in prison."

Snorting again, Lovisa stood. "Come play City?"

"Between you and me," said Katu, "I don't think we have a choice."

THE BOYS COULDN'T convince Katu to stay for dinner, because Katu had a date.

"A date!" Viri squealed. "Who do you have a date with, Katu?"

"A lovely woman who happens to be one of my doctors," Katu said.

"Can't you bring her here for your date?" said Viri, a suggestion that sent Lovisa into a fit of coughing at the notion of Katu trying to romance someone over dinner at the Devrets' house, in the company of three constantly interrupting little boys.

So Katu went away, but Lovisa stayed. She was shy around Mari's parents at dinner. She didn't want their eyes or their questions; but then she always found herself watching them curiously, trying to listen in on their conversation with each other, because they actually enjoyed each other's company. They never minded if the boys amused themselves with an increasingly loud conversation of their own.

Mara, who was an Industry rep in Parliament, announced tonight that the zilfium vote, originally scheduled for December, was being pushed to late spring.

"What?" said Lovisa. "Why?"

"Now that a military use has been found for zilfium, we all need more time to research and debate," Mara said. "It's one thing to open Winterkeep to trains and faster boats. Explosive weapons is a whole other matter."

"But aren't the weapons going to be destroyed?" said Lovisa, who knew the rumors. "Didn't the blueprints burn in a fire at the queen's hotel?"

"Even so, what was invented once can be invented again," said Mara.

"Well then," said Lovisa, "is it safe to ban a weapon in Winterkeep if the other nations in Torla are likely to be developing that weapon for themselves? And anyway, shouldn't Queen Bitterblue be part of the conversation, since she has so much zilfium?"

Mara considered her approvingly. "Have you chosen a party, Lovisa?"

The old familiar impatience rose in Lovisa at this tiresome question. "Doesn't that choice generally come down to where one's self-interest falls?"

Mara's eyebrows rose. "At what cost?" she said. "Arni's bank would flourish beyond our wildest dreams if war came to Torla. War is expensive. Nations and people go into massive debt. Debt creates loans, and loans make banks rich. You understand, Lovisa? But if the day comes when you see me voting yes on any measure that's a step on the path to war, I hope you'll take me to the doctor to have my head checked."

She turned to her husband, took his hand. "Promise you'll have me removed from office," she said to him.

"I promise," he said. Then he leaned forward and kissed her mouth, right in front of everyone.

As DINNER WAS ending, the son of the house came home.

"Ah," said Mari, entering the dining room, tall and cheerful, bending down to kiss first his father's cheek, then his mother's. "I wondered if you were here, Lovisa, when you didn't show up at dinner in the dormitory."

"You found me," said Lovisa.

Then, after dinner, she waited until the boys had pulled Mari into some sort of long and complicated card game, then slipped out on her own.

She needed to think, by herself. And Lovisa was still shy around Mari. Being at his house was a way of being near him without actually having to figure out how to be with him. Lovisa kept getting a sense that Mari wanted something she did not currently want. It would probably come to a conversation, sometime soon. Now, however, felt like the time for waiting. She was being careful.

Anyway, Lovisa needed some fresh air, and the stars above; she needed a long walk, to settle some of her swirling thoughts about the queen's offer. *I could figure this out better if I were standing on a cliff above the sea,* she thought, then snorted at herself, knowing Nev would like that she'd had that thought.

As she neared the campus dorms, she saw Nori Orfa on the path ahead, talking to a girl Lovisa recognized as the sister of one of Mari's friends.

"Oh, hi, Nori," she said airily as she reached him. "I'm writing a letter to your girlfriend. Any message you'd like me to pass on?"

The poisonous look that crept into Nori's face was extremely satisfying, because it was ugly. It made the girl with him hesitate, then take a small step back.

Inside the dormitory, Nev's door was open. Lovisa considered passing on by, but she couldn't quite. Something drew her to Nev's doorway, some understanding that even if she couldn't talk to Nev about the queen's secret offer specifically, talking to Nev about something else—anything—might still help. Nev had that effect.

Nev was watering the plants in her window, from a tin watering can with a long, graceful spout. When she saw Lovisa, she shot her a tiny smile. "How are you?"

"Fine. You?"

"All right."

Nev was suffering these days from a small heartbreak. Not Nori; she seemed to be coping fine without Nori. But her fox, Little Guy. The fox had apparently decided not to bond with Nev, and wasn't living with her anymore. It had something to do with Quona Varana, though Lovisa didn't know the details. She only knew that neither human nor fox should be allowed to break Nev's heart like that.

Lovisa had offered to share Worthy with her. Laughing, Nev had told her she must have Worthy to herself. "Don't worry about me," she said. "I'm surrounded by animals in my life. You keep the one that's yours. You need him."

It was the sort of protectiveness that warmed Lovisa with surprise, then always made her think sharply of her father. Benni had been her protector too, when she was younger. But this protectiveness from Nev, which showed up in a lot of different ways, was different. When people tried to approach Lovisa on campus, Nev's shoulders could get very big and swaggery, her face very unwelcoming. It made some tight thing inside Lovisa, some sense of guilt or obligation, relax, in a way she'd never relaxed with her father. Lovisa hadn't worked out the difference. It was one of the things she'd been thinking about recently.

"You look tired," said Nev now.

"People keep asking me my political party," said Lovisa, rolling her eyes.

"Do you have to have a party?" said Nev. "Couldn't you just have beliefs?"

"That's a nice idea," said Lovisa, "but then who would vote for me?"

"Running for something, are you?" said Nev, with a crooked grin.

"Definitely not."

"Do you want to come in? Or just hover in the doorway?"

Sometimes Lovisa got confused about whether Nev was flirting.

Did she want Nev to be flirting? And then she would worry that she was hanging around Nev the way she feared Mari was hanging around her; and Mari was her oldest friend and Nev was Mari's ex; so could there possibly be anyone more complicated for Lovisa to be having these confusions about?

And then Nev would give her a sly grin and invite her in, and Lovisa would stop caring about Mari. Then get confused and worried again, then remember who she was. She was Lovisa Cavenda. Lovisa Cavenda was a person who would just ask Nev outright about it one day, plain and straightforward. And then she would deal with Nev's answer, whatever it was. She had a feeling Nev would deal with it too.

Lovisa entered and sat on the rumpled blankets of Nev's bed, patting around for Little Guy before remembering that Little Guy was gone. Nev leaned in her window comfortably, with her arms crossed.

"Who would *you* vote for?" Lovisa asked Nev.

"Someone who gave silbercows a voice in government," Nev said, without hesitation.

"Really?"

"Really. I think it's a travesty that they're unrepresented. Also, someone who protected my family and understood our needs in the north. Someone who cared for the land."

"That sounds more like a Scholar in name," said Lovisa, "but not necessarily in practice."

"Maybe you should decide what you want to change in the world," said Nev, "instead of which party to join."

"I think you're being too idealistic."

"If you start waxing poetic about how it's because I'm a northerner who talks to glaciers, I won't make you any tea," said Nev.

Now Lovisa was grinning. "What kind of tea?"

"What kind do you want?"

"Something that'll help me make an important decision."

"Hm," said Nev. "How about I make you something harmless that won't interfere?"

"That sounds fine."

Nev set her little pot on her stove, then came to sit with Lovisa, cross-legged, while the water boiled.

"What are you trying to decide?" she asked.

Lovisa spent a moment finding a way to express it without revealing the queen's offer. "I've been thinking about my father," she said. "About how he used to protect me."

"How did he used to protect you?"

Lovisa shrugged. "My mother would have these rages. I would run to my father, knock on his library door. He would sit me in his favorite chair, fuss over me. Order me some tea or something nice to eat. If my mother came looking for me, he would hold her off at the door, telling her he was handling it. It was nice. It's one of the reasons I've always felt like my care of my little brothers is inadequate. I never held my mother off from them."

Nev sat up straight, something hard in her face. Lovisa shrank, certain Nev was angry at her for not protecting her brothers better.

"Lovisa," Nev said. "Do you understand that it was never your job to stop your mother from hurting your brothers? That was the job of your *father*."

This seemed wrong to Lovisa, for she was big. Her brothers were little. The big protected the little.

"It was my job too," she said.

"With your father there?" said Nev. "As big as he was, the man that he was? I've seen him, Lovisa. He would leave you to defend your brothers?"

"It's not that simple," Lovisa said. "My mother was his wife. He had obligations to her."

"After you would spend that time in your father's library," Nev said. "When you were little. What happened next?"

"What do you mean?"

"Well? Did your mother forgive you?"

"No," Lovisa said. "Of course not. We would come out for dinner. She would wait for my dinner to be served. Then, before I could eat it, she would take me away from the table and put me upstairs, in this room in the attic where she took us for punishments."

"And your father would sit at the table?" Nev said. "And watch you go?"

"Yes," Lovisa said, startled by the question. "But he wasn't the one I'd crossed. It was my mother, you understand?"

At the sudden, soft sorrow in Nev's face, Lovisa went quiet, thinking. Then gradually, inconsolably, sad.

"Oh," Lovisa said. "I see."

CHAPTER FORTY-FIVE

LOVISA WAS SITTING on a bench Nev had shown her after Lovisa had complained that there was no place to think in Ledra. The bench was at the Cliff Farm, overlooking the water.

"I sit there sometimes and look for silbercows," Nev had said.

So now Lovisa sat there too, occasionally smelling a whiff of manure that reminded her of Nev's home in the north. The light was falling, stars beginning to prick the violet sky. Lovisa had used to sit in the dorm foyer and watch people, pulling information into herself to consider later, to fit into the puzzle of who was doing what, and why. She still did that. But now she also sat here, looking out across the sea and sky. Like the dorm foyer, this cliff was a place on the edge of something.

Lovisa had gone to Gorga Balava, her professor, after class on Monday, demanding an explanation from him about zilfium pollution.

"Surely you've read the studies, Lovisa," he'd said, squinting at her with a puzzled expression. On his arm, his silly fox was wearing a hat with two ear holes and a pom-pom, tied with a ribbon under her chin. "You should talk to a scientist, or a Scholar."

She'd gone to Gorga exactly because he was an Industry rep, not a Scholar. "I'm not asking you to explain what pollution is," she said scornfully. "I'm asking you to explain why you don't *care* about it."

"I do care about it."

"Just not enough to do something about it?"

"What should I do, Lovisa? Let Winterkeep's industries fall behind the advances of the rest of the world? So that no one will trade with us, no one will send students to our schools, or take our opinions and resources into account when larger decisions are being made?"

"You could insist on research into other fuels besides zilfium," said Lovisa. "You could try to get the rest of the world to care about the problem. You could break the Varanas' monopoly on varane production. You could ask someone other than your self-interested Ledran friends for ideas. You could try to inspire people!"

Gorga's eyes had gone rather bright as he watched her rising agitation. "This is the start of an excellent list, Lovisa," he'd said. "What would you think of an independent study next term, examining these questions more fully?"

ON HER BENCH on the cliff, Lovisa was trying to come to a decision about the queen's offer when something extraordinary happened.

A vibration grew around her, starting low, then pushing itself into her consciousness. It was a sense of something swelling, impossibly, in the sea. And it was dark on the water, the light falling fast. But Lovisa saw.

What was it that she saw? Looking back later, Lovisa was never sure what the honest answer was to that question. She saw a mountain, black in silhouette, rising out of the ocean. It had long, winding, wavering legs. And it was making a dreadful, almost unbearable noise, maybe not the kind her ears could hear—it was hard to tell what part of her body was hearing it—but the kind that flooded every cell with a need for the terrible, loud pressure to stop.

One of the mountain's long legs was holding something. An object with hard edges. Slowly, the leg lifted the object into the air, water streaming down from its surface. Then the leg placed the object gently on the beach to the left of Lovisa's cliff, nearer to the city.

The mountain receded. Gradually, mercifully, so did the noise.

At her bench, Lovisa was standing. "Icositetrapus cyclops!" she was shouting aloud to the air. "Icositetrapus cyclops! What? What?" turning in circles, looking for someone to talk to. Someone to whom to say, "Did you see that?" and demand, "What *was* that?"

She was alone.

Lovisa sat down, stood up again, sat down. She couldn't begin to understand it. Nor could she believe it, except that at the water's edge on the sand to the left, a large, oblong shape that had certainly not been there before was cast ashore, like a beached ship.

In fact, the more Lovisa looked, the more she believed that it *was* a beached ship.

She began to be frightened that she was losing her sanity. When, a moment later, voices and images appeared in her mind unbidden, her fears sharpened into a certainty.

Then she saw the small, smooth shapes out at sea, gliding, playing in the sunset water. Silbercows? Is that what was happening? Had they noticed her? Could they possibly—

Yes. She felt them, like a soft touch brushing against her heart. They were calling out to her, wanting to talk. To her!

We heard you, they said, *in the north. We heard you say you're sorry.*

It wasn't words; it was pictures, ideas. Feelings. Lovisa felt breathless, dizzy, but she thought she understood.

It's not your fault, they told her.

What? she said, not sure how to talk to them, not sure what to say. *What just happened?*

That creature you saw just now, they told her. *It wasn't the Keeper. Not exactly. The Keeper is a story. That was our big, strong friend. She's real.*

How did one talk to silbercows? She tried it again. *I don't understand,* she told them.

That ship on the beach is the Seashell, they told her. *With two bodies trapped inside. Mikka and Brek.*

Lovisa was cast into a new kind of shock. *What?* she cried out. *You brought us the* Seashell? *How did you do that?* Why *would you do that?*

It's the evidence you need, they told her. *There's a lock on their door.*

Evidence?

Evidence that they were murdered, they told her. *Our friend is big. She's big enough to move ships. We want to help you humans, so you'll help us. We know you need true things for your courts.*

You know that? Lovisa said. *How do you know that?*

Why wouldn't we know that? they said. *We talk to humans. We're part of your world. Some humans are our friends. Do you know the small human who lost the ring?*

The queen? said Lovisa, incredulous.

They asked her, *Can you come down to the water?*

LOVISA WALKED NORTH, to a place where steps in the cliff led down to a little beach. It was a different beach from the one where the ship was sitting. She didn't want to go anywhere near that beach, for human voices had begun to sound down there, calls of amazement, shouts. "Did you see that? Did you hear it?" She didn't want to be part of their speculation, their wonder. Their horror, when they discovered the bodies inside. Lovisa didn't want to see any more bodies.

When she got down to the water, the silbercows were waiting for her, floating some distance from the shore. She didn't know how to get close to them. She had no boat. When one of them swam up close to the beach, so close that Lovisa was frightened for its safety, she walked right into the water.

It was freezing. Aghast, she strode in up to her thighs, suspecting she was ruining her shoes, her trousers, her coat, and remembering, of course, that she no longer knew where the money would come from to buy new things. The Devrets, probably, which wasn't right. But Lovisa was beyond that just now. She'd watched a sea monster—the silbercows had said it wasn't the Keeper, but when she told her brothers this story, they would make it the Keeper—*everyone* would make it the Keeper—lift the *Seashell* out of the sea. It was just the sort of thing the Keeper would do. Who cared about her clothes? The ocean had shared a secret with her. A monster had reached out and delivered a miracle. This world kept wanting to be bigger than she was letting it. Why did she keep trapping herself inside small things?

Lovisa had never been so close to a silbercow before. Physically, it was little more than a dark shape rising from the water before her, but in her feelings and her mind, it was a great deal more. As it talked to her, she felt, to be honest, as if her brain were trying to rise out of her skull. It wasn't an entirely pleasant feeling. Her body became awash in a sadness that she understood was the silbercow's sadness. She began to cry, at the thought that her parents had done something to hurt this creature. *I'm sorry,* she started saying again. *I'm sorry.*

It wasn't your fault, the silbercow said.

Maybe that was true. But Lovisa was beginning to understand that it was her legacy. *I'm going to make up for it,* she said, not knowing what it meant, but certain, in that moment, that it was true. *I'm going to protect you.*

I believe you're going to try, said the silbercow. *I can feel the fire in your heart.*

Lovisa saw then that the silbercow was holding a tiny, hard ring in its mouth. She understood that she was supposed to take it. She held out her hand.

The silbercow dropped the ring into her hand. It was cold and wet and small. She understood that she was now tasked with returning it to the queen.

Then she understood something else. A sort of doubtful apology from the silbercow, on behalf of their monster friend, who was very unhappy. Unhappy about the ship? About the drowned humans? Lovisa wasn't understanding this part entirely, but she did understand that the silbercow wanted to know if she had any . . . it was hard to believe, but the silbercow wondered if Lovisa had any sparkly baubles. Any shiny human thing she didn't care about. If it could be worn as a ring, so much the better.

For the monster? Lovisa asked, thoroughly confused.

Yes.

The monster wants a sparkly bauble?

It would make her very happy.

From her state of mental chaos, Lovisa did an inventory of her person, because if the monster wanted a sparkly bauble, she wanted the monster to have a sparkly bauble. She had some snacks and one of Worthy's milk rags in her pockets, all sodden now, but no baubles, and she wore no jewelry. Then she remembered something. Reaching into the front of her coat, she pulled the string with the attic room key over her head. She held it up, considering it. In the twilight, the purple stone sparkled and the metal of the key glimmered silver.

She felt a sort of relieved sigh coming from the silbercow, and considered that the key had a steel loop at the top. If someone really wanted to, they could wear it as a ring.

Or a necklace, the silbercow said, *around one of her eye-stems.*

Uncertain, but deciding, Lovisa held the key out to the silbercow, who took it gently in its mouth. Lovisa felt a thank-you, then the silbercow turned and took off. It had happened so fast, the relinquishing of that key. Lovisa looked for a sign of the silbercow streaking across the water, but it was gone.

Will you come talk to me again? she cried out desperately.

Yes, Lovisa Cavenda, said the silbercow, in a fading voice. *You will be our friend.*

LOVISA WALKED BACK to the city, dripping water, stomping her feet hard to warm them. The ends of her coat began to form a frozen sort of shield around her legs.

When she reached the tall, brightly lit hotel where the queen was staying, she stood outside for a moment, watching snowflakes hit its glass windows, then slide down like rain.

It had taken her so long to give up that key, the key to her cage. But it was a cage that no longer existed, because she'd destroyed it, by herself. Freeing Bitterblue was freeing herself. What would've happened if she hadn't?

Now the key had moved on, to the bottom of the sea, where it belonged. It was someone else's treasure. She'd received the *Seashell* in return, the missing link for the Magistry in the story of her parents' crimes. Those two murders would be added to the charges against her father.

There was more. Lovisa had seen something today. She had a story to tell. She thought it might even be an inspiring story. "The Keeper is a fairy tale," she could say, "but what I saw was real. Are you so sure that the silbercows are making things up?"

What if her story could make people want to hear new voices, new ideas? What if Lovisa was discovering that she agreed with Nev that silbercows should have a voice in Parliament? What if she made it a political experiment, to figure out what words, what way of telling her story, would get other people to think so too? She was sixteen. That was still young, wasn't it? She'd already wasted a lot of time. What if she started now? Who could help her? Gorga? Mara? Nev? How long would it take her to learn all she needed to know?

Staring up at the windows of the foreign queen, Lovisa was beginning to understand how much she wanted a bigger world than she'd
ever been promised as a child. There were monsters in the sea who
returned lost items, and silbercows she could talk to, and a pig wandering the Devrets' heat ducts. There were smugglers pulling off
questionable feats of engineering in the north, and glaciers calving
icebergs into the sea, and problems here in Parliament, for people to
argue about as if they cared. Some of them actually did care.

And she was thinking now not about what it would mean to her
brothers if she did or didn't testify against her father, but about what
it would mean to her. What did any of this mean to *her*? What had
her father done to *her*? Her father had lied to her, playacted. He'd
pretended to be her ally against her mother, then betrayed her repeatedly. He'd killed a boy she'd brought home. He'd compelled her to
do desperate and destructive things—set fire to a house, throw an
explosive egg—to save other people. And now, finally, he'd put her in
the position of having to decide whether to tell the truth about him,
then live with the consequences forever.

I believe you think you love me, Papa, she thought, *in your way. But
I'm worthy of more.*

She stepped into the light of the hotel's entrance. The guards,
recognizing her, glanced dubiously at the sodden lower half of her
coat, then let her in.

SHE FOUND THE queen and Giddon in an upstairs library, sitting
on a sofa together, eating cake that, inexplicably, had flaming candles
stuck into it.

"Lovisa," said Bitterblue in a glad voice, patting the space beside
her. "We're celebrating Giddon's birthday. Have some cake." Her eyes
were wide and trusting. Bitterblue's eyes had used to track Lovisa anxiously, as if Lovisa was about to do something desperate. Lovisa had

known what Bitterblue had been thinking then. She'd understood why the queen had asked her questions to distract her, or created jobs to keep her away from a cliff's edge. Lovisa was grateful, for the queen had been right.

Now Lovisa could feel herself standing on solid ground. The queen had offered to shoulder her burden, but Lovisa wanted strong shoulders of her own, to carry well whatever she was given.

She indicated the state of her coat. "I'm a mess," she said, "so I won't sit down."

Abruptly, Giddon stood and left the room. "Have you been in the sea?" the queen asked.

"Something like that."

Giddon came back with a towel. "Oh," Lovisa said, touched by this thoughtfulness. "Thank you."

She took a moment to rub down her coat and legs. Then she said, "I've been thinking about your offer."

"Yes?" said Bitterblue.

"I'm grateful," said Lovisa. "For that, and for everything." She took a careful breath. "I've decided that it's my truth. I'll say it myself."

The queen's eyes were bright. "You know you can always change your mind?"

"I know," said Lovisa, who wasn't going to change her mind.

The queen nodded. "I'm proud of you."

"And now," said Lovisa, reaching into her pocket, enclosing the small, cold ring in her hand, and holding it out to the queen. "Are you ready for a little magic?"

Cast of Characters

From Winterkeep

ADA BALAVA: An importer of Monsean zilfium.

ADVENTURE FOX (ADVENTURE, AD): A blue fox bonded to Ferla Cavenda.

ARNI DEVRET: The father of Mari Devret. A banker.

BENNI CAVENDA: The father of Lovisa Cavenda. An owner of a shipping business, an importer of Monsean zilfium, and an Industry representative in Parliament.

DAVVI: The father of Nev. A builder.

DEV DIMARA: A zilfium shipper and a Scholar representative in Parliament.

EARMUFF: A blue fox bonded to Gorga Balava.

ELLA: A housemaid at the Cavenda property in Torla's Neck.

ERITA CAVENDA: A brother of Lovisa Cavenda, seven years old. Observant.

FERLA CAVENDA: The mother of Lovisa Cavenda. The co-owner of a silver mine with her brother, Katu, a Scholar, and the President of Winterkeep.

GORGA BALAVA: A professor in the school of politics and government at the Winterkeep Academy and an Industry representative in Parliament.

KATU CAVENDA: The brother of Ferla Cavenda, with whom he co-owns a silver mine. The uncle of Lovisa Cavenda. A traveler and adventurer.

THE KEEPER: A mythical undersea creature in the fairy tales told by the silbercows. The keeper of the planet, she exhorts silbercows and humans to help her protect the earth and the sea.

KEP GRAVLA: A student at the Winterkeep Academy and a childhood neighbor of Lovisa Cavenda and Mari Devret.

LITTLE GUY: A blue fox kit living with Nev in the dorms of the Winterkeep Academy.

LIV: The cook at the Cavenda property in Torla's Neck.

LOVISA CAVENDA: A student of politics and government at the Winterkeep Academy. The daughter of Ferla and Benni Cavenda. The sister of Viri, Erita, and Vikti Cavenda. The niece of Katu Cavenda.

MARA DEVRET: The mother of Mari Devret. An Industry representative in Parliament.

MARI DEVRET: A student of medicine at the Winterkeep Academy. The son of Mara and Arni Devret. The oldest friend of Lovisa Cavenda.

MIRNI TIMA: An importer of Monsean zilfium.

MINTA VARANA: An airship engineer and an importer of Monsean zilfium. The sister of Quona and Sara Varana. A Scholar politically.

NEV: A scholarship student of animal medicine at the Winterkeep Academy, from Torla's Neck. The daughter of Davvi and Nola and the granddaughter of Saiet.

NOLA: The mother of Nev. A healer through massage.

NORI ORFA: A student of animal medicine at the Winterkeep Academy, from Torla's Neck.

ONA: The firekeeper on Trader's Beach.

PARI PARNIN: A student at the Winterkeep Academy.

QUONA VARANA: An animal doctor and an environmentalist. A professor of animal medicine at the Winterkeep Academy. The sister of Minta and Sara Varana. A Scholar politically.

SAIET: The grandfather of Nev. An animal doctor.

SARA VARANA: A Scholar and the Prime Minister of Winterkeep. The sister of Minta and Quona Varana.

TA VARANA: A student at the Winterkeep Academy. The daughter of Minta Varana.

VERA: The proprietor of a bath north of Ledra. An airship smuggler.

VIKTI CAVENDA: A brother of Lovisa Cavenda, nine years old. Quiet.

VIRI CAVENDA: A brother of Lovisa Cavenda, five years old. Curious.

WORTHY: A pig.

From the Royal Continent

ASHEN: The mother of Bitterblue and the previous Queen of Monsea. From Lienid. Deceased.

BARRA: An adviser to Queen Bitterblue.

BITTERBLUE: The Queen of Monsea.

BREK: A previous adviser to Queen Bitterblue. He drowned in Winterkeep with Mikka.

COBAL: The Estillan envoy to Winterkeep.

CORAN: An adviser and doctor to Queen Bitterblue.

FROGGATT: Queen Bitterblue's foremost adviser.

GIDDON: One of the leaders of the Council. A dispossessed Middluns lord and a friend of Queen Bitterblue.

HAVA: A Graceling, Graced with the ability to change what people see when they look at her. A spy for Queen Bitterblue and secretly Bitterblue's half sister.

HELDA: The caretaker of Queen Bitterblue's domestic affairs and her spymaster.

JOFF: A lord from southern Estill.

KATSA: The founder of the Council. A Graceling, Graced with survival. From the Middluns. A friend and mentor of Queen Bitterblue.

LECK: The father of Bitterblue and the previous King of Monsea. A Graceling, Graced with the ability to tell lies that people believe. A psychopath. Deceased.

LOVEJOY: A cat.

MIKKA: The previous Monsean envoy to Winterkeep. He drowned in Winterkeep with Brek.

PELLA: A lord from central Monsea who had an affair with Queen Bitterblue.

PERIWINKLE (PERRY): The Lienid envoy to Winterkeep.

SKYE: A Lienid prince, the sixth son of King Ror and Queen Zinnober of Lienid. A cousin of Queen Bitterblue.

TRINA: A Graceling, Graced with finding things. Originally Estillan, she escaped to Monsea with Giddon's help.

ACKNOWLEDGMENTS

THANK YOU, KATHY Dawson, for your keen guidance and insight.

Thank you, Faye Bender, for your tremendous help and support.

Thank you, Jen Loja and Lauri Hornik, for making me safe under your wings.

Thank you, Catherine Cashore, Dorothy Cashore, Laura Chandra, Hannah Gómez, Margo Rabb, Alix Reid, and Marie Rutkoski, for your feedback on early drafts that nudged me toward the book I was trying to write. Thank you, Regina Castillo, for your copyediting magic.

Thank you, Theresa Evangelista, Kuri Huang, Jessica Jenkins, Jennifer Kelly, Dana Li, and Ian Schoenherr, for creating an object of beauty.

Thank you, Elyse Marshall, Emily Romero, Felicia Frazier, Debra Polansky, and the entire team at Penguin Young Readers Group, for everything each of you does, adeptly and tirelessly, to connect me and my book with readers.

Thank you, Judy Blundell, Laura Chandra, Eve Goldfarb, Deb Heiligman, Marthe Jocelyn, Barb Kerley, Kevin Lin, Betsy Partridge, Margo Rabb, Marie Rutkoski, Natalie Standiford, Rebecca Stead, and Tui Sutherland, for conversation after conversation that kept me grounded and helped me untangle the knots.

Thank you, Kevin Lin, for every single thing.